PENGUIN BOOKS

Cinderella Girl

Carin Gerhardsen was born in 1962 in Katrineholm, Sweden. Originally a mathematician, she enjoyed a successful career as an IT consultant before turning her hand to writing crime fiction. *Cinderella Girl* is the second title in the Hammarby series, novels following Detective Inspector Conny Sjöberg and his murder investigation team. Carin now lives in Stockholm with her husband and their two children. She is currently working on the seventh title in the series.

Cinderella Girl

CARIN GERHARDSEN

PENGUIN BOOKS

PENGUIN BOOKS

Published by the Penguin Group

Penguin Books Ltd, 80 Strand, London WC2R ORL, England

Penguin Group (USA) Inc., 375 Hudson Street, New York, New York 10014, USA

Penguin Group (Canada), 90 Eglinton Avenue East, Suite 700, Toronto, Ontario, Canada M4P 2Y3
(a division of Pearson Penguin Canada Inc.)

Penguin Ireland, 25 St Stephen's Green, Dublin 2, Ireland (a division of Penguin Books Ltd)

Penguin Group (Australia), 707 Collins Street, Melbourne, Victoria 3008, Australia
(a division of Pearson Australia Group Pty Ltd)

Penguin Books India Pvt Ltd, 11 Community Centre, Panchsheel Park, New Delhi – 110 017, India

Penguin Group (NZ), 67 Apollo Drive, Rosedale, Auckland 0632, New Zealand
(a division of Pearson New Zealand Ltd)

Penguin Books (South Africa) (Pty) Ltd, Block D, Rosebank Office Park,
181 Jan Smuts Avenue, Parktown North, Gauteng 2193, South Africa

Penguin Books Ltd, Registered Offices: 80 Strand, London WC2R ORL, England

www.penguin.com

First published in Sweden as *Mamma, pappa, barn* 2008
This translation first published as *Playing House* by Stockholm Text Publishing 2012
First published in Great Britain as *Cinderella Girl* in Penguin Books 2014

001

Copyright © Carin Gerhardsen, 2008
This translation copyright © Paul Norlén, 2012
All rights reserved

The moral right of the author and translator has been asserted

Set in 12.5/14.75pt Garamond MT Std
Typeset by Jouve (UK), Milton Keynes
Printed in Great Britain by Clays Ltd, St Ives plc

ISBN: 978-1-405-91407-9

www.greenpenguin.co.uk

Cinderella Girl

1964

Sleep now, go to sleep now; make it quick. Shut your eyes and leave your mouth half open so it looks convincing. Breathe slowly, evenly, even though your heart is pounding like a fist in your chest. But where there's a will, there's a way.

Now he hears the steps on the stairs, gentle steps, not hard, angry steps like before; now they are soothing and forgiving. He hears the door open and close again – oh no, it's one of those nights. But his breathing is even, sighing, perfect. His head is angled slightly on the pillow, a trickle of saliva works its way out of his mouth and down his cheek. The impression has to be of complete relaxation, even though every muscle in his body is so tense it hurts, but that's not noticeable; it cannot be seen.

'Are you sleeping, little man?' the hated voice whispers in a smooth, sugary-sweet tone. 'I was thinking we'd go to sleep as friends. That's always nice, isn't it?'

His eyelids always betray him.

'I can see you're awake. Your eyelids are twitching. Don't be silly; you're not going to hold a grudge, are you? We only want what's best for you; you know that, don't you? Now let's make up, pretty please?'

Then it's impossible to keep his eyes shut and he has to wipe away the spit that's trickling into his ear. And then the skinny, cold hand with the long, dirty nails slips inside the pyjama top. His whole body freezes and he stares at the man with a look full of loathing and fear, but the monster doesn't notice it. He notices a little twitching of the eyelids, but can't see a whole body in revolt.

Now clatter starts up in the kitchen and the whole house resounds with rattling china being put away in cupboards and clinking silverware placed in drawers. He winces when a patch of sensitive skin in his belly button gets caught for a moment by a long fingernail. The finger twirls around for a while in his belly button – which seems to have direct contact with his belly in an unpleasant, almost painful way – before making its way further down into the pyjama bottoms.

At that point he usually disappears from the room and out on to the football field or down to the shore to catch tadpoles, but this time he is standing by the railway tracks, looking through the windows at people in a passing train, and for some reason that image becomes engraved in his memory. It is neither pleasant nor disagreeable, but it's as though there's no way to get rid of it. From then on he always finds himself beside that train as he disappears into himself, away from himself. But he doesn't know that yet. The rails are screeching as they meet the onrushing train.

A Friday Evening in September, 2007

She sets him down on the rug by the bed while she removes the sheets. His screaming is almost unrecognizable now, the round face red from exertion. It's half past ten, and for four hours she has been trying to get him to sleep. But with his sore throat he can't keep the dummy in his mouth, and without a dummy it's hopeless. The Calpol no longer helps; it hurts to swallow so he's eaten almost nothing, and he can't keep the penicillin down on an empty stomach. She is so tired after three days that exhaustion has become the norm. But not once has she raised her voice; she has not blurted out a single harsh word. That feels like a victory.

All this time a countdown is going on inside her. She is counting the days, hours and minutes until Mats comes home again. As of now four days, ten hours and thirty minutes remain. He is in Japan at a technical seminar, but his mobile phone doesn't work there, so she can't even call him for a few encouraging words. It's just as well; it would only upset him to know how they are doing, and she would probably start crying and let her resolve turn into self-pity.

She rushes into the bathroom with her arms full of vomit-soiled linens and crumples the bundle into the washing machine. Out of habit she picks up a few pieces of clothing in similar colours from the laundry basket and stuffs those into the washer too, before she adds detergent and sets the over-filled machine at 60 degrees.

The child's screams suddenly stop and in the silence she hears her own stomach growling. She doesn't feel the hunger, but takes a detour through the kitchen to pick up the last brown-speckled banana from the bowl on the counter. Just then the howling from the bedroom resumes. She hurries back and picks up the boy, sits down at the foot of the unmade bed, lays the child on his stomach across her knees and strokes his back. On the TV in front of her she is trying to watch an American movie with the sound off, while the banana fills her mouth and her left hand monotonously caresses the inconsolable infant.

After only a few more minutes the movie is over and the credits quickly scroll past. She turns off the TV, gets up laboriously with the little one sobbing in her arms and goes over to the window. Two middle-aged men pass on the pavement across the street and a young couple is visible a little further away. No one carries an umbrella — evidence that the weather is clearing up. The driving rain that came down for most of the day has finally subsided.

She tries to set the boy on the windowsill, holding him by the hands, but he isn't interested and instead kicks his legs furiously without putting his feet down. She lifts him up, lays his head against her shoulder and sniffs his hair. It is damp with sweat and the child's screaming cuts like knives into her ears. Her eyes ache from lack of sleep and she has a hard time keeping them open. For a moment she unwillingly admits that she is feeling sorrier for herself than for the deeply loved but tormented little person in her arms. She is struck by a tangible desire for revenge, against some nameless, elusive, abstract being that cannot be conquered. With a sigh she gets up and goes out into the hall, carrying the boy. Before she puts the key in the lock she hesitates for a moment, thinking that at this time on a Friday evening the risk of burglars is probably greater than the risk of fire. Then she carefully locks the door from the outside.

* * *

The apartment was bubbling with laughter and happy voices. It was one of those evenings when everyone seemed to be in a good mood, no one was sulking or causing trouble. Most of them were sitting in the kitchen because Solan was in the living room with some new guy. It was clear the couple didn't want company because they had shut the doors to the hall and kitchen. No fewer than nine people were crowded around the kitchen table. On the floor, leaning against the refrigerator, Elise was sitting with a drink beside her. Across from her sat Jennifer, and she too was sipping a blend of moonshine and Coke.

Their apartment was almost always full of people. Even before noon folk started stumbling in for coffee and sandwiches, if anyone had gone shopping. Their mother kept her home open to all her buddies, but they had to supply their own food and drink. It had been hard for her to say no before, but finally she steeled herself and had put a stop to the guests' raids on the refrigerator and cupboards. And they had respected that. She made sure there was always food for the girls' breakfast and that they got going in the morning. She would send one of them down to the supermarket at Ringen, not because she was lazy – Elise knew she really would have preferred to do the shopping herself – but because she was ashamed to be seen outside. But Elise and her sister seldom ate at home; usually they ate out when they got hungry and sometimes with friends. They got money for clothes, toiletries and dinner. So they managed okay. Their mother was able to hold things together, even though their lives looked a bit different from most others.

By early afternoon the first bottles would be opened at the coffee table in the two-bedroom apartment in the Ringen complex. After that people came and went all afternoon and into the evening. Things did not settle down until close to midnight. It was not unusual for some of their mother's drinking companions to pass out and spend the night there.

The girls went to school during the day and then mostly roamed around town or went to friends' houses. They had a separate room that they shared, but for the most part they avoided being at home as long as the partying was going on. Instead they tried to stay away. Their mum's parties didn't usually lead to fights, but the conversations were often loud and you had to be careful not to rile someone who wasn't in a particularly good mood. Elise and Jennifer usually tried to make themselves invisible as they slipped into bed in the early hours.

But now it was Friday night, the weekend beckoning without school or other obligations, and their mother had recently acquired some money. Everyone was in high spirits around the kitchen table, where bottles crowded against glasses and full ashtrays. Elise and Jennifer were not unaffected by the elated atmosphere. Normally they would have sneaked past without anyone paying attention to them, but tonight they'd been called into the kitchen and offered drinks and cigarettes by the noisy group around the table.

Elise started to feel pleasantly relaxed even after the first gulp. She took a deep drag on the cigarette and closed her eyes. She intended to keep this one for herself, and besides, she knew tonight it would be easy to get her hands on more. Her allowance was usually not enough for cigarettes, and if you begged from friends you had to be content with butts. She took a substantial gulp from the glass and looked at her big sister. Everyone said they were alike, but she did not see many similarities. Jennifer was two years older, cool and self-confident, and always had an answer for everything. Elise was a pale copy, with low self-esteem, bad posture and ridiculous, small breasts that could not compare with Jennifer's. Even these characters in the kitchen made a distinction between them. Jennifer was the grand prize to pull down on your lap on a night like tonight, but she almost always refused them in her confident way. Then they might start pretend-sobbing, and beg and plead to change her mind, but she would just shake her head and roll her eyes. Only then did they ask Elise the same thing, but she usually refused because Jennifer had. Sometimes she sat on Dagge's or Gordon's or Peo's lap, simply because she couldn't bear to say no – or because she wanted to feel appreciated for a while.

'What are you going to do tonight?' Elise yelled over the din to her big sister.

'Don't know. Maybe see Joakim, maybe not, whatever,' Jennifer called back.

Jennifer had a boyfriend. Well, Elise had boyfriends too, off and on, but Jennifer had a real boyfriend. A man. Joakim was twenty-four years old and had a beard. The boys Elise went out with had voices that had just started to change. They had peach fuzz and they were childish and silly. But Jennifer had a real man and now she wasn't sure if she wanted to see him! He was also sweet and considerate. Elise could not recall even meeting that kind of guy. She had seen them at a distance once, and Joakim was holding on to Jennifer almost like he owned her. Like, 'This is my girl and I'm proud of it.' And then he had looked deep into her eyes and caressed her cheek so tenderly and carefully, as if she might fall apart at the slightest touch. Elise wanted that kind of man herself. She wanted him.

'What do you mean "whatever"?'

Jennifer emptied her glass with one gulp and Elise did the same.

'Uh, I don't know.'

'Aren't you still together, or what?'

'Maybe, maybe not. Yeah, but he's so . . . It doesn't matter. You want another?'

'Sure. Get me a smoke too.'

Jennifer got up and ploughed her way between chairs and legs and swaying bodies over to the kitchen table. Dagge threw out two big hands, took firm hold of Jennifer's hips and pulled her teasingly down on his lap, but she bounced up again, grabbed a bottle and a pack of cigarettes, and quickly wriggled back to her spot by the kitchen cupboard.

'Hey, listen up, kiddo. What kind of attitude is that?'

8

Dagge blurted out in a loud, hoarse voice. 'You take my wine and I don't even get a little hug!'

Dagge was a blond, red-faced character with small bloodshot eyes and big hairy ears. Strangely enough he had a fairly fashionable shirt on, but his jeans were spotted with paint and had a reek of old grime that wafted all the way over to where Elise was sitting.

'Maybe you'll get one if you're nice,' Jennifer replied coolly while she filled her glass and her sister's with luke-warm white wine.

Elise shuddered at the thought of even grazing against those jeans.

'I'm the one who should get a hug, damn it; it's my wine,' her mother yelled.

Embarrassing as always. She was more tolerable when she was in one of her silent, semi-depressed moods. Tonight, however, she was up and talkative. Wanted to be seen and heard. Elise didn't want to see or hear her; she tried not to think about her.

'Yeah, yeah, but you owe me one,' Dagge went on, and the conversation shifted to debts and injustices and suddenly everyone around the table had something to say.

Jennifer offered Elise a cigarette, took one herself and then stuffed the pack, not missed by anyone, into the front of her blouse. Elise lit her own cigarette and handed the lighter over to Jennifer.

'Are you going out, or what?' asked Jennifer.

Elise knocked back half of the contents of the glass with a disgusted grimace.

'Yeah, I guess so,' she answered. 'I'm seeing Nina. You don't have any money I can borrow, do you?'

'Right, like I have any cash. Just ask one of them. They seem to have money today.'

She made a gesture towards the table, knocked back the rest of the sour wine and got up to leave. Elise felt her cheeks burning; the drink put her in a good mood. Made her feel courageous.

'Jennifer, wait!'

'Yeah?'

'Listen, can I borrow your jacket?'

'What fucking jacket?'

'The leather jacket. From Gina Tricot.'

'So what am I supposed to wear?' Jennifer asked crossly.

'Can't you wear a different one? Please, just tonight?'

Maybe Jennifer felt a little tipsy too, because suddenly she gave in.

'Okay, but I've got to have it tomorrow.'

'I promise. God, that's awesome.'

'It's in the hall. I'm out of here,' said Jennifer.

Elise remained seated on the floor, smoking until the ember burned the tips of her fingers. Then she emptied the glass, dropped the butt in and listened to the hissing sound it made. She went over to the table, noticing that she staggered a little.

'Can anybody loan me a couple of hundred?' she asked, but no one volunteered.

'What do you mean loan? You'll never see that money again,' her mother complained.

'Like I can afford that,' Gordon muttered.

'And if I could, I wouldn't give it to you!' Peo howled.

Monkan just shook her head and the others didn't seem to even notice Elise; they kept on talking about other things.

She went out to the hall and felt in the pockets of the jackets hanging there, without finding anything. She took Jennifer's leather jacket down from a hook and pulled it on. After a quick look at herself in the mirror she went out to the stairwell, slamming the door behind her. The time was half past ten.

* * *

'What kind of damn girl?'

'Just a regular girl.'

'"A regular girl." She has a name, doesn't she?'

'Her name's Jennifer. I've told you that before.'

'That sounds like a good name for a slut.'

'She's not a slut, she's nice.'

'Nice! You ugly piece of shit, how the hell could you get a "nice" girlfriend? She's messing with you; don't you get that?'

Maybe his dad was right. Joakim wasn't much to look at and Jennifer was cute as a doll. He had never had a girlfriend before. Jennifer was his first. True, she was eight years younger, but she was his. Wasn't she? She must be; they'd slept with each other and she had asked him to go along on the Finland cruise tomorrow. And now she'd called and asked if they could go out together.

'Maybe she is. But I'm glad I have someone. I'm leaving now.'

'Oh no, mister, oh no, you're not. You're staying here and taking care of your mother.'

A malicious smile split his father's face into two grotesque halves and Joakim started to feel sick.

'But she'll be fine; she's going to sleep soon.'

'You're staying home,' his father said dryly without looking at him, taking a deep drag on his cigarette.

He didn't bother blowing out the smoke; it stayed inside him. Joakim felt the tears forming a lump in his throat. He wanted to see Jennifer so much; he *needed* to see her. What if she could see how pitiful he was, always doing what his dad told him to do. To her he acted tough and worldly wise, so far as he could, and he was tall and had a beard and smoked and used snuff. True, he wasn't supposed to, but his father didn't notice because he was a smoker himself. Deep down Joakim had a feeling that he was deceiving her. He was twenty-four years old and she was sixteen. He hid behind a beard and sunglasses, and she thought he was a big, strong man, even though any man at all could see he was a wuss.

'But please, Dad, I have to go out,' he pleaded. 'I've spent the whole day with Mum. It's Friday night, and –'

'You do as I say. Go in to your mother now, so I don't have to look at you.'

Joakim felt his worry turning to desperation, but he wouldn't give up so easily – not this time.

'I'm not going to,' he croaked in a voice that broke from the held-back tears. 'I won't do it, I'm going out! You can't rule my life; I can do what I want! I'm an adult!'

'I see, so now you're suddenly so grown up,' his father hissed between clenched teeth, and only now did a few streams of smoke make their way out of his nostrils. 'I haven't seen any signs of that.'

His father was right; he was a failure. After a few meaningless years he had left high school with miserable grades.

They had determined that he had difficulties reading and writing, but he wasn't mechanically oriented either. The few jobs available were not meant for someone like him, and further studies were out of the question.

But his father had found a way. When his mother got too ill to work, he hired Joakim as her personal assistant. For that he got food, lodging and a minimal amount of pocket money. He also delivered newspapers in the mornings and with the money he had scraped together he intended to get an apartment at some point. A life of his own.

'I'm leaving now anyway; I don't care what you say,' Joakim snuffled, starting to back up in the direction of the door. 'And tomorrow night I'm going to Åbo with Jennifer,' he added, regretting it the moment he said it.

'The hell you are!' his father roared, leaping up from the armchair and coming towards him with huge strides, the cigarette still in his mouth.

Joakim ran through the hall and heaved himself against the outside door, but the security chain was on. While he was desperately trying to coax it out of its holder he felt his dad's arm taking hold of his neck from behind. His Adam's apple was pushed in with such force that he felt like he was choking. He tried to drive an elbow into his father's stomach, but the grip only got harder. With no chance of fighting back, Joakim was forced to turn towards his father and he felt his neck crack with an unpleasant sound. While he gasped for air his father took the opportunity to ram a fist into his stomach and he fell down doubled-up on the hall rug. After another kick in the stomach, and one across the mouth and nose, things calmed down and he was left lying, half in a stupor, on the floor in the darkened hallway. He sensed how his father lumbered back to the armchair in the living room and impassively started rustling the newspaper.

In his mind's eye he saw Jennifer – her round form in tight jeans, her soft, glistening lips and happy, grey-blue eyes that at any moment, unexpectedly, might take on an introverted, almost shy expression. Tomorrow he would dance with her on the Finland ferry and he would treat her to colourful drinks in the bar. They would sleep together; he would get to touch the soft, downy-white skin that peeked out between her waistband and her top, and he would taste her warm, shimmering lips.

He must have fallen asleep because when he opened his eyes the lights were off in the living room. After carefully moving his arms and legs to make sure nothing was broken, he pulled himself up on to all fours and, supporting himself against the door, slowly got up. His belly ached, and he avoided touching his throbbing nose as he stumbled to the bathroom as quietly as he could. He closed the door behind him before he turned on the light and looked at himself in the mirror. One half of his face was covered with dried blood and his upper lip was split and swollen. As he gingerly felt his nose, it made an unpleasant crunching sound around the bridge. He wet some toilet paper under the cold tap and dabbed his nose and split lip. Then he carefully washed the uninjured parts of his face and brushed his teeth.

He put the toothbrush and toothpaste into a washbag and took it with him into the small corridor outside the bathroom, where he dug a gym bag out of a cupboard. He emptied the workout clothes into one of the wire baskets in the cupboard and replaced them with a few pairs of clean underwear, a shirt, a pair of jeans and the washbag. Then he snuck back out to the hall and tied his trainers in the dark.

Then he did something he had never dared to do before: he put his hand in the inside pocket of his father's coat, hauled up his wallet and counted three thousand kronor. He took fifteen hundred, returned the wallet, tucked his own jacket under his arm and the bag over his shoulder, and slipped out to the stairwell. He took a look at his watch and saw that it was only half past ten.

* * *

Conny Sjöberg tidied up and Åsa packed. The family – five children aged between two and nine, Åsa, and himself – had spent Friday evening with his mother, who lived in an apartment in Bollmora, a half-hour drive south of the city. It was late by the time they had got home, and once all the children were in bed Åsa started gathering up clean clothes and toys for the next day. She and the kids were taking the train to Linköping to visit her parents for a few days. Simon and Sara had Monday off from school and Åsa was not teaching that day, so they would not return until Monday evening.

Sjöberg opened the dishwasher, pulled out the baskets and turned over the cups to tip out any water that had collected. Then he went over all the five rooms of the apartment with a meticulous gaze, making sure all the bits and pieces had been put in their proper places. Not until everything was in order could he relax and enjoy his home.

It was the same at work; he couldn't concentrate on

a task if there were papers and binders spread out across the desk. Binders neatly set up on the bookshelf behind the desk, loose papers in tidy piles, and office supplies, such as the pen holder and hole punch, symmetrically lined up at a good distance from the work surface itself; this created a calm, harmonious work environment with no unnecessary disruption.

When he had finished he put the kettle on and made a few sandwiches with the meatloaf from yesterday's dinner. He lit the candles on the kitchen table, poured hot water over the tea leaves and set the teapot on the table.

'Complaining and criticizing as always,' said Åsa as she sat down.

'She's just that way, I guess,' sighed Sjöberg.

'And yet she's so considerate and nice to the kids. And to us too. Why does she have to be so hard on herself?'

'I guess it's insecurity. She's shy, that's all. Low self-esteem. Doesn't really know how to behave, but has a sense that she does everything wrong. Class and education complex.'

'There's always something wrong with the food, the sweater she's knitted has turned out ugly, and the coffee is too strong. She's always criticizing herself – never us though, and that's good – but the food *does* taste unappetizing after she's pointed out everything that's wrong with it while we're eating. It's really a shame she's that way, that she can't be happy about anything.'

Sjöberg served the tea and poured a heaped tablespoon of sugar into his own cup.

'She's happy when Sweden wins,' he said with a wry smile.

'Sure, but that's not real joy – that's just sport. Where does this interest in sport come from anyway? Older women aren't usually interested in sport, and she's very concerned about not being different.'

'Well, Dad was interested in sport, I guess maybe that's where it came from. And she doesn't read. I suppose it's good that she's interested in something.'

'Well, I didn't mean it like that,' said Åsa, taking a bite of her sandwich. 'It's great that she's interested in hockey and football and athletics and skiing and all that, it's just a little odd, you have to agree. It doesn't fit the image somehow . . . What was she like when your dad was alive?'

'I don't remember.'

Sjöberg washed down his sandwich with a few gulps of hot tea.

'I only remember that she was very subdued while he was in the hospital. Not much was said about it, and I never got to visit him. I was so little, I must have been about three.'

'That's another thing that's strange about your family: you *think* he had cancer. How come you don't *know* that?'

'But Åsa, you know how she is! She doesn't remember anything, or at least she just doesn't want to talk about it.'

'Exactly! It would be interesting to know what you were like as a child, for example. Were you naughty, did you sleep well at night, did you have a dummy or did you suck your thumb, how old were you when you started to walk, and so on. You can't find out any of those things. And you don't remember all that much either,' she added.

'I grew up in a working-class home, you grew up in an

17

academic home,' said Sjöberg. 'Everything I know I've had to learn on my own. I bought my first book with my pocket money. You just opened your mouth and they poured knowledge and education into you.'

'Oh, my little disadvantaged child,' said Åsa with half-genuine, half-pretended tenderness, stroking him on the cheek. 'In any case I love you most in the whole world.'

Sjöberg took his wife's hand and kissed the back of it. A slight noise came from the little boys' room and they both froze for a moment. Just when the danger seemed to be over, the scream came and Åsa ran off on tiptoe, so as not to disturb the other children.

Then the phone rang.

'Who was on the phone?' asked Åsa when she came back into the kitchen. 'Do you have to work?'

'No, it was my mother,' sighed Sjöberg. 'She fell down from a stool and seems to have broken a rib. I have to drive back over there and see how she's doing. I may have to take her to casualty.'

'If it's not one thing it's another. She's not in any great danger though?'

'No, she's feeling okay otherwise. She got herself into bed, but apparently it hurts. I'm sorry I have to take off.'

'A man's got to do what a man's got to do. I'll go to bed anyway,' said Åsa. 'Give me a kiss when you come back.'

'It's already ten-thirty; it's going to be really late.'

'It doesn't matter. Let's hope we at least get a little time together first thing tomorrow.'

'I'll get up, whatever happens,' said Sjöberg. 'I can always take a nap during the day if I need to.'

He kissed her on the forehead, took his jacket and car keys, and disappeared into the dark stairwell.

* * *

The Pelican on a Friday was always crowded and noisy, but this evening the venerable beer hall on Blekingegatan was even more packed than usual, if that were possible. Hard to say whether it was the end of the month or the persistent rainfall outside the gigantic multi-coloured window that drove people into the warm room. Customers were crowded around the oak tables and at the bar, and by half past ten their combined voices had increased even more in intensity. The high ceiling and tiled floor made the sound bounce so that sometimes it was easier to hear what was being said in another corner than at your own table.

Petra Westman and Jamal Hamad sat shouting to each other over their empty beer glasses. They had been fortunate to secure a table a few hours earlier when an elderly couple had got tired of waiting to be served and left. Petra and Jamal were in no hurry; they patiently overlooked the stressed staff running past several times without noticing them at their table, partly obscured by a large pillar in the middle of the room.

But now a waiter showed up, a tall, good-looking guy in his mid-thirties with dark hair gathered in a ponytail. According to the badge on his chest his name was Firas, and he delivered the two large beers they had ordered a few minutes earlier from one of the waitresses.

'*Shukran,*' said Jamal.

'*Ahlan,*' answered the waiter, meeting his gaze with curious blue-green eyes. '*Men wen hadrtak?*'

'*Lebnen. O anta?*'

'*Suria.*'

'*Anjar?*' asked Jamal with a crooked smile.

The waiter hesitated for a moment, but then leaned over and hissed in his ear, '*Ana rabian honek . . .*'

Then he gave Jamal a thump on the back that Petra interpreted as friendly and hurried away towards the bar. Jamal laughed out loud as he watched the waiter, who turned around and winked before disappearing into the throng. Petra looked at her colleague with equal surprise and admiration.

'Now my whole body is tingling,' she laughed, raising her glass.

'On account of me or Firas?' Jamal smiled, responding to her toast.

'Both. Or to be more exact, the language.'

'A little *Fish Called Wanda* alert there?'

'Exactly. You do remind me a little of John Cleese. What were you talking about?'

'Our origins, you might say.'

'And that's what you were laughing about?'

'Apparently. Now let's change the subject,' Jamal said, making another toast.

'Feminine?' said Petra a little later, shaking her head. 'In what way? Do I trip around on high heels or what?'

'Sure, don't you?' Jamal winked at her and continued. 'What's wrong with being feminine? Would you have been happier if he'd said you had a masculine posture? You know, a bow-legged footballer's walk? No, I think he was referring to your challenging way of swinging your chassis, Petra. Booooty,' he added, exaggerating his lips to prolong the 'oo' sound, as if to emphasize how silly he thought the word was.

Petra could hardly keep from laughing. She took a big gulp of beer, wiping the foam from her upper lip with her index finger.

'Would it be better to have a centre of gravity like you then, between your shoulders?' she snorted. 'I can only interpret that to mean you're putting on a show. Ruffling yourself up like a male peacock to attract females.'

'And look how well it works! Here I am, sitting with Stockholm's best-looking policewoman . . .'

Jamal laced his hands behind his neck and looked at her with a playful gleam in his eyes. Petra liked what he'd said. The problem was that she didn't know whether he meant it or if he was just pulling her leg. Even though she'd known him for a long time, she never really knew how to take him.

Their conversation was about a course they had attended during the day, along with twenty other hand-picked Hammarby police officers. It was called 'Centring on Body Language' and the main idea was that you could influence the impression you made on people around you with your posture. The point was not to change, but rather to use and develop what you already had.

Each participant had to take a short walk before the critical but amused eyes of the others, after which the location of that particular person's centre of gravity was analysed. If you wanted to make an authoritative impression, for example during the arrest of a suspect, you wanted your centre of gravity in the right place and not in your pot belly (like Jens Sandén) or your feet (as Petra imagined would be the case for Einar Eriksson). All in all the class had been an enjoyable break from the daily grind, and they had probably picked up one or two useful tips as well.

'Anyway, birds ruffle their feathers up because they're cold, not for any other reason,' Jamal continued.

His brown eyes glistened in the glow of the candle on the table. When he smiled his teeth seemed blindingly white against the summer tan that lingered on his face.

'But sweetie-pie, come and let me warm you up then.' Petra stretched across the table with a feigned compassionate expression on her face and took one of his hands between hers. It was soft and warm.

'I didn't know you knew so much about birds,' she continued.

'No, I never cease to amaze.'

'Then perhaps you can tell me what species the police commissioner belongs to? He's good at puffing himself up.'

'Brandt? I thought you said he was sexy,' Jamal answered.

Petra let his hand fall back on to the table.

'Knock it off,' she said wearily. 'They put those words in my mouth. It was his deputy – what's his name, Malmberg – who put me on the spot there. What could I say? I had no interest whatsoever in commenting on the police commissioner's way of walking. Malmberg suggested sexy and I smiled and nodded. Embarrassed.'

'"Yes, maybe so" is what you actually said,' Jamal laughed.

'Yes, maybe so. What the hell could I say? "No, I really don't think so, more like unsexy"?'

'You said you thought the police commissioner was sexy.'

'It was Malmberg who said that.'

'I think it was Holgersson actually.'

'Yes, maybe it was. He's a real creep.'

'He is? I think he's a lot of fun,' Jamal smiled mockingly. 'Apparently he reads you like an open book. Sniffs out your intimate feelings for the police commissioner.'

Petra let out an audible sigh and knocked back the last of her beer.

'But what do you think Brandt meant by "feminine"?' she asked with a hint of a worried frown.

'I think he meant . . .' Jamal looked at her for a moment with a serious expression before he continued. '. . . sexy,' he finished the sentence and burst into laughter.

Petra threw out her arms and shook her head.

'I'll treat you to one more,' said Jamal, getting up.

Petra watched him as he made his way over to the bar with the two empty beer glasses in his hands. He dismissed the whole embarrassing situation as a joke, but personally she had a hard time seeing anything funny about it.

After consuming massive quantities of beer, an hour or two later they went their separate ways. Outside the metro entrance at Allhelgonagatan Petra suggested they could keep drinking, but Jamal said he was getting up early the next morning and he intended to take a brisk walk home before sleeping off the buzz. When she asked about his plans, he revealed that he was going to Nacka to play golf.

'Golf?' said Petra. 'You don't play golf, do you?'

But her brain was working on a completely different question: Nacka? So you're involved with Bella Hansson after all?

'Well, I don't know yet,' Jamal smiled. 'I've never tried.'

After a quick hug and a kiss on the cheek, Petra rushed down the steps with a centre of gravity that seemed to be somewhere down in her diaphragm.

* * *

Even though it was late in the evening, there were a lot of cars out making noise, splashing muddy water on to pedestrians and bicyclists, and saturating the air with stinking exhaust fumes. Nina was already waiting outside the Pressbyrån shop at the Ringen shopping centre on Götgatan when Elise showed up.

'Shit, you look really hot!' said Nina.

The colourful lights from the shops' neon signs were reflected in the sunglasses on her head.

'Where'd you get that jacket?'

'Uh, it's not mine,' answered Elise. 'I borrowed it from Sis.'

'Are you drunk?'

Elise laughed.

'Got some from my old lady. And you?'

'Not yet,' Nina replied. 'But we're going over to the Crocodile, aren't we?'

'I don't have any money. Can I borrow some from you?'

'Hey, look at that old man there.'

Nina whispered even though the man she was looking at was inside Pressbyrån and the doors were closed.

'He's so fucking ugly! He's a paedophile, a real dirty old man,' Nina continued.

The man was browsing through a magazine, and with his back turned towards them Elise couldn't see what he looked like. But at least he didn't wear a low-brimmed hat or turn up his coat collar for protection from their stares.

'How do you know that?' Elise asked. 'Has he been after you or – ?'

'No way, as if! But I've heard about him from other girls. He drools over little girls and gropes them and carries on. Are we going?'

'But I don't have any money. Can I just borrow a hundred?' Elise begged.

'I barely have enough for myself. Sofia and Magda are already in the Crocodile; I'm going there anyway. Why don't you go home and get some money, then I'll see you in a while?'

Nina went off unconcerned and Elise remained standing on the pavement, not really knowing what to do next. Nina turned around a few moments later, waved and called with a happy smile, 'Hurry up!'

Elise cast a glance through the Pressbyrån window and her gaze fell on the old man Nina had called a paedophile. He was still standing in the same place, reading magazines for free, but there were lots of people in the shop and the assistant was probably distracted.

Elise remembered a programme she'd seen on TV. It was a documentary about some young girls in Malmö who were on the street for various reasons. You couldn't see their faces and their voices were distorted. Elise thought their friends probably recognized them anyway.

One of them said she was saving up for a horse of her own. She was thirteen.

After a few minutes' consideration, Elise went into the shop. Her eyes swept across sweets and ice cream, sandwiches and drinks. Then she gathered her courage and sidled up to the man to see what he was reading. Sure enough, he was looking at naked girls. She looked quickly around. None of the other customers was within earshot if she spoke in a low voice.

'Do you want to see some of the real thing?' she asked, not looking at the man beside her.

He checked behind him to make sure it was really him she was talking to and then turned back to the magazine.

'Some what?' he asked guardedly, without looking up from his magazine.

'A naked girl.'

'How much do you want?' he asked unperturbed.

So he had done this before. Nina was right.

'A hundred for tits, three hundred for pussy,' Elise answered with simulated experience.

'And more . . . ?'

'That's all,' said Elise.

He put the magazine back in the rack, but still did not look her in the eyes.

'You'll get two hundred,' he said, starting towards the door.

She followed with her heart pounding in her chest. It was both exciting and a little scary. Like the start of something new and dangerous.

Friday Night

His mother was lying in bed when he arrived. She didn't complain about the pain; she just stated factually that probably she'd broken a rib because her chest didn't feel right. Sjöberg asked whether he should call for an ambulance, but he knew she wouldn't want to cause any fuss and bother. The ambulance staff had much more important things to do and what would the neighbours think. He helped her carefully up on to her feet, put her coat over her shoulders and led her out to the car. Then he went back into the apartment and gathered together some underwear and toiletries in a bag. At the last moment he happened to think of her handbag; then he turned off the lights and locked the door.

In the car, en route to the hospital, his mother told him that she had climbed up on a stool to put away a tray in a high cupboard after they had left her earlier that evening. She had lost her balance and tumbled to the floor.

'The trouble I'm causing you now! I keep you up, and poor Åsa is all alone with the children.'

She shook her head and looked out of the side window.

'Mum, the children are asleep and Åsa is too,' said Sjöberg soothingly. 'I can't complain either, I'm off tomorrow. You're the one I'm worried about; you could have asked me to put away that tray. You shouldn't do that sort of thing, Mum, not at your age.'

'I know. You don't notice that the years pass.'

'So how does it feel now? Are you sitting comfortably?'

'I don't feel it as much while I'm sitting.'

They sat in silence for a while and Sjöberg thought about what Åsa had said earlier. His mother was a rather strange character, he had to agree with that. He was just so used to her. She was now seventy-four and he was forty-nine. She had been a widow for more than half her life. What had it really been like for her? How did it feel then, when she was left alone with him? Feelings were not something they had talked about at home. Life went on as usual and it was neither good nor bad. It was what it was.

'How did Dad die?' he suddenly thought to ask.

His mother hesitated for a moment.

'He got sick,' she replied.

'But what kind of illness did he have?'

When she didn't answer his question right away he continued, 'Was it cancer, or – ?'

'I never asked for details,' she said with a sharp tone in her voice. 'You never understand what those doctors say anyway.'

Sjöberg sighed. That's how a typical conversation went, always had. The world is so big and incomprehensible. You yourself are little and insignificant and what good does it do to get involved, to stick out, to be seen or heard? The best you could do was to avoid attracting attention, keep your faults and doings hidden, and mind your own business.

Once at the hospital, they had to sit in the A&E waiting room for several hours. Sjöberg left for a few minutes to get them some weak coffee from a vending machine; otherwise they mostly sat leafing through old newspapers. They didn't speak much – you don't in public – but when new patients showed up they both looked up curiously for a few moments. His mother refused to lie down in the waiting room and remained patiently in her seat until her name was called at about one-thirty.

The female doctor confirmed that several ribs were broken and his mother was taken in a wheelchair to a ward where she would stay, at least overnight, for X-rays and observation. Sjöberg tucked her into bed and promised to be in touch the next day.

When he finally left she was already asleep; it was almost two-thirty in the morning.

Sjöberg yawned as he came out into the corridor. He looked around for some clue to which direction might take him out of the large hospital. A little further down the long corridor he spotted some signs and made for them. A couple of nurses came towards him and just as he was about to ask them the way he stopped short. He stood rooted to the spot with a stupid expression on his face and at first he could not manage a word.

One of the nurses was much too familiar, with her flowing dark-red hair and her lively green eyes. She was the woman in the window, the woman who had tormented him at night for many months. Lately in his dream her facial features had started to blur into a kind of general female appearance, because it had been almost a year since he'd last seen her – Margit Olofsson. But the hair was always the same, and now here he stood, stammering, not knowing what to do. This is ridiculous, he thought.

This woman doesn't know about my absurd dreams. They had only met two or three times the previous year, during a murder investigation, and had not exchanged many words. What was the matter with him? Her neutral expression changed to recognition and she was already smiling broadly when he finally came out with an awkward greeting.

'Hi,' he said. 'Margit Olofsson . . .'

'Inspector! Good job, remembering my name after such a long time. I must have been a prime suspect!' she joked.

The other nurse continued on her way along the corridor and they were left alone together. Sjöberg couldn't think of anything to say, so Margit Olofsson continued, 'What are you doing here? Is there another murder case?'

'No, my mother broke a couple of ribs, so I drove her here. We've been in casualty since eleven o'clock, and she's spending the night for observation. Do you work at this time of night?'

'Yes, periodically. But tonight has actually been pretty quiet, so it's no problem.'

Sjöberg didn't know where the idea came from, but without thinking he heard himself saying, 'May I get you a coffee?'

In order to play down what felt to him like a minor social transgression, but which presumably meant nothing to Margit Olofsson, he added, 'I feel like I need a cup of coffee, so I don't fall asleep behind the wheel.'

'Why not?' Margit Olofsson replied. 'I'll just go and tell them I'm taking a break. Wait here so I can pilot you through the labyrinth here at Huddinge!'

*

'So how is she doing now?' asked Margit Olofsson as they sat facing each other in the hospital cafeteria with their coffee.

'Pretty good, I guess. They're going to X-ray her to make sure she hasn't punctured a lung or anything. She may get to go home as early as tomorrow.'

'I'll look in on her. What's her name? Sjöberg perhaps?'

'Yes, Eivor. And how are you doing? And – what was her name – Ingrid?'

'I don't have any contact with Ingrid Olsson now. I never knew her well; it was only for a few weeks that it worked out that way.'

'The good Samaritan . . .' said Sjöberg.

'Yeah, yeah,' said Margit Olofsson self-deprecatingly. 'Things are fine with me anyway. Two happy children who've left home. A husband in the painting business and personally . . .'

'Isn't he happy then?' Sjöberg interrupted.

'. . . I've been idling around here for thirty years.'

She finished the sentence, but now she looked at him thoughtfully. Sjöberg felt like he was blushing, but hoped it didn't show. Why did he ask that? What had got into him? Was he really sitting here flirting with Margit Olofsson, an extremely peripheral person from an old murder investigation? It was definitely time to drive home.

'Well, I guess he's happy in his own way. And I in mine,' she answered cryptically, with a slight, almost imperceptible smile. 'And you?'

During the few seconds Sjöberg took to consider how he should answer that, he was flooded by an almost irresistible urge to tell her about the strange dream. She aroused peculiar feelings in him, which he couldn't really put into words. It wasn't love, in any event not the kind of love he had for Åsa or the children. Not a communion of souls either, because what did they have in common? Nothing apparently, at least nothing he could discern behind the outer shell of the person he'd encountered up to now. Was it desire? Absolutely not. Margit Olofsson – who was certainly decent-looking and not at all lacking in charm – did not have much of what he would normally be attracted to in a woman.

Even so, he was drawn to her. There was something about this person that simply made him want to crawl into her arms and weep. He wanted to tell all the secrets of his heart and pour out his innermost thoughts to her. Was the same maternal aura that had caused Ingrid Olsson to ask her for help now sucking him in too? He didn't think so. He already had all the love, concern and friendship he needed. Margit Olofsson stirred up his emotions in a way he did not recognize from his almost half-century of living. He had to get out of here, collect himself.

'Oh yes, no reason to complain,' he replied, the words sounding as if they had come from his mother rather than himself.

They sat out the rest of her half-hour break and talked about themselves and their lives, aspects both important and trivial. When Sjöberg finally got in the car to drive home he did not think he had exposed too much of himself. He had not mentioned the dream.

Saturday Morning

Hanna stayed in bed for a long, long time, waiting for the familiar sounds. Even though the blinds were down it was completely light in the room. She didn't feel tired at all, but she tried to go back to sleep anyway. Mummy said that if she woke up before anyone else, she had to stay in bed and try to fall asleep again. But now she just couldn't stay in bed any longer. She decided she had to get up and play, no matter what, with the door closed. She crept out of bed and took down a puzzle from the shelf. She chose the green box with Pooh on the lid, opened it and scattered the pieces on her little table. The table was red with yellow chairs. Daddy and Hanna had painted the furniture together, but Mummy had painted the blue flowers on the seats with a very small brush.

When she finished the Pooh puzzle she prepared some make-believe food on her stove. In the oven she found a battery-powered mixer and whipped a little cream for Magdalena, the brown-eyed doll with long, dark, flowing hair and a pink dress. The mixer buzzed loudly, and she suddenly thought that maybe the noise had wakened the others. But it was still just as silent in the apartment.

Her nappy was heavy after the night and was hanging uncomfortably under her red and white striped nightie. Her stomach was also starting to rumble, even though she usually didn't care much for breakfast. What could she do to wake Mummy without getting yelled at? If she screamed, maybe ... that she'd had a horrible nightmare ...

'Mummy, Mummy!' she called. 'Mummy, come here! Help!'

Nothing happened. Hanna opened the door a little and called out again, but it was still completely silent. Suddenly it struck her that her little brother was quiet too. Even though he had been screaming and screaming nonstop for days. Lukas had a sore throat and a fever and took medicine, but he still didn't get better, Mummy said. Maybe his sickness had passed, now that he'd stopped screaming? Then Mummy would finally have a little time left over to play with her too, and not just be always occupied with Lukas.

Hanna stuck her head through the doorway, pushing back a strand of fair hair that was hanging down in her face. She had long hair that Mummy would put up in a ponytail or pigtails in the morning, so it wouldn't get into her eyes when she played. She was three years old and went to preschool several days a week, although not today because today was Saturday. Hanna knew that, because you kept track of such things when you were as big as she was; Saturdays were especially easy to remember, because then you could buy sweets and drink pop.

So Mummy would just have to be angry. Hanna couldn't stand waiting any longer; she tiptoed out to the living room. The bedroom door stood wide open and there was full daylight inside. That was strange; were they sleeping with the blinds up? She sneaked up to the doorway and looked carefully into the room. The big double bed was where it always was, but it was empty. There were no covers, no pillows. There was no Mummy or little brother either.

Hanna stood quietly for a long time, without really understanding what she saw, but then she crept up on to the empty bed and started to cry.

* * *

With a jerk he sat up in bed and screamed. He had never done that before. Åsa, with a hardened parent's ability to go straight from deep sleep to being wide awake, sat up just as quickly and looked at her husband in alarm. Then she caressed his back with big, gentle movements and he put his hands over his face and rocked slowly back and forth.

'What were you dreaming?' Åsa asked carefully. 'You've never done that before.'

Sjöberg did not answer, simply shook his head in distress and sighed. They remained like that for a long time, and then he whispered, 'There's a woman in a window.' He hoped she didn't hear him. 'She's looking down at me and I'm standing barefoot in the grass.'

Then he fell silent.

'That's it?'

'That's it.'

'Who is she?' asked Åsa.

'I don't know,' Sjöberg said quietly.

'You've only slept for a few hours,' said Åsa. 'It's not time to get up yet. Lie down again and I'll stroke your back.'

He lay down beside her obediently, with his back turned towards her. She drew her hand through his blond hair a few times and then brought it slowly across his shoulder, arm, back and down to the lower back. He was sweaty and his entire body was still tense, despite Åsa's gentle caresses.

The dream had been the same as so many times before. He was standing barefoot on a lawn wet with dew, looking down at his feet. He wanted to look up, but something held him back. His head felt so terribly heavy that he was barely able to raise it. He exerted himself with all his strength and managed at last to turn his face upwards, but still he didn't dare open his eyes. The back of his head pulled down towards his shoulders and he didn't want to move.

At last he opened his eyes. And there she stood again in the window, the woman with the dazzling dark-red hair like sunlight around her head. She was dancing for him up there in the window, before finally meeting his gaze. But she only seemed surprised. So strange. He raised his arms up towards her but lost his balance and fell headlong backwards.

The dream was becoming clearer every time he had it. And although the woman had not always taken her shape, now it was Margit Olofsson standing in the window, mocking him. Since the woman in the dream had assumed Margit's features, the dream had become that much more unpleasant. Why, he didn't know. It had been unpleasant enough, without the woman in the window having a name. He wanted to push the dream out of his mind, but he failed. It encircled his thoughts like a fog bank.

Careful to conceal how tense and upset he was, he turned around in bed. He took Åsa in his arms and buried his face between her cheek and shoulder. Her hair smelled of celery. When Åsa ate celery her whole body smelled of it for hours afterwards. She smelled like Åsa, and that was the most marvellous scent he knew. How he loved this woman. But then, as they made love in the darkness, it was still Margit Olofsson he saw before his eyes.

* * *

Elise was still in bed, silent and still. Maybe she was asleep; she didn't respond and her eyes were closed. Jennifer had a feeling her little sister had thrown up a few times during the night, because she had kept running into the bathroom. She had come home fairly early, but she hadn't said much and she'd looked terrible. Dead drunk probably. You couldn't tolerate much at that age; she was only fourteen after all. Jennifer closed the door to their room and went out to the hall.

The door to the living room was still closed, and Jennifer had no idea who or what was concealed behind it. Maybe it was Solan and her guy. Someone was sleeping in there anyway, because she heard heavy breathing and sometimes a snore. It was probably a frightful mess in there too. She wasn't even going to set foot in the kitchen. It stank of sour beer and old cigarette butts, rubbish everywhere. Gordon was lying on the kitchen floor, fully clothed and with nothing to cover him, but under his head he had a rolled-up rag rug as a pillow. He was lying completely still with his mouth open, and she couldn't see whether he was breathing. He might just as well be dead, she thought, but just then he let out a muffled whimper. She looked contemptuously at the floored wreckage of a person and thought how today Elise would have to do the cleaning; she was going to have fun.

Jennifer reached for the leather jacket on the hook and put it on. With an accustomed movement she tugged up the blonde hair that was inside the collar and let it fall down over her shoulders. Then she left the disaster area behind her, a bulging bag over her shoulder; she did not intend to come back within the next thirty-six hours.

Fanny and Malin were waiting for her outside the Intersport shop at the corner of Dalslandsgatan and Götgatan. And Joakim. He was also standing there, a little further away. She didn't know why; she had suggested they meet at Central Station, but here he was anyway. For some reason she felt ill at ease and avoided looking at him, greeting her friends instead.

At first she pretended not to see him. Joakim didn't know how to interpret that, what he ought to do, but after some consideration he gathered his courage and went up to the girls, making a show of being unconcerned. Jennifer didn't react at all at first, but finally gave him a distant glance. Only now did she see that his face was completely battered.

'What the hell happened to you?' she cried out. 'You look freaky!'

Joakim didn't know whether he should tell the truth or come up with an excuse, so he chose the simplest way and told her what really happened.

'Uh, Dad had a fit,' he answered nonchalantly. 'That's the way he is.'

Malin and Fanny were staring at him with admiration and then looked enquiringly at Jennifer, who seemed embarrassed.

'Hmm,' was all she said. 'Well, this is Joakim. A friend. He's coming along tonight. Or . . . ?'

She turned to Joakim with a look that said it didn't matter either way.

'Of course,' said Joakim. 'That's what we said.'

The situation felt strange. Jennifer was not like she usually was, now her friends were here. It was almost like she was ashamed of him. Usually she was so gentle and straightforward. Of course, yesterday when he needed her most she hadn't answered when he tried to reach her on her mobile. Instead of being with Jennifer, he'd spent the night in the city, wandered the streets around Sergelstorg, ridden the night bus, had a couple of beers by himself and killed a few hours at a McDonald's. Now he just wanted to hug her, but he couldn't when she was like this. Instead he placed his hand on her shoulder and squeezed her upper arm a little. Jennifer didn't react at all, but took off towards the stairs down to the metro over at Ringvägen, walking quickly.

'Come on, let's go get the tickets,' was all she said.

In the metro carriage they all stood, even though there were plenty of seats. The girls babbled on about this and that but did not draw Joakim into the conversation; after a while he sat down on a seat near them. He studied Jennifer, her facial expressions and movements, without listening to what they were talking about.

With her self-confident manner she was everything he wasn't. She was relaxed and natural and in a quiet way she was automatically the centre of attraction in every situation. Not to mention how good-looking she was. He wanted to hold her; he wanted her to smile that smile at him again. He wanted to dance with her, kiss her neck and stroke her gleaming hair.

What had happened? Was she tired of him, or had there never been anything between them? Was it just a game, a whim for her, and now everything was over and without his having understood the rules of the game? Or was she just shy in front of her friends? Before there had only been the two of them.

Suddenly he felt unsure about going along on this Finland cruise; maybe it would turn out completely different from how he had imagined it. He didn't have his father's permission either, so maybe it would be just as well not to go. Then he remembered how his father had attacked him the night before and he hesitated no longer. Of course he would go along on this trip. With a few beers under his belt he would feel fine. Jennifer would lighten up and get giggly and cuddly and he would take care of her and treat her to everything she wanted. Of course he would go along.

He smiled at her and she seemed to have sensed his gaze on her back, because suddenly she turned towards him and gave him what might be a hint of a smile. And then immediately started gossiping with her friends again. Maybe they were talking about him, because sometimes they looked over at him too. In contrast to Jennifer, their smiles were friendly.

As they made their way up out of the metro at Central Station, Joakim stayed a few steps behind the girls; Jennifer turned around every now and then to make sure he was still there. And at the entrance to the Viking Line office in the bus terminal, to his surprise she stopped and waited for him. When it was their turn in the line she took him by the arm before they went up to the counter. He felt his face turning bright red, but hoped it wasn't noticeable under his beard and wounds.

The woman behind the counter looked startled when she saw Joakim, and it struck him that his current appearance would scare the wits out of anyone. Maybe that was why Jennifer had kept her distance. But she was standing close beside him now, holding her arm under his.

'We've booked tickets to Åbo this evening,' said Jennifer.

'And the name was . . . ?'

'Jennifer Johansson.'

'So, how old are you?' the woman asked, studying them suspiciously over her reading glasses.

'We're twenty,' said Jennifer, nodding in her friends' direction.

'And you?' she said, looking at Joakim without concealing her distaste.

'Twenty-four,' Joakim replied.

'I see. Can you prove it?' said the woman in an ice-cold voice.

Joakim took his wallet from the back pocket of his jeans and fished out his ID. Her gaze flicked back and forth between Joakim and the ID card; apparently she could visualize Joakim going berserk in the bar on *Viking Cinderella*. Finally she nodded and her gaze swept over Joakim, Jennifer's arm under Joakim's, Malin, and finally Fanny.

'And you then?'

Fanny pulled out her fake driver's licence and they got their tickets without further questions.

Saturday Afternoon

Her tummy was screaming with hunger now. Hanna did not understand how Mummy could take Lukas and move away without giving her something to eat first. It was obvious that they had moved away; Mummy had taken not only her handbag but the sheets too. Hanna found pillows and covers on the armchair in the bedroom – Mummy probably couldn't carry them – but the sheets were gone, so they must be sleeping somewhere else. Mummy and Lukas weren't hiding anywhere in the apartment; instead they had disappeared while she was asleep. She'd known it the whole time: Mummy only loves Lukas. Even though he screams and throws up.

At first Hanna was very sad, but that had passed. She still thought Mummy was mean, so it didn't matter that she had moved away. It was just nice not to be nagged all the time. Now she mostly felt angry. And so hungry that she was starting to feel sick. She knew where the saucepans were, so it was just a matter of getting started. It couldn't be that hard. She took out a saucepan from the cupboard under the stove and placed it on the counter. Then she dragged the child's chair all the way from the dining-room table to the sink, climbed up on it and turned on the water. She took a firm hold of the saucepan with both hands and held it under the running water.

'Ouch!'

One hand ended up under the stream and the scalding hot water caused her to let go of the saucepan; when the saucepan landed in the sink hot water bounced against the edge and up into her face. She almost lost her balance, but at the last moment managed to grab hold of the counter. She screamed and screamed while she crawled back down to the floor, but no one came to her rescue.

The pain in her face subsided fairly quickly, but the burned hand was throbbing and soon turned completely red. The tears streamed down her cheeks and she lay as if paralysed on the kitchen floor, howling. She hoped that Mummy, despite everything, would hear her and come running like she always did when Hanna hurt herself. But she knew that it wouldn't happen this time; Mummy had got tired of her at last. Why did Hanna nag and whine, why did she have to be so difficult all the time? Mummy had warned her many times and said she couldn't put up with any more fussing. Now she'd had enough and taken Lukas with her and moved away. Without Hanna. And it probably served her right.

When she had recovered somewhat, the hunger pangs asserted themselves again. Hanna resumed her hunt for something to eat. Something that didn't need to be cooked. She went through cupboards and drawers methodically until she found the sweets. She'd ventured up on the chair again to hunt in one of the upper cupboards, where deep bowls and large platters were stacked. Here Mummy hid old bags of sweets from parties, a box of chocolates, a bag of lollipops, a tin of gummy bears and a bag the contents of which Hanna could not see. She poked around a little with one arm and everything except the box of chocolates crashed down to the floor. After a few more attempts she managed to push it so far forward on the shelf that she could grasp it with her fingers. She climbed carefully down from the chair, sat down on the floor and stuffed her mouth full of sweets. Mummy wouldn't like it, but then she should have stayed here with Hanna if she wanted to say no.

When she was full she wiped her sticky fingers on her nightie and got up. Her nappy was now so heavy that one Velcro fastening had come loose. Hanna peeled off the other one too and freed herself from the burden, which thudded on to the kitchen floor. She wandered aimlessly around the deserted apartment before she sat down on the floor in front of the TV in the living room. She rubbed her sore hand and studied the buttons on the remote control apprehensively. It was impossible to know which of the many buttons she should push to get it to work, but after she randomly played with the keypad for a few minutes the TV suddenly came on.

She remained sitting there, in front of an incomprehensible programme with women and men wearing strange clothes and speaking a peculiar language, her thoughts fluttering around. At last she felt fairly comfortable, with her belly full and the room filled with TV voices. But her hand still hurt. It would really be nice if Mummy or Daddy could come anyway and blow on it so the hurt would go away. But Daddy would be gone for many days, she knew that. And Mummy had moved away.

But maybe Mummy would stop by anyway to visit her? Then Hanna would be really happy and nice and not nag or whine at all. She would show Mummy that she could do better and that she had done everything right when she had to take care of herself. She would sleep in her own bed and make nice drawings for Lukas. She would take a bath and wash her hair – without shrieking. She would not take out a lot of toys unnecessarily and she would put the ones she was finished playing with back in their place. When Mummy saw that she would change her mind and move back home again.

Finally, when she couldn't keep her eyes open any longer, she lay down on the parquet floor and fell asleep, secure in the company of the TV.

Saturday Evening

After checking in and getting their room keys they went down to the cabin to drop off their bags. It was a four-bed cabin with two lower beds and two upper beds that opened out from the wall. There was also a small bathroom with toilet, sink and shower.

Malin and Fanny quickly laid claim to the more comfortable lower beds. Jennifer grumbled a little and suggested they draw straws, but Joakim was not at all bothered. Up above, you could be alone. He tossed his bag up on one of the upper bunks and Jennifer's on the other, but he was hoping that one bed would be enough for both of them.

Another group of both girls and guys had joined up with them at the terminal and was sharing another two cabins. They were all younger than Joakim; none of the girls appeared to be older than twenty, perhaps twenty-three for the guys. Everyone knew everyone, except Joakim, who knew only Jennifer. But that was enough for him.

Jennifer suggested they go straight to the duty-free shop to buy drinks, and everyone was in favour. They had to stand outside and wait for a while, until the boat had put out. Jennifer was once again reserved towards him, but Joakim decided to take matters into his own hands. He put a pinch of snuff under his lip and went around and introduced himself to everyone. To the question of what had happened to his face, his brief reply was simply that he'd been in a fight. This explanation did not seem to upset anyone; just the opposite. The ground under his feet gradually felt steadier.

He introduced himself as Jennifer's boyfriend, which was received with some surprise, but it was also apparent that this inspired respect. Jennifer was certainly a sought-after prize and he got a feeling that with this revelation he had made a considerable move up the status ladder. Now that their relationship was established she couldn't just ignore him, and the boys in the gang would keep their hands off her. Only Jennifer seemed indifferent, and she did not respond to his smile.

The shop opened and everyone bought what they wanted without being carded. On board the attitude towards suspected minors was more relaxed than it had been at the ticket counter and during boarding; the fake IDs had been left in back pockets and handbags. Joakim ended up being one of the last of the group in line at the till, and when it was time to pay for his beer Jennifer slipped in alongside him and put her arm around his waist.

'Hi!' he said, happily surprised at the sudden change in her manner.

He placed his arm around her shoulders and gave a little extra squeeze.

'Do you want anything?' he asked.

'Yes, this,' she answered, nodding at the basket she had in her hand.

'I'll get that,' said Joakim. 'Put it through the checkout and we'll get all this together.'

When they walked out of the store Jennifer said apologetically, 'Thanks, that was super nice of you! Student aid doesn't go very far.'

'Are you short of money?' asked Joakim.

'Usually,' answered Jennifer, 'but it'll work out.'

'Take this,' said Joakim, handing her a five-hundred-kronor note.

'You're so sweet,' Jennifer smiled, putting the money in her jeans pocket.

They went back down to their cabins as a group, where the long night's partying got under way. Joakim was gathering the courage to sound Jennifer out. He had hoped they would be able to get some time to themselves in the cabin, but in vain. It didn't really matter, however, once the liquor and Elephant beer started flowing he grew more confident and it brought results. Jennifer unexpectedly stayed put after he pulled her on to his lap, as he sat on the bed in one of the group's other two cabins. He held on to her and breathed in the scent of her newly washed hair without her pulling away. Everything was like normal again. He had been right to introduce himself to Jennifer's friends as her boyfriend, and now he was there drinking and enjoying himself like everyone else. The intoxication increased and Jennifer turned and kissed him on the mouth. He responded to the kiss and felt even more than before that he wanted her to himself.

'Come on, Jennifer, let's go to our cabin,' he whispered through the golden-blonde hair, but she squirmed and giggled disarmingly.

'Not now, Joakim, later. I want to party. Can't we stay with the others and have some fun?'

He went along with her gladly. Now they were back on track and he was exhilarated, proud and in love. He knocked back half a can of beer in one go and opened another. Jennifer was drinking vodka and Coke, and he wondered how her small body could tolerate so much, but on the other hand she was not exactly inexperienced.

Sitting next to him on the bed was Andreas, who looked to be about nineteen. He was broad-shouldered with an athletic appearance and a Nike T-shirt that fit snugly around a pair of muscular upper arms. He too had a big wad of snuff under his lip and Joakim toasted with him. Andreas told Joakim about a trip he'd taken to Kos during the summer, while Jennifer entertained herself – still from her position on his lap – with Malin, Fanny and two of the other guys. The noise level was high; a portable CD player boomed from the floor at one end of the cramped room and the music drowned out all the other conversations in the cabin.

Some time later, when Joakim was involved in a discussion with Andreas about a four-year-old girl who had been kidnapped in Portugal, Jennifer got up with a glass in her hand and left the room. People were running in and out of both cabins so Joakim assumed she wanted to mingle a little in the other one. Even though he really wanted to follow her immediately, wherever she was going, he remained sitting out of politeness until the conversation started to run down. Then he slipped over to the other room and scanned Jennifer's already seriously intoxicated friends. They had been joined by two guys who appeared to be about Joakim's age; to general amusement they were bellowing Finnish drinking songs. Jennifer was nowhere to be seen. He opened the door to the bathroom, but she wasn't there either. He went back to the first cabin, but that bathroom was empty too.

'Where'd Jennifer go?' he called to Malin, who replied with a shrug.

Fanny didn't know either, so he went and tried the door to their own cabin, but it was locked and no one answered his knocking.

Suddenly the fun of sitting and drinking with a gang of inebriated teenage strangers disappeared and he left the party unnoticed to find Jennifer. He searched down long corridors lined with doors, over to one of the stairwells and then up to a level where there was more than just cabins. He went systematically through all the shops, restaurants, bars, dance floors and gambling rooms, but without finding her. A hint of a headache was sneaking up and he gave up searching for the moment and sat with a can of beer at a table near the windows in the upper dance hall.

* * *

Suddenly she had just had enough. They were all so childish, especially the boys with their pathetic teenage bellowing. The giggly, shrill girls weren't much better. Joakim was different of course, although when they saw each other this morning something had changed. Something was wrong; it didn't feel right any more. He shouldn't have been there, uninvited, shouldn't have watched her with that look, although she had actually liked it before.

Yearning. Like a dog. Her feelings for him were simply gone; she was tired of him. She just couldn't think of what to do to end the whole thing, what she should say.

After aimlessly drifting around for a while, preoccupied by her thoughts, she found herself on the topmost deck. It was half past nine and so far there were few people in the large dance hall, but soon they would be flocking in, once people had finished dinner. There were a few scattered groups in the big hall, mainly at the window tables. Another group was sitting around the long bar.

She braced one foot against the footrest and heaved herself up on to one of the tall stools closest to the entrance in the half-moon-shaped bar. The bartender was turning glasses further down and did not seem to have noticed her. Syrupy-sweet dance music echoed in the mostly empty space and she was thinking about what to order when an older man sat down on the bar stool next to hers. Automatically she turned towards him, but he took no notice of her, looking instead at the bottles lined up on the shelves behind the bar. He had a somewhat slovenly, almost ravaged appearance: unpressed white shirt, unwashed hair that was too long over his ears, and he didn't seem to have shaved for several days. Jennifer could see that he was continually tensing his jaw.

'What are you drinking?' he asked suddenly, still without looking at her.

He sounded almost unfriendly and a shiver of distaste passed through her.

'Nothing,' Jennifer answered, preparing to leave.

'What are you doing in the bar then?' he continued.

'I was going to get a beer, but –'

'Two beers!' he called to the bartender, who nodded in response.

'But I don't want —'

'I realize that,' the man interrupted her again. 'Things don't always turn out the way you want, do they?'

He turned towards her for the first time and openly let his gaze sweep over her body. He hardly seemed interested in her face. His eyes were rather small and he looked harried. She had no desire to talk to this man, but she would probably have to endure it until the beers were finished; a beer was not cheap, after all. Jennifer didn't know where to direct her gaze, so she started fumbling in her handbag for her mobile phone. She had turned it off when Joakim started calling her and sending text messages, but now she turned it on again to have something to do with her hands. As soon as the phone was on it signalled that she had received several messages. They were all from Joakim, and she couldn't bear to think about him right now, so she turned the phone off again.

It struck her that maybe she should make a slight gesture of gratitude towards the man, since he was treating her to a drink, so she rooted out a packet of mints from her bag and extended it to him without saying anything. But he just shook his head with the same forbidding look. The bartender came with the two beer glasses and she took a few substantial gulps from hers at once, while the man paid with a crumpled hundred-kronor bill that he fished out of his back pocket.

'Thanks,' said Jennifer, but then couldn't think of anything else to say, so she sat in silence, gazing down into her beer.

'So you're drunk again today,' he said suddenly.

Who was he? He was seedy, but not enough to be part of her mother's gang and besides, she knew them all pretty well by now. Jennifer hesitated for a moment before she answered.

'What do you mean, "again"? I don't get drunk every day exactly.'

She looked around self-consciously to avoid looking him in the eyes; her gaze fell at last on her own hand, nervously fingering the beer glass. She quickly raised the glass to her lips and took in half the beer at one go. He placed one hand on her shoulder, but not to calm her.

'Yesterday and today,' was all he said.

Jennifer tried to pull away from his hand, but couldn't. She looked around again and made eye contact with a man sitting at a table just behind them. The hand was pinching her shoulder a little harder now, and she turned towards the heavy-handed man and looked him right in the eyes.

'What the hell are you talking about?' she spat out. 'I'll get drunk if I want to.'

He hissed at her with his mouth twisted in a malicious grin.

'You shouldn't carry on like that, you little whore!'

Her shoulder hurt now and she finally managed to twist out of his grasp.

'I'm sitting here peacefully and then you come along and start bothering me. And talking a lot of fucking shit! What the hell do you want from me?'

Once again she felt a hand on her shoulder, but this one belonged to someone else. She turned around and saw it was the man from the table behind who had come up to them.

'Are you coming any time soon?' he asked in a friendly

voice, but a little urgently, as if she was part of his group and had only gone away for a little while.

Jennifer quickly let herself down from the tall stool. In passing she grabbed her handbag from the bar.

'Gotta go now. Thanks for the beer,' she said with a contemptuous smile.

* * *

Where could she have gone? If she was with strange people in another cabin, there was no point in searching for her. If she was on one of the upper decks, they must have passed each other in all the stairs and corridors. But what was she really up to? Everything had felt so good before, when she was sitting curled up in his lap, carrying on like all the others. Why had she just left, without giving the least hint of where? She had kissed him, damn it! Besides, she had hinted that they had a long evening ahead of them – together. Once again it felt as if she didn't want him, that in reality she was looking for something else. But what? She didn't seem particularly interested in any of the other guys in the group, even if she interested them.

Joakim had no idea how Jennifer functioned. They really didn't know each other. They saw each other now and then, but not as often as he would like. He knew nothing about what life was like for her at home, about her family. That was the kind of thing she didn't talk about. He had no idea what she did during the week either. Sure, she went to school, that much she had told him, but that didn't seem to keep her from seeing him in the middle of the day if she wanted to. Did she have interests, did she play sport, what did she do when she wasn't in school and wasn't with him?

As he sat there thinking about their relationship – or whatever you wanted to call it – she was like a blank sheet of paper. He knew nothing about who she was or how she viewed things. On the other hand, she didn't know much about him either.

They had met only about a month earlier, in August, when it was still summer and warm outside. They met on Götgatan, in front of the building at Ringen where she lived. Jennifer had been to the shop to redeem bottles and do some shopping. She told him that she put the groceries in the paper bag she'd brought the empty bottles in. Just as they were passing one another on the pavement, the bottom dropped out of the bag. He helped her gather up the groceries then ran to the 7-Eleven on the other side of the street to buy a new bag for her.

Completely unperturbed by people looking at them, she'd directed all of her attention at Joakim. He noticed that she had a way of laughing with her whole face, not just with her mouth, and her eyes sparkled at him until he was completely weak at the knees.

A few days later they ran into each other at McDonald's, where they were sitting at separate tables. Jennifer caught sight of him and came up and asked if she could sit down at his table. She had been in a rowdy mood then, interested and talkative, and when they had finished eating she asked if he wanted to have a beer at one of the outdoor cafés on Medborgarplatsen. Taken by surprise by her direct manner, he agreed. They got drunk, and although he was much older, she was the one who took the initiative. Joakim felt free and a little wild in her company; she didn't ask annoying questions and didn't demand anything. She bubbled away and seemed to appreciate him as he was. Jennifer dragged him around to various places and after they had been snogging for a while in the bar at the Green Hunter she'd pulled him into the toilet.

It had been a magical evening and there had been a few more like that, before her interest in him seemed to subside. It was now almost two weeks since they'd had such a good time together. She blamed it first on one thing, then another, and sometimes – like yesterday – was simply unavailable or didn't show up when they made a date.

Joakim was at a loss about what to do, but he thought the whole situation was unpleasant. He knocked back the last drops of beer and pushed the glass away. Just as he was getting up to leave he caught sight of her. Far away, in the other part of the dance hall and half hidden by the long, semicircular bar he saw her from behind. Slouched in an armchair and with a reddish drink in her hand, she sat talking to two middle-aged men in suits.

Joakim froze mid-movement. He turned completely cold inside when he saw how she gestured and laughed with the two strangers. Why was she acting like that? He was the one she was here with; who were those men? They both seemed to move a little closer to her. One placed his hand on her thigh; the other stroked her cheek. She didn't pull away and didn't seem the least bit bothered. On the contrary, she laughed again and again – he could see that from the way she moved her shoulders. She held out her glass and toasted them and they brought their glasses next to hers. Dance music was playing through the loudspeakers and Joakim was sitting too far away to hear the clinking glasses or their voices. But he'd had enough. He felt his worry turn to rage and knew inside that it was all over now. Definitely over.

* * *

Jennifer tried to tell herself that she was only looking for excitement. But she knew there was something else besides – attention, not just from Joakim, not just from the usual losers who filled her world. Right now this felt right. And it would tomorrow too. The thought of poor Joakim flitted through her mind, but to hell with him, he was an adult; he could take her as she was or not at all. She was the smith of her own happiness; that was enough. She wasn't prepared to be the smith of Joakim's too.

She felt pleasantly tipsy; now if she could just keep this perfect level of intoxication going. Not get more drunk, not get sober.

'Are you here alone?' asked the darker and thinner of the two men.

They both spoke with that wonderful Finnish accent, and even though they sounded like Moomintrolls she thought the dialect only reinforced their manliness.

'No, I'm here with a few friends. I just got a little tired of them,' Jennifer replied apologetically. 'They're so . . . immature.'

'That's not good. We'll have to cheer you up a little. We're very mature,' laughed the other one. 'What's your name?'

'Jennifer.'

57

'I'm Erik,' said the huskier one, 'and this is Henrik. We've been on a business trip to Stockholm. What are you drinking?'

'Tequila Sunrise,' she answered, thinking it sounded glamorous.

'What the hell. That is mature,' the one named Erik grinned, getting up and going over to the bar.

Jennifer felt herself blushing a little, and glanced at the clock over by the bar as if to divert their attention.

'So, how old are you?' asked Henrik, placing his hand on her shoulder.

'Almost seventeen. How old are you?'

'What do you think?' he countered. 'We're two men in our prime.'

'Forty-three,' she guessed, and Henrik nodded appreciatively.

'Not bad, not bad at all. At our age, you know, you don't really like talking about your age. Do you have a boyfriend?'

He gathered up the papers they had been looking at before they rescued her from that disgusting man, and placed them in a briefcase on the couch beside him.

'Well, what should I say? Sometimes, sometimes not.'

Henrik was not content with that, and persisted.

'Okay, but right now?'

After quick deliberation she answered with a half-truth.

'No, I can't really say that. Maybe he thinks so, but I'm not involved with him any more.'

Well, that was that. There was something about the situation with Joakim that made her uneasy, but now it was over. Once she'd formulated them and the words were spoken, it became the truth. But Henrik didn't give up.

'So is he here on the boat, the poor guy?'

And now Jennifer lied; she didn't want to think about it any more, much less talk about it.

'Hell, no!' she said. 'Do you think I'd take him along on a trip like this?'

Erik came back. He set two large beers and a reddish-yellow drink, decorated with orange slices and a piece of kiwi neatly arranged on a toothpick, in the middle of the table. Henrik handed out the glasses and extended his own towards Jennifer.

'Cheers to freedom then,' he said, winking at her.

Erik did the same and Jennifer responded with a smile. The drink was not as strong as she'd hoped and she soon emptied it.

'You're a real pro at drinking,' said Erik.

'That was just fruit juice. They're a little stingy with the alcohol, I think. I'll go get a beer instead, then you know what you're getting.'

'No, no, what the hell, our treat,' said Henrik. 'But you know what, let's go down to our cabin instead, where we've got some real stuff. What do you say, Erik?'

Erik agreed, the two men finished their beers and all three left the bar and made their way towards the lifts.

Their cabin was higher up in the boat than Jennifer's, but not high enough to have windows. This cabin also had room for four people, but Erik assured her that he and Henrik were the only occupants. Henrik uncorked a bottle of Finnish vodka that he pulled out of a bag from the duty-free shop, mixing the alcohol with orange juice in some toothbrush glasses. Jennifer and Henrik sat down on one lower bunk with Erik across from them.

He's handsome, thought Jennifer. He and Henrik were talking about something and joking and laughing, but she wasn't thinking about what they said so much as how they said it. Henrik was handsome too; tall and dark, maybe a little too thin. He looked almost dangerous, with his cheeks scarred by something, probably teenage acne. He was better dressed, with a slightly more refined style than his friend, but Erik on the other hand had a kind of bitter humour and a dimple in his chin that appealed to her. He was a bit more rugged and had streaks of grey in his medium-blond hair, but it suited him.

Jennifer had always been attracted to older guys, but they were both considerably older than what she was used to. Real men, simply. In their prime. Different from the blokes her mother dragged home, or the peach-fuzzed geeks her own age, for that matter. No, she would probably choose Erik, but it could go either way. There was something exciting about both of them and to top it off, that mature, manly self-confidence. It was like they owned the world, they didn't need to look around to see what people thought. Nothing worried them. They were the ones who set the agenda; they didn't accommodate other people.

'Cheers again, kiddo,' said Henrik, placing his hand on her thigh.

He could do that, completely unruffled, without risking anything. He placed his hand on her leg and then the leg was his. He spoke to her as if she were little and he was big, and she could calmly lean back and let herself be taken care of on his terms. It was natural and obvious and she felt comfortable. With Joakim it was different. Suddenly it occurred to her what the problem was with him. Even though he was much older, it was Jennifer who was in charge, and that wasn't the way she wanted it.

They talked and drank and everything felt completely natural. She found herself far from her everyday world and far from her friends and their loud teenage drunkenness. She had taken yet another step into the adult world; Joakim and his yearning and fumbling were forgotten. It was not long before Jennifer was perched on Henrik's lap. Erik moved over and took her place on the bed. Suddenly she caught sight of a ring on his finger.

'Are you married?' she laughed.

'Yes, I've been married for a long time. Far too long,' he answered, looking deep into her eyes.

Jennifer didn't really understand what that was supposed to mean, whether it was good or bad, but she was held fast in that long gaze. His face was close to hers now and she could sense the aroma of his aftershave and the heat of his breath. Henrik's hands suddenly caressed her legs, the inside of her thighs, and wandered playfully up over the button of her jeans. She sank even deeper into Erik's gaze and his face approached hers until their lips met.

Practised hands groped their way in under her top, cupped her breasts, and she could feel hot breath on her neck; damp, warm lips on her face; several hands – hands everywhere. Two pairs of hands, two pairs of lips, two men playing with her body. Her sight was clouded by a kind of nameless yearning; she sank into the alcoholic stupor and let go.

*

When she woke up a few hours later she was alone in a cold, sticky bed. Her mouth was completely dry and a hangover was already making itself known in the form of a pounding headache right behind her eyes. What had really happened? What was she doing here? Shit, now it came back. Why did they just leave her like this? Damn it.

She propped herself up on her elbows and looked around the room. A half-full glass had been left on the floor below the bed, begging to be emptied. Jennifer took a look at the clock on the wall-mounted radio: one o'clock – not really late at all. She had no plans to go to bed early, so she knocked back the lukewarm drink and staggered into the bathroom for a quick shower and fresh make-up. The headache had already retreated somewhat and her spirits had recovered. She picked her clothes up from the floor, brushed them off and got dressed.

As she was bending down to put on her shoes she noticed a bundle of extra blankets and pillows under one of the beds. But there was something else too – in the middle of the soft pile of bedding she glimpsed the black briefcase Henrik had had beside him on the couch up in the bar. After a few moments of hesitation she decided.

For no real reason she pulled out the briefcase and cracked open the lid. Besides paper and pens, a calculator and a pair of gloves there was a diary. She couldn't resist picking it up and leafing quickly through the thin pages, until her gaze stopped at the owner's name on the inside of the leather-bound binder. Carefully she put the diary back where she found it, closed the briefcase again and pushed it under the bed.

In the little cupboard right inside the door, two jackets

were hanging. After turning almost all the pockets inside out, she finally found what she was looking for: a small bundle of business cards, carefully tucked into an unassuming navy-blue folder of velvety fabric. The same information was printed on all the cards and the business name was not familiar. She memorized the names Fredrik Grönroos and Gustav Helenius, put the business cards back in the inside pocket of the jacket and left the cabin.

* * *

When Hanna woke up it was already dark outside. The floor beneath her was wet, as was her nightie. The hunger was back again, worse than before. The sweets had satisfied her for a while, but now she needed food – like Mummy and Daddy would make. She took off the damp nightie, drying the pee from the floor as best she could using the nightie as a rag. To please her mum and dad, as she told herself, she stuffed the damp bundle into the laundry basket in the bathroom.

The rest of the sweets were still on the kitchen floor. There was only salt liquorice left, and she couldn't imagine eating that even in an emergency. A sandwich would have been good now and she knew where the bread was kept, but even if she got up on one of the tall stools she still could not reach that far, up to the cupboard over the refrigerator. Instead she tried to open the refrigerator door, but it was stuck fast.

This was not the time to give up, she felt instinctively, so she stubbornly dragged a chair all the way over to the refrigerator and climbed up on it to get a better grip on the handle. The chair left obvious scratches on the floor and that would not be appreciated, she knew, but the damage was already done. Hanna tugged and pulled on the obstinate door, and just as she was about to give up it finally surrendered. It turned out to be the freezer she had opened, but that would just have to do. Her skin got goose pimples from the icy cold blowing out on her bare body as she systematically pulled out the drawers in the freezer, one at a time. At last she found a packet she recognized: hash. That was also one of her very favourite things.

She got on her knees on Daddy's chair at the kitchen table and tore the freezer tape from the packet. The contents had clumped together inside. She tapped it on the table, carefully to start with and then more violently. Finally a few crumbs and then a large, frozen chunk of potatoes, onion and meat fell on to the table. The small pieces could easily be eaten; they melted quickly in her mouth and gradually took on a familiar taste. The large clump of ice, on the other hand, was harder to attack; she bit into it like an apple, but did not manage to get even a little bit loose. She was goose-pimply and her temples felt so cold that it was painful. Her teeth could not bite through the frozen block and Hanna suddenly felt herself getting angry. She took the stupid clump and threw it on the floor with a howl, causing a whole bunch of little frozen cubes to come loose. Yet another meal was eaten on the floor and even though her teeth ached and she was so cold that she was shaking, she felt rather content afterwards. Her stomach was full and she had shown that she could take care of herself, even get food.

She swept together the leftovers on the floor with her

hands and put them in the packet, which she left lying on the kitchen table. Then the phone rang. She rushed out into the hall where the phone was mounted on the wall. She tried to make herself as tall as she could, but she could not possibly reach the furiously ringing apparatus. She jumped up and tried to get hold of the cord to the receiver, but failed again and again until the telephone stopped ringing.

What if it was Daddy calling from Japan? Or what if it was Mummy who did care about her a little after all and wanted to hear how she was doing? She sank down on to the floor with tears running down her cheeks. How could Mummy do this to her? Silly, silly, silly Mummy, who only likes Lukas. At that moment she hated her and hoped she would die over there in her new life where Hanna was not allowed to be.

She was sitting on the cold tiled floor, with her hands in her armpits to get warm, when she suddenly happened to think about the door. She had not even tried to open the outside door. Opening it and running out and making noise in the stairwell and disturbing the neighbours was so forbidden that she had not even thought of it before. But the rules must be different now. Could Mummy have meant Hanna to live alone here in the apartment for the rest of her life without even being able to go out and shop?

She pulled herself up from the floor and went over to the wrought-iron gate. It looked closed, but Mummy had not locked it and the gate simply glided open when she pulled on the grating. Then she reached for the door handle and pulled it down. Nothing happened. The door was locked. But there was a knob higher up and if she could turn that the door would surely open, so she went back to the kitchen again to get the child's chair.

This time she pulled hard and managed to really lift the chair, a little at a time. She did not want to make any more scratches. It was quite far from the kitchen to the hall, but at last she was there. She climbed up on the chair, full of expectation, and made a half-turn on the knob until it stopped, at the same time pushing down the handle. Nothing. The door would not budge. So Mummy had locked her in. Could that really be so? She could believe many things about Mummy, but she never would have imagined that she would want Hanna to starve to death.

Hanna climbed carefully down from the chair again and carried it over to the telephone, so that she would be prepared next time it rang. If it rang. She shivered, still freezing after her ice-cold dinner. Her whole body was cold, except her right hand, which throbbed angrily from the hot water that had splashed on her that morning. She went to the children's room to look for some clothes to put on. Just as she had pulled out one of the drawers in the dresser and yanked out a little white T-shirt with a strawberry on the chest from one of Mummy's neatly folded piles, the phone rang again.

This time she would make it; the child's chair was already by the phone. One ring: Hanna started running towards the hall. Two rings: she was at the chair and starting to climb. Three rings now: she would make it, she was already halfway up. Four rings: she reached for the receiver, but with the dark-red, tender back of her hand she bumped against a framed photograph of herself and Lukas that was hanging on the wall. It hurt so much that she pulled her hand away wildly, losing her balance and falling headlong from the chair. She fell to the side where there was a bureau with metal knobs sticking out from the drawers. One of them struck her across the mouth and another one tore a gash in her cheek as she fell. She landed on her back on the hard, cold tiled floor, her hair fanned around her head like an ash-blonde wreath. The phone rang a fifth time and then it was silent.

* * *

Sjöberg took the opportunity to live like a bachelor whenever the rest of the family was out of town. This was something Sandén – who cared little about his health – was always open to, but which Sjöberg seldom indulged in. If you decide to have five kids you have to bear the consequences. This evening, however, they would party.

Sjöberg could not quite shake off the unpleasant mood of his dream and felt slightly nauseous all day. The dream, which he usually had once or twice a month, had started haunting him several times a week. And it had such a powerful effect on him that it never really left him in peace, not even during the day.

When Sandén had called to suggest they meet for a beer, Sjöberg happily accepted the invitation. He was on the way back from visiting his mother at Huddinge Hospital. She would be there for another twenty-four hours according to the medical staff, but was feeling good for the most part.

At four o'clock, when Sjöberg showed up at the little pub, the Half Way Inn on Swedenborgsgatan, Sandén was already perched on a bar stool by the window waiting for him. He could not have been waiting long; the two pint glasses in front of him were untouched. Sjöberg cheerfully greeted his old partner-in-crime, but was given a reserved smile in return. He did not understand until Sandén turned his whole face towards him.

'What the hell happened to you?' Sjöberg exclaimed. 'Do you have a black eye?'

Sjöberg could not conceal his amusement. Sandén was big enough to take care of himself and if something had happened to the lout, he no doubt had himself to blame. He was good-hearted by nature, but he could be a bit too aggressive for his own good.

'Ran into a door,' Sandén replied, nonchalantly drumming against his glass with his fingertips.

'Ha,' said Sjöberg. 'Classic.'

Sandén wrinkled his face into a grimace that was supposed to look distressed, and said in a quivering voice, 'It's Sonja. Spouse abuse.'

'Oh boy,' said Sjöberg, affecting sympathy, well aware that Sandén's wife was a gentle, peaceful soul who would never harm a hair on his head. 'We'll have to call the men's crisis centre. They can save a place for you at a shelter.'

'No, damn it! Call the women's crisis centre, I'd rather stay at a women's shelter. Cheers.'

He stopped his drumming and brought the glass up to his mouth. Sjöberg pulled off his jacket with a broad smile, hung it on a hook under the table and sat down. Sandén pushed the untouched glass towards him and Sjöberg took a generous gulp.

'What happened really?' he asked, more serious now.

'Oh, it's that damn Pontus,' Sandén sighed. 'Jenny's boyfriend.'

Jenny was the older of Sandén's two daughters. She was twenty-four and had slight learning difficulties. Right now she was not working or going to school; Sjöberg was also keeping his eyes and ears open for available jobs simple enough to suit Jenny. Quite recently she had moved in with a guy Sjöberg had never met, but who was, according to Sandén, an unpleasant character who was exploiting her. Jenny was an incredibly nice person and gullible besides. Sandén had hinted that she probably went along with almost anything this Pontus asked her to do.

'Did he beat you up?' said Sjöberg.

Sandén answered by pulling air into his mouth to a toneless 'yes'.

'What? You got beat up by some little punk?'

'Well, he's not that little . . .'

'You have to report him,' said Sjöberg excitedly. 'Tell me now, what happened?'

'I probably thrashed him first,' said Sandén, lowering his eyes.

'Seriously? The guy is an idiot, but you didn't really resort to violence, did you?'

'He assaulted Jenny. She had ugly bruises on her arms and her whole back was scraped up on some old trunk they have in the apartment.'

Sjöberg felt completely cold inside. Jenny had never had it easy with her handicap; it was too mild for others to really notice, but too serious for her to manage a normal job. During the past year she had been happily in love, something her parents had welcomed but also worried about.

'Why, I don't know; she wouldn't hurt a fly,' Sandén continued, taking a gulp from his glass. 'But when I found out I went crazy and hit him. That little piece of shit hit back, so Sonja had to intervene. But his black eye is probably worse than mine,' he added with a cheerless laugh.

Sjöberg shook his head. 'That was childish, Jens. The kid can report you to the police, you know that. Is it worth it? Will anything be better for Jenny, if you're done for assault?'

'Listen, that's exactly what he intended to do. Then I pointed out to him that if he did, I'd report him for assaulting Jenny. He answered that he didn't have any problem with that. He thought life in jail would be harder for me than for him. Being a cop. How do you respond to that? He's right.'

'Yes, how did you respond to that?'

'I offered him ten thousand kronor to forget the whole thing, move out of the apartment and break off contact with Jenny.'

'Did he take the bait?'

'He's going to think about it.'

'Jenny will be heartbroken,' said Sjöberg.

'Yes, but we're here for her. He's an idiot if he doesn't take up an offer like that. Ten thousand is a lot of money.'

There was nothing to add. Sjöberg absentmindedly fingered his glass and sat with his eyes fixed on the Scottish plaid wallpaper.

After a while Sandén broke the silence. 'Is that supposed to look "genuine British"? Who the hell ever saw plaid wallpaper in a real pub? They're too funny, those Scotsmen . . .'

Sjöberg, who had just emptied the last contents of his

glass, started laughing, and beer sprayed out of his nose and mouth. Sandén started laughing so hard that people turned around, and the oppressive mood quickly lifted. Sandén never let sorrows and grief put a damper on his good time.

After another two beers they moved on to Portofino on Brännkyrkagatan. The restaurant was full and they did not have a reservation. Sandén, however, ate at the excellent little Italian restaurant often, so Marco, the owner, managed to conjure up a table for them at lightning speed. After a superb pasta meal with wine and grappa with coffee, they found themselves at the Cadier Bar at the Grand Hotel of all places, shortly before midnight. Sjöberg had suggested a simple beer at some place like Akkurat on Hornsgatan, where they had a number of varieties to choose from. But Sandén was in an extravagant mood and was determined to spend the rest of the evening at a piano bar. Because these days there was only one left in Stockholm, they ended up at the Grand Hotel.

Together, they had endless topics of conversation. They had a long shared history because they had worked together ever since the police academy. Their families happily socialized a good deal too. Sandén's daughters no longer lived at home, but the jovial Sandén and his wife, both fond of children, were not bothered by the presence of the Sjöberg children at family gatherings.

The pianist was playing 'Fly Me to the Moon', and the tipsier members of the audience sitting closest to the keyboard were singing along. Sjöberg and Sandén stood further away at the bar, each with a beer. The noise, the music and the relaxed atmosphere that prevailed in

71

Sandén's company surrounded Sjöberg like a warm embrace, and he found himself feeling euphorically free of demands. With Jens he could just talk, there was no attitude, no scrutinizing glances. They had already taken each other's measure twenty-five years before and there were no personality analyses left to make. And besides, Sandén was fun. The laughs came often when he got going, and Sjöberg could already feel how hoarse he would be in the morning. His bad dreams, his obligations were pushed from his thoughts. He was just taking in life with all his senses.

It was then that Margit Olofsson emerged from the throng of people over by the piano and approached them.

'Hi, Conny!' she called happily, to make herself heard over the buzz and the music.

'Look who's here!' Sjöberg answered in surprise, spontaneously putting his arm around her. The way you do when you meet an acquaintance in a crowded bar, he told himself. Sandén looked, perplexed, from one to the other. He knew he recognized the woman, but the connection between her and Sjöberg was an unsolvable equation.

'Don't you recognize Margit, the nurse? Ingrid Olsson's benefactor?' said Sjöberg, with a friendly pat on her shoulder.

'Exactly! It's you!' Sandén exclaimed, still looking a trifle perplexed.

'We met yesterday, at Huddinge,' Sjöberg helped out. 'When I was there with my mother.'

'That explains it,' said Sandén cheerfully. 'I was starting to wonder whether you were on a friendly footing with all the old witnesses and murderers and victims and relatives . . .'

'Jens . . .' said Sjöberg urgently.

'Jens Sandén,' said Sandén, extending his hand to Margit Olofsson.

'Yes, I recognize you too,' said Margit, still smiling. 'Are you out celebrating a solved murder, or . . . ?'

'We're celebrating Conny's recovered youth,' Sandén answered quickly. 'He's a temporary bachelor and enjoying his freedom without five snot-nosed kids around his ankles.'

'And you?' Sjöberg added.

'We're a group of nurses celebrating a birthday. Not mine,' she added, raising her hand in a deprecatory gesture.

'Is he here, that eighty-year-old guy in a nurse's uniform?' Sandén asked in his customary outspoken manner.

'Gunnar? Sure! He's not one to say no to a party,' Margit laughed. 'He's sixty-three, I should point out, and it's his birthday. He wanted to go to a piano bar and this seems to be the last one in town.'

Sjöberg treated her to an Irish coffee and the three of them remained standing, chatting for a good while in a relaxed manner. Now and then one of Margit Olofsson's co-workers came over and exchanged a few words, but then quickly left again. When all three finally started thinking it was time to go home, Margit's colleagues had already left. Sandén got into a taxi, and Sjöberg and Margit Olofsson accompanied each other in the direction of the Old Town.

As soon as Sandén left them, the mood changed. They talked about her and him, about him and her. Sjöberg felt as if they were in a bubble, screened off from the world, from reality. The romantic undercurrent was tangible now, with Sandén's boisterousness gone, but this time it did not feel wrong. Now there was no sober self deciding what he could and couldn't talk about, nothing to determine how long his smile could last. When he placed his arm around her as they were walking it felt like a completely natural gesture.

When a little later he pulled her to him and kissed her, nothing stopped him or warned him. In some strange way he felt as if he had come home. He sniffed her beautiful hair, with a fresh scent of shampoo and cool September night air. He suddenly felt completely relaxed. They remained standing like that for a long time; he with one hand around her waist and the other somewhere in her long hair, his mouth pressed against her forehead. Just then Sjöberg was not speculating about motives; not his own, not Margit's. A group of teenage girls on bicycles passed them shrieking loudly, but Sjöberg took no notice of them. He was still in his bubble and he did not want to come out. He took her face in his hands and turned it up towards his own. He looked for a long time into Margit's glistening green eyes before he kissed her again.

He followed her to Slussen and there they separated without a word.

Early Sunday Morning

It must have been extremely late because almost everyone had gone to bed. A dreary atmosphere had settled over the large vessel. Here and there budget travellers and drunks were sitting or lying down.

Jennifer did not have a watch, but she was tired and needed to sleep. Her legs felt unsteady, so it took her a while to make her way back to the cabin. Even though her head was surprisingly clear, she did not really know whether she was in the right end of the boat. A wave of nausea passed over her and she looked around for a toilet. Behind the one-armed bandits and video games she caught sight of one. She staggered there as quickly as she was able, but had to swallow several times so as not to vomit on the wall-to-wall carpet.

She rushed into one of the cubicles and did not have time even to close the door behind her. The vomit came cascading out of her mouth. As much ended up outside as in the toilet. It was only liquid; she had not eaten for hours. The effort made her sweaty and she reached for a roll of toilet paper that someone had set on the cistern. She needed to wipe off the sweat and blow her nose, but the paper on the roll was damp and crinkled. Hoping it was only water, she managed to poke loose a piece of wet tissue and wiped her face.

Suddenly she heard the door slam behind her, but in

her foggy condition she did not have the energy to turn around.

She felt a movement by her left ear and heard a voice hiss, 'You shouldn't be so nosy, you fucking little cunt.' Just as she started with terror and was about to turn around, she felt warm hands in a rock-solid grip around her throat.

She tried to scream, but she could not get out a sound. Her larynx was being pressed into her throat with great force. Through her bulging eyes, the white tiles on the bare wall in front of her turned first pink, then red. At last it felt as if her eyes had burst. The hands released their hold, and she collapsed over the vomit-covered toilet.

Sunday Morning

Petra Westman was running through the fog on the cobble-stones along Norra Hammarbyhamnen, from the police building at the far end of Östgötagatan over to the Danvik canal and back. She ran past one boat after another, some with pretty bunting and others with colourful lanterns hanging above well-tended decks. Right before Barnängs-bryggan there was a fishing boat for sale. She looked out over the black water, rippling in the wind. In the distance she saw Hammarbybacken; the hill looked green and deso-late, at this time of year just a reminder of the winter activities several months away. Except for the distant roar of early morning traffic, it was completely silent.

It was only six-thirty but she had already been running for twenty minutes. Now she was on her second round and turned off in the direction of Vita Bergen, running up Tengdahlsgatan towards the allotments. The air was cool and damp with a scent of autumn, even though the trees had not yet started losing their leaves. Garden furniture and barbecues were still out; summer flowers adorned the pots outside the houses.

A door shut somewhere behind her and instinctively she twisted her head. She didn't see anyone. She never used to be like this. Before, she would have just forged ahead, pos-sibly noting that she was not the only one awake at this hour on Sunday morning, but paying no attention to the sound.

Peder Fryhk was in safe custody at the Norrtälje prison and would not get out for at least three years, probably more. Petra had not been involved in the arrest, had not been questioned by the police, had not testified at the trial. Her name did not figure at all in the investigation of Fryhk and his systematic rapes. Besides her, only the prosecutor Hadar Rosén, forensic technician Håkan Carlberg in Linköping and Fryhk himself knew that Petra was one of his victims.

And one other person. The Other Man. Carlberg had found that the semen in the condoms she took with her to Linköping after the rape belonged to two different men, one of whom was Peder Fryhk. The other was unidentified.

Petra had had plenty of time to think since she had been drugged and raped last November. She had revealed her first name to Fryhk, no more. She said she worked as an insurance agent at Folksam; he had no reason not to believe her. Presumably he had gone through her wallet; he must have wanted to know who he was dealing with. So okay, he had her surname too, and personal identification number. But he had probably been content with that. He hadn't examined her wallet carefully enough to find her police identification – well hidden behind her driver's licence – had he? Maybe he had, but there was still no reason for him to suspect that Petra was behind the arrest. She had played her part well, blamed herself for being hungover and given him a tender farewell in the morning. Without leaving any traces after her personal crime scene investigation.

But there were still a few things that pointed to a different conclusion. Peder Fryhk's basement was full of video recordings of his other rapes. He must have preserved his souvenir of the one of Petra too, but no such film had been found. Why? Where had that tape gone?

Fryhk was a former foreign legionnaire. Intelligent, educated, cunning. Senior anaesthetist at Karolinska Hospital with a great deal to lose: nice house, high position in society and a good reputation. And yet he did it, again and again. Raped. In his own home, videotaping the whole thing besides. And he finally lost. Everything.

The Other Man held the camera. Artfully panned the scene, changed angle to capture the action from various perspectives, zoomed in. And raped. But without ever allowing himself to be filmed. He was more careful than Fryhk, not as self-sacrificing. Perhaps he had more to lose? Could you lose more than Peder Fryhk? Hardly. But the Other Man was not prepared to lose everything.

Fryhk duped his victims, lured them home. He risked being recognized in town, but relied on his charm and on the memory gaps and the feelings of guilt of the victims. The Other Man never left any memories with his victims. And Fryhk was obviously loyal; he had not uttered a word about a co-perpetrator. A real soldier. His lips had been sealed when he was questioned about who held the camera during the rapes in his house. Despite false promises of a reduced sentence, he had kept his mouth shut.

And Petra was stuck in a limbo of uncertainty. She had been raped by a man without a name and without a face. The police did not know that this cameraman was also a rapist, and the efforts to find him had come to a standstill long ago. But now someone was calling her at night; not often, but not so infrequently that she could simply shrug it off. Once or twice a month she was woken in the early hours by the phone, but no one was there when she answered. The Other Man could not know her number; it was unlisted and so he couldn't have found it in the phone book. Yet that was just what worried her. That it was him calling, that he wanted to punish her for putting Fryhk in jail. Frighten her into silence. Crush her to show his power. Wasn't that what rape was about? Power. That was what worried Petra Westman. And the fact that he existed. Was out there, alive and kicking. Free. The Other Man.

She had been running for longer than usual now, but still did not feel especially tired in the dew-fresh September morning. She flowed along at an easy pace; the half-awake paper boy she encountered was startled as she zipped past. Otherwise, as far as she could see, the area was completely deserted. When she had almost reached the allotment area she left the street and took the small stairway between the apartment buildings up to Vitabergsparken. She ran on the gravel path between muddy, well-used lawns, past the amphitheatre and the closed outdoor café over to the turning area by Stora Mejtens Gränd. There was a smell of rosehips and wet tarmac.

In the fog she could still not see Sofia Church up on the hill, but suddenly she caught sight of something else. To her left there were dense thickets next to a Falun-red wooden house, and deep inside the thicket was something big and blue, almost entirely covered by branches and leaves. Curiosity made her change direction and she jogged over to the bushes, leaned down and pushed the branches apart. It was a baby's pram insert, upholstered in navy-blue cloth with small white dots. It looked nice, not much used, and her initial thought was that some self-obsessed, pimply adolescent marauders had taken the frame of the pram and thrown the insert into the bushes. She took hold of the edge on one side with both hands and pulled it firmly towards her. She managed to get it halfway out through the resistant branches, and got ready for another tug just as she took a look down into the insert.

There was a little person inside, with closed eyes and a light-blue cap, tucked into a foot muff. Instinctively she rose from her crouching position and threw all her weight into the bushes. Thorny branches tore through her thin leggings and scratched her skin. She held the branches away from the child with her body while she leaned over and carefully picked up the whole foot muff, with one arm under the child's neck and the other at the foot end. Something in the little face made her think it was a boy. She put her cheek against his but could not tell whether he was breathing.

Then she ran, with the child in her arms and blood seeping from the scratches on her legs, over to the substantial doors that led into the garden of the house. She tore at them but they were locked. Then she rushed off towards Stora Mejtens Gränd. Despite her haste, she noticed a neatly parked pram without an insert on the grass on the other side of the turning area. With her hip she pushed open the gate to one of the houses on the street and rushed the few steps to the porch and up the outside stairs. While she kicked at the door she rang the doorbell, shouting all the while that she needed an ambulance.

After half an eternity the door was opened by an elderly woman who immediately let her in, indicated an unmade bed in a room off the hall and hurried away to call for the police and an ambulance.

'The child is suffering from hypothermia and may be injured – he may be dead!' Petra called to the woman. 'I found him in the park. He may have been there a long time.'

She pulled down the zip on the foot muff and placed the boy on the bed. He showed no signs of life and felt very cold. While she puffed deep breaths on to his face, she massaged his arms and body to get him warm. She took hold of his lower leg and bent it as if to pump life into him. Finally she simply took him in her arms and tried to encircle his entire little body with her own. She was sitting like that with tears running down her cheeks when the paramedics finally showed up.

* * *

Ewa Tuominen was tired. A co-worker was sick, so she'd had to work a double shift and was more than an hour behind schedule. She had been cleaning on *Viking Cinderella* for ten years and was used to most things, but when she opened the door and saw the mess in the toilet she let out an audible sigh. And to top it off, there was a young woman lying there asleep in the midst of it all, in a very uncomfortable position besides. A bit of bare back could be seen between her jeans and her leather jacket. She shouldn't be lying there; anyone at all could attack her.

Just as Ewa gave the lifeless creature a light tap on the foot, it occurred to her that something was not right. Her position was unnatural. Even the most intoxicated person could not sleep like that. The girl did not react at all to her touch either. Ewa began to panic, her pulse started to race and she stood there with her hand in front of her mouth for a few seconds while her brain whirred. Then she decided to call the doctor immediately, rather than try to search for the girl's pulse. She backed up a few steps, out into the laundry room, and dialled the emergency number, the ship's doctor's mobile phone.

Doctor Magnusson, who arrived almost immediately, could tell right away that the girl was dead. When he turned her over and saw the onset of bruising on the throat, he decided to leave the girl lying there. Without a doubt this was a matter for the police. He told Ewa Tuominen to lock the toilet and contacted the ship administrators. In an hour or so they would be arriving at Åbo.

* * *

Hanna spent the whole night on the hall floor. Once she woke up, her head hurting and the wound on her cheek throbbing. Her mouth was tender; it felt completely swollen. The floor below her was so cold that she was shaking. She did not have the energy to get up and make her way to the nice warm bed, but she managed to crawl the short distance to the hall rug. She had been lying there in the only position that was comfortable. When she woke up early in the morning she was curled up in a foetal position, with her uninjured cheek against the rug and her hands clasped under her chin.

She moved her burned hand carefully over her cheek, which was covered with dried blood. When she came to the wound itself she winced with pain and pulled her hand away. But she did not cry: she simply screwed her eyes shut and gritted her teeth, the way you should when things were tough. 'The only thing to do is grit your teeth,' Mummy always said when Hanna cried, so that's what she did now. It was the first time she'd done this, but it was already too late. Mummy was gone. There was no point in crying when there was no one there to console her anyway. Her hand and her mouth hurt terribly too, but in comparison with the wound on her cheek and the awful headache, she barely felt them.

What was she going to do? It felt like a lot of days had passed now. Would Daddy be coming home soon? Or did he know that Mummy and Lukas had moved? Would he maybe live with them instead? But Daddy liked Hanna very much, she thought. Daddy was not as strict as Mummy, and he always played with her when he came home from work in the evening and Mummy only paid attention to Lukas. Yes, Daddy would surely come home to Hanna when he got back from Japan.

Then almost without her noticing it there was poo on the rug. She must start paying more attention to that and use the toilet instead. Mummy had said so many times, but it just never happened. There were so many other things to think about all the time. But now she had to get up and put things away before Daddy came home. Forget how much it hurt all over and clean up after herself. She got up laboriously and remembered the urine-soiled nightie. She staggered into the bathroom and pulled the nightie out of the laundry basket and went back to the hall. After she dried and rubbed for a while it was still not clean, but much better, so she carried the sticky rag back to the bathroom and pushed it down into the basket again. Her hands smelled bad. When you've pooed you have to shower, she thought, but that would be hard. The whole bathroom would get wet, the walls and ceiling, and water might splash all the way out into the bedroom and Mummy didn't like that. Hanna decided to take a bath instead. And wash her hair. Then Daddy would be happy when he got home and think she smelled good.

She knew how to do it: she put the plug into the plughole and turned on the tap. At first the water was cold, but then it got warmer. Hanna sat on the toilet seat and watched the water flowing out of the tap and down into the bathtub. Her head felt very dizzy. Sometimes she had to look with one eye to see clearly. Her teeth were chattering and she longed to creep down into the warm water, but she did not dare climb in before the tub was full. She did not like the roar of the running water.

After a while she turned off the tap and got into the bathtub. It was so nice! She sat down carefully, but just then she heard the phone ringing out in the hall. Oh, why did it have to ring right now? She had to answer, had to talk to someone. Quick, quick! Heaving herself to her feet, she skidded on the slippery bottom but managed to catch herself by pure reflex. Her chin missed the edge of the tub by a hair's breadth. But she wasted time and now the tears were coming again, although she tried to hold them back. She tried again and stood up more carefully this time, and climbed down on to the floor. But before she had even left the bathroom the ringing stopped.

So she slunk back to the bath and settled down in the warm water again. With a damp hand she tried to wipe away the tears from her cheeks. The square tiles on the wall in front of her flowed together and she was no longer able to make the effort to see them clearly. Even though she had slept for the whole night and had only just woken up, she once again fell into a deep sleep.

* * *

Joakim woke up with a start at a knock on the door. He pushed himself up on to his elbows in the bed and looked around, half asleep. The bed that Jennifer should have slept in, because she was not in his, was untouched. Below him he could see Fanny lying quietly in her bed. He glanced at his watch and saw that it was only seven-thirty.

There was another knock and now he heard movement in the bed below him and assumed that Malin was stirring. Fanny was still completely quiet. Suddenly through his clouded condition he remembered how the night before had degenerated and he started to feel sick. It was warm in the cabin and he felt sweat breaking out on his upper lip. There was another knock, harder this time.

'Open up, it's the police!' a voice called in a Finnish accent from outside.

Now Fanny too started moving; she complained with her face in the pillow, 'Damn it, open the door, Joakim!'

'Coming!' he called back tamely, wriggling out of bed and down on to the floor.

Before he opened the door he glanced down to check whether he had something on. When he saw that he was wearing underwear he opened the door. Outside stood two men, neither of them in a police uniform. One however was holding up what might be a police ID. Joakim stepped instinctively to the side and let the police come into the cabin.

'Nieminen, detective chief inspector with the Åbo police,' the policeman standing closest to him introduced himself in his melodic accent. 'This is Inspector Koivu. What's your name?'

The other man stood in the background and studied several sheets of paper. When Joakim gave his name, he made a note with a pencil. Both police officers looked in towards the girls, who were now sitting up in bed, curiously looking over towards them.

'And you girls?'

They said their names and more notes were made.

'I need to ask for your ID,' Nieminen continued commandingly. 'Please take them out. Who's sleeping here?' he then asked with a gesture towards the vacant upper bunk.

'Jennifer, but she didn't sleep here last night,' Joakim answered.

'Jennifer Johansson?'

'Yes.'

'Do you know where she was last night?' Nieminen asked. 'Since she hasn't been here?'

The girls got out of their beds and started rooting in their bags. None of them really knew what to say, which made the policeman impatient.

'Well, when did you last see her?'

'I haven't seen her since we were with the guys next door getting primed a little,' Malin answered. 'That was pretty early in the evening.'

Fanny nodded in agreement and added, 'You ought to know, Joakim. She's your girlfriend.'

Joakim looked down at his feet in embarrassment, not knowing what to say.

'I see, you're the boyfriend,' said Nieminen.

'Well, I don't know,' said Joakim lamely. 'Or, well, it's hard to say. What's this all about?'

'A dead girl was found in a toilet. We think it may be Jennifer. If there aren't any relatives on the boat, I have to ask one of you to come along and look at her.'

Joakim sat down on Malin's bed.

'We just need to look at your ID first.'

Malin and Fanny extended their ID cards, their real ID this time. It was probably best not to do anything stupid at this point. Joakim reached for his jeans, which he'd thrown on the floor at the foot of the bed, and pulled his wallet out of the back pocket.

He handed the whole wallet to Nieminen, who simply gave it to his colleague. None of the young people said anything; they looked wide-eyed at the two policemen, not really grasping what was going on.

'So, are you the one who's coming with us?'

Nieminen directed himself to Joakim, who mumbled something inaudible in response and started pulling on his trousers.

'I'm very sorry about this. But it's good if we know for certain as soon as possible; it'll help us know what we have to go on,' said Nieminen, in a friendlier tone now.

Koivu gave the young people back their ID cards while Joakim pulled on his T-shirt.

'We'll need to talk to you more during the day, girls.

Until then, try to remember what you were up to and when, and what Jennifer was doing during the evening and night.'

Joakim and the two policemen disappeared through the door, which closed by itself behind them.

When they got out of the lift on one of the upper decks Joakim saw that barricade tape had already been put up in various places. A number of uniformed policemen made sure that no unauthorized persons went past. Joakim could not think clearly. He was brought to a room, which according to the sign outside was the ship doctor's consulting room. This too was guarded by a policeman in uniform. The two men escorting him exchanged a few words with each other in Finnish and then unlocked the door and pushed him into the room ahead of them. The door closed behind them and Joakim took a few hesitant steps forward. He felt as if his legs were going to fold under him, and instinctively he held his breath.

On a cot by one wall lay Jennifer. Of course it was her. But the liveliness in her face, which was an odd flame-red colour, was gone. Her forehead looked freckled, as did her closed eyelids. On her throat a few large, light-red marks were visible that he did not recognize. And her lips no longer glistened. She still had on her black, waist-length leather jacket, and her belly could be glimpsed in the gap between her trousers and her top. Joakim was struck by the terrible stillness. Not a sound could be heard; even the policemen seemed to be holding their breaths.

Then the silence was broken by a drawn-out whimpering sound that issued from Joakim's mouth. The sound grew louder and at last he put his hands in front of his face and let the tears flow. He turned quickly around and rushed towards the door.

'Let me out of here!' he pleaded. 'It's Jennifer – I don't want to see any more! Let me out, let me out!'

'I don't know what she was doing last night,' Joakim had to admit when he was questioned a short time later by the Finnish police inspector, in a room adjoining the doctor's consulting room.

He had been told that the ferry was in Åbo and that no passengers would be allowed off until everyone on board had been questioned. That had no significance for him, except that it would be a while before they got back to Stockholm.

'Was she murdered?' asked Joakim, even though he already knew the answer.

'It looks that way. Strangled, presumably. In one of the toilets.'

'So anyone could have done it?' asked Joakim.

'It's not usually just anyone who does this sort of thing,' the policeman answered with a joyless smile.

He now clasped his hands before him on the table and cleared his throat, as if to start again.

'And you were, or you weren't, or to some extent you were her boyfriend. Were you really her boyfriend?'

Nieminen acted appropriately and even kindly towards Joakim, but he was not able to conceal his suspicion very well. That was probably how he had to be in his occupation. Joakim felt ill at ease and squirmed in the chair, still shaken up after his encounter with the expressionless face of death.

'Yes and no,' he answered uncertainly.

Even he did not understand what their relationship had been, so how could he explain it?

'I guess you could say we were together sometimes, sometimes not.'

'So you exploited her just as it suited you? You're twenty-four and she was sixteen. Wasn't she a little young for you?'

'Maybe so.'

Joakim could only bear to answer one question at a time, and the policeman's insinuation that he had exploited Jennifer had to remain unchallenged. Had he? He had been in love with Jennifer. That was for real. Until yesterday. Until he had seen her preening for those old men in the bar. Then all his tender feelings and hopes had faded. After that he had felt only anger. And contempt. At first he was hurt, but he'd been hurt many times before. You can't go around bleeding all the time, so he forced the wounds to heal quickly. But they always left ugly scars.

'Tell me about yesterday evening. Tell me about Jennifer.'

'We were partying in the cabin next to ours, for an hour or two maybe. Jennifer and me and a few others. She was sitting on my lap. People came and went. There was a party in the cabin next to that one too; the door was open. Same group. I didn't know anyone besides Jennifer to start with; the others were her friends.'

'Were you drunk?'

'Yes, I guess I was. That's, like, the point. Everyone was drunk.'

'Everyone was drunk? They were just young kids. How did they get on the boat to begin with?'

'It wasn't too hard. I had to show ID, but not the girls. I don't know about the others.'

A half-truth, but Joakim saw no reason to mention anything about fake IDs.

'What happened to your face?' Nieminen asked unexpectedly.

Joakim had not looked in the mirror since yesterday and had completely forgotten how he looked. Instinctively he brought his hand to his nose and felt it carefully.

'Got beat up,' he mumbled.

It went against his instincts, but he could not lie before the penetrating gaze of this policeman.

'My dad,' he added. 'It was my dad.'

'Is your dad with you on the trip?'

'No, damn it. It was on Friday. He gets a little angry sometimes,' Joakim said in an effort to downplay it.

'I see. And then?' Nieminen continued.

'Jennifer left. I thought she'd gone into the other cabin. After a while I went to look for her, but she wasn't there either. I tried the door to our cabin, but it was locked and it was quiet inside. We only had two key cards, but I didn't have either of them. So I searched in the toilets, but she was gone.'

'And you were content with that?'

'No, I went out and searched for her on the boat. I searched everywhere, but I couldn't find her.'

'What time was it when you discovered she was gone?'

'Nine, nine-thirty maybe. I don't know for sure.'

'And then?'

'I took the lift up to the top floors to look for her. I searched everywhere. In the bars and restaurants, at the disco, everywhere, but she was nowhere. So I had a beer up there by the big dance floor.'

'Where did you think she'd gone?'

'No idea. Sometimes she acts that way. Just disappears. You don't really know where she's coming from. But after a while I caught sight of her up there. She was sitting at the other end of the place, with two men. They were older, in suits.'

'Did you go up to her then?'

'No, I didn't. I sat there for a while and then I left.'

'Why did you do that? She was your girlfriend, after all.'

That suspicious gaze was evident now. Yes, why *didn't* he go over to her? How could he put his disappointment into words? How could he explain to the policeman that it was Jennifer who controlled their relationship, despite the age difference? That he followed Jennifer's lead, that he had never had a girlfriend before her. And that she had started to see through him.

'I guess I didn't care about her,' he answered nonchalantly. 'As far as I was concerned she might as well sit there and show off for those old blokes.'

'How did you feel then? Were you offended?'

'I just felt like she wasn't my girlfriend any more. It was over,' Joakim lied.

'And what did you do then?'

'I went to a different bar and had a few more beers,' he lied again. 'Then I went to bed.'

'And those men – would you recognize them?'

'Don't know. Maybe.'

'What did they look like?'

'One was dark and one was fair-skinned, I think. I don't remember more than that.'

'Were they Finnish? Swedish?'

'No idea. I was sitting too far away.'

'We'll get back to you,' said Nieminen with a gesture towards the door.

* * *

Just as the ambulance was leaving Stora Mejtens Gränd with the baby, the police showed up. Petra thanked the woman, whose name was Ester Jensen, for her help and apologized for the trouble and the mess she left behind. She said that she was a police officer herself and that they would come back and speak to her again during the day.

Then she went out on to the street to meet the police. Petra knew both of the patrol officers as acquaintances. One was a harmless character named Staaf. The other one's name was Holgersson, an oaf with his centre of gravity between his shoulder blades. He swayed as he walked in a way that made it look like he was about to fall backwards. His pumped-up upper arms presumably prevented him from letting his arms hang along his sides like a normal person, or else he deliberately held them that way. He had also participated in Friday's course in body language. With a sting of irritation she recalled that he might have been the one who had put the word 'sexy' in her mouth when they were discussing the police commissioner's gait.

Staaf gave her a smile of recognition. Holgersson also

had a hint of a smile on his lips, while his eyes were directed at parts of her body other than her face.

'Hi,' she said, nodding at them. 'I'm the one who found the child.'

'Oh, shit,' said Staaf.

'Let me show you where it was,' said Petra, going down towards the park with the two policemen in tow and over to the bushes where she had found the boy.

With a gesture she stopped them and then, as carefully as she could, walked over the still dew-wet grass and up to the bushes. Instinctively she felt Holgersson's eyes on her back. Or that vicinity; she was quite sure where he was looking. Form-fitting sports leggings were not her garment of choice in Holgersson's company.

'He was lying in here,' said Petra, managing with a single tug to get the pram insert out of the bushes.

Then they went over to the turning area where the pram was. Now she saw that it was damaged. One of the wheels was crooked and the steel frame was buckled on one side. She carefully set the insert on top of the frame and let the two cloth handles fall down on the little bed.

'These must belong together,' said Petra. 'They match, even if the pram itself looks a little battered. We'll have to cordon off a pretty big area,' she said, sweeping with her hand in the direction of the bushes, twenty-something yards away.

Yet another police car showed up, and Holgersson ordered the two policemen who got out of the car to start fencing off the area. Petra told them about her macabre discovery and then took another look on her own around the discovery site, trying to think through the situation. Only now did she feel the throbbing in the scratches on her legs. She glanced down and realized that she would have to throw away the expensive Nike leggings.

Someone must be missing the child, she thought. Someone must be completely desperate right now, chasing around searching for the blue pram with white dots. We have to find the boy's parents. But then it struck her: that's not my job. I'm just a witness; I ought to leave and head home.

She went back over to the turning area. The barrier was almost ready now. Out of habit, she took a look in the bin she passed as she came out on to the path again. Nothing special. It was not her job to root in bins and look for tracks in the grass. Staaf and Holgersson and their colleagues could take care of that.

'I'm taking off now!' she called to Staaf, who was standing further down on the hill. 'You know where to reach me. The woman at number 10 knows you're coming. Good luck.'

'Thanks. We'll be in touch,' Staaf answered, raising his hand in farewell.

A little further away, Holgersson was standing on the lawn, looking after her with a smile that was hard to interpret. With a slight shiver, she turned around and started walking towards the allotments. Without really knowing why, she stopped by a municipal sand box, containing sand to grit icy roads, that was behind a fence she passed. She went to the gate, opened it and walked over to the sand box. She pulled the end of the sleeve of her hoodie down over her fingers and, with the cloth between her hand and the plastic, cracked open the heavy lid. She remained standing like that for a few seconds before she let the lid down with a bang.

'Holgersson! Staaf!' Petra Westman shouted. 'You'll have to expand the cordoned-off area. I think I found the mother.'

Sunday Mid-morning

At quarter to six Sjöberg woke up, even though he really could have slept as long as he wanted. You're getting old, he thought, before the memories of the night before washed over him. The first thing that struck him, strangely enough, was a sense of well-being. The subdued lighting and convivial glow of Saturday evening still rested like a filter over his thoughts. He was even smiling to himself at the memory of Margit's warm embrace and the smell of her hair. When she looked at him with those honest, open, understanding eyes he was intoxicated; it made him feel at home somehow.

'At home?' he said out loud to himself.

What did that mean – at home? At home; that was here, of course, with Åsa. And then came the guilty conscience. But not completely. Not the way it should have. It should have hit him like the kick of a horse in his gut, but instead it slipped past him like a cat and settled down quietly in a corner of his awareness.

The hangover he should have had was almost non-existent. He went barefoot out to the hall and retrieved *Dagens Nyheter*, Sweden's daily newspaper. Then he stopped into the kitchen where, just in case the hangover made itself known, he drank three glasses of water, and found a pen. Instead of sleeping for those extra hours, he lay down in bed again and managed to solve almost all of the Sunday crossword. When it was almost quarter to seven he got up and prepared to drive out to Huddinge Hospital.

His mother had improved considerably and the X-ray images did not show any serious consequences from having broken her ribs. Sjöberg drove her home to Bollmora and helped her up to her apartment, which was on the second floor. After taking cups down from the cupboard above the kitchen counter, his mother made coffee, while Sjöberg looked for a binder on the bookshelf in the bedroom. When he found it he sat down at the kitchen table to help her pay the month's bills. He flipped back and forth through the papers, in search of the right plastic folder. Suddenly his eyes fell on something he hadn't seen before.

'What's this? Björskogsnäs 4:14. It's a title deed for a piece of property. Do you own a piece of land?'

'No, I don't think so,' his mother answered guardedly, not turning towards him.

She picked up the coffee pot and started pouring coffee for them both.

'Would you like some milk? It's good for your stomach.'

'I don't have any problems with my stomach, Mum. Why do you have this land? Where is it?'

'It must be something left behind after Dad. It's nothing.'

'Mother, of course it's something. It's a bit of property. Where is Björskogsnäs?'

'I'm so bad at geography, you know. I really have no idea.'

She was still standing with her back to him, so he stood up and went over to the counter to look her in the eyes.

'Are you lying to me?' he asked.

'Lying! Pah!' she said simply, carrying the cups to the kitchen table.

She set them down, directed her attention to the binder instead, turned a few pages ahead and then said, 'Here are the bills. The chequebook and envelopes are on the bookshelf.'

Sjöberg did not understand. Other than that it was pointless to try to talk to his mother about something she did not want to talk about. He drank his coffee and looked out of the kitchen window at the cloudy grey sky while she wrote her cheques. Finally, after Sjöberg had checked through the bills and cheques one more time, she put them in their envelopes and sealed them. Sjöberg understood that he really had no right to root in his mother's business. If she wanted to have a secret property, she was perfectly entitled to. But yet – he just could not leave the subject like that. So much in their life together had remained unspoken and unexamined. He felt dissatisfied with all the evasive manoeuvres, with his mother's way of constantly navigating away from troublesome topics of conversation, always flinching from what wasn't simple.

'So, was it something he inherited?' Sjöberg persisted. 'Did Dad inherit the property from Grandma and Grandpa?'

'I don't know, I'm telling you! Now let's just forget about it!'

His mother did not often raise her voice. It was best to shelve the matter. And pretend nothing had happened, in the customary Sjöbergian manner.

'I'll go to the supermarket for you, Mum. What do you need?'

They made a shopping list together. An easy task that did not involve any discussions.

* * *

Hanna opened her eyes and discovered that she could not breathe. She did not know where she was. Terrified, she started to wave her arms. Then she remembered she was still in the bathtub. She slid up into a sitting position, coughing and spluttering, and finally managed to take a deep breath again. She knew of course that you couldn't sleep in the tub. When she had calmed down she stood up. Her whole body ached; it hurt almost everywhere. She moved slowly and carefully now; she did not want to do more damage to herself. Remembered that she was going to wash her hair, but did not have the energy. Had to sleep now.

She climbed over the edge of the tub and reached for a towel, moving at a snail's pace. She dried her whole body softly and carefully, almost dabbing it. Then she dropped the towel on the floor and staggered into her parents' bedroom. She could not see clearly but, squinting through one eye, she managed to focus on the covers on the armchair. She took hold of one of them and pulled it with her over to the bed. Crawled up, thought there ought to be a sheet, before she pulled the cover over herself and fell asleep again.

* * *

'Conny, it's Petra.'

Sjöberg was at the Ica supermarket with a trolley full of shopping.

'Listen, something's happened here. You probably need to come in.'

'I thought you were off today.'

'I thought so too. I was out jogging this morning – in

Vitabergsparken. I found a baby pram insert in some bushes, pulled it out and in the insert there was a little baby. There was a baby in the bushes! I didn't know whether he was alive or dead. I ran with him to a house and tried to bring him back to life. Then the ambulance came.'

'Oh, shit. Do you know how he's doing now?'

'No, I haven't had time to find out. I helped the patrol officers fence the area off – it was Holgersson and Staaf and a few others.'

'Good,' said Sjöberg. 'They'll be sure to contact the boy's parents. Someone must be missing him.'

'Conny, that's just it. I'd finished here and was just going home –'

'Yes?'

'You know how curious I am, and I couldn't resist opening the lid of one of those municipal sand boxes as I went past –'

'And?'

'There was a woman lying there. The body of a woman. I don't know for sure, but I assume it's the mother.'

There was silence for a few moments. Then Sjöberg continued matter-of-factly, 'How did she die?'

'Her skull was completely crushed. Someone put her in that box. I don't think this is a case for patrol officers.'

'Where are you now, Petra?'

'I'm still in Vita Bergen.'

'What's going on?'

'They've photographed the discovery site, and they're in the process of photographing the rest now. I called Bella, and a few of her men have already started combing through the area. She's on her way here from a tennis court somewhere. The medical examiner is also on his way. We've cordoned off a large part of the park. I'm going to call the hospital and check the boy's condition. Just hope he's not dead too . . . Poor, poor baby. We need to take this over now.'

'It looks like you've already done that. Good work, Petra. Call in Einar, Jamal and Sandén. It helps if everyone has seen the crime scene. I'll talk to the police commissioner. We'll contact the prosecutor's office later. I'm out in Bollmora right now. I'll be there within an hour.'

'The reporters, Conny. What should I do with them? They're already here. This is going to be on the news this afternoon.'

'Just take it easy. Say that we found the body of a woman, but we don't know more than that. Let them take their pictures. They don't know about the child?'

'No, they don't seem to.'

'Good. We'll leave it like that.'

Sjöberg put his mobile phone back in the inside pocket of his jacket. He paid for the shopping and walked quickly back to his mother's apartment. After helping her put away the groceries, he said a quick goodbye, got in the car and drove in towards town. Momentarily incapable of focusing, he let his thoughts flutter between sand boxes and Margit Olofsson, mysterious land titles and abandoned infants.

* * *

'Yes, I saw her in the bar.'

The bartender Juha Lehto held the photographs he'd been given by Nieminen, who sat opposite him, studying the bartender over his glasses. The interview was being conducted in swivel chairs at a window table in the dance hall on the upper deck. At tables around them staff and passengers were being questioned by other police officers. All of the almost two thousand people on board would be questioned before those disembarking in Åbo would be allowed off and the ferry could return to Stockholm.

'Are you sure it was her?' asked Nieminen.

'Yes, I recognize the jacket,' said Lehto, pointing at the picture the crime scene photographer had taken a few hours earlier. 'I recognize the face too. She was very pretty.'

He said this with a gesture towards the other photo, a copy of her ID card.

'What time was this?'

'I would say it was nine, maybe nine-thirty. There were very few people in the bar.'

'Was she alone?'

'No, she was in the company of an older man. He may have been somewhere between fifty and sixty. Although I don't think they were together actually. At first I thought so, because they came in at the same time and he ordered for both of them.'

'What did he order?'

'Beer, I think. But he wasn't very nice to her. She seemed upset.'

'Did you hear what they were talking about?'

'No, but he took her roughly by the arm and looked angry. Or mean rather. I was just about to say something to him when another man came up that she seemed to know and stood between them. She went and sat with him at a table right next to the bar.'

Lehto pointed towards a table at the other end.

'Over there, just to the left of the bar. There were two Finnish men sitting there together. Well-dressed, in suits. It looked like they were working, but they stopped when the girl sat down with them.'

'The man at the bar, then, the unpleasant one – was he Finnish too?' asked Nieminen.

The bartender hesitated for a moment before he answered.

'No, he was Swedish,' he said. 'He had no accent, as far as I could tell. He just got up and left when the girl had gone.'

'What did he look like?'

'Ordinary. Nothing special about him that I noticed. Other than that he had an aggressive attitude, like I said.'

'This man, do you recognize him?'

Nieminen showed the bartender another photograph – the picture they had taken of Joakim earlier in the morning.

'No, I don't think so,' answered Lehto. 'Should I?'

'He was sitting at one of those tables at about the same time and said he saw her together with the two Finnish men. He said he ordered a beer.'

'It was probably from my colleague who was waiting tables. We take table orders sometimes when there aren't many customers. I don't remember him anyway.'

'Do you think you'd be able to point out those men we were talking about?'

'Doubtful. Not the guys in suits anyway. Possibly the one at the bar, but I don't know.'

Nieminen let the bartender return to his work and made yet another note on his pad before he called the next man.

* * *

Joakim was in the breakfast lounge, absentmindedly toying with a rye roll with liver pâté. The mood on the boat was subdued, the conversations at the tables around him quiet. He felt completely empty inside. He needed to eat, but the very sight of the sandwich turned his stomach. He looked at the seagulls diving through the rain-soaked air outside the windows, but he did not see them. At the same table as him, but a few seats further away, a Finnish father sat with two boys about ten years old playing cards. The chair across from him was pulled out and someone sat down, but he took no notice of that either. Instead, he continued his listless staring out the window. Until a voice mercilessly roused him from his musings.

'Well, that put a real damper on this trip, wouldn't you say?'

Joakim turned and looked blankly at the all-too-familiar face without answering. At first he was struck by a sense of unreality. It could not be true, not this too. He could not react, did not know how he should react, whether to be frightened or even relieved. Relieved at the domesticity of the situation, relieved in the security that the balance of terror was restored.

'That was one pretty girl, by the way.'

Joakim could not get out a word.

'Yeah, the one in the bog, I mean. The body. Although a little sluttish, in my opinion. She got in over her head, you might say.'

Only now did he hear, only now did he understand what he was seeing and hearing.

'Dad, that was Jennifer. My Jennifer,' he said quietly.

'I thought as much,' said his father with a scornful smile. 'I thought the name sounded familiar.'

'Have they questioned you?' asked Joakim.

'Depends on what you mean by questioning. They asked me my name and where I live and whether I knew anything. And then they showed photographs and asked if I recognized her. But I said I didn't. So it was over quickly. And you?'

'She was my girlfriend, Dad. Of course they questioned me. I've seen . . . the body.'

He turned his eyes away and let them linger again on something far away outside the window.

'You would have,' said his father. 'I guess you saw it when you killed her.'

Joakim winced and looked his father right in the eyes.

'I didn't kill her,' he hissed. 'Why are you saying that?'

His father only gave him a cunning smile in response.

'What are you doing here anyway?'

'What am I doing here? I'm keeping an eye on you, of course. I seem to recall saying you couldn't go on this trip.'

'But what about Mum?' said Joakim. 'You couldn't leave her home alone, could you?'

'Couldn't I? You did.'

His father smiled at him maliciously.

'I did not! You were home. She has to be cared for –'

'Listen, she's not going to starve to death,' his father interrupted.

Joakim got up suddenly and left, his father's gaze burning into his back.

Sunday Afternoon

Chairs scraped across the wooden floor and notebooks thudded on to the table. For once everyone was on time for the briefing in the blue oval office at Östgötagatan 100. The explanation was that they were all coming from the same place – McDonald's on Götgatan – except Bella Hansson, who took a detour to Forensics, and Hadar Rosén, who came from his summer cabin in Roslagen. Instead of his usual grey suit, today he was wearing jeans, a checked flannel shirt and wellingtons. He looked like he had come straight from his garden. His almost-six-foot-six frame was in a reclining position as Sjöberg opened the meeting.

'Sorry to interrupt your weekend, Hadar. And everyone else too, for that matter. But this case has priority, as you all understand. If Westman could go over everything for us, we'll try to get a general picture of what happened.'

Petra, who had been rushing around outdoors in thin exercise clothes all morning, was sitting with her hands wrapped around a teacup to warm up. She had still not had time to shower and change after her morning run. But Bella Hansson and Hamad were also in workout clothes and did not appear to have showered. She knew that Hansson had spent the morning at the tennis court, but when Hamad showed up in a tracksuit too she had a feeling he had come from the same place. For some reason she did not really like that.

Petra told her story and was interrupted only by a few scattered questions from Rosén.

'We have a roughly five-month-old boy fighting for his life at Karolinska,' she summarized in conclusion. 'The boy does not have any apparent injuries, but he is dehydrated and suffering from hypothermia. He must have been there for a while before we found him. We have a dead woman, who may be the boy's mother or nanny, in a municipal sand box near where the child was found. Based on what has been determined so far, she was at least subjected to blunt force to the head. I think we can assume she did not put herself in the sand box. She has not been identified yet. No notification of a missing person has gone out on the boy and no child that age has been reported missing in the Stockholm area. On the other hand, there are a number of missing women who might match the description, but we'll have to look more closely at that.'

'Bella, what does the medical examiner's office say?' asked Sjöberg.

'Because the woman has not yet been identified, they want to wait before starting to cut into the body. Otherwise – severe skull injuries, blunt force, probably sufficient to kill. Both legs broken in several places. A lot of haemorrhaging on the lower body. I have her clothes, but haven't had time to look at them closely. And as was said, no form of identification has been found on her person or anywhere else in the park.'

'No ID,' muttered Sandén. 'Did she have anything interesting in her pockets?'

'Not a thing,' Hansson replied. 'A few tissues, that's all.'

'So no money, no wallet. No keys?'

'No keys.'

'If she didn't have any keys on her, that suggests that either someone was at home – someone who ought to have missed her and the child by now – or else someone, let's say the perpetrator, took them.'

'What about rings?' asked Hamad.

'No rings either. But there are marks on the left ring finger.'

'So presumably she was married.'

'Or had been,' Sandén filled in.

'How long has she been dead?' asked Sjöberg.

'Too soon to say. The medical examiner will send an initial report this evening.'

'Any ideas about what might have happened to her?'

'It looks like she was run over, but presumably she did not get the skull injuries from the car. We're looking for blood at the scene.'

'She may have flown a little, you mean? Into a tree, for example?' Sandén interjected.

'Yes.'

Gabriella Hansson – brief and factual as always. No unnecessary speculation, just direct answers to concrete questions.

'And the pram?' asked Westman. 'It looked battered.'

'The damage on the frame itself is a match in terms of height with the broken legs. We'll investigate the pram further.'

'So we have a possible scenario to work from,' Sjöberg observed. 'Woman with pram hit by car. Hit-and-run accident, to put it simply.'

'In that case it was an uncivilized bastard, who emptied

the victim's pockets, hid the body, and left the baby to die in the woods!' Sandén exclaimed.

'Maybe the driver panicked,' Sjöberg suggested. 'Einar, you search for missing persons who may match this woman. Or the child, of course.'

'The dad will probably get in touch with us before I've got anywhere,' muttered Einar Eriksson.

Sjöberg ignored the grumbling. Eriksson just was that way; it was not worth bothering about, and he did good work.

'And then find out from all the garages whether any cars come in that match the damage to the pram,' Sjöberg continued. 'Petra, you keep us informed about the boy's condition. We need a photo of him too. Jens, Jamal and Petra will get the door-to-door operation going in the area. Big effort. We need witnesses, but above all we need to find out who the dead woman is. Hansson, you keep in contact with the medical examiner. As soon as you know anything about when she died, I want to know so we can pursue witnesses. We need a few other things too for identification: fingerprints, teeth, clothing, model of pram, all that kind of thing.'

Sjöberg was interrupted by a cautious knock at the door.

'Yes?' he called to Lundin, the young constable who was serving as receptionist for the day and was now hazily visible through the frosted glass in the door.

Everyone's eyes turned towards the self-conscious Lundin as he cracked open the door.

'Phone for Conny Sjöberg. It can't wait,' he added apologetically.

'Connect it in here,' said Sjöberg, opening his notepad.

Sandén pushed the phone across the table to Sjöberg, who purposefully clicked out the nib of his pen while he took two quick gulps from his coffee cup.

The call took longer than expected and when he was finished he put down the receiver with a sigh.

'Things seem to be piling up a bit,' he said wearily. 'A sixteen-year-old girl has been found strangled in a toilet on a Viking Line ferry. She was murdered during the night in Swedish waters and is registered on Götgatan, up by Ringen. So the case falls on our desk. The Finnish police have taken care of the job so far and we'll get help from them going forward too. But we'll be leading the investigation.'

'Holy shit. Two children on the same day.' Sandén said what everyone was thinking.

'I'll lead this investigation,' Sjöberg continued. 'Jamal will work with me. Petra will have to take over Vita Bergen. You'll manage it. Jens will work with you. And Einar will have to work with both cases. If that doesn't hold up, we'll have to request reinforcements, but let's try it this way to start with.'

Petra Westman had never before been responsible for an investigation. Now she felt proud and a little nervous at the same time. Nervous with respect to the older, considerably more experienced Sandén, but he patted her encouragingly on the shoulder and gave her a quick wink. Humility was one of Sandén's attributes; during all the years at the heels of Sjöberg he had never shown any signs of jealousy or envy, and that in turn was a sign of another of Sandén's traits: contentment. He took things as they were, seldom worried and never let himself get discouraged.

'You can get going now.' Sjöberg was addressing Westman and Sandén.

'I'm here if you need me,' he added, with a reassuring smile at Westman. 'The rest of us will start this new case.'

'And me?' asked Einar Eriksson, his face clearly displaying a feeling of having been slighted in some way.

'It's important that you get started with Vita Bergen as soon as possible,' Sjöberg said nonchalantly. 'But it would be good if you took five minutes to get familiar with this boat case first. Even if the ferry doesn't come back to Stockholm until early tomorrow.'

Eriksson let out an audible sigh. Westman and Sandén left the conference room and Sjöberg reported what he had learned on the phone.

'And the body?' asked Hansson when Sjöberg was done. 'What happens with it?'

'It will remain in Åbo. I don't know how long for. I'm not familiar with the practice in these cases. Perhaps you can find that out, Bella? There are no visible signs of rape – her clothes were in order – but according to the Finnish medical examiner she appeared to have been sexually active during her last hours. That's the only thing that's come out so far. Talk to Kaj Zetterström at pathology; then you can take whatever action the situation requires. Maybe go over there.'

Sjöberg emptied his coffee cup and pushed it aside. Einar Eriksson looked at his watch, stood up and left the room.

'And with that the five minutes are up,' said Sjöberg

with a resigned expression when the door to the conference room had shut.

'Well, this is going to be a heavy-duty assignment,' Hadar Rosén observed. 'A hell of a lot of people to be questioned and half of them in Finland. Has the girl's family been informed?'

'No, I guess that's the first thing we'll have to see to,' Sjöberg sighed. 'I'll do it.'

'We'll have to ask them to send a passenger list,' said Hamad. 'So we have something to work from.'

'Yes,' Sjöberg agreed, 'and a list of staff. Einar will run the names against the crime register to start with and get the Finns to do the same thing. Otherwise there's probably not much we can do before the ferry arrives tomorrow. Then there'll be a mass meeting on board the boat. You'll have a lot to do, Bella.'

'No problem,' Hansson answered with a cool smile. 'We'll take Vita Bergen this evening, sleep for a few hours and be at the end of the pier with our bags early tomorrow.'

'How many people can there be on one of those Finland ferries?' the prosecutor asked.

'Evidently this one can hold up to 2,480 passengers,' Sjöberg replied. 'These ferries are a real marvel. But I don't know how many there were on this trip.'

'Just be sure to have enough people with you,' said Rosén. 'That's a lot of passengers to question.'

'We'll have to make some kind of probability calculation. We'll start with the boyfriend and his circle of friends, look for the men in the bar – the Swede and the two Finns.'

'And if we don't find our murderer there, this investigation is going to be a drawn-out affair,' Rosén sighed, shaking his head.

'I know,' said Sjöberg. 'But if this is an unpremeditated crime, there will be someone who saw something. If it's not, we'll solve it through detective work.'

'Just make sure it gets done,' the prosecutor said urgently. 'When there are children involved, or young people –'

'Will you be there tomorrow?' Sjöberg interrupted. 'On the boat?'

'I'm coming,' Rosén answered. 'What time are we talking about?'

'Maybe as early as six. I'll be in touch when I know for sure.'

'Then perhaps we can consider ourselves finished here?' asked Hansson, striking both palms on the table. Her intense but absent gaze showed that mentally she was already in the lab, busy charting the technical circumstances around a woman's cold autumn death in a park in central Stockholm.

Sunday Evening

When Hanna finally woke up again it was already starting to get dark outside the bedroom window. She stayed in her parents' double bed for a while to determine whether she could see and whether the whole situation was for real or just a scary nightmare.

'Mummy!' she called out hopefully into the apartment.

No answer. She called again, louder this time. Still no answer. She pulled the cover over her head.

'Mummy, you have to come home now,' she murmured quietly to herself. 'This isn't fun any more. Let's play something else now.'

Then she felt how hungry she was; her stomach was screaming for food. She slid carefully down from the bed – she had to do everything carefully now. With both hands she took hold of the cover and put it around herself like a cape. It dragged behind her as she tiptoed out to the kitchen. But the cover was heavy, so she dropped it at the threshold to the kitchen and went into her bedroom. The white T-shirt with the strawberry on the chest was still lying on the rug and she pulled it over her head. In the bureau drawer that was still open she found a pair of knickers and a red corduroy skirt, which she also managed to get on with some effort. Then she went back into the kitchen.

The packet with the frozen hash was still on the table.

She turned the packet upside down over the tabletop and shook out what was left. It wasn't frozen any more! It was ready to eat, and it was good. The hash tasted almost as good as if it were hot. She took whole fistfuls of luke-warm meat and potato cubes and stuffed them in her mouth. It was so wonderful to eat real food that she forgot she was sad. Almost everything felt better now; the only thing that was not better was the wound on her cheek, which really hurt. But Hanna gritted her teeth.

When she had finished the whole packet of hash she pushed one of the chairs at the kitchen table to the counter, climbed up on it, and turned on the water slowly so she would not burn herself if it was too hot. She tried the tap in different positions and finally got it to give out cold water. Then she took a glass from the dish rack, filled it halfway and drank.

That was when she happened to think about the tele-phone. If no one was going to call her, she would have to make a call herself. All you had to do was push the little buttons, and then someone would answer. She slid down to the floor and went out into the hall. The child's chair was still there below the wall phone. She climbed up on it and was careful not to get too close to the knobs on the drawers of the tall hall bureau or the framed photo. She picked up the receiver, as she had seen others do, and aim-lessly pressed buttons. She could hear a ringing sound and she waited for a while but no one answered. Hanna hung up and tried again. Suddenly she heard a voice in her ear.

'Hello.'

It sounded like a man.

'Hello,' said Hanna.

'Who's calling?' the man said crossly.

'It's Hanna, of course,' Hanna answered. 'Is this Daddy?'

'No, it's not. You've got the wrong number.'

Then he hung up. But Hanna was determined. She tried again, many times, until she heard another voice at the other end.

'You have reached the Larsson family. No one can take your call right now, so please leave a message after the beep.'

'Is Daddy there?' asked Hanna.

Beep, it said in her ear; then there was silence.

'Hello, I want to talk!' Hanna called to the answering machine, but it remained silent.

Then she hung up, but she was not going to give up so easily.

'Hagström,' said a voice in the receiver.

'Hi,' said Hanna.

'Hi there! Is this Emma?'

The voice sounded friendly. It reminded her of Mummy's.

'No, it's Hanna. Is this Mummy?'

'No, sweetheart, you've probably dialled the wrong number.'

'What number should I call?' asked Hanna.

'Why don't you try your mummy's number?' the voice said cheerfully.

'My mummy is gone,' said Hanna.

'That's not good,' said the voice. 'So where is your daddy?'

'He's in Japan. He's coming home in a whole lot of days.'

'That's terrible. You know, you really shouldn't play

with the phone. I think it's best if you stop doing that now. But it was nice talking to you anyway. Bye now.'

And then there was a beeping in the receiver again. Hanna sighed and hung it back on the cradle. You could find nice people when you called like this anyway. She would not give up. No, she would call and call until someone came and rescued her. That's exactly what she would do.

After a few more failed attempts she finally got a bite again.

'Dahlström.'

It was an old lady who answered. Her voice sounded really old.

'Hi, this is Hanna.'

'Hi, Hanna!' the old lady said cheerfully.

'What's your name?' asked Hanna.

'My name is Barbro.'

'Do you know my mummy?'

'No, I don't think so,' Barbro replied.

'So why do you want to talk to me?'

'Well,' the old lady answered hesitantly, 'weren't you the one who wanted to talk to me?'

'Yes,' Hanna agreed, 'because my mummy and daddy are gone.'

'What are you saying?' said Barbro. 'Who's taking care of you then?'

'I'm doing it myself,' Hanna answered with some pride.

'But honey, how old are you?'

'This many,' said Hanna, holding three fingers up in the air. 'But soon I'll be this many.'

Four fingers in the air now. The old lady was silent for a moment.

'You're not at home all alone, are you?' she asked.

'Yes, I am.'

'So where is your mummy?'

'She moved. She only likes Lukas, and I'm a big bother.'

'I don't believe that,' said Barbro firmly. 'I think you sound like a very nice, good little girl. And your daddy?'

'Daddy is in Japan.'

'But someone must be taking care of you.'

'I manage almost everything myself. I had hash. Although I hit myself so there was blood and I want Daddy to come home now and kiss it and make it better.'

'Are you joking with me now, Hanna, or are you really all by yourself?' Barbro asked in a worried voice.

'I'm not joking. Can you come and rescue me? I don't want to be alone any more.'

'Hanna, first you have to tell me where you live. Do you know the name of your street?'

'Sweden?' said Hanna hesitantly.

'Do you live in Stockholm, do you know that?'

'Yes. And in Sweden.'

'What's your last name?'

Hanna did not know the answer, so she didn't say anything.

'Is your name maybe Andersson or Pettersson? Hanna Karlsson maybe? Do you know that?'

'My name is Hanna Birgitta,' Hanna said contentedly, but Barbro did not seem to think that was anything special, because she just continued asking her questions.

'What does it look like where you live? Are there a lot of cars and shops and things?'

'Yes,' Hanna answered. 'And summer cabins.'

'Listen, Hanna,' said Barbro eagerly. 'Can you go to the window and look out on the street? Just set down the phone – don't hang up – and then come back and tell me what you see when you look out. Can you do that?'

'But it's dark outside.'

'There must be streetlights so you can see a little anyway?'

'Hmm,' said Hanna again, setting the receiver down on the bureau, like the nice lady said, and went over to the living room window.

When she came back to the phone she dutifully described what she had seen.

'There's a castle here. It's really big and yellow, with blue and red squares on it. And letters. And then there's a tower at the very top, where the princess lives.'

'So no summer cabins?' asked Barbro.

'Yes, summer cabins too. And a castle.'

'Do you know anyone who lives in your building?'

'Just Mr Bergman, but he's always angry.'

'Hanna,' said Barbro seriously. 'Listen to me now. I'll come and rescue you, but it may take a little time. I want you to eat properly. You have to be a clever little girl now. You must not open any windows, and don't touch the cooker or any electrical wires. Do you understand that, Hanna? It's very important that you do as I say.'

'I'll be good,' said Hanna convincingly.

'If the phone rings, you should answer it and tell the caller the same thing you told me. And then try to be a happy girl, and I'll hurry to come and rescue you. It may take a while, but you mustn't give up. Do you understand?'

'Yes,' said Hanna.

'Bye now,' said the old lady. 'Take care of yourself now. Be careful.'

Barbro almost sounded like she was about to start crying, but could that really be? She was big after all.

'Bye-bye, Barbro,' said Hanna happily, to cheer up the kind lady.

Then she hung up the phone and sat on the hall mat to wait.

* * *

Deep down he was grateful that Hamad was with him. Sjöberg had done this many times before, alone, but it never got any easier. And now – the girl was sixteen, just a child. After they got the Finns to fax over the names and addresses of passengers, and the time approached for Sjöberg to leave for the address at Skanstull, Hamad noticed that his head was sinking lower and lower.

'I'll come along,' he said. 'For moral support.'

Sjöberg meant to tell him not to, but at the same time he felt so relieved that he hesitated and Hamad continued.

'Sooner or later I'll be the one standing there, so I might as well get used to it.'

But it did not turn out the way either of them imagined.

'It's open!' someone bellowed from inside the apartment when they knocked for the third time.

There was a strong smell of soap in the stairwell, but even more of fried onion. They carefully opened the door to the apartment on the second floor, looked at each other before stepping over the pile of flyers on the floor in the hall and took the few steps to the nearest room, which proved to be the kitchen.

Three women and a man were seated at the table, talking away in loud voices. Yet another man, dressed in shoes and a jacket that were both too warm for the season, was sitting on the kitchen floor, comfortably leaning against one of the lower cupboards with a half-empty wine bottle in his hand. On the table there were beer cans, bottles and several cups of something that clearly was not coffee.

No one in the gathering took any notice of them, so Sjöberg cleared his throat loudly. No reaction.

'We're from the police,' he said in a resounding voice, and a woman with her hair in a long braid actually looked up at him for a moment before she painstakingly put out her cigarette in a beer can.

Just as Sjöberg was about to speak again the cigarette was extinguished and the woman shouted in a hoarse voice, 'Hello! Can you all shut up now! The cops are here.'

Then it actually got quiet in the kitchen, and through clouds of smoke the two policemen saw five pairs of tired eyes turn towards them.

'Conny Sjöberg, Violent Crimes Unit, Hammarby,' said Sjöberg, holding up his police ID. 'Jamal Hamad, the same,' he continued, gesturing towards his colleague. 'Which one of you lives here?'

'She does,' said the man at the table, pointing at a woman with tangled, shoulder-length dyed-blonde hair.

The woman straightened up a little and looked at them with an attempt at a smile.

'Are you Lena Johansson?'

She cleared her throat, but instead of saying anything she simply nodded in response.

'Are you the mother of Jennifer Johansson?'

'Yes,' she said, taking a quick puff on her cigarette.

'Can we perhaps talk privately in another room?' asked Sjöberg.

The woman shrugged, scooted the chair back and got up on unsteady legs, a beer can in her hand. She went ahead of them into a simply furnished living room and tumbled down on one of the two worn plush couches on either side of a low table. The lacquered pine surface was covered with circular stains only partially concealed by a thin layer of dust and ash. Sjöberg and Hamad sat down on the couch opposite her. The conversation started up again in the kitchen and soon the voices were just as loud as before.

'I have some bad news to tell you,' Sjöberg began.

The woman looked at him uncertainly. The police probably didn't talk that way when the neighbours had complained.

'I'm sorry to say that Jennifer is dead.'

She did not seem to take the information in, but continued smoking her cigarette instead, apparently unperturbed, saying nothing. Sjöberg waited quietly for her reaction.

'I haven't seen her for a few days,' she said after a while. 'She's in Finland, I think.'

'Lena, she's dead. Jennifer is dead. Do you understand what I'm saying?'

'I'm not stupid. Even if I may be a little drunk.'

She spoke with a calm, slightly drawling voice, and her eyes wandered back and forth between the two policemen.

'I also have to tell you that Jennifer was murdered,' said Sjöberg.

She sat quietly for a few seconds before she said anything.

'Did it hurt?'

Finally, some kind of healthy reaction, Sjöberg thought.

'It probably hurt,' he answered factually. 'Jennifer was strangled. It presumably took a while, but she didn't have to suffer too long. She's in Åbo now. She was murdered on a Finland ferry. We don't have any suspects yet. Do you have any idea who would do something like that to Jennifer?'

'No,' her mother answered, still equally blunt. 'You'll have to ask Elise.'

'Elise?'

'My other girl. But she's not home right now.'

'Is there anyone else in the family?'

'No. Just the three of us.'

'Do you have any friend or relative you can ask to come over?'

Laughter and noise from the kitchen. She tapped a long pillar of ash down into the beer can.

'We want to give you a little time to digest this terrible news,' said Sjöberg, 'but we will need to speak further to both you and Elise.'

'Really?'

'Preferably as soon as possible. Can we come back tomorrow afternoon?'

'I'm sure that will be fine. But I don't know whether Elise will be home then.'

'I want you to make sure that she is. It would also be nice if you could be completely sober then.'

Sjöberg felt ashamed when he said that; he did not want to sound threatening, but he was forced to continue. 'Otherwise we'll have to bring you in for questioning, and I'm sure you would prefer us not to do that.'

Lena Johansson mumbled something inaudible in response and let her gaze rest on a random point on the yellowing wall behind them.

'We're extremely sorry about this, I hope you understand. There is help available if you need it. You can call this number any time, day or night,' said Sjöberg, handing her a card. 'I'll see to it that someone comes here too, someone you can talk to. But try to ask a friend or relative to stay with you as support.'

The card left a long trail behind it on the dusty tabletop. The friends in the kitchen were laughing. The woman twisted her neck and looked absentmindedly in their direction. Sjöberg and Hamad got up from the couch at the same time.

'We'll meet here tomorrow afternoon then,' said Sjöberg. 'Some time between five and six. We are truly sorry about what happened.'

He hoped that Lena Johansson was too.

* * *

It was almost ten when Petra got back to the police building. She, Sandén and a few reinforcements had been door-knocking in the area around Vitabergsparken, but as far as she knew none of them had produced any interesting information so far. The medical examiner Kaj Zetterström had called and estimated the time of the woman's death at some time between Friday evening and Saturday morning.

Petra froze inside when she heard that. Could that little baby have been lying outside in the cold for more than twenty-four hours before he got care? In a park in central Stockholm without anyone noticing him? He must have stopped crying before it was morning. Because he must have cried. The doctors at Karolinska had not found any injuries, just that he had hypothermia and was dehydrated. He had a severe throat infection too. According to what they said the last time she spoke to them, he would not have lasted much longer. But now his condition was stable. They thought he would recover without any lasting damage, although they could give no guarantees.

No one had contacted them yet. No one missed the little boy and his mother, or perhaps babysitter. It was disgusting that you could be so isolated in a city, surrounded by people. So alone in a large community. The hunt for witnesses had become simpler once they had an approximate time to work with, but despite that no one they had spoken to so far had seen or heard anything. She had visited the ever-friendly and helpful Ester Jensen on Stora Mejtens Gränd again. She lived near the discovery site and had not gone out on Friday evening, but she had not noticed anything either.

They had a difficult, extensive job ahead of them. Vitabergsparken was surrounded by apartment buildings. They had only covered a fraction of them before they had to quit for the day. Petra sent home the police officers who were supposed to be off for the weekend and the increasingly fatigued Sandén. She suspected he had been up late the night before, but he hadn't complained.

The lights were off in all the offices along the dimly lit corridor, except in Einar Eriksson's, where the midnight oil was burning, she thought ironically. Einar was not one to exert himself unnecessarily, but he did what he was asked and pretty well besides, even if it was seldom without complaining. As she passed his office, she hesitated for a moment before she stopped after all. She knocked lightly on the open door and stepped in. Eriksson did not look up but continued to stare at the screen in front of him.

'It's too dark in here,' she said with solicitude in her voice that she did not feel. 'You'll ruin your eyes.'

He muttered something under his breath, still without looking at her. The office smelled musty in a way that Petra unconsciously associated with beard stubble.

'Have you found anything?' she continued.

'I've produced an extensive list of previously convicted passengers on the Finland ferry. No murderers, though. I haven't found any missing infants, if that's what you're wondering. No missing mothers of infants or babysitters either. But I can tell you that the pram is an Emmaljunga, 2003 model.'

'An '03,' said Petra pensively, and was about to say something else when her mobile phone rang.

She pulled it out of her pocket and assumed it was Sjöberg, as it usually was when the display read 'Blocked number'.

'And here's a list of sales locations in Stockholm,' said Eriksson, apparently undisturbed by the ringing. 'New and used. And here's a list of childcare centres in the area.

I don't have anything else for you yet,' he said in conclusion, returning to his searching on the computer.

Petra suspected he hadn't met her gaze once during the conversation. She wanted to say something encouraging, but instead she picked up the lists and left the office to answer the call.

* * *

'And what was your name again?'

'Barbro Dahlström.'

'Where do you live?'

'Doktor Abelins Gata 6,' answered Barbro.

'Where's that?'

'It's on Södermalm, but that's not important –'

'I'll connect you to the Hammarby Police Department,' the female voice interrupted.

'No, wait a moment. It doesn't matter where *I* live; the girl might live anywhere in Stockholm.'

'Then you should call the county detective unit. You'll have to call back tomorrow.'

'In that case I'll try the Hammarby Police anyway,' said Barbro irritated, surprised at her own stubbornness.

'Very well.'

After a few seconds, giving Barbro a little time to think through how she should express herself, a male voice answered at the other end.

'Hammarby Police, Lundin.'

'I would like to make a report concerning a small child

whom I think is in danger,' said Barbro, deliberately skipping the courtesies.

'Does this concern a report of a violent crime?' asked Lundin.

'No, not exactly, but I would like to speak to someone.'

'Then I'll connect you to a patrol officer.'

'Fine. Thanks,' said Barbro.

'Holgersson,' answered an authoritative voice, before Barbro even heard a ring.

'My name is Barbro Dahlström and I have received an unpleasant telephone call –'

'Then this isn't the number to call.'

'Yes, but that's what I'm doing now anyway,' she said with increasing irritation. 'This is important. A little girl called me – not someone I know, she called at random and happened to get me – and told me that she was at home all alone. She must be pretty young, because she didn't know for example what her last name was or where she lived. But she spoke extremely well otherwise –'

'To the point,' said Holgersson sullenly. 'I've got lots to do.'

'Yes, the point is just that no one is taking care of her. Her father is out of town, she says, and her mother has moved. She hurt herself and is making her own food. She wants me to come and rescue her, but of course I don't know where she lives. You have to help me.'

'How could I do that? You said you don't know where she lives or what her name is.'

'You're the police, for God's sake!'

'But I'm not a psychic.'

Barbro bit her tongue; she must try to remain calm now.

'I know that her name is Hanna. And that she lives in Stockholm.'

'Stockholm's a big city. I suggest you contact the county detective unit.'

'But I have managed to get certain details about the surroundings of the building where she lives.'

'Hmm.'

'Are you writing down what I'm saying?'

'No,' answered Holgersson. 'Like I just said, you'll have to contact the county detective unit about this. Good luck with that.'

The conversation was over. In no way did Barbro feel convinced that the county detective unit would take her more seriously.

* * *

It might be too late, but it had been a hectic day and Sjöberg felt he ought to call Åsa. Check how they were doing. Justify his existence, though he was not sure why that should suddenly be in question. He sat down at the kitchen table with a glass of milk and a cheese sandwich, smelling again the aroma of Margit Olofsson's modest perfume in his nostrils. It had come and gone all day; the power of the olfactory memory could no. .. .. He took a bite of the sandwich and tried to recall the aroma of Åsa's perfume instead. Pleasures, he thought. But it didn't work; he could only smell cheese. And Margit. He reached for the phone and dialled Åsa's number.

'Did I wake you?'

'No problem, we just got the kids to bed. What are you doing?'

'Just got home. I've been working all day.'

'Working? Haven't you been at the hospital?'

'Sure, I drove Mum home this morning, helped her shop and all that. Now we've got two bodies and an abandoned infant on our plate.'

Sjöberg briefly related the events of the day.

'You must be really tired,' said Åsa when he was finished. 'Weren't you going out on the town last night, you and Jens?'

'Yes, I should go to bed now.'

'*Were* you out, or what?'

'Yes, we were. I'm completely done in.'

'So where did you go?'

Åsa was curious, as always, but why shouldn't she be? They were in the habit of telling each other about things they did. Not to be controlling, but out of interest. Genuine interest and the desire to share each other's lives.

'First we had a beer at the Half Way Inn. Then we had a bite at Portofino.'

'Portofino! On Brännkyrkagatan? Are you kidding me?'

'Kidding? Why would I do that?'

'You and I were supposed to go there!'

Åsa was upset, and Sjöberg felt himself also starting to feel angry. He was an adult, damn it!

'So when? In seventeen years, when the kids have moved out?'

He regretted it as soon as he said it, but Åsa did not give it up.

'That place is really expensive!'

'Really expensive, I don't know . . . But there's nothing to keep you and me from going there too, is there?'

'Maybe our budget. If you're throwing away our money on a night out with Sandén.'

'We just had pasta! Since when do I have to ask for permission to go to a restaurant?'

'Goodnight.'

And then she hung up. Åsa was mad. Sjöberg had not been prepared for that, but for some reason it was not completely unwelcome. The subject of how the evening developed after dinner at the restaurant had not come up.

Monday Morning

Petra Westman had two dozen police officers, Sandén among them, out knocking on doors. So far no witnesses had been found, nor could anyone give them any useful information about the dead woman or the child. The medical examiner had determined earlier that morning that the woman was indeed the mother of the child – a piece of information that Petra received with some relief, in terms of the investigation, trying not to think about the implications for the child.

Petra herself was at a children's health centre on Barnängsgatan, hoping to find a paediatric nurse who recognized the dead woman or her son. This was the first children's health centre she had visited. Every child goes for periodic check-ups by a nurse, and the younger the child, the more often it is weighed and measured. The woman looked Swedish, as did the child. Somewhere in the country there must be a nurse who would recognize them both, hopefully in Stockholm and preferably on Södermalm.

The waiting room was already full of people. The majority were mothers with infants, but a few of the children were big enough to crawl and walk. A father was sitting at a little table being served make-believe food by his daughter on a plastic dining set.

'Mum,' a four-year-old boy called from a red plastic car, 'can you push me?'

The mother was a woman in her thirties trying to read *Parents* magazine while she nursed a baby.

'Not now, Hugo,' she answered quietly, so as not to disturb the infant she had in her arms. 'The baby needs food.'

Then it occurred to Petra for the first time that the woman might have more than one child, that there might be siblings who were also missing their mother. But in that case they must be in good hands, she told herself. Perhaps they're out of town, with a grandmother or their dad. Perhaps the parents were divorced. They had to find out who this woman was. They could hardly publish a picture of her when the only one they had was of an obviously dead person, with severe skull injuries besides.

A nurse came into the waiting room and looked around as if she were expecting someone in particular. A good sign, thought Petra. They recognize their patients. She went up to the nurse and addressed her in a low voice, keeping her back to the others in the waiting room so as not to attract unnecessary attention.

'I need to speak to you. My name is Petra Westman and I'm from the police.'

The woman, who was in her fifties, looked at her in surprise.

'Of course. I was just going to call a patient, but that can wait a moment. We'll go to my office.'

She looked around the waiting room and caught sight of the family she was expecting.

'There's Otto!' she said to the nursing mother. 'It will be your turn soon. I just have to take care of this first.'

She showed Petra into her office, closed the door behind them and extended her hand.

'Well then, my name is Margareta Flink. What's this about?'

Petra explained her errand in a brief, factual manner. The nurse looked at her bemused.

'I'm going to show you several pictures. One of them is extremely unpleasant. I'm sorry about that, but I have to.'

Petra held out the photographs.

'I'd like to know if you recognize either of them. The woman is about thirty-five.'

The nurse instinctively recoiled from the appearance of the dead woman, but she studied the pictures carefully before she answered.

'Unfortunately I don't recognize either of them. This is not one of my mums, I'm sure of that.'

'I'll need to ask all your colleagues here the same question,' Petra continued. 'Right now seems to be the best opportunity. I'd also like to get a list of all the other children's health centres around here.'

'There are only a few, but I'll write them down for you,' the nurse answered willingly.

'Are new mums assigned to a children's health centre,' Petra asked, 'or can they choose any one they want?'

'You are automatically assigned to a children's health centre in the area where you're registered. But of course you can be registered somewhere other than where you live. There are a few private alternatives too, in the Stockholm region. Those are available to anyone.'

'Would you be able to include those on your list?' Petra asked.

Soon she had a relatively short list in her hand, but

when she found out how many nurses worked at this children's health centre alone, and how many children each nurse was responsible for, she realized she had a huge job ahead of her. Stockholm was big, Sweden even bigger. Perhaps the woman and the child were not from Stockholm or even Sweden.

It was undeniably very strange that no one had missed them yet, after sixty hours. Or was that really so strange? If the woman were a single mother, it might well be the case that she had no daily contact with anyone at all. She died on a Friday night and only now was it a weekday again. She was almost certainly on maternity leave, if she even had a job. How often did Petra herself call her parents or acquaintances? Not that often. If she didn't have a job, weeks would probably pass before anyone really missed her.

In any event, the woman probably lived in the vicinity of Vitabergsparken with her child. Theoretically she could have been just visiting, but then someone should have missed her almost immediately. So we'll start with the children's health centres in that area, thought Petra, and search outwards from there.

None of the other nurses at the children's health centre on Barnängsgatan recognized the woman in the picture either. One nurse was sick and Petra had to visit her at home, which was not far away. The ill nurse talked to her, coughing and sniffling, but she did not have any new information to offer either.

On the way to the children's health centre on Wollmar Yxkullsgatan she went into a 7-Eleven to buy a banana and a bottle of mineral water. Ahead of her in the queue was a young mother with a small child hanging in a carrier on her front. The mother was also pushing a pram. Petra was wondering why you would bring a pram if you were going to carry the child anyway, but in mid-thought she was shocked to realize that the pram was done up in navy-blue fabric with small white dots and looked just like the one in Vitabergsparken. Petra was not the sort of woman who looked at baby prams and their contents with a longing gaze. In fact she had never in her life paid much attention to a pram's appearance. It must be like with cars, she thought. You naturally notice one that looks like your own. If you're really interested, you notice other types too, and connect the owner with the model.

'Excuse me, may I ask you something?'

Petra carefully placed her hand on the woman's shoulder.

'Do you know or would you recognize anyone who has a pram like yours?'

The woman turned around and both she and the child looked at Petra with wide eyes, before the woman answered with some surprise.

'No, I don't know anyone who has one like it. But you do see people around now and then who have one.'

'Do you say hello to each other or . . . ?' Petra asked stupidly.

The woman snorted.

'Sure, that happens sometimes. Or you just smile at each other or nod with a kind of mutual understanding.'

It was her turn and she paid for her items. Petra got out of the queue, letting those behind her go ahead, and continued stubbornly.

'You probably think I'm being a nuisance now, but

I would like to ask you a couple of questions. I'm a police officer and I need help with something. Do you have time? It will only take a few moments.'

'Sure.'

They left the pram near the queue and moved away from the till, further into the shop.

'Perhaps you are aware that we found a dead woman in Vitabergsparken? We haven't been able to identify her yet. But she had a pram similar to yours, so I thought maybe you had noticed her. The picture I have is unpleasant – can you handle it, do you think?'

Petra asked herself why she was being so careful with this woman. She'd had no such scruples when she'd spoken to the nurses at the children's health centre. It must be the child on her chest making me soft, she thought.

'Okay then,' answered the young mother, evidently more interested now.

Petra held out the photographs and the woman studied them with an expression of disgust and sorrow combined. She slowly shook her head and gave them back.

'I'm sorry,' she said, 'but I don't recognize either of them. Is the baby dead as well?'

'No. He was found nearby, but he survived. Thanks for your help anyway. You gave me an idea. About the pram, I mean,' said Petra. 'Perhaps someone will recognize the pram, if nothing else. By the way, where did you buy it?'

'Oh, I don't remember. You buy a lot of things, you know. For the first child. This was big sister's pram first and we went all over looking for a pram, changing table, cot, finding a babysitter –'

'And when was big sister born?'

'December 2003.'

'Thanks again,' said Petra, setting aside her items in a basket of apples and going out on to the street. Her mobile phone was already at her ear as the door shut behind her.

'Einar, it's Petra.'

'Yes, I'm sitting here with a long list in front of me of boys born in March, April and May of 2007.'

'That's good. This search process takes a lot of time –'

'Yes, mine too.'

'I think it's embarrassing that we haven't been able to identify the victim yet. We'll have to take a chance at this stage. We have to focus the search. I want you to start calling around to all these families, and do it in wider and wider circles from a starting point in Vitabergsparken.'

She could hear how bossy she sounded. Eriksson was much more experienced than her, yet she was the one giving orders. Perhaps she could express herself differently, a little more gently. But why should she even need to worry about that?

'And ask whether they have a polka-dotted pram, or what?'

'Yes, of course. And where the mother and son are. Besides that, Einar, I want you to start by focusing on families where there is also an older sibling aged three or four. Also ask whether they know any other family that fits this pattern.'

'All right, but it's really nice to find this out now, when I've already produced the information –'

'We can trade, you and I, if you'd rather run around to all the children's health centres?'

She bit her lip and took a deep breath. It was always just as well to accommodate Einar Eriksson. It served no purpose to get too irritated by him. If you wanted work done – and he did do a good job – it was best to let him have his way. And she almost felt a little sorry for him. It couldn't be fun having his attitude towards everything and everyone.

'Einar, I'm sorry about the extra bother. It just suddenly struck me that the baby probably has an older sibling, because the pram is from 2003.'

'Or it might very well be a hand-me-down, or bought used or even borrowed.'

'That's true, but I still want us to try this. We have to start somewhere. For that reason let's start with boys born in March, April or May 2007, registered in the area around Vitabergsparken and with an older sibling born in 2003 or 2004.'

'Sure, sure,' said Einar Eriksson.

'Take careful notes about every call. The ones you don't get hold of you'll have to phone again, until you get an answer. Okay?'

'Sure,' answered Einar Eriksson, making no effort to conceal his antipathy.

* * *

Barbro Dahlström was starting to get really irritated. Admittedly she could not assume that the police were not doing their job, simply because she had been treated rudely when she spoke to *one* of them. But she was quite convinced that Holgersson at the Hammarby Police had not taken her seriously. Earlier in the morning she had called the police switchboard again, and asked to be connected to the county detective unit. She was not able to speak to any detectives, only to the receptionist. The person she should talk to was 'not in at the present time', so she had been encouraged to call back after eleven.

'A ticklish matter,' said Detective Nyman, who was now back in the office.

'I realize that,' said Barbro as politely as she was able. 'On the other hand, can it really be all that hard to figure out who called me yesterday evening?'

'What time did you say it was?'

'I don't remember exactly. It must have been around eight o'clock, but that has no significance because I only had one call the whole evening, and it was from this girl.'

'I'll see what I can do,' said Nyman.

'That's not good enough,' said Barbro in a sharper tone now. 'You have to promise to do something about it immediately.'

'I will, but it may take a little time.'

'How long?'

'Up to a week usually.'

'And in a prioritized case, like this? Involving a child in obvious danger?' Barbro hoped it would pay to go on the offensive.

'A whole day at best. It depends on the work load of the provider.'

'Can I call Telia myself and apply pressure?' Barbro offered.

'No, that won't work,' Nyman replied, and Barbro

could have sworn he was smiling as he said it. 'The police have special access and private individuals can't request that type of information.'

'Then can I rely on you?' Barbro coaxed further.

'I think you should, Mrs Dahlström. I'll be in touch as soon as I know more.'

* * *

Sjöberg sat on the metro, summarizing to himself the morning's events on *Viking Cinderella*. Hamad, Eriksson, Hansson, Rosén and he had been met by their counterpart from the Åbo police, Nieminen, and several other Finnish police officers in the company of the ship's captain. After first taking a look at the crime scene itself, they were treated to breakfast and had a meeting in one of the conference rooms on the boat. Nieminen outlined the current situation and reported on the meagre results from the questioning so far.

It had been determined that the persons of most interest in the investigation – besides the boyfriend, Joakim Andersson, and the other young people in the party – were the man that Jennifer Johansson had been seen with in the bar and the two gentlemen in suits she met afterwards. None of these men had made themselves known during the introductory interviews, and the girl had not been observed after she had been seen with them. For that reason it was decided that the search for these three individuals should be given highest priority, from both the Finnish and Swedish side.

*

The bartender Juha Lehto was taking a few days off and was now with his Swedish girlfriend, who lived in an apartment by Thorildsplan. That was where Sjöberg was headed after the morning's work on the Finland ferry. The door opened almost immediately when he rang the bell.

'That was fast. No problems finding a parking spot?'

Lehto spoke with a lilting Finnish accent, but even though he spoke very well it was clear that Swedish was not his native language. In Nieminen's case it had been hard to tell whether he was actually a Finnish Swede or simply spoke excellent Swedish.

'I took the metro,' Sjöberg answered. 'Once you've found a parking spot on Söder, you don't want to give it up.'

He hung his jacket on a hanger and, being well brought up, left his shoes on the hall mat. Lehto showed him to an arm-chair in the sparsely furnished living room. Although he had gone to bed early the night before, Sjöberg had not slept long. He ignored how tired he was and instead sat leaning forward with his interlaced hands hanging between his knees.

'Coffee?' asked Lehto, sitting down at the table when Sjöberg declined.

'You've done this before,' said Sjöberg, 'but I want you to do it again. Tell me in your own words as much of what you recall from that evening as possible. I'm going to record our conversation. I hope you don't mind.'

Lehto shook his head and from his trouser pocket Sjöberg pulled out the MP3 player he had got from Åsa as a birthday present and activated the voice-recording function. He had been using it more and more like a Dictaphone, and with a nod at the bartender he asked him to start.

'It was fairly early in the evening,' Lehto began, and

then told how Jennifer Johansson and the considerably older man had shown up in the bar at about the same time.

Lehto thought for a little while before continuing.

'She was good-looking, that girl. Really good-looking. It probably occurred to me that she shouldn't be sitting there with him. He was too old for one thing, and seedy besides. I've thought about this quite a bit, but I can't really put my finger on what it was that made me think he looked a little down at heel. I remember that he had on a white shirt. It was probably wrinkled or dirty, otherwise I wouldn't have thought that. And I think he was unshaven. And not in a trendy way. I don't think he was drunk. He wasn't fat. There was nothing special about his appearance that I noticed. That's the best I can do, unfortunately.'

Lehto threw out his hands in an apologetic gesture and continued trying to explain what he thought seemed threatening in the situation and how the girl was then approached by another man.

'So you think they knew each other, Jennifer and that other man?' Sjöberg asked.

'I got that impression, but they may have just been pretending. She went with him and sat at their table.'

'That man at the bar, where did he go then?' asked Sjöberg.

'He just left. Without finishing his beer.'

'Did he pay?'

'I don't remember if he left money on the bar or if he had already paid earlier. He left anyway.'

'How old was he?'

'He must have been fifty or sixty.'

'How old are you?'

'Thirty-one.'

'Could he have been forty or seventy?'

'No.'

'Do you recall whether he had a dialect?'

'I'm not good at Swedish dialects, I have to admit. I don't think he was from Skåne anyway.'

'Those other men then,' Sjöberg continued. 'Can you describe them?'

'They were a little older than me. In their forties, I would say. Cool guys, yuppie types. Both of them had suits on, looked like businessmen. Quite handsome, both of them, it's fair to say. I only saw them when they were ordering at the bar.'

'What did they have to drink?'

'The girl had an umbrella drink. I don't recall what the guys were drinking.'

'Do you remember how they paid?'

'Cash.'

'But you don't think you would recognize either of them?'

'Not the Finnish guys, I don't think. Maybe the guy at the bar.'

'And this kid?' said Sjöberg, holding out the photograph of Joakim Andersson. 'Do you recognize him?'

'I've thought a lot about that, but I really don't remember serving him.'

'It was fairly early in the evening. If you had served him, would you have noticed?'

'You mean considering the injuries on his face?'

'Yes.'

'You have no idea how many people I meet who look like that.'

When Sjöberg had left Lehto and made his way to the metro platform, where he was now standing, waiting for the train, he called Lotten, their cheerful receptionist.

'Where have you been hiding? Einar's the only one here.'

'It piled up a little over the weekend, as you may have heard. We're all out on the job. Do you miss us?'

'Always,' Lotten chirped.

'And how's Pluto doing?'

Lotten was an unusually enthusiastic dog person. Her dog – an Afghan whose name was not Pluto at all, but something pretentiously French-sounding – and the care-taker Micke's standard poodle sent each other Christmas cards and even birthday cards. Sjöberg often asked himself whether these birthdays were celebrated once a year or seven times, but he never got around to asking. Presumably because he would not be able to ask without sounding contemptuous and – her dog obsession aside – he had nothing but respect for this positive, bubbly person who made any situation whatsoever easier and more pleasant.

'"Pluto",' answered Lotten with feigned annoyance, 'has a slight cold, otherwise he's just fine. Listen, I have a message.'

Efficient and factual as always, despite the cheerful wrapping.

'A journalist from *Aftonbladet* called who wanted to talk about the infant in Vitabergsparken. I didn't know whether I should refer her to you or Petra or what I should do –'

'Wait,' he interrupted. 'I can't hear anything right now.'

The train pulled into the station and Lotten's voice was drowned in the noise of the underground. Sjöberg got into one of the carriages and resumed the call.

'What did you say? Infant?'

'Yes, she mentioned the infant in Vitabergsparken. I didn't think it was officially –'

The doors closed and the train left Thorildsplan.

'What's her name? Telephone number?'

The receiver started to crackle.

'. . . text . . . call back . . .'

'Now I'm losing you!' shouted Sjöberg. 'Put Petra on it! I'll be in after lunch!'

* * *

After checking off Wollmar Yxkullsgatan and Hornstull from her list of children's health centres without success, Petra went back to the police building to compare notes on the situation with Eriksson and Sandén. Hopefully she would have time to consume something edible too. She had just stepped into her office when Lotten called.

'I have a journalist from *Aftonbladet* on the line. She's been after you all morning.'

'Us?' said Petra.

'Yes, she has questions regarding the infant finding in Vita Bergen.'

'Did she use that phrase, "the infant finding"?'

'Yes, she did actually,' Lotten laughed.

'She'll have to talk to Conny. I have no authority to speak to the press.'

'I called Conny,' Lotten explained. 'He said you should do it.'

'He did? The last time I spoke to him he thought we should keep this low profile.'

'But now it's already out.'

Petra sighed. Yes, apparently it was. There was always someone who couldn't resist calling the tabloids. After brief consideration she came to two conclusions: that it must have been the young mother in the 7-Eleven who had been tempted by a little extra cash, and that a little media attention on the infant boy in Vitabergsparken was perhaps what they needed to get somewhere.

'Okay, put her through,' said Petra, tossing her jacket on to the desk.

She had never communicated directly with the press; Sjöberg usually took care of that. But if you were responsible for an investigation, then you were. It was just a matter of biting the bullet and being careful not to say too much. And not to leave room for personal interpretation.

'I've been told that you're the one leading the investigation,' the reporter said after she introduced herself. 'How do you spell your last name?'

Petra spelled her name and hoped she would not regret this conversation.

'I've heard that you not only found a dead woman in Vitabergsparken last Sunday,' the journalist continued, 'but also an infant. Comments?'

Petra explained how it all hung together, and described the boy's appearance and age, including clothing and the pram.

'And no one has called in?' asked the reporter.

'That's correct. But we would be grateful for any information,' she added to forestall the journalist and at the same time seem accommodating. 'Serious information.'

'Do you have any photos we can publish?'

'At the present time we've decided not to release any photographs,' Petra answered in a voice she did not recognize. 'We hope of course that very soon we will be in contact with relatives.'

'There is apparently an older sibling in the picture?'

'We know nothing about that,' said Petra firmly, visualizing the young mother in the 7-Eleven taking out her phone as soon as Petra had left.

'But the pram is a 2003 model. So it could be that way?'

'Naturally there is such a possibility,' Petra answered diplomatically, 'but it may just as well be the case that the pram was borrowed or bought used.'

Then they devoted a few minutes to classifying the crime. The phrase 'murder with robbery' came up, but Petra tried to characterize it as 'an alleged hit-and-run accident'.

When the call was ended, she was not sure whether she had done a good job or if it had been a complete fiasco. That probably depended on the current mood of the headline writer, she decided with a sigh, as she left the room to find her colleagues who were less burdened with responsibility.

Monday Afternoon

She was starting to feel inadequate. She did not trust that Nyman at the county detective unit. What if the poor girl really had been abandoned by her parents! Then a week was too long. If only she had caller ID, she could have traced the number Hanna was calling from herself and found out where she lived. And she could have called to console her and offer help. If it were really needed. Perhaps it would turn out that the girl was not alone after all, and then the problem would be resolved. But Barbro could not get the thought out of her head; she had to do something.

The girl had talked about summer cottages in the middle of the city. Barbro came to the conclusion that she must have meant allotments. The probability that the girl would have dialled a Stockholm area code before Barbro's own number must be very slight. On that basis she reasoned that the call was local, that the girl was in Stockholm, in an apartment with a view of allotments. Where else could she look? She had to start somewhere.

She sat down at the computer in the kitchen and turned it on. Barbro was generally not keen on technical gadgets. As long as the landline telephone worked, she kept it. What reason was there to change? And caller ID – what would she do with that? If the phone rang, she answered it, no matter who called. A mobile phone and answering machine were not for her either. If she wasn't home when they called, they could just try again. That had worked in the twentieth century and quite likely it still did. Besides, being retired, she did not have unlimited resources.

But it was different with the computer. She could hardly live without her beloved computer. The indispensable search engines helped her to solve crosswords, book trips and theatre tickets, and best of all kept her up to date on what was happening in cultural Stockholm. True, it was an extra expense, but it was worth every penny.

A quick search on Eniro showed that there were thousands of Bergmans in Stockholm. Couldn't Hanna's neighbour have been named Liljesparre instead? No, she would have to attack the problem from a different angle. Four minutes later she found what she was searching for: a list of all the allotment areas in Stockholm, on the website of the Greater Stockholm Allotment Association. There were a lot, almost eighty, but she told herself not to panic and to visit them one at a time. She could start with the ones that were closest and then work outwards; taking them one by one and keeping her eyes open for yellow castles and angry old men by the name of Bergman.

Barbro Dahlström was seventy-two years old. She had been a high-school French and English teacher, and had been a widow for thirteen years. Every autumn, together with some retired friends, she would hike in the French Alps, stay at hostels, eat and drink well. Now, at the end of September, it was time to walk off the added French pounds.

She made herself a few sandwiches and put them, along with a Thermos of coffee and a bottle of ordinary tap water, in the small backpack that she used when she was out walking. This time however she left the walking sticks at home and went out into the mild Indian summer.

First she went towards the Eriksdalslunden allotments, to which she had walked many times. After that she intended to walk around Södermalm, clockwise. She realized that it would not be possible to do that in a single afternoon, but she had to take one day at a time. In her ears she had Radio P1. Sometimes, when she got tired of the serious voices, she changed to a music station. She had received the small portable radio from her daughter as a Christmas present a few years ago and was now so attached to it that to be on the safe side she always carried reserve batteries in her backpack.

Eriksdalslunden and the extensive Tantolunden allotments produced nothing. No yellow castles were to be seen, but she worked systematically and searched anyway for the name Bergman on the directory boards of every nearby building.

After searching without success through the allotments in Årstalund she allowed herself a rest, removed the earplugs and ate her sandwiches sitting on a park bench, accompanied by the sound of the water of Årstaviken lapping against the shore. Some ducks were rooting in the sand between two large willows that had grown in a way that made them look as if they were falling headfirst into the water, with their branches spread out, as if they were trying to catch each other in mid-fall. In her mind she constructed an image of little Hanna. How old could she be? Certainly much too young to be able to manage by herself. Five maybe? Six?

Barbro realized that it was very unlikely that she had been

left at home alone. You don't let such a small child take care of herself, even for a short time. Not in today's Stockholm, with all the electrical appliances, heavy traffic, criminals and paedophiles, corrosive detergents, toxic pharmaceuticals, high windows; she hardly dared think about all the hazards that might entice a curious little person without supervision. Her mother must only have been gone for a few minutes; down to the laundry room or rushed off to the store.

But what about the hash? Hanna said she had had to get food for herself. She also said that she had hurt herself and that she wanted her daddy to come home from Japan and kiss it and make it better. True, the girl could have a lively imagination, but Barbro's instinct told her this was for real.

Barbro Dahlström finished her picnic, carefully rewrapping one of the sandwiches in foil and putting it back in the little backpack. Then she took off again. A promise was a promise.

* * *

The reception area was suddenly full of young people and Lotten had her hands full taking everyone's information. They were all aged between fifteen and eighteen. Sjöberg had forewarned her that he had called in Jennifer Johansson's group of friends from the Finland boat for questioning at one o'clock, and here they were, about a dozen of them. Despite the serious atmosphere, as teenagers do they took up too much space and sounded like there were three times as many. A few boys were lounging in a group of armchairs, some of the young people sat on a pair of benches along the wall, while others wandered around. There was nonstop talking on mobile phones.

One of the girls stood crying and a couple of friends consoled her. Maybe she had more reason than the others to grieve for Jennifer Johansson, thought Lotten, or else she just wanted attention. On one bench another girl sat crying by herself. The boys tried to look neutral and carried on as usual. But Lotten saw the sorrow and consternation in their eyes, and remembered that it was not easy being a teenager. Everyone had a facade to keep up.

And then there was Joakim Andersson. He too had been called for questioning, but he did not join the others. Instead he stayed apart by the window overlooking the turning area and gazed out towards the apartment buildings by the Hammarby canal. He stood quietly with his hands in his pockets and appeared not to be affected by the tumult around the other young people.

* * *

When Sjöberg came in, aware of being a few minutes late, he took a quick look at the various constellations of young people in the reception area before he went up to Lotten.

'Is that Joakim over there – by the window?' he asked.

'That's right,' Lotten replied. 'He nodded at a couple of the girls when he arrived, the ones named Fanny and Malin, but except for when he came up and reported in he's been standing over there by himself the whole time.'

'He hasn't talked to anyone?'

'No. No one has approached him either. I guess they're

afraid of being confronted with his grief. You know how youngsters are –'

'I'm not sure I do. Maybe they're afraid of him.'

'I think he looks nice,' said Lotten. 'Nice, and sad.'

'How can you see that behind the beard?' Sjöberg snorted.

'You sound a little cynical, Conny,' Lotten said. 'That grungy style is trendy.'

'He's twenty-four. What was he doing with a sixteen-year-old girl?'

'When did you get so conservative?'

'He's probably the one who did it. Who else? Bear in mind, Lotten, that this prejudiced statement is based on many years of experience,' he added jokingly. 'This is a pretty lively group!'

'Just be glad you're not a teacher, like poor Åsa.'

Suddenly and unexpectedly ill at ease at the mention of his wife, he made to go.

'Send Joakim up to me in five minutes. Jamal should start with those girls, Fanny and Malin, separately. After that, it doesn't matter.'

He let go of the door behind him, threaded his way past the young people and took the stairs up to the second floor in a few quick steps.

* * *

'So until that episode in the bar you considered Jennifer your girlfriend?'

'Yes, more or less,' answered Joakim, watching Sjöberg set an MP3 player on the table between them.

'What do you mean by that? Did you have other girl-friends too?'

'No, not like that –'

'Maybe she had other guys?'

'Maybe she did. I don't know. I don't think so.'

'Now I think you should try to explain to me what kind of relationship the two of you really had.'

Joakim let out a heavy sigh. What should a relationship be like? How do you explain feelings? He was not a verbal person, but now for the first time in his life he was forced to explain things that could not be put into words.

'What kind of relationship . . .' Joakim repeated like a faint echo.

'Well, tell me how you met. We have to start somewhere.'

Now it was easier. There were good times and actual events he could describe. Joakim told about their initial meeting, how the shopping bag fell apart, about evenings drinking at the bar, and walks hand in hand. But soon they found themselves in the grey vacuum that followed after the first few ecstatic weeks with Jennifer.

'Do you know what I think?' said Sjöberg. 'I think Jennifer was your first girlfriend. Is that right?'

'Yes,' Joakim answered quietly, not daring to look the chief inspector in the eyes.

* * *

Sjöberg saw the boy's eyes light up as he talked about the first few weeks with Jennifer. He had guided him out into deeper and deeper waters, and now he felt himself relenting as the truth became clear. The boy was twenty-four and had never had a girlfriend. In light of this, it was much easier to understand how hard it was for him to describe his relationship with Jennifer. Joakim Andersson had nothing to compare it to, no tools to evaluate what they had had together.

Sjöberg could imagine how the girl gradually began to see through this inexperienced, uncertain young man. Twenty-four would sound good to an experienced sixteen-year-old, but under the tough surface, behind the beard and the sunglasses he now had pushed up on his forehead, she glimpsed something completely different and started to feel embarrassed. Perhaps what she sensed behind the facade he put up was a sensitive and delicate personality, but she needed resistance, someone as big and strong on the inside as he appeared to be on the outside.

'It's nothing to be ashamed of,' said Sjöberg in an attempt to soften his earlier harsh tone. 'Some time has to be the first time for all of us. But now I want you to describe what you were doing – in detail – from the time you woke up on Friday morning until the police knocked on the door of your cabin yesterday morning.'

'Friday morning?' Joakim looked perplexed. 'What does Friday have to do with this?'

'I'll decide that. Let's hear it now.'

'I delivered papers in the morning, between four and eight. Then I was home all day. Nothing happened in particular.'

'Delivering newspapers – that's your job?'

'Yes.'

'How often do you do that?'

'Just a few days a week.'

'That's not much income. What do you live on?'

'I live at home. I don't need that much money.'

'So how do you spend the rest of your time?'

'I'm mostly at home,' he said, but Sjöberg gave him a challenging look.

'I take care of my mum,' he said at last. 'She's ill.'

'I'm sorry to hear that. What kind of illness?'

He asked because he wanted to form an image of Joakim Andersson's life, what it was like at home, the family circumstances. He wanted to look into the dark corners, dig out secrets, penetrate into his private sphere.

'She's handicapped,' Joakim answered, a little too loudly. 'Disabled. She can't walk!'

He spat out the words, with an almost triumphant facial expression – unexpected anger, perhaps he felt offended? Like a child who swears, thought Sjöberg, who hurls out all the bad words he knows, with the fear of repercussion shining in his eyes. The young man across from him had just said something forbidden, something he never mentioned, perhaps was not allowed to say. He had revealed a family secret.

'Oh dear,' said Sjöberg, trying to sound factual and neutral. 'That must be hard for her. Is she getting the care she needs?'

'I take care of her. I told you that.'

'And your dad, what does he do?'

'He works at a bank. Swedbank in Farsta.'

'Do you help out with the care of your mother or do you do most of it yourself?'

'Dad feeds her if I'm not home. Otherwise I'm the one who takes care of her.'

'I see, so you were at home taking care of your mother all day last Friday. And then, in the evening?'

'I was going to see Jennifer, but that didn't happen.'

'What happened instead?'

'Dad wouldn't let me go. He didn't like her.'

'Had they met?'

'No, but he didn't like that I had a girlfriend. I said I was going to go anyway and that we were going to Finland on Saturday.'

'And then?' Sjöberg gestured towards Joakim's mangled face.

'He knocked me down. I don't know if I fainted or fell asleep. When I woke up he had gone to bed anyway. I threw a few things in a bag and left.'

'Does he always mistreat you like that?' asked Sjöberg.

'Sometimes. He has a bad temper.'

Sjöberg noticed how Joakim Andersson excused his father, tried to give him a legitimate reason for hitting him.

'Do you hit back?'

'No. What good would that do?'

'And where did you go?' Sjöberg continued.

'I walked around all night. Looked for Jennifer. Sat in a McDonald's. Rode the bus.'

'Did you sleep at all?'

'A little, on the bus.'

'Why didn't you go to Jennifer's?'

'She didn't want me to go round to hers.'

'Why is that?'

Joakim answered with a shrug. Sjöberg had a strong feeling he knew why, but he did not share his suspicions.

'So you must have been extremely tired and irritable on Saturday?'

'Not that I remember. I guess I didn't think about it that much.'

'What was that day like?'

'In the morning I waited for Jennifer outside her building, until she came out. Fanny and Malin were there too and then we took the metro to Central Station and bought the ferry tickets.'

'How well did you know Jennifer's friends? Malin and Fanny, for example.'

'I'd never met either of them before.'

'And none of the others on the boat either?'

'No.'

'Why do you think that was? That she didn't let you meet her friends?'

'But she did. On the trip to Finland.'

'But before?'

'I don't know. Maybe she intended to break up with me.'

'Were you worried about that?'

'Not worried exactly. Well, maybe. It didn't feel real that she would want to be with me. And she was so strange towards me at the end. She could be really happy one moment and other times – well, then it was as if I didn't exist.'

'And how was it on that day?'

'More or less like that.'

'So it fluctuated?'

'She was mad at me the whole day, until the pre-party in the cabin. Then it changed. Then she disappeared. I'm sure you know the rest.'

'I still want to hear it in your own words,' said Sjöberg. 'Tell me everything that happened after you got on board the boat.'

Joakim talked and Sjöberg coaxed and listened. An hour and a half later he let him go, went out to the kitchenette in the corridor and served himself a cup of coffee, then he phoned Lotten and asked her to send up the next young man.

* * *

Jens Sandén had a late lunch in the office with Petra Westman and Einar Eriksson. He would have preferred to go out to eat, but Eriksson stubbornly refused to eat anything besides his own packed lunch. Petra was stressed and in a hurry to be off again, so she and Sandén wolfed down a sandwich and a cup of coffee in the conference room, while Eriksson had beef stroganoff, heated up in the microwave. They quickly reviewed the situation and Eriksson delivered his latest lists of prioritized addresses.

After a brief run-through for the foot soldiers, Sandén again found himself knocking on doors in the area around Vitabergsparken. He was working first north along Barnängsgatan, to then continue with Bondegatan and its cross streets between Skånegatan and Åsögatan, all the way up to Klippgatan. Outside a yellow building in the same block as the Transport Museum that housed a storage company, according to the anything-but-modest sign, he caught sight of a woman in her sixties bending over a navy-blue Emmaljunga pram with small white dots.

Sandén stopped beside her and cleared his throat before saying, 'I see, so Grandma's doing the babysitting today?'

The woman straightened up and gave him a friendly smile.

'Yes, my daughter is at the dentist and I'll just be babysitting for an hour, but it's no picnic when they're this small.'

She shook her head slightly in a gesture of resignation. Sandén took a look in the pram. The child appeared to be sleeping soundly, so he assumed that Grandma was doing just fine.

'How old is he?' he asked out of curiosity.

Sandén took a chance on the baby's gender, but he had apparently guessed correctly, because the woman answered without further comment that the child was six months old. After introducing himself and explaining his errand, he took the photographs out of the inside pocket of his suede jacket. The first one he showed her was of the boy.

'This little boy has a pram similar to your grandson's here. Do you recognize him? He's about five months old.'

The woman studied the photograph for a while but then shook her head.

'It's not easy. It's really hard to see the difference in such small children, unless they're close to you. No, I can't say I recognize him.'

'This is his mother. Do you recognize her?'

'Oh my!' she said behind the hand that had flown up to cover her mouth.

'I'm sorry, but there's no other way –'

'But I do recognize her,' the woman interrupted. 'I've chatted to her several times. I run into her in Blecktornsparken now and then. I usually go there with this little boy's big brother. There's such a fun playground there, with rabbits and everything.'

'And what was she doing there?' asked Sandén, who already feared the worst.

'Oh my God!' the woman exclaimed, her eyes moist. 'There's a big sister too, you know. A little girl – how old can she be? A little younger than Edvin – my grandson, that is – yes, three or four, I'd say. A bright, happy little girl, talkative and lively. Where is she now?'

'We don't know, but hopefully she's in good hands. Perhaps she's with her father – do you know if he's around?'

'No, I don't really know. The few times we spoke it was mostly about the children and their games, the weather and such. They weren't deep conversations, you understand.'

'Did you ever see her in the company of anyone else?'

'Not as far as I remember.'

'Do you have any idea where they live?'

'No, I don't think she mentioned that. They could live anywhere. Blecktornsparken is probably the most popular playground on Södermalm.'

'Did she have an accent? Or perhaps some dialect you recall?'

'I'm quite sure that she was Swedish. She had no accent at all, and both she and the girl looked as Swedish as can be. But dialect . . . No, I don't think so. In any event nothing noticeable, I mean from Skåne or Gotland or such.'

'How did she look?' Sandén continued insistently. 'For example, was she smartly dressed?'

'As far as I remember there was nothing remarkable about her clothes. She looked like a mum with small children. Practical clothes, nothing she'd want to keep from getting dirty, but not slovenly in any way. She was very friendly; not everyone you meet is.'

'Did you notice whether she seemed afraid or to feel threatened? Did she seem worried?'

'Not at all. On the contrary, she seemed extremely content and relaxed. She took the time to talk to me. And she was sweet with the girl. The girl was pretty lively as I said and demanded a lot of attention. She was at that age where they fall down and hurt themselves all the time. She wanted her mother to push her on the swings and play, and her mother mostly did what she asked.'

'When did you last see her?'

'It must have been sometime in the spring.'

'You never saw her anywhere other than Bleck-tornsparken?'

'No, I didn't.'

The baby started whimpering in the pram and Sandén felt he had got all he could for the time being.

'You've been a great help,' he said sincerely. 'We'll need to speak to you again, so I would be grateful if I could get your contact information. Name, address, and telephone number.'

'I would be grateful if I could get yours first,' said the grandmother with a hint of sarcasm.

'Oh, excuse me. Naturally,' said Sandén, awkwardly pulling out his police ID.

The woman studied it for a moment and then took the pen and notepad and wrote down her contact details.

'You'd better give that child back before he really gets going,' Sandén said.

The boy was wriggling in the pram and the little face was screwed up alarmingly.

'Thanks again,' said Sandén.

'Don't mention it. Just see that you arrest whoever did this.'

Then she went off with the pram and left Sandén to his no-longer-hopeless assignment.

He took his mobile phone out of his jacket to call Petra Westman when it started vibrating.

'Hey, Jensy! Pontus here.'

Jensy? Was Pontus messing with him? Or was this just a pathetic attempt to be friendly? Never in a million years would he play happy families with that piece of shit. Especially now, when the whole thing was finally over. Because he was sure that it was. With the offer of ten thousand kronor, this chapter in Jenny's life should be a thing of the past. Sandén knew what he was doing. The boy liked money. He was a wheeler-dealer through and through, but not in a legitimate-feeling way. He had no education to speak of, showed no signs of cultivation or any noteworthy intelligence. Despite that, he liked to give the impression of having lots of money; he talked in vague terms about investments here and there, spewing Wall Street clichés about his clearly dodgy – as far as Sandén could tell – business ideas.

And everything had to be flashy. Expensive, brand-name clothes and stylish, trendy places. Places that Sandén had the impression his beloved little Jenny was never taken to. The few times all three of them had been in the same room there had been talk *about* Jenny, not *with* Jenny. As if that creep thought of her like a sweet little dog. Or a piece of furniture. And Sandén had his suspicions about which one.

He had known from the first that this guy would only

mean trouble. It was not just his oily, pseudo-yuppie appearance – a real yuppie would have a real job, Sandén assumed – but, above all, the fact that he was interested in Jenny at all. That in itself said a great deal. What twenty-six-year-old of normal intelligence falls for a younger girl with learning difficulties? It was so unlikely that Sandén was convinced that it couldn't be for real. Jenny was an attractive girl, so in that respect she was good enough for Pontus. And she was devoted to him. She was devoted to anyone who showed her the least bit of appreciation, and that was a charming quality. In most cases. Not with men, however.

Reluctantly Sandén forced himself to see his daughter as a woman who was sexually active. And Jenny's devotion presumably made her good in bed. He hated thinking about it, but at the same time he could not let himself close his eyes to the truth. Pontus was exploiting her, exactly how he refused to go into – that was the limit. And then he'd hit her. That was hard to understand; Jenny would not hurt a fly. Maybe Pontus did it just because he felt like it. But there must be an end to that now; there *would* be an end to that now.

'What's on your mind?' said Sandén, with as much contempt as he could muster in his voice.

'I've been thinking about your offer.' Cheerful voice. Offhand.

'And?'

'It's generous, certainly, but I guess I would have expected a little more.'

Extortionist, thought Sandén. The bastard has a system of picking up girls with learning difficulties in order to be bought off by their families. We need to put an end to this.

166

'Same old Pontus.'

'I was thinking about fifty thousand. Deal?'

'I never want to see you again. You have to be out of the apartment before Jenny comes home.'

'Yes, baby.'

The guy was not all there.

'Deal?'

'Deal,' Sandén heard himself say before he ended the call with a shudder.

* * *

Petra was sitting in the waiting room of a children's health centre by Gullmarsplan, browsing through a well-thumbed copy of *Nursing Guide*. At this point she was fed up with the rose-tinted picture of motherhood in *We Parents*, and she promised herself never to open that magazine again. Even if she had a reason to. Which she hoped she would have sooner or later. She had two nurses left to confront with the unpleasant pictures; none of those she had questioned so far recognized the mother or the boy.

The chorus of 'I Don't Feel Like Dancin'' blared from her pocket, and the eyes of about ten mothers and four older siblings turned towards her. Time to change ringtone, thought Petra, as she walked past the sign with the crossed-out mobile phone and slipped outside to answer the call. It was Sandén, who told her about his meeting with the woman with the polka-dotted baby pram.

Petra sighed.

'Then we're on the right track anyway. We just have to keep working to try to find the girl and the father.'

'Do you think we should release this to the media?'

'Already done.'

'I thought Conny said –'

'Yes, I thought so too,' Petra interrupted. 'But he changed his mind. I got a call from a reporter at *Aftonbladet* who had got wind of the boy. I just provided a few details. So any moment now I'll be disgraced.'

'"Police detective Petra Westman in hair-raising hunt for merciless woman-killer." No, damn it, Petra, you're going to be promoted,' Sandén laughed.

Her mobile beeped in her ear.

'Someone else is calling. Were we finished?'

'Yes, I'll be in touch.'

With the push of a button she let call number two through.

'Westman,' said Petra.

'Hi, Petra, it's Roland.'

The voice sounded . . . positive. Petra struggled for a few moments to place this 'Roland'.

'Brandt,' said the voice. 'Roland Brandt. Remember me?'

'Of course, please excuse me. I just didn't make the connection.'

The police commissioner – what business in the world could he have with her?

'You're going to be promoted,' Sandén had joked just a few moments earlier. You don't get promoted because you answer a few questions from a journalist. More likely fired, she thought. But the voice sounded friendly.

'What are you doing?' asked the police commissioner.

Hi, this is Roland. What are you doing? What was this really about?

'I'm, uh, working on the Vita Bergen case,' Petra replied uncertainly. 'Trying to find someone who can identify the victim.'

'Good, good. So you're in the field?'

'Uh, yes,' Petra answered stupidly.

The field? What was going on with him?

'Would you care to drop by and see me a little later, when you're in the neighbourhood?'

The silky smooth voice was on the border of ingratiating. Could this be the calm before the storm? Did he want to lull her into a sense of security before he dealt her the death blow?

'Sure,' answered Petra. 'How long will you be there?'

'I'll be waiting for you,' said the police commissioner with an audible smile.

'Okay,' said Petra, hoping that Brandt would deliver some parting words.

He did not.

'See you later then,' she tried again, hearing immediately that her words didn't sound as formal as she'd intended.

'Okay,' said the police commissioner softly. 'Take care.'

And with that the call was over.

'What the hell . . . ?' mumbled Petra, standing stock-still and staring foolishly at the phone in her hand.

Then she shook her head to bring herself back to reality. She put the mobile on silent and went back into the children's health centre.

* * *

Sandén rang every doorbell in the building, but no one was home. At the last attempt, on the ground floor, he finally got a response. A man in his seventies opened the door and glared at him through bright-yellow glasses. He was skinny and a little stooped, dressed in a checked blue flannel shirt and jeans, and with a cigarette in his mouth. He might have been the caretaker, thought Sandén, if the building had one. Sandén held out his police ID and explained who he was.

'You are Mr Bergman, I presume?'

'Yes. What's this about?'

'I just want to ask a few questions. It won't take long. The family with children who live upstairs – the Hedbergs – do you know where they are?'

'How would I know?'

'I need to talk to them,' said Sandén.

'Then ring their doorbell, not mine,' the old man answered grumpily.

'Of course I already have, but apparently they're not at home,' said Sandén, not hiding that he was now starting to get irritated. 'That's why I'm asking you: Do you know where they're hiding themselves?'

'They're out of town, I would think.'

He seemed a little shaken after all by Sandén's harsh tone.

'Why do you think that?'

'Because they do that every now and then.'

He took a puff on his cigarette, and without taking it out of his mouth blew the smoke out of the other side.

'They're probably on a "weekend away",' he added with contemptuous emphasis.

'What makes you think that?' Sandén continued unperturbed.

'They're so *refined*. He runs around in a suit all day.'

'I see. Blimey. Where do they usually keep their pram?'

'In the apartment,' the man answered with an unwarranted smile.

'Always?'

'Listen, at first that damn pram was blocking the way down by the entrance, but I told them off and since then we've been spared that.'

Sandén sighed. Bergman had given true neighbourliness a face.

'And when was this?'

'Maybe six months ago.'

'What does the pram look like?'

'It must be black, maybe. Or blue.'

'Is it by any chance dotted?'

'Maybe it's dotted. Or checked. Or striped or flowery, damned if I know.'

'I would like you to look at a couple of photographs –' Sandén began, but he was interrupted.

'There's probably no point in that, inspector, because I'm as good as blind.'

Sandén stopped mid-motion and pulled his hand back out of his inside pocket.

'So you can't see my face now, for example?' he asked with surprise.

'Exactly. I see that you have a body and a head, and we'll have to be grateful for that.'

'So what do you think about my suit?'

The man thought before he answered.

'Listen, I can distinguish a white shirt from a dark suit, if that's what you're wondering.'

He was clearly not slow on the uptake anyway.

'Thanks for your help then,' Sandén ended the conversation, holding back the sarcastic tone he would have preferred.

He went back up to the fourth floor and rang the bell several more times. He crouched down and put his eye to the letter box, but inside it was completely quiet. With a muffled groan he managed to straighten his somewhat overweight body, after which he made a note on his list and hurried down the stairs.

* * *

Hanna was mumbling something in her sleep as she lay on her back, snugly encased in the two down duvets on her parents' unmade bed. She turned on to her side and only a few wisps of tangled hair and a little foot poked out.

Late in the afternoon Hamad and Sjöberg finished the interviews with the young people, without finding out anything new. Their misgivings were not confirmed; both Jennifer's mother and sister were at home, and fortunately they were alone in the apartment. Lena Johansson seemed almost sober and perhaps that was why today she looked, if possible, even more lost and worn out than she had on Sunday.

'Thanks for waiting,' Sjöberg began. 'I'm sorry we're so late.'

They went into the living room and introduced themselves to Elise, who looked scared, sitting curled up on the couch with her arms around her knees. She was red-eyed from crying and avoided making eye contact.

Sjöberg set the MP3 player on the coffee table and noted that someone had wiped it clean since they were last here. The kitchen, too, was somewhat more presentable, Sjöberg noticed as he passed it. He had a feeling it was the girl who had tidied up after the party the previous evening. Her mother looked like she had just woken up where she sat, collapsed at the other end of the couch, her hair in disarray. With a quick movement Elise tapped a cigarette out of the pack on the table in front of her mother and lit it with trembling hands. Her mother did not seem to notice, or else she didn't care.

'How do you feel today?' Sjöberg asked carefully. 'This must be hard for you . . . ?'

Elise turned her eyes towards the dirty living room window. She did not react to the question, so Sjöberg let his gaze wander to the mother instead.

'Yes,' she answered with uncertainty in her eyes and an almost ingratiating expression on her face.

Perhaps she was making an effort now to react in the manner she thought was expected of her. Perhaps the sorrow was much greater on the inside than it appeared. Perhaps she felt no pain at all. It was impossible to know what was going on in this person's mind. Was she accustomed to disparaging looks or was she perhaps completely dulled after years of substance abuse? This catastrophe was probably just one in a series of disasters that had struck her over the years.

'You don't know . . . You don't really know what you should do.'

Elise was staring out the window, apparently unaffected by the conversation. Sjöberg studied her clean profile and was struck by the likeness to her sister. He wondered about the caprice of nature: two such beautiful daughters coming out of a person like Lena Johansson. Lena Johansson could never have been beautiful. Even overlooking the wrinkles, swollen eyes, large-pored and scarred skin, what remained was average-looking at best.

'No. It must be extremely hard to pull yourself together after something like this. We're doing our utmost to arrest the perpetrator, if that's any consolation. For that reason we need to ask both of you a few questions, if you're up to it.'

'Oh, I'm sure we'll manage. Won't we, Elise? We have to help the inspector now.'

She looked imploringly at her daughter, but got no response. Elise reached towards the table for the ashtray, pulled it to her and set it on her lap.

'Tell me about her boyfriend,' Sjöberg began. 'Because she did have a boyfriend, didn't she, Elise?'

Elise squirmed a little on the couch and answered quietly, her eyes moving between the cigarette and the ashtray.

'His name is Joakim. He's twenty-four years old, I think. But I don't know if they were together any more. They were supposed to go out last Friday, but she decided not to, it seemed like.'

'Did she say that?'

'She said that *maybe* she was going to see him. If she felt like it.'

'Have you ever met Joakim?'

'No.'

'What did she say about him?'

'Nothing in particular, as far as I remember. I guess he was nice.'

'Were you close to each other, you and Jennifer?'

'I don't know exactly. I don't think so. We share a room. Shared a room.'

Elise took a few deep puffs on the cigarette and let the smoke out of her mouth in small, well-formed rings. A random thought passed through Sjöberg's mind: Smoking is better suited to overweight, older women.

'Well, what did she do then? Last Friday? Did she see him?'

'I don't know. I went out. When I came back she was here anyway.'

'And what time was that?'

'Twelve-thirty maybe.'

'What were you doing?'

'I was just out. Hung out for a bit down on Götgatan. Saw a friend. Nina.'

'Were you at home on Friday evening?'

Sjöberg had turned to the mother, who seemed to have lost focus. She did not appear to be listening to what was being said. He could see how she pulled herself together when she was spoken to.

'I was at home, yes. Last Friday.'

'And Jennifer,' Sjöberg coaxed further, 'was she at home or did she maybe go out for a while?'

Lena Johansson looked embarrassed and answered, stammering, 'Don't remember . . . yes . . . no . . . No, I really don't remember, I have to say.'

Sjöberg imagined that Friday evening was presumably not very different from Sunday evening. There were probably not too many evenings that Lena Johansson could actually account for.

'Did you have guests then too?' Hamad chimed in.

'She always has guests,' Elise clarified.

'Who was here last Friday?' Hamad continued. 'Perhaps you remember, Elise?'

'The usual,' she answered tonelessly. 'Monkan, Gordon, Peo, Solan. Dagge. Some strange guy that Solan dragged here. Bengtsson and Lidström. That tall, ugly jerk with no teeth. What the hell's his name?'

She turned towards her mother and looked at her with a blank expression.

'John,' she answered, nervously picking at the cuticle of one thumb and not looking up.

'John,' Elise repeated. 'And the Finn. I don't remember any others.'

Hamad wrote down everything that was said and Sjöberg continued.

'You and Jennifer – were you usually present at these parties?'

'No, not that often.'

'And what about on Friday?'

'We sat in for a while.'

'Did you get drunk?'

Elise hesitated, perhaps deliberating what answer would benefit her the most. The truth? Or a modified version?

'I was drunk,' she said. 'Not really drunk, but a little drunk.'

'And Jennifer?'

'We drank more or less the same amount. Maybe she drank more after she left. I don't know.'

'Do you offer the girls alcohol?' Sjöberg directed to the mother, more out of curiosity than as a reprimand.

'They steal from me. What can I do? And you took my smokes with you when you left, didn't you?' she said to Elise, who did not comment on the accusation.

'So you were in kind of a rowdy mood on Friday, Elise?'

'Yes, but I didn't have any money . . .' Elise began, but bit her lip as she said it. 'We were supposed to go out, but Nina and I just walked around a little. Didn't do anything special,' she added.

Sjöberg noted the slight change in the way she spoke, the sudden sharpness at those words. He wondered what kind of foolishness this girl had been involved in, but decided to drop the subject for the moment and only come back to it if it proved necessary.

'Why didn't you go on the Finland trip?' he asked instead.

'I guess they didn't want me along,' Elise answered with a shrug and looked at something outside the window, uninterested again.

'Do you know if there was anyone who disliked Jennifer, anyone who threatened her?'

'Who would that be? Everyone wanted to be friends with Jennifer. And all the guys were hot for her,' she added.

'Did she have many boyfriends?' Sjöberg asked.

'Before she did. Not any more, I think. She thought the boys were so childish. Well, and then there was Joakim of course.'

'Yes, he is a little older. A little more mature.'

Sjöberg listened to the echo of his words and thought he sounded like an old man talking to a child. Empty phrases, awkward attempts to put himself on a level that actually did not suit either of them. She – a child? Hardly. And he – wise from the experiences of a long life? He dismissed the thought.

'Hmm,' said Elise.

'She had nothing going with any of the blokes who always hang around here?' Hamad suggested.

'Hell, no!' she exclaimed, spitting out the words. 'If you saw them, you wouldn't even ask.'

She cast a contemptuous look at her mother, who did not respond.

'There were no jealous former boyfriends who bothered her?'

'No,' Elise answered.

Lena Johansson adamantly refused, as Sjöberg had feared, to go to Finland to identify the body. The two policemen left the Johansson family's home without having got a single solid piece of information. Still, their picture of Jennifer was that much clearer now. A sixteen-year-old, precocious in many ways, from a broken home, with a poorly functioning family and a shaky life in other respects too. A sixteen-year-old with a mind of her own, with certain social ambitions, but apparently no occupational or academic ambitions. Accustomed to taking care of herself, unaccustomed to emotional ties. Accustomed to going her own way, unaccustomed to outside demands.

You could see traces of their common upbringing in little sister Elise, but not much of the vitality that seemed to have characterized her older sister. What would life be like for Elise without her dominant big sister? Even though they did not appear to have *communicated* with each other, they must have *talked* to each other, exchanged words and opinions. Who would be there now for Elise?

* * *

Barbro was tired. She was sleepy, and her feet were sore. She should have ended the day's trek hours ago, but instead she sat down on a bench, finished the rest of the coffee in the Thermos and had the last sandwich. While she ate she considered going home and calling that Nyman again, being a little pushy. But when the sandwich was finished she felt stronger and dismissed that thought. Calling him now would not get her anywhere; she would only be giving in to her fatigue and backing out of what she had set out to do. She would finish off Zinken too before the day was over, and anyway it was better to wait to put pressure on the county detective unit until a full day had passed. Perhaps then, despite everything, Nyman would have managed to get the information from Telia she had tried to pressure him for.

Now it was starting to get dark. Barbro had completed what she'd made up her mind to do, but obviously, she was forced to admit to herself, without success. True, she had found no fewer than two apartment buildings in the vicinity of Zinken's allotments where the name Bergman was on the directory inside the front door, but there had been no yellow castle to be seen. And it was doubtful whether the allotments could even be visible from the windows in those buildings.

When she had finished Krukmakargatan she finally decided to make her way homewards, and chose Zinkens väg through the green belt instead of the same route back. As she was walking across the turning area which for her marked the start of Zinkens väg, she passed for the second time several low, red buildings with an adjoining play area, all surrounded by a green fence. On the wall was a sign announcing that the Pipemaker Preschool was inside, perhaps christened after the old tobacco factory in the vicinity. A random thought occurred to Barbro and prompted her to open the gate and go over to a closed door. Doubtful that anyone would still be there, she rang the doorbell anyway, and to her surprise someone immediately opened up. It was a young woman about twenty-five in a jacket and gym shoes, with a bag hanging over her shoulder. She showed all the signs of being on her way out.

'Excuse me for bothering you,' said Barbro, 'but I need to ask a few questions. You work here at the preschool, I assume?'

'Yes, I do,' the woman answered, 'but now I'm closing for the day.'

'I can see that, but this will only take a minute. First, I'd like to know whether you know a little girl named Hanna? Hanna Birgitta to be more precise. Unfortunately I don't know her last name, but I know she has a brother named Lukas.'

The woman thought for a moment before answering.

'I know a few Hannas, but I don't think any of them has a brother named Lukas. How old is she?'

'Unfortunately I don't know that either,' Barbro replied, 'and that's what the next question is about. How old do you think a girl is who doesn't know her last name and who says how old she is by showing fingers?'

'Well, that does depend on how grown-up she is of course,' said the woman, by now with an amused gleam in her eye.

'This girl is very grown-up,' Barbro hurried to say. 'She knows colours and speaks extremely well. Uses whole sentences.'

'Then I would guess three, four at the most. At five they usually know their last name. And then they're usually very particular about half years,' she added with a laugh. 'There is a big difference between five and five-and-a-half, and I'm guessing she doesn't have half a finger?'

Barbro smiled back and thanked the woman for her help. But inside she felt growing worry. The answers she got only confirmed what she seemed to remember from her own daughter's childhood but hoped was wrong. The abandoned girl was no more than four, more likely only three years old.

* * *

Lena Johansson was tired. Of most things, but above all tired of herself. She was thirty-seven years old, but on the rare occasions she looked at herself in the mirror, she thought she looked much older. She had never been a beauty, but her early life had been easy. Even though many of the girls in school were prettier, there was something about her, her attitude to life, that made schoolmates flock around her, including the boys. The same way it had been for Jennifer. Elise was from a different mould, more withdrawn. Both of them were extremely good-looking; they got that from Janne.

Janne and she were the same age and had met during high school in Södertälje. He was a survivor, grew up in a family of substance abusers with parents who abdicated their parental roles early on. Apparently unaffected by his background, he had everything the boys she grew up with were missing. He was big and strong, practical and industrious. He also had a kind of adultness about him that she had not encountered before, a well-filled wallet in his back pocket and a way with words that could bowl anyone over.

But above all it was his recklessness she fell for. His lack of respect for rules and authority and his attraction to adventure, to what was forbidden. She was an only child and her parents were much older than those of her friends. Maybe it was because they had not given her any siblings, or maybe it was to compensate for their advanced age that they spoiled her and gave her so much freedom.

As soon as they left high school – she from the two-year social work programme, Janne from the construction programme – they packed their bags and left Södertälje for the big city. Within a few days Janne had got a job at a construction site, and soon he had also talked his way into a sublet on the apartment where she and the girls still lived. She soon got work at a screen-printer's in Västberga, where she was very happy.

But after six months Janne broke his arm and went on sick leave. It was a typical Janne thing: he had been working up on a roof without a safety rope, slipped and fell several storeys down on to a lower roof, and the only consequence was a broken arm. The old guys who'd seen the whole thing said he had a guardian angel. When Janne couldn't work they rented out the apartment and travelled to Thailand with the money they had saved. It was a marvellous time: sun-drenched beaches, cheap to live and parties around the clock if you were so inclined. And both of them were. To start with she had been hesitant about all the drugs that were in circulation, hallucinogenic mushrooms and cheap diet pills that made you dance for days on end, but in Janne's company she felt secure and let herself be talked into things she otherwise would not have dared try.

After almost a year of travelling they returned home, got married and had the children. But Janne could never really settle down again. He continued to experiment with drugs, and Lena knew he was not sober even during work hours. He became indifferent and nonchalant, and when the news of his death reached her from a bridge construction site west of the city, she was crushed but not surprised.

Elise was a newborn then and life collapsed. Right after the accident Lena's mother died of cancer and not long after her father, who was fifteen years older, died too. But she had never betrayed her girls. Despite all the sorrows and distress she had not given up; she had always been there for them. Consoled and nursed them. For their sake she pulled herself together, even if it hadn't always been easy. No new blokes after Janne, no drugs. Except alcohol, which she had never been able to give up, although she had promised herself many times that she would quit. And here she was now, staring at herself in the bathroom mirror. She was red-faced and bloated, swollen and wrinkled. And crying did not make it any better.

With tears streaming down her cheeks, she sat down on

the toilet seat and let out her grief for her daughter. For the first time since she had got the news of Jennifer's death she gave in to her feelings. In her mind she saw her beloved little girl, naked and pale on a shiny metal stretcher in a white-tiled room. An unbearable sight. She needed something to drink.

Monday Evening

That morning Hanna had thought ahead and taken all the packets out of the freezer. She could tell from the wrappers what was inside. Now she was on her knees on Daddy's chair in the kitchen eating cold but no longer frozen meatballs straight from the table. This was her second meal of the day. In the morning she had found an unopened packet of liver pâté in the refrigerator and after hesitating for a long time she had finally used the big knife to open it. And she had succeeded, without cutting herself. Then she had eaten the entire packet without anything to go with it, but it had been good and she had felt full.

In the morning she played for a while in her room, but it had felt lonely. Even though no one besides herself was in the apartment, she felt more secure when she was in one of the rooms where the rest of the family *usually* were. She loaded her little doll's pram full of toys and pulled it into the living room. Then she spent most of the day with her toys in front of the TV. Even if most of what was happening on the TV screen was incomprehensible, it felt better to be in a room where there was sound and voices. When she started to feel tired in the afternoon, she lay down to sleep in her parents' bed and did not wake up until the sun was going down.

'Silly Barbro,' she said out loud to herself.

That silly Barbro, who had promised to come and

rescue her. True, she had said it would take time, but now Hanna had waited a really long time. And no one had called all day. Not even Mummy. Mummy could at least call and talk to her for a little while. Even if she didn't want to live here any more. Hanna had tried calling, but no one ever answered. She stuffed another meatball into her mouth and it was so big her mouth was completely full.

'Gilly Gaggo' came out when she tried to speak.

It sounded funny. She laughed and pieces of meatball flew out of her mouth.

'Gilly Gaggo,' she said several times, until it started to sound like 'silly Barbro' again.

The meatballs she couldn't eat she put back into the packet, which she left on the table. At preschool the children who were potty-trained had to go to the toilet to pee after eating, so Hanna did the same. It actually went really well. She had only got pee on her underwear once today and then she had managed to stop herself and run into the bathroom to finish peeing. Daddy would be proud of her if she could do that sort of thing when he came home. If he ever did come home.

As she was standing on her little white stool washing her hands after using the toilet, the phone rang. For the first time all day the phone was ringing. Without bothering to dry her wet hands, she rushed out into the hall, climbed carefully but not slowly up on to the children's chair and picked up the receiver.

'Hello!' she called, but there was silence on the other end.

'Hello! Hello! Is this Barbro?'

No answer, but still she felt as if someone were there. She happened to remember what Barbro had said; that if someone called – whoever called – she should tell them the same thing she had told her.

'My mummy has moved away and Daddy is in Japan and I'm all alone!'

The words poured out of her like a flood.

'Can you come and rescue me, because I fell down and hurt myself and there was blood although it's almost gone now. I can't come out because Mummy locked me in 'cause I'm so noisy. Barbro was supposed to come and rescue me, but that was days and days ago and I'm all alone.'

Still no answer, but now she was sure she heard someone breathing, so she continued.

'I can see a castle from my window. A nice, yellow castle with a tower for the princess and red and blue squares on it. And letters . . .'

'I know where you live,' a husky voice suddenly said in the receiver.

'You do?' said Hanna surprised. 'Then come and save me, please, please! I won't be noisy, I'll be good.'

'That sounds nice,' the man said in a slightly drawling voice.

'What's your name?' asked Hanna.

'Björn,' the voice replied.

Hanna did not know that a man could be called that. She thought it sounded sweet, and a little strange too. But she didn't say so. She did not want to make the man sad.

'What's your name?' asked the man.

'Hanna. Do you think that's a nice name?'

'I think it's a very nice name,' the man said politely. 'Are you the only one home?'

'But I already said that! Are you coming now?'

'I can't come this evening, because it's already too late. But maybe tomorrow?'

'Yes!' Hanna cheered. 'Will it take long?'

'Well,' the voice answered hesitantly, 'that depends on what you think is a long time. First you sleep all night and then it's tomorrow. I'll come when it's dark outside.'

'But Mummy locked me in and I can't open the door,' Hanna suddenly realized.

'We'll figure that out tomorrow. I have a lot of keys. I'm sure one of them will fit your lock. Do you have any food?'

'I've been eating meatballs that I found in the freezer. And liver pâté. But there are no more sweets.'

'Then I'll bring some sweets with me when I come tomorrow. And maybe hamburgers, would you like that?'

'Yes, that's good! I like that!'

'You must be very dirty, Hanna. Are you?'

'I took a bath, but I got water in my nose and –'

'You shouldn't do that,' said the man. 'We can take a bath tomorrow, you and me. I'll bring hamburgers and sweets, then we'll have a little party and then we'll take a bath so you get really clean and nice.'

'Yes, we'll do that,' said Hanna.

'But listen, don't tell anyone about this. It will be our little secret . . .'

'Okay,' said Hanna. 'I promise to do just what you say. I will never be naughty again, I've decided that.'

'That's good. Bye for now, Hanna.'

The call was over, but Hanna was as happy as a lark. Once again she had something to hope for, and she was so exhilarated that she stayed up late that evening. Not until the voices and the music that had been streaming out of the TV all day were replaced by an angry buzzing did she withdraw to the bedroom, curl up in a foetal position in the big double bed and fall asleep.

* * *

She never would have believed she could feel this way. She, who always had such a hard time concentrating in school, now had nothing in her skull besides this one incident; those moments when she had done the stupidest thing possible. How could she be so dense? Nothing was worth this anxiety. And all for a couple of stupid hundred-kronor bills.

She had barely slept since it happened. She pictured those empty, hazy eyes, eyes that wandered back and forth over her but never met hers, that gaze that looked at her without seeing. The hand that moved up and down, up and down. Those strange sounds, repeated, again and again. The fingers that pawed her, that sought their way between her thighs as she sat with her legs parted, her skirt pulled up and her knickers in her jacket pocket. Again and again she had to say no, to push back; again and again there he was.

At last, after an eternity, that drawn-out, smothered shriek, the gaze turned inside out, the wallet lying there begging to be stolen, the disgust, and a moment's inspiration. The voice that echoed in her head long afterwards, the words that were still hanging there: 'You damn little whore! What the hell are you doing? I'll –'

And then her jump, the screeching tyres and car door slamming. But she was already away from the car, running for all she was worth. Before she turned the corner she looked back towards him one last time – suddenly he was out of the car, intending to run after her instead. Then she was out of earshot, could no longer see him. She had run incredibly fast and he could not catch up with her.

Still he was there all the time. She was so afraid that she hardly dared leave the apartment. What if she ran into him again, what would she do? When she did go out she took the back way, out towards Tjurberget. She did not dare set foot on Götgatan. She took long detours to avoid the area around the cursed Pressbyrån shop.

The wallet was burning a hole in the wire basket of clothes under the bed. She did not even dare open it, did not dare take the money she had wanted so badly that she had committed her first crime. She had no idea what she would do with it. She could not get rid of it, because what if he found her and demanded the wallet back. She could not imagine keeping it either; she was having a hard enough time as it was, without having to share a room with the cause of her misfortune too.

And then she sometimes thought of Jennifer. Jennifer and *her* misfortune. This wallet problem had occupied her mind so much that she had not had time or really been able to start grieving for Jennifer. Jennifer was gone; she was dead. Murdered. But Elise was occupied with other things. She felt a sting of bad conscience for Jennifer's sake. Everyone else was grieving for Jennifer. Elise missed her, of course she did. But it was also nice to be left alone. To have the room and her thoughts to herself. Jennifer would have teased her, laughed at her if she had known what she'd got herself into. If she were here.

Who would miss Elise if she died? Absolutely no one. Her mum would escape that inconvenience too and could party as usual with her disgusting pals. Nina and her other friends? They might shed a few tears for the sake of appearances, but then she would be forgotten. Life had to go on. If you didn't take up any room on earth, there was no vacuum when you died. But Jennifer had left a big vacuum behind her.

Then she happened to think about Joakim. With his beard and those friendly eyes. Maybe he missed Jennifer. Yes, of course he did.

If they had been together. Of course, that wasn't crystal clear exactly. Maybe he was the one who had killed her. That's usually how it was. Jealous boyfriends or married men or exes – they were usually the ones who murdered women. She shuddered as she pictured Joakim and Jennifer. He a head taller, with his strong hands around her throat. Jennifer terrified, spluttering, gasping for air. A long, long time later she finally gives up; he lets her go and she collapses.

And then that wallet again. She tried to think logically. Wallets get stolen all the time. She wasn't the first thief in the history of the world. What happened to thieves? They mostly went free. Otherwise – what then? The police arrested them and they had to serve their sentence. What might that be in her case? Prison? Not likely for a first offence. A fine? Juvenile detention? She would end up with a criminal record. So what? That was nothing to worry about.

Still this paralysing state of terror. It was that gaze. The eyes that saw, yet didn't see. She had no more worth than a cigarette butt under a shoe to that disgusting pervert. But yet – he wouldn't kill her just because she stole his wallet. People weren't that sick. Unless, it suddenly struck her . . . unless there was a lot of money in that wallet.

She was lying on her back with her hands clasped behind her head, staring up at the underside of Jennifer's bed. Years earlier she had taped a poster of Robbie Williams up there. The tape had yellowed and curled up at one corner. The room still smelled faintly of Jennifer's perfume. It was quieter than usual. She could hear a few voices from the kitchen, but most of her mother's friends had not shown up today. Maybe they had found some other place to hang out this evening.

Otherwise her mother went on as if nothing had happened. It was possible that somewhere inside the fog she was grieving for Jennifer, that she had some feelings for her girls, but it didn't show. Whenever she talked to sober people, like the two police officers who had visited them in the afternoon, she had such a hard time pretending to be sober that you could not see the person behind the awkward attempts to appear normal. All Elise noticed was how artificial and ridiculous her mum was; her efforts to precisely pronounce all her consonants made her words overly drawn out and the 'r's ridiculously prominent. On such occasions Elise was ashamed of her mother. She liked her better when she was really loaded, like she usually was. Then at least she was herself.

Elise sat up on the edge of the bed. With a deep sigh she leaned over and pulled out the wire basket. She removed a few layers of clothing and there it was. A thin wallet of what looked like black leather. She weighed it in her hand as if to get a sense of what it might contain. Then she opened it very carefully, as if she were afraid it would fall to pieces or explode in her hands. It contained no credit cards, just a medical card, an ICA supermarket card, a Co-op card and a membership card for Buylando. In the bill compartment she found six five-hundred kronor notes: three thousand kronor. That was a lot of money to her, but was it to him? Was it enough for him to take the law into his own hands, hunt her down and perhaps hurt her? She did not know for sure. But now she knew who he was. He stared at her with a serious expression from his driver's licence. She knew his name, his personal ID number and his address. But what could she do with that information?

* * *

Conny Sjöberg was sitting with Hamad in Eriksson's office, ploughing through the lists of staff and passengers on the big boat. Einar Eriksson had produced new lists: lists of names sorted by gender, age and nationality, lists of families with children, lists of convicted individuals, individuals who appeared in crime investigations, who were in contact with social services, minors, and lists organized by various other criteria.

Sjöberg realized that the time was approaching when they would have to broaden their search for the perpetrator. But it was certainly the case that with these long lists as a basis for investigation, it would take for ever before they would even get through all the interviews. One of these people had murdered Jennifer Johansson, but it was not likely that it was just a passing stranger. Whoever it was, the person in question had probably had strong reasons to take the girl's life. It must be someone she knew from before, someone in her circle of acquaintances, someone she had met in some context, a shadow from the past who was also on the boat, perhaps for the sole purpose of killing her.

Or else it was someone she had just met on the boat, someone she had found out too much about or someone whose feelings she had wounded and who killed her without premeditation. Whoever the killer was, Sjöberg wanted to believe that there must be a loose end to tug. There must be witnesses, he thought. There must be witnesses to something that led up to this murder.

The Finnish police were working hard to locate the two businessmen Jennifer had been seen with in the disco. Sjöberg hoped this would produce something soon. For their part, trying to identify the solitary Swedish man in the bar seemed much harder. But if that man was the murderer, if he had made this trip purely to kill Jennifer Johansson, he had presumably had no travel companion and would therefore be easier for them to find. Eriksson was working on a compilation from Viking Line of all the single men who had reserved a ticket in a separate cabin or in a shared cabin with strangers. That list – together with the list of convicted persons – could be important. If the man in the bar really was a person of interest in the investigation, that is. There were a lot of 'ifs', but for the time being Sjöberg was pinning most of his hopes on this man.

An autopsy had been performed on Jennifer Johansson. There was nothing unusual: no pregnancy, no trace of abuse, either recent or otherwise. No sign of disease, no conceivable cause of death other than strangulation. Strands of hair from a number of different persons had been found on her. They might have come from anyone at all on the boat, been snagged on her clothes in the crowd on the dance floor or been on the toilet floor where she was found. They might also belong to the murderer.

It had also been determined that Jennifer Johansson had been sexually active during her final hours. The semen had yet to be analysed. It was most likely Joakim's, but if not, that might suggest new approaches. Had the murderer raped her? Hardly. Not at the murder scene anyway; that would have been far too risky in a public toilet. Not to mention the cramped cubicle. But perhaps she had willingly had intercourse with him in the toilet and then been murdered? That was possible. It was also possible that she had intercourse with the murderer earlier in the evening. Or with someone else on the boat. There were many possibilities, but the semen would sooner or later lead them to an individual who had lied to them or withheld important information.

While he gulped down the last of his coffee Sjöberg covertly studied Hamad. Jamal Hamad, the man with the phenomenal memory. There was nothing wrong with his own memory, but Hamad's was something else entirely. He sat purposefully looking through the many pages of Eriksson's lists. Sjöberg watched his eyes moving back and forth, back and forth across the lines with great concentration. His own eyes started to ache after a while and he wanted to discuss one or two points with his colleagues, but Eriksson was pecking away at his computer with a gloomy expression and Hamad only mumbled something brief in reply, without taking his eyes from his papers. His mobile phone beeped and when Sjöberg saw that he had a text from Åsa he took the opportunity to go out into the corridor to escape the monotonous job for a few minutes.

'Kids sick, staying with Grandma. Lots of hugs, don't work yourself to death,' it read. Evidently he had been restored to favour. The message had been sent earlier that afternoon, but there could be serious delays in forwarding text messages with that confounded provider. He deleted the message and entered the number of his in-laws.

'I just now got your message,' he apologized when he got Åsa on the line. 'What's going on?'

Åsa let out a deep sigh on the other end.

'Both Simon and Sara have chickenpox,' she said tiredly. 'We might as well stay here so I get a little help from Mum and Dad.'

'But what about you? Don't you have to work?'

'I'll take a few days' paid leave. I'm due back at work on Thursday, but if it's not possible, it's not possible.'

'Chickenpox,' said Sjöberg dejectedly. 'Doesn't that last a few weeks?'

'About a week. But it's contagious too,' said Åsa with an ironic laugh. 'So if the others come down with it, it could be a month before we're through with this.'

'Everyone else has two children; why do we have to have five?'

'Well, you should have thought about that before!'

'But you can't bring infectious children home on the

train either. I'll have to come down and pick you up with the van. How sick are they?'

'It's no big deal, just a slight fever,' answered Åsa. 'But there's an awful lot of complaining about the itching. Take it easy for a few days anyway, then we'll have a rethink.'

'And the little brats, they're probably healthier than ever, I'll bet?'

Sjöberg was referring to the two-year-old twin boys they had adopted when they were just newborns. Their biological mother had been a drug addict and completely unaware of her pregnancy when she suddenly gave birth to twins shortly before her death. Sjöberg, who had come across the mother through a case he was working on, regularly visited the babies at the hospital after they were born. He did not hesitate to add another two children to the three they already had, and Åsa had not been hard to convince. But Jonathan and Christoffer were two lively little boys, to say the least.

'Sure, but Grandpa is delighted,' said Åsa.

'I can believe that, he doesn't have to clean up after them. So how are you doing? Are you tired?'

'Exhausted,' Åsa answered truthfully. 'But there are three of us. That makes it easier.'

'I'll do my duty,' said Sjöberg. 'Just so we get you all home.'

'You don't need to think about that right now. How's it going with the murders?'

While he updated her he felt an intense longing for Åsa to come home. His life partner and great love. He needed her, and he wanted her with him. A couple of days of the bachelor life was more than enough. Now he wanted his family back. Besides, he wanted to seek consolation in Åsa's arms, wordless consolation, just to feel that they were together. He'd pushed the incident – or whatever it should be called – with Margit Olofsson aside. It was hidden somewhere deep inside. No further action would be taken. End of story.

When Sjöberg returned to the others, Eriksson announced that the compilation of male, single travellers on *Viking Cinderella* was now ready. How could he get so much done without getting up from his chair? About fifty men who had reserved a solo trip across the Baltic were listed. Under Hamad's supervision, those who lived in the Stockholm region would be questioned, starting the next morning. Sjöberg took on the task of visiting Jennifer Johansson's high school, to get a clearer picture of her with the help of her teachers and classmates. He could not cope with any more lists, so he decided to call it a day, but Hamad and Eriksson were still in their seats when he left the police building.

* * *

Petra had been back in her office for a while, tackling one task after another in order to postpone her visit to the police commissioner for as long as possible. From the tone he had used on the phone she could not figure out what he wanted. And she was not sure how her first official media appearance had gone. Was there any reason to worry?

On her way back to the police building she had bought the damn tabloid and now she read through the article for the umpteenth time. It filled one page. One *whole* page, but only *one* page. It wasn't small, but it wasn't that long either. However, for Petra's mental well-being, it was too much. She did not want to appear in the press at all. She did not at all care for the idea that Peder Fryhk and the Other Man could read about her in the newspaper and discover that she was a police officer. The article did not include a picture of her, only a picture that had been published previously showing her with her back to the camera in her torn leggings, along with some other police officers inside the cordon in Vitabergsparken. On the other hand, she was mentioned by name in several places in the article: 'Police detective Petra Westman, who made the macabre discovery . . .'; 'The child may have an older sibling, Petra Westman from the Hammarby Police Department confirms'; 'Westman admits that the police have not managed to identify the dead woman.' There. That could be a reason for repercussions from the leadership team. The journalist's choice of words was not one hundred per cent favourable to Petra. The word 'admits' signalled secretiveness, and 'have not managed' hinted at failure on the part of the police. The general public may like that sort of thing, but not the police administration.

Petra sighed and got up. It was time to take the bull by the horns and present herself to the police commissioner. She went to the end of the corridor and took the lift up to the top floor, where the bigwigs and some of the admin staff had their offices. During the ride she rehearsed what she realized was a weak defence: the words that the reporter used in the article were not hers and she had been ordered to do the interview despite her lack of experience in communicating with the media.

The door to Brandt's office was closed and she knocked gently.

'Yes,' came from inside the office, and Petra straightened up, opened the door and went in.

'Petra!' said the police commissioner, getting up with a broad smile. 'Welcome!'

Petra smiled back and he came towards her with his hand outstretched. Petra was prepared for a formal handshake, but he wrapped both his hands around hers. When he released his grip he showed her to one of the armchairs by the window with light pressure on her lower back. Petra sat in the indicated seat while he stood looking down at her with an expression that she could not interpret. His chest, she thought. He looked like he was about to tip forwards. His centre of gravity is in his chest. À la Groucho Marx.

'Coffee?' he asked.

'No, I'm fine, thanks,' Petra answered with a deprecatory gesture.

'Mineral water?'

'Mineral water is fine.'

'Two mineral waters,' he said into the intercom on his desk, and then came and sat down in the other armchair.

Between them was a round table small enough so that he could easily reach over and place his hand on her shoulder as he asked, 'How's the investigation going? It seems a bit sluggish.'

The touch made Petra stiffen, but she answered in as relaxed a way as she was able.

'Yes, you might say that. We're completely occupied just trying to identify the woman. And no garages we've talked to have seen a car that matches the damage to the pram and the victim's injuries.'

There was a knock at the door and Brandt pulled his hand away with a natural movement. A classic, middle-aged secretarial type, complete with twin set and pearls, came in with a tray with two glasses and two bottles of mineral water, which she placed on the table between them. She nodded amiably at them both without saying anything and left the room, closing the door behind her.

'I see, it's going slowly, you say,' Brandt said, looking at her the way you look at a little child who has fallen down and hurt herself.

Petra poured mineral water into a glass and took a sip while Brandt continued to observe her, with his head at an angle.

'But I'm sure it will pick up soon,' said Petra in a tone that was supposed to sound hearty.

'I'm sure it will,' said Brandt. 'I read about you in *Aftonbladet*.'

'About me?' Petra laughed. 'That was mostly about the case, wasn't it? I only answered a couple of questions.'

'And you did just fine.'

What a horrid gaze. This must be what they mean by 'he looked deep into her eyes'. Must get the conversation moving now, thought Petra, so we can get this over with.

'That's nice to hear. I tried to stick to the point. Not to say too much and not to leave room for free association. You don't think –'

'And you were in the picture too,' the police commissioner interrupted. 'You looked good.'

Broad smile.

'That must have hurt,' he said, moving his eyes down to her crossed legs. 'Your leggings were in tatters.'

'Ah, it was no big deal,' said Petra, squirming in the chair. 'I had to get the child out of those bushes. You have to sacrifice yourself sometimes,' she added with a laugh that in her ears sounded borderline hysterical.

Which quite exactly reflected her state of mind. The police commissioner's gaze was wandering slowly back up to her eyes.

'Do you like children?' he asked unexpectedly.

Petra did not know what to do. She considered not answering at all, just getting up and leaving, but she managed to overrule her instincts and calm down. For the sake of my career, she thought. Don't ruin all future prospects with a single impulsive action. The guy is mentally ill, that's quite clear. But let him be that way, let him eat you with his eyes and say strange things, humour him just this once.

'Yes, I do,' she answered, letting the air out of her lungs slowly so that it would not be perceived as the sigh it really was. 'I like children a lot.'

When he did not answer but simply sat staring at her, Petra felt compelled to say something more. The silence was unbearable.

'But you don't think I made a fool of myself? In the interview? I don't have any media experience and I was worried about that –'

'Petra, come here,' Roland Brandt interrupted, his voice dripping with honey. 'Don't worry, you did an excellent job. Come here.'

He waved her over. Petra was about to lose her composure, but she could not sabotage this. Just hold out, she thought, getting up and taking two steps in his direction.

'You are *doing* an excellent job, Petra,' he said, extending his left hand towards her.

Her own hands were hanging loosely by her sides and she left them there.

'As proof of my appreciation I was thinking about treating you to dinner this evening,' he said, smiling at her as if he were Santa Claus.

'That's not necessary,' Petra said quickly. 'I'm glad you like what I'm doing, but I have to work this evening.'

He took her hand in his and pulled her to him. Petra did not dare resist, because doing that would be to officially acknowledge that she took the whole thing as a pick-up attempt and not as a friendly gesture.

'Like what you're doing,' Brandt oozed. 'Yes, I'd say that, Petra. And there are others who can work tonight. I've already reserved a table for us at Mathias Dahlgren this evening at eight o'clock. That's not something you say no to.'

'I'll have to do that anyway, Roland,' said Petra, hearing how strange that sounded; of course she was not on first-name terms with him. 'I have other plans this evening.'

Now she felt a tug on her arm. What was he trying to do? Completely unbelievable; he was trying to pull her down on to his lap. She made herself strong, unwavering, and remained braced against the floor, hand in hand with the police commissioner. This sort of thing does not happen in reality.

'I do too, Petra. I was thinking that we could continue up a few floors once we've eaten.'

A few floors up? Petra did not understand what he was talking about. But she had no doubt about his intentions when his hand released hers and instead took hold of her right buttock. That was the last straw. She took a step back, out of reach of the police commissioner who was puffed up in the armchair with a satisfied grin.

'I'm sorry I need to say this,' said Petra, no longer hesitant, 'but I can only interpret this in one way. You're coming on to me. And that last thing could be considered sexual harassment.'

Then she turned away from him and headed for the door.

'Are you joking with me, Petra?' said the police commissioner.

Petra pushed down the handle.

'I thought you said I was sexy?' he continued with something in his voice that Petra could only take to be triumph.

The door opened.

'That's not what I said,' Petra answered, ice cold. 'Someone else put those words in my mouth.'

Petra left Roland Brandt and went out into the corridor without turning around. The words 'don't leave room for free association' echoed in her ears.

Tuesday Morning

Sjöberg had a headache. He'd been in bed by eleven the night before, after wolfing down some leftover fish fingers and macaroni from a container in the fridge. Exhausted, out of pure habit he solved the daily puzzle in the newspaper before turning off the bedside lamp. He had been so tired that he fell asleep as soon as he closed his eyes.

Five hours later he was woken by his own scream. Margit Olofsson's face, beautifully framed by the abundant red hair like flames around her head, was there again with its tranquil expression. Puzzled, she looked at him, and danced a few steps up in the window, and then he fell. Released his hold on the world and fell.

Even though he still felt completely wiped out he could not go back to sleep. The morning paper had not yet arrived, so he got up and turned on the TV, clicking between vapid programmes on the cable channels before he heard the thud in the hall and wondered whether it might be Joakim Andersson putting the newspaper through the letter box. After reading every page of the newspaper in the total silence of an empty apartment and then eating a hearty breakfast in peace and quiet, he got dressed and went to work.

Now he was drawing up guidelines for the day's interviews while he massaged his temples. It was just past seven and it would be as well to try to reach as many of these single gentlemen as possible before they left for work. He had actually meant to assign this task to Lotten, but she wasn't in yet, so he might as well do it himself. Just as he was about to pick up the receiver, his mobile phone rang. It was the medical examiner, Kaj Zetterström, calling from Åbo, where he had gone to take part in the autopsy and arrange transport home for the body.

'Are you awake this early?' asked Sjöberg.

'We're an hour ahead of you. Are *you* awake this early?' Zetterström countered.

'Yes, today I am. Why'd you call, by the way, if you didn't think I was in?'

'You *aren't* awake. I called your mobile. Meant to leave a message. I don't even know where you are.'

'I give up, you win. How's it going over there?'

'Have you talked to Nieminen?'

'Today? No, not yet. Should I have?'

'He tried to contact you on your mobile. I'm sure he left a message.'

'That damn provider!' Sjöberg swore. 'The voice messages seem to get stuck along the way somewhere. Sometimes I don't get them for hours. Okay, you tell me instead.'

'The reason I'm calling is to tell you that the boyfriend's – Joakim Andersson's – DNA doesn't match the semen.'

'Oh boy. I don't know if that's good or bad, but at least he's telling the truth. On that point,' added Sjöberg.

'But not on all points, it appears,' said Zetterström. 'What Nieminen had to tell you was that they've located those men in suits. The ones she was sitting with in the bar.'

'Good work! Finally, a breakthrough.'

'Wait, let me tell you. Nieminen is a sharp guy; he didn't know for sure it was them, but he had a feeling, so he told them that they'd been seen in the bar with the girl.'

'Did he question them together?' Sjöberg asked.

'Yes, he saw them at work. They're consultants of some kind – whatever that means – and share an office. The Finns will look into their business and see what they really do. Anyway, Nieminen had a mental advantage, so to speak, because he caught them in a lie about the girl. They had said earlier, of course, that they didn't recognize her. That was a little dodgy to say the least under the circumstances. Suddenly they both confessed, not only that they'd been with her in the bar but also that they'd had intercourse with her in their cabin. Both of them.'

'I'll be damned. How old are they?'

'In their forties.'

'Poor kid. Why put yourself in such a situation? Did they rape her, do you think?'

'There are no signs of rape, and both these customers deny it consistently. But it's impossible to say. She had a blood alcohol concentration of 0.15.'

'So why did they lie about that?' Sjöberg asked. 'It just makes the situation worse for them.'

'Because she was sixteen and they are forty, maybe,' Zetterström replied cynically. 'Or maybe because they're both married.'

'Or because they're involved in shady dealings and don't want to attract attention,' Sjöberg suggested.

'The Finns are checking up on that, as I said.'

'You said that Joakim doesn't seem to have told the truth on all points. What did you mean by that?'

'Those gentlemen – Helenius and Grönroos are their names – say they went out again, when they were finished with the girl, and partied some more. When they came out into the corridor, a man was standing there. They maintain, and are quite convinced, that he was the man in the photograph they were shown – Joakim Andersson, that is. They say it was obvious that he had been waiting outside, but when they came out he immediately started to walk away, pretending he was on his way somewhere.'

'And they've withheld that information from us!' Sjöberg exclaimed with irritation. 'The girl they'd just had sex with has been murdered and they keep silent about something that could possibly convict the murderer. What bastards. "Didn't want the wife to know . . ." No, put those bastards away. I hope they're smuggling dope or something.'

'Maybe they're lying,' Zetterström interjected. 'They might have made that up, just to direct suspicion elsewhere.'

'All the better in that case,' Sjöberg muttered. 'Listen, the forensic techs over there, are they doing a good job? Or shall we send Hansson over?'

'I don't think that's necessary. They seem serious.'

'Everything found inside that loo should be analysed. To the minutest detail. Everything should be matched against those men in suits and Joakim.'

'Don't tell me,' Zetterström defended himself. 'I'm just the messenger.'

'I'll talk to Nieminen. Is he there?'

'We're not working in the same part of the city.'

Sjöberg thanked him for the information and ended

the call. Then he dialled Nieminen's number and dis-
cussed what he had learned from Zetterström. Nieminen
also told him that five hundred kronor had been found in
Jennifer Johansson's jeans pocket. That was not by any
means an eye-catching sum of money, but the thought
still struck Sjöberg that perhaps she had sold herself to
the two Finnish men. He asked Nieminen to send over
pictures of them. They agreed that Stockholm would
continue working on the man in the bar and also apply
further pressure to Joakim Andersson, while the Åbo
police would question all the single male travellers who
left the boat in Åbo, and of course follow up on Helenius
and Grönroos.

Hamad showed up at the door, fresh and well-pressed
as always.

'Slept well?' he asked.

'No, damn it. I have such weird dreams. But you look
energetic. Did you stay long last night?'

'I stared at those lists for a while longer.'

'How do you manage it? And why?'

'I don't know. It's like I want to savour the names. So
that they're there if I need them. Maybe see if any bells
start ringing.'

'So, did they?'

'No, but you never know. Sooner or later maybe.'

'I've spoken to Zetterström and Nieminen. Come
in and sit down and I'll tell you about it. Is Eriksson
here yet?'

'Think so. I'll go get him.'

Sjöberg reported on the current situation for his two
colleagues, after which Eriksson slunk away. Sjöberg

realized that he had a lot to do on the Vita Bergen case so he let him go when he had finished his summary.

'We have to call in Joakim Andersson,' Hamad suggested.

Sjöberg shook his head. 'I'm curious about that family, so I think I'd rather go to him. Check out the atmosphere. Meet the mother. If I'm lucky maybe I'll see that brute of a father too, if he hasn't left for work yet.'

Sjöberg glanced at his watch. Half past seven.

'You know the kind of hours they have at the bank. He might very well be home still,' he continued. 'I suggest you get to work on those solo travellers immediately. Call them or get help from Lotten and bring them in at, say, fifteen-minute intervals. I'll aim to be back from the school around twelve, so count me in after that and we'll divvy up the job.'

'Speaking of families,' said Hamad. 'When you think about the Johansson family ... What a strange group! Those girls have grown up in that environment; they don't know anything else. In Sweden you're so vulnerable. Even if there isn't a dad, there should at least be grandparents and aunts and uncles and cousins, neighbours, whatever. There ought to be someone who cares. I think it's the welfare state's fault. It's like you don't need to be responsible for anyone else. Society does it for you.'

He was silent for a few moments, as if considering what he had said. Sjöberg waited for him to continue.

'I guess what I'm getting at is that maybe it isn't a co-incidence that something like this happened to Jennifer Johansson in particular. Who knows what trouble she invited? Home for her was an environment where all the individuals were dangerous in their own way, to themselves and to others. How could she distinguish something really dangerous from what was run of the mill to her? She could have ended up in any sort of company, done any kind of stupid thing. Maybe she did do something incredibly stupid or saw something really ugly.'

'And so she only had herself to blame?' Sjöberg said provocatively, as if to take the edge off the seriousness of it all.

'More like the other way round. She had no chance to defend herself. That's what I mean. That story with the Finns in the cabin. How much do you know about life if you go along with something like that?'

'Way too much,' Sjöberg said.

'Or too little. I'm not so sure this incident really has anything to do with the murder, but it's an indication if nothing else. An indication that Jennifer Johansson was capable of quite a lot.'

'Or that she wasn't capable of anything,' said Sjöberg. 'That she was a reed in the wind. Being blown around, unable to control her own fate.'

'Is that the impression you have of her? That she was a victim who let herself be controlled by others?'

'No, it's not. But whatever happened to her, she was innocent.'

'She was sixteen. Just a kid. We'll get him, Conny.'

'We'll get him,' Sjöberg agreed.

* * *

When Barbro had arrived home at her apartment on Doktor Abelins Gata on Monday evening it was already getting dark. She was tired, hungry and dissatisfied. After a quick dinner, she fell asleep like a clubbed ox and slept for the whole night without interruption.

When she woke up she was rested and angry. Mostly at herself because she had not got going earlier the day before and had to give up her search after the Zinken allotments. But also at the whole situation. If a little three-year-old girl really had been abandoned by her parents, how could the police not take it more seriously instead of simply shifting the responsibility on to an overloaded telephone service provider? Deep down she knew the answer. It was no more complicated than that they didn't believe her, and perhaps they were right not to. *Hopefully* they were right in this particular case. She wanted nothing more than for Hanna simply to be a child with a lively imagination who made crank calls and invented scary stories while her mother was in the laundry room. At the same time, Barbro did not like the idea that she might be perceived as a confused old lady, just seven years after retiring as a hard-working academic and pillar of society. She felt hurt, in short. Her nose had been put out of joint.

Now a full day had passed since she talked to that Nyman fellow at the county detective unit, and Barbro did not intend to leave him alone. It would be best to act before her fury subsided. She remembered a story she had recently read on the Internet, about a man who woke up in the night and discovered that there were thieves in his garage. He called the police and told them what was going on, but they answered that they had a lot to do and no cars were available. A little later the man called again and said that the police could cancel his previous report, because he had shot the intruders. Two minutes later six cars showed up and the crooks were arrested.

'I thought you said you'd shot the thieves?' said one of the policemen.

'I thought you said you didn't have any available cars,' the man replied.

The idea crossed Barbro's mind that she should blow the whole thing up. Pretend that the girl said her mother was dead in the apartment. But she dismissed that idea. If it turned out the whole thing was a misunderstanding, she might be taken to court for false reporting and she was not prepared to take that risk.

She imagined that Nyman – by his tone alone – judged her to be a hysterical version of Miss Marple, and she intended to convince him otherwise. Now she would take on the role of angry terrier. Still in her pyjamas, she steeled herself and reached for the phone with her teeth bared.

'This is Barbro Dahlström. We spoke yesterday, as I'm sure you recall, and now I want to know whether you've managed to locate that call I received on Sunday evening.'

Pure facts, no prattle about little girls left alone – that would only make her seem emotional and unreliable.

'The provider has been informed,' answered Nyman.

Barbro wondered whether he was telling the truth.

'As I said, it may take a week if they have a lot to do,' he continued, 'and most of the time they do.'

'You also said that it can take twenty-four hours in pri-oritized cases. Like this one,' Barbro added.

'Well, this is not exactly a typical example of a priori-tized case,' Nyman began, but Barbro was quick to counter him.

'It may turn out that that's just what it is. If you find a dead three-year-old in a few days, perhaps you'll regret not making this a higher priority. I think we should try to avoid that.'

'That sounds ominous,' Nyman laughed in the receiver. 'But I'll do what I can. Besides, it hasn't really been twenty-four hours yet.'

Barbro glanced at the clock; it was only quarter past eight. Perhaps she ought to be grateful that he was even at work at this time. But she did not feel particularly grateful. On the contrary, she had a strong feeling that he was not taking her seriously this time either.

'How hard can it be?' she said in her sternest tone of voice. 'See that it gets done, then you'll be rid of me. I'll be in touch during the day.'

Barbro ended the call, feeling no less frustrated but even more resolved to succeed in her project. With an angry snort she shook off the detective's condescending tone and half an hour later she locked the door and was on her way out for yet another day among the allotments of south Stockholm.

* * *

Not surprisingly, it was Joakim who opened the door at quarter past eight. He gave Sjöberg a look first of surprise, then fear.

'I was in the neighbourhood,' Sjöberg explained. A white lie, he told himself. 'I thought you could avoid a trip to the station today.'

Joakim looked at him, and Sjöberg could see his mind was racing behind the anxious eyes.

'I know you have your mother to take care of,' Sjöberg continued when he got no response. 'I have a few questions I'd like to ask you, if that's all right. May I come in?'

'Uh, sure,' Joakim stammered, taking a few steps backwards.

He remained standing there, in the entrance hall, and Sjöberg got a feeling that Joakim did not want him to go any further into his home. But he stepped out of his shoes anyway and took a few steps in Joakim's direction, without taking off his jacket. Joakim stood as if rooted to the spot and looked at him desperately.

'Well,' said Sjöberg with exaggerated calm. 'Shall we go in?'

Joakim leaned against the wall and let him past. Sjöberg went into the living room and glanced towards the three-piece suite. 'Is this a house search or something?' Joakim said.

'Not at all,' Sjöberg answered calmly. 'I'm just looking around a little.'

He continued into the small kitchen, which only held a breakfast nook for two, by a window overlooking an inner courtyard, and a worktop with cupboards above and below as well as a cooker. On the opposite wall were the fridge and freezer and a tall cupboard that might contain cleaning things or food. The room had a somewhat shabby air, but it was clean and things were put away.

'So where's your mother?' he asked, apparently unperturbed.

'She's sleeping,' Joakim answered quickly. 'What were you going to ask?'

Sjöberg was already on his way out of the kitchen and answered with a counter-question.

'Is this where she's sleeping?'

He went back through the unimaginatively furnished living room, with its bookshelf without books, the conventional suite and a TV that had seen better days. On the table was a half-full ashtray. In the windows hung yellowed half-transparent curtains, framing a few surprisingly vigorous monsteras. Across from the hall a small corridor with a cupboard ran past a bathroom and ended in a wall with two closed doors. Voices were coming from inside one of the rooms, like from a radio or TV. Sjöberg knocked carefully on the door and looked at Joakim with a smile that he meant to seem good-hearted.

'You don't need to . . .' Joakim implored, but Sjöberg disregarded the sympathy he felt and let his curiosity guide him.

He pushed down the handle and opened the door, determined not to reveal any reaction.

The little room was completely taken up by a double bed. On the wall above the foot of the bed a TV was mounted. Spread-eagled on the bed was a woman, dressed in an enormous, light-blue garment like a housedress. The woman was bare legged, and the gigantic blocks of her legs led up to a gigantic body. Layer upon layer of massive rolls of fat were spread out over the bed; the head was like a colossal pumpkin without a neck, and her skin was dry, cracked and scaly.

Sjöberg had never seen anything like it. This was not a person; this was a monster lying there on the bed before him. In the middle of that giant head was a little face, with a mouth, nose and two small embedded eyes, looking at him in terror. As he had resolved, Sjöberg managed to conceal his immediate reaction of horror and disgust, even though he could not have imagined what he would encounter behind the door. He gave her a friendly smile and introduced himself with exaggerated heartiness.

'Good day, good day. Conny Sjöberg is my name. From the Hammarby Police.'

She still looked terrified, but answered in an uncannily light, beautiful voice, 'Good morning.'

Sjöberg did not know what to say next. He considered leaving after a few polite phrases, but after a moment of hesitation the official in him took over.

'You appear to need professional care. Is it Joakim who takes care of you?'

'Yes, and he does it very well. We get along fine.'

'Do you ever see a doctor?'

'No, I'm not sick exactly . . .'

She switched her gaze from the frightening stranger to her son.

'Why did you bring the police here?' she wanted to know, but Sjöberg answered for him.

'This is just a routine matter. It has nothing to do with you. I'm here because we're investigating a murder. An acquaintance of Joakim's was murdered. Didn't you know about that?'

'No,' she answered with surprise, looking at Joakim as if she expected an explanation.

The woman was spending her life in this bed. God knows for how many years she'd been here, cut off from the outside world, disconnected from all responsibility, happily ignorant of what was going on beyond her bedroom.

'You can't carry on like this,' Sjöberg asserted. 'This is indefensible. You need medical care. You can't lie here like this, it won't do. Joakim can't be solely responsible for you in this condition. He has no training for this sort of thing. He's twenty-four years old and has his whole life ahead of him. I'm going to contact the social authorities. It's my duty.'

'But what will people say?' was the only thing that came out of her mouth.

How he loathed that phrase. Those words that controlled life for so many people in this country. He had a mind to tell her that she should have thought of that earlier. But what did he know about what had driven her into this room? Perhaps it had been a way for her to escape, thought Sjöberg. Perhaps she had eaten herself away from her husband's abuse of her son, eaten herself away from the hardships of life and into the corner of the world that was her own. A hiding place where there was only room for her, where she was cared for without being in an institution, a place where she was free from harsh words and accusations. She had become a family secret, an eyesore that must be kept away from the world. But what she really was, thought Sjöberg, was a monument. A monument to this family's secrets.

He turned to Joakim, who was standing behind him in the corridor, looking at his feet.

'Now we'll get to those questions,' he said, but then he caught sight of the other door and on impulse decided to find out what was behind it too.

He opened the door and looked into a bedroom that was smaller than the other one, furnished with a single bed, wider than normal, and a bedside table. The blinds were drawn, but despite the darkness Sjöberg could see that the bed was unmade. At first he saw only an ordinary bedroom, like any other, and furnished like the rest of the apartment without any attempt to make it cosy. But as he was about to close the door he was struck by the insight that more than one person slept in this room. On a chair in one corner were clothes that must be Joakim's, tossed into a heap. Over a valet stand in front of the window hung a cardigan and tie that evidently belonged to the father. In the bed he saw three pillows and two blankets. He remained standing in the doorway, unable to bring himself to say anything, for a long time. What could he say? What should he say?

'So, this is your bedroom?' he asked simply.

Joakim nodded self-consciously.

'And your dad's?' Sjöberg added, in a tone that was as neutral as he could make it.

'Uh-huh,' mumbled Joakim.

Sjöberg felt a growing sense of unease. A distaste for the whole situation, for this musty, run-down, cramped little apartment with its gloom and its colourless walls. A suspicion was taking shape in his mind, a suspicion that this family had more secrets than he had at first thought.

He closed the door and went back out into the living room.

'Can we sit here?' he asked Joakim, gesturing towards the dark-green suite.

'Sure,' Joakim answered guardedly.

They each sat down in an armchair and Sjöberg tried to brush aside what he had just seen. He put the MP3 player on record and tackled his actual business.

'We have been able to chart another few hours of the end of Jennifer's life,' he said matter-of-factly.

Joakim showed no reaction.

'You said the last time you saw her was when she was sitting in the dance hall together with two considerably older men, is that so?'

'Yes.'

'When they'd had a few drinks they left the bar together, all three of them.'

'Yes,' said Joakim tonelessly.

'Then they went to the two men's cabin.'

No comment.

'I think you already know this, Joakim. Am I wrong?'

Joakim did not say anything, just looked down at his hands.

'You're not answering, Joakim. I want you to answer me when I ask you a question.'

'Shouldn't I have a lawyer then?'

'You're not suspected of anything. Yet.' Sjöberg emphasized. 'But I do get suspicious when you refuse to answer questions and when you lie to me. Wasn't it the case that you followed them to the cabin and stood outside until they had finished whatever they were doing inside? Wasn't that how it was?'

Joakim let out a heavy sigh and answered without looking Sjöberg in the eyes, 'Yes, I guess that's how it was.'

'Why didn't you tell us that to begin with?' asked Sjöberg, even though he already knew the answer.

'Then you would just think I'd followed her.'

'But you did, didn't you?'

'Yes, but then. You'd think that I killed her.'

'And you didn't do that?'

'No.'

'But you did follow her. Why did you do that?'

'I wanted to know what she was doing. What she was thinking.'

'About the two of you, you mean?'

'Yes.'

'What do you think she thought about the two of you?'

'I don't think she thought about me at all.'

'That's just what I think too,' said Sjöberg provocatively. 'I think she'd lost interest in you.'

Joakim did not answer, did not change his expression. Sjöberg studied him for a while in silence before he continued.

'Well, what do you think Jennifer was doing there in that cabin? With those men.'

No answer.

'Joakim, you must answer when I ask you something. I can take you down to the station if you prefer.'

'They . . . They probably had sex,' Joakim almost whispered.

'Yes, they did, Joakim. They had sex. That must have been a bit of a shock to you. That she would betray you like that.'

'Not exactly. I didn't expect anything else.'

'You didn't expect anything else,' Sjöberg repeated. 'Personally I would have been extremely angry in that situation. I think you were too. I think you were so angry that you did not know what to do with her. So you kept track of her the whole evening. Followed her when she left. Waited until an opportunity arose when you could be alone with her. When no one was looking. Like in the toilet behind the gambling machines. And then you strangled her. That's what I think.'

'I didn't kill her,' said Joakim. His voice betrayed him and it sounded thick when he spoke.

'I think you did, Joakim. You killed her, and you had planned it for several hours. You just waited for the right moment.'

'That's not true.'

'We're going to find out the truth. There are traces of the murderer inside that toilet. If we find as much as a strand of hair from you inside there, you're caught.'

'You won't. I wasn't there. Besides, it wouldn't be so strange if you did find traces of me on her; she was sitting on my lap at the pre-party.'

'So what did you do, Joakim? What did you do when you discovered that Jennifer was having sex with two strange men in that cabin?'

'I just stood outside, because I wanted to know. I wanted to know for sure what they were doing. I stood there for several hours, because I didn't know what else to do. Then they came out.'

'All three of them?' Sjöberg interjected.

'I don't know. I only saw the men, and then I left. Pretended that I just happened to be passing by.'

'And then?'

'Then I just wandered around. I didn't know what to do.'

'Did you meet anyone who can confirm that?'

'I saw a couple of the others in the group a few times. But I kept away from them. Didn't want to talk to anyone.'

'And when you went to bed the girls were already asleep?'

'Fanny and Malin, yes.'

'So they can't tell us what time it was when you came back?'

'Apparently not. Or I guess they would have.'

'That was a bit of bad luck. So what time was it?'

'Two, maybe.'

'But how did you get in? You told us yourself you didn't have a key.'

'I banged on the door until Fanny opened it for me.'

'She has no recollection of that.'

'That's what happened anyway.'

'This doesn't look very good for you, Joakim,' Sjöberg summed up.

'No.'

'It was stupid of you to lie to start with.'

'I know,' said Joakim.

'But now you're telling the truth?'

'Yes.'

'Nothing you want to add or change?'

'Not that I can think of.'

'You know,' said Sjöberg forgivingly, placing a hand on Joakim's shoulder, 'I hope this holds up for you. Understand, we don't want to catch you in any more lies.'

Joakim nodded gloomily.

'You should move away from here,' said Sjöberg, getting up from the chair.

When he left the apartment Joakim was still sitting, staring blankly into space. Sjöberg made his way down the stairs with heavy steps and out on to the street.

* * *

Jenny had been heartbroken when they visited her on Monday evening in the apartment at Brommaplan. Extremely sad, but not unreasonable. Together with Sonja and her younger sister, Jessica, Sandén had finally got Jenny to understand that a life with Pontus was a bad life. That he really didn't care about her, but was only using her as it suited him. He was a disagreeable character who abused her. Sandén did not say a word about the fact that it was him who had asked Pontus to pack his things and never show his face again, that he had actually paid him to do it. It was hard enough for Jenny to be abandoned by her great love believing that he had simply got tired of her. She didn't need to know the whole story; all three of them were in agreement about that.

They took turns sitting with her, consoling and explaining.

At the same time they cleaned up the apartment, eradicating all traces of Pontus. They invited her to sleep in her room at home on Önskeringsvägen, but she would not have it. She wanted to stay in the apartment, even though Pontus was gone. She did not even agree to have one of them stay with her overnight; she was sad but not incapable of taking care of herself.

At last she asked them to leave her alone. After glancing incessantly at the clock on the wall, she said she needed to sleep, that she couldn't bear any more talk about Pontus and the future. Sandén was struck by a suspicion that Pontus might show up again anyway, that they had arranged something and that she was waiting for him to come. He asked her, nicely but firmly, if that was the case, and she looked him in the eyes and promised it was not.

He was content with that, because Jenny could not lie. Sandén smiled to himself at the memory of Jenny as a child, when you occasionally discovered that all was not as it should be in the pantry.

'Jenny, some sweets have disappeared. Did you take some?'

And then those glistening blue eyes, with a glimpse of worry in them, would honestly meet his. 'Yes, Daddy, I took eleven.'

'Eleven sweets? How could you do that when you knew I would be angry?'

'I was so hungry. I couldn't stop myself.'

And you can't lie either, little Jenny, he thought. It had never occurred to her that she could blame her little sister or simply deny it. It was part of her disability. It was hard enough to understand the world around her. Trying to describe events that had never taken place was beyond her.

For that reason he was not worried as he got out of the car on Spinnrocksvägen at Brommaplan on Tuesday morning. If Jenny said that Pontus did not intend to show up again, that's how it was. Seen from her perspective at least. He opened the front door with the code, made his way up to the second floor and rang the doorbell to his daughter's apartment. Or his apartment, to be more exact. He and Sonja were listed as owners of the studio flat – a precautionary measure when they had bought it for her that they did not regret now.

Jenny did not open the door for him, and he could hear nothing from inside the apartment when he put his ear to the door. He rang once more without getting a response and then he tried the door to reassure himself that it was locked, which they had carefully instructed her that it must be, whether she was out or at home. It was not. The door glided open and he took a step into the hall and called his daughter's name. Still no answer. He carried on into the room without taking off his shoes and looked anxiously around. He noticed that the bed was unmade; then the bathroom door suddenly opened and Jenny came out in a bathrobe with her hair wrapped in a towel.

'You have to lock –' he began before catching sight of the man behind her.

Sandén was completely taken aback. Jenny had not lied to him; it was not Pontus who looked him in the eye with a smile that should have been self-conscious but was not. It was a completely different man who, naked, squeezed past her in the doorway and, totally unconcerned, walked over to the living room couch where he started pulling on his clothes. He was tall and muscular, dark and unshaven.

'Who the hell are you?' Sandén said at last, a thousand thoughts buzzing through his mind.

'Who the hell is that?' he then asked Jenny, who stood frozen, looking both terrified and desperate.

'Daddy, you can't just come here without calling first,' she answered pitifully. 'I have to have a life of my own.'

'Who the hell is that?' he asked again, turning towards the man, who seemed to be in no hurry.

'Get out of here,' he said then, surprising himself with the decisiveness in his voice. 'There'll be no breakfast here. Out!'

'Sure, I'm leaving,' said the man. 'Take it easy.'

Sandén watched in silence until a minute or two later he

left the apartment with a wave in Jenny's direction. She responded with a distressed smile and sat down on the edge of the bed. Sandén sat down beside her and put his arm around her. It had never been easy for him to scold his oldest daughter, and this time he was not sure it was necessary.

'What are you doing, Jenny?' he asked gently. 'What was that?'

'That was Dejan,' said Jenny.

'Dejan? Where did you find him?'

'He's a friend of Pontus,' she answered, not looking at him.

'A friend of Pontus? What the . . . ? You were sitting here crying last night, because you were so sorry that Pontus had left. And then you drag home one of his buddies? And maybe it wasn't the first time either.'

Jenny shook her head.

'Pontus is not allowed to hit you, but I could understand him being angry about this. Can't you see that, Jenny?'

She did not answer, but leaned her head against his shoulder. He caressed her gently on the cheek.

'You can't carry on like that,' Sandén continued. 'It's not love, if you have two guys at the same time. And he seems to be a real dodgy type. Don't see him any more, Jenny, promise me that.'

He turned her face up so that he could look her in the eyes.

'Can you promise me you won't see Dejan any more?'

'I think so,' Jenny answered, looking as if she meant it.

'And you have to promise to keep the door locked. Always.'

'I promise. But you can't show up here without calling first.'

'Okay,' Sandén answered dejectedly. 'But it was lucky I did this time, otherwise I wouldn't have found out about this Dejan. And then I couldn't have helped you.'

'I don't want help.'

'I'm your dad. I'll help you when I think you need it.'

'Get me a job then.'

'I'm trying, Jenny, you know that. And Mum too. It'll work out. It just takes a little while.'

After spending a little more time with his daughter, and eating his second breakfast of the morning, he had to leave her. Gloomily he got in the car; the endless traffic on Drottningholmsvägen did not put him in a better mood.

Tuesday Mid-morning

She finally made up her mind. She thought about talking to Nina about it, tell her about the mess she was in and ask for advice. But there would be no point. With Nina you could talk about everyday things: school, friends, gossip, clothes, parties. But serious things she just shook off with a laugh. For her, nothing was serious enough for anyone to get hung up on, or 'harp on about' as she would put it. And Elise was probably perceived the same way because they were almost always together.

Nina had called when she heard about Jennifer, but it was a brief conversation, she had had to rush off somewhere. Elise could picture Nina in the centre of things, eagerly answering everyone's questions about the murder between classes. But she couldn't be bothered to find out how Elise was doing. And she would just laugh at this wallet story, Elise was sure of that. But Elise was having a hard time shrugging the whole thing off. She felt guilty about the crime itself, and shame about the whole prostitution thing, or whatever you wanted to call it.

After a lot of back and forth and yet another sleepless night, she finally came to a decision. For once she was going to do the only right thing. She would go to the police with the damn wallet and turn it in; she would say that she had found it, that it was full of money but she hadn't touched anything. Not stolen a krona. She hadn't either.

She'd had the wallet for days; she'd thought about the money but hadn't taken it. She'd halted her criminal career almost before it started. Now she would erase her stupid act, delete it from her memory once and for all.

With renewed courage she entered the police station in Hammarbyhamnen. She looked around the enormous lobby before she went up to the reception desk.

'Hi,' said the receptionist. 'How can I help you?'

'I want to hand in a wallet I found,' Elise answered, trying to look self-confident.

'I see, then you need the lost property department. Go along the corridor over there and turn right. Then just follow the signs.'

'Thanks very much,' said Elise, starting off in the direction she had been shown.

Just as she was passing the stairs she glanced up and caught sight of a familiar face. One of those cops from yesterday, the dark one, was heading right towards her. Before she could turn away, he noticed her and smiled in recognition. What should she say? He would wonder what she was doing there, and she could not tell him the truth. He would assume that someone from a family like hers would keep any money she found.

'Hi, Elise,' said Hamad, extending his hand towards her as if they were business acquaintances.

She shook hands with him and hoped that her uncertainty was not too obvious as she returned his smile.

'What's on your mind?' he wanted to know.

Of course he thought it was him or his colleague she was looking for. She could not spit out a word.

'Was there something you wanted to tell us? Did you happen to think of something we ought to know about?'

'I . . . I just wanted to know how things are going,' she said.

'We're doing our best,' said Hamad. 'Will you come up to my office for a moment, so we can talk?'

He put his hand on her shoulder and it felt as if he were pushing her into something she was not at all prepared for. But now there was no turning back. Now she could only do as she was told, so she followed him up the stairs, along a corridor and into an office. He showed her a chair, and she sat down. He sat down behind the desk and looked at her with his brown eyes, trying to look friendly.

'Would you like anything?' he asked. 'Tea, coffee?'

She shook her head. She just wanted to get out of there – as quickly as possible.

'Don't you go to school?'

'I can't handle it right now,' she answered. 'It's a little tough, with everything.'

What she said was true, but not the way he thought.

'I understand,' he said. 'It's going to take time to get back into your normal routine again. But it's probably good if you go to school anyway, so you have something else to think about. See people.'

That compassionate look – how she loathed it. She recognized it from certain teachers, the school nurse, the social worker. She didn't ask for compassion, but certain people could not look at her any other way. There was something unpleasant about that look: he wanted to break her, coax out something small and weak in her that wasn't there. He wanted to get her to cry – which she never did – and then uncover it all, revelling in her bad upbringing. She shuddered and squirmed a little in the chair to cover it up. She did not want to be seen as a victim; she had to get that man to look at her as something else: an adult who didn't need that velvety tone of voice and his compassionate looks.

'How's it going? Have you caught the murderer?' she asked, more curtly than she intended.

He straightened up and put his fingertips together.

'No,' he answered. 'Not yet. But we will. We have lots of people to question, perhaps hundreds, so that will take time, but we're going to get him.'

'Him?'

'Yes, we believe it's a man. You have to be strong to strangle a person with your bare hands.'

He studied her in silence for a few seconds, no doubt waiting for some kind of reaction, but she didn't intend to give him the satisfaction.

'You haven't thought of anything new?' he continued. 'Something you wanted to tell us? Did Jennifer have any enemies? Did she maybe do something really stupid, something that someone made her pay for?'

Jennifer, she thought, never did anything stupid. Jennifer knew what you could and couldn't do; she never went over the limit. She was always just right, never too much, never too little.

'No, I can't think of anything,' said Elise. 'I just wanted to find out whether you've made any progress.'

'We have,' said Hamad. 'The investigation's moving forward all the time, but not as quickly as we'd like, perhaps.'

'I guess I'll go then,' said Elise, starting to get up.

'Don't hesitate to call or drop in if you want to tell us anything or if you just need to talk.'

Need to talk? thought Elise. I don't need to talk to you, you slimy creep.

At last she was out of there. She went back along the corridor and down the stairs. Took a look over her shoulder to reassure herself that no more unpleasant surprises awaited her, before she went to the lost property department. She handed in the wallet anonymously, saying that she did not remember where she had found it. With a light shudder as the doors closed behind her, she left the police building and walked rapidly up towards Skanstull.

* * *

The mood among Jennifer Johansson's classmates and teachers was subdued. In the room where he met the class and their tutor, there was a framed photograph of Jennifer and a candle had been lit for her. A beautiful bouquet of flowers added a touch of warmth to the arrangement, and Sjöberg could not help wondering whether Jennifer had ever been given flowers during her lifetime.

This day, like the one before, would be devoted to discussion and counselling rather than the timetabled subjects – which Sjöberg imagined was as educational as regular lessons. After saying a few words to the whole class, he spent a few minutes with each of them separately, and the picture was consistent: Jennifer Johansson had been popular and in some understated way a leader, without making too big a show of herself in the process. And the idea of any possible threat to her was dismissed as pure nonsense.

Those of Jennifer's teachers that he had an opportunity to meet during the morning seemed to share that perception. They also told him that although she had the capacity to get good grades, she totally lacked the motivation to achieve them. Which did not surprise Sjöberg in the least. Nor did his consultation with the school counsellor, whose contribution only reinforced what Sjöberg already knew about Jennifer.

Tuesday Midday

Sjöberg was now back on Östgötagatan and had just concluded a rather boring interview with a congenial furniture dealer from Bålsta, whose only purpose for the trip had been to have a little fun, to 'put his dancing shoes on', as he put it. He had achieved this aim so successfully that he could provide the address and phone number of a female passenger he promised could confirm that he hadn't been up murdering young girls at three o'clock in the morning.

Just as the recently divorced fifty-eight-year-old closed the door behind him, the police commissioner called and offered reinforcements in the form of human resources. Leadership was usually stingy with that type of offer and Sjöberg always strove to manage the workload with the personnel he already had at his disposal. It was a question of trust. He had no interest in relying on the judgement of an unknown colleague, however talented. Extra staff tended to take on too much or else nothing at all. Sjöberg had no problem delegating responsibility, but he was not prepared to lose control of the investigation just to speed it up.

'Thanks, but no thanks,' he answered curtly. 'On the other hand,' – Sjöberg grasped the opportunity – 'I know that Lotten in reception would really like a little help with simpler tasks. Sandén's daughter has slight learning difficulties and is looking for work right now. Give her a chance.'

The police commissioner muttered something incomprehensible at the other end and changed the subject. 'And the Vita Bergen case?' he asked. 'How's that moving along?'

That was quick, thought Sjöberg. Brandt not being particularly interested in personnel issues was one thing, but he had so little interest in the murder of Jennifer Johansson that he dropped it after half a minute. No insightful, detailed questions that might lead Sjöberg's thoughts in a fruitful direction, no proposals for action. Roland Brandt, in Sjöberg's opinion, was an incompetent pen pusher, if that. He seemed mostly to like showing off and looking important. But that was both good and bad. He had to assume that Brandt was relying on Sjöberg's ability to lead investigations, and it was nice not to have the police commissioner sniffing at his heels.

'You'll have to speak to Westman about that,' Sjöberg replied, 'but I guess it's roughly the same situation there.'

'Yes, that was just what I wanted to talk to you about,' continued Brandt. 'How is she conducting herself actually, that Westman?'

Actually? Sjöberg became wary. What was he after now?

'Very well,' Sjöberg answered quickly. 'Petra Westman always conducts herself very well. Otherwise I wouldn't have turned the responsibility for the investigation over to her. Besides, she usually works longer days than anyone else, so it's likely the investigation will move ahead faster than if someone else were responsible. Like me, for example,' he added with a laugh, to take the edge off the tension that he instinctively felt radiating from the receiver.

Brandt laughed too. In a 'between us guys' way, thought Sjöberg, who had no intention of cultivating any such relationship with the police commissioner.

'But I think she gives a somewhat unstable impression, don't you?'

'Not at all!' Sjöberg replied sharply.

Not that tone, he said to himself. Don't make an enemy of the police commissioner over some silly misunderstanding.

'That interview yesterday,' Brandt continued. 'In *Aftonbladet* –'

'I thought she dealt with it admirably,' Sjöberg interrupted, but in a rather friendlier tone.

'I don't know about that. The rhetoric was a little iffy, I would say. From what she said you might get the impression that the police aren't doing their job properly. And Conny, you know what I think about that warped view of the police.'

'It was quite clearly the journalist who chose to take that angle. Petra obviously expressed herself quite differently.'

'You trust her?'

'Completely,' Sjöberg answered honestly.

'Then I would like you to take a look at an e-mail I got from her the other day,' said Brandt and Sjöberg was certain he could hear Schadenfreude in his voice. 'I'm forwarding it to you now.'

He felt his palms starting to sweat as he turned on the computer monitor. What in the world could Petra have done? His e-mail pinged and Sjöberg double-clicked to open the message from Brandt. He started by checking the original sender and time of the forwarded e-mail. Petra was the sender; there was no doubt of that. And the message was sent last Friday at 11.58 p.m. That worried Sjöberg even more. It was undeniably a time of night when perhaps not the most sensible decisions were made.

He took a deep breath, moved his eyes down to the message field and read the text. It seemed inconceivable that Petra could have written this. But evidently she had. Brandt sat quietly on the other end of the phone, obviously waiting for a reaction. Without a word Sjöberg clicked on the attached document and studied it for approximately three seconds while his brain processed what he was seeing. Then he closed the document again as quickly as he could and let out a deep sigh.

'Well?' he heard Brandt's expectant voice say in the receiver.

'I . . . I don't know what to say,' Sjöberg stammered. 'I don't believe my eyes.'

'No, it's not surprising that you start to wonder,' the police commissioner agreed.

'Was she even in the building when this was sent?' The thought struck Sjöberg. 'We have to investigate that. It may have been someone else who –'

'I've already done that,' Brandt interrupted. 'The log from her pass card shows that she came in at 11.44 p.m. and left the building at 12.06 a.m.'

Sjöberg wiped his palms on his trouser legs, sighed again and turned off the monitor. He could not bear to look at it.

'I'll talk to her,' he said tiredly. 'I'll be in touch when I've investigated this.'

* * *

The weather was not as nice today, but it was still relatively warm and it did not look like it would rain. During the morning she had managed to investigate the buildings around the allotments on Långholmen but that had taken longer than one might expect. For one thing there was a lot of walking, and another – above all – the investigation process itself. She had to visit every building that might conceivably have the slightest view of the garden cottages and then assess whether they could really be visible from any of the apartments in the building.

Searching for the name Bergman on the directory in every stairwell was not exactly straightforward either. Sometimes the directory could not be seen from outside the door. Then she had to either wait until someone showed up or call on the entryphone to be let in. As a rule if anyone was home they were unwilling to open the door for her, so now she pretended she was the postwoman and the code wasn't working. A few times she had been able to see the directory from outside but the text was too small for her to read. That was why she had brought binoculars with her today, to at least solve that problem.

And could the old prison building from the 1840s be perceived as a castle in a little girl's eyes? It was possible, but nowhere had she found a building with a view of both the garden area and the 'castle', in which there also lived an apartment dweller named Bergman. When she had finished Långholmen her legs were so tired and she was so hungry that she was forced to take a lunch break, even though only one allotment area remained before she completed the search of Södermalm. Now she directed her steps towards her last destination in that part of the city, the Barnängen allotments by Vitabergsparken.

She realized that sooner or later she would be forced to start taking public transport. She considered having a taxi drive her around to the various allotments, but decided that was not really financially feasible for her. There was not much of her small pension left over for such extravagances, and just the thought of being rushed by a ticking taxi meter while she inspected stairwells left her in a cold sweat. And she did not own a bicycle. Cycling around among hot-tempered Stockholm motorists was not for a woman in her seventies. As the plan stood, she would walk as much as possible and take the bus and metro as needed.

The little girl's voice echoed in her head. She had spoken so well! She spoke quite clearly and formulated her ideas remarkably well. She was certainly a talented little child. Precocious. She could take care of herself, find food when she got hungry. But she didn't know what her last name was. She could not say how old she was or where she lived. How could you leave such a small child at home alone? It was just not possible. Hanna was a little devil, a child with a very lively imagination. She had discovered the telephone and started pushing buttons, making crank calls when her parents turned their backs. That's how it must be. The alternative seemed implausible. What was she doing, chasing all over the city on the basis of a three-year-old's prank? Pure madness. But that's how it was with intuition. It told her something different.

Barbro's body was stiff and her calf muscles were sore. She was used to walking long distances, but yesterday she had walked for almost seven hours with only a few short breaks, and that was more than she and her friends usually did. Yet she did not really feel satisfied with her efforts. It would have been better if she could have checked off all of Södermalm yesterday. But that was how it was. She quickened her pace a little as she left Götgatan and moved on to Bondegatan.

* * *

'What time should the next man be coming in?' asked Hamad.

'Let's see now . . . Yes, it was one-thirty,' answered Lotten, turning towards him.

Behind her on the notice board a number of postcards were pinned up, all depicting dogs of various breeds, but there were also serious items, such as the list of names and times that Lotten produced for him. He had already dealt with several, but none of the interviews had produced anything.

'Listen, that girl you talked to before – did you know her?' Lotten asked.

'Which girl?'

'That young thing, pretty, blonde . . . You took her up to your office.'

'Right, Elise. She figures in one of our investigations.'

'So what were you talking about?'

'About her sister. She was the one who was murdered on the Finland ferry. Why do you ask?'

'Just curious,' Lotten said. 'I was wondering how you knew each other, that's all.'

Hamad was not satisfied with that answer.

'How's that? Do you think that I . . . with a fourteen-year-old girl?'

'Oh, Jamal! Of course I don't think that! A grown man . . .'

Hamad rolled his eyes and had started to leave when Lotten suddenly thought of something.

'But listen,' she said to his back.

He stopped and turned towards her again.

'Yes?'

'Did you call her in?'

'No,' answered Hamad. 'She just wanted to find out how things were going.'

'But that's not why she came here . . .'

He retraced the few steps back to the reception counter and said, 'I assume it was. What do you mean?'

Lotten looked at him, surprised herself at her possible discovery.

'She found a wallet, she told me. She asked for the lost property department.'

Hamad did not know what to believe. First he thought just that: she found a wallet, nothing strange about that. But when he realized that Elise Johansson had lied to him, it put the matter in a different light. She had not said a word to him about a wallet. What had really happened when they met in the hall by the stairs? Yes, she really had said he was the one she was there to see; she hadn't mentioned the wallet or the lost property department. She had looked a bit anxious, certainly, but on the other hand he had not expected anything else. The girl was here to turn in a wallet, but lied about it. What could that mean? It might mean two things, Hamad reasoned. Elise had found a wallet but suspected that he would not believe that. Or – most likely – she had acquired the wallet some other way and then regretted it.

'Thanks, Lotten!' he called, already running to the lost property department. 'You're worth your weight in gold!'

'Yes, indeed, there was a young girl in here with this,' Ivarsson at the lost property department confirmed, producing the wallet. 'She found it, she said. Couldn't remember where. But I don't think she found it, 'cause then they usually leave their name and address. They don't say no to a little reward at that age. And there's a lot of money in it too. I'm guessing she got cold feet.'

'Have you got hold of the owner?' Hamad asked.

'No, he hasn't been informed yet.'

'Good. I don't want you to inform him either. I'll take care of this for the time being.'

Hamad went up the stairs at a half-run and into his office. He sat down at the desk and set the wallet in front of him, a thin little thing in back-pocket format, black imitation leather, with nowhere for coins. In the bill compartment he found three thousand kronor. A lot of money to a fourteen-year-old. It must have been hard for Elise to abstain from spending it, he thought. The wallet had spaces for six cards, but contained only five: a medical card, ICA and Co-op cards, a membership card for a video-rental chain, and a driver's licence. One Sören

Andersson, born in 1954, stared at him with a vapid expression. He looked ordinary, if a little dishevelled.

* * *

'The only thing we have to go on is that there's a big sister,' Petra Westman stated dejectedly.

'And that doesn't make it any more fun,' said Sandén.

'No, it will probably be harder for her than for the boy to grow up without her mother. He's not going to remember what she was like.'

Petra and Sandén were having a quick, fairly unhealthy lunch together at McDonald's on Götgatan. Normally Sandén would at least try to take a longer break, but they were short on time and wanted to meet up anyway to summarize the investigation. They sat strategically located in one corner, near the street, speaking in low voices.

'Have you talked to the hospital today? How's the kid doing?' Sandén asked.

'He's going to pull through,' Petra answered. 'He just has to gain some weight and get over the throat infection. But where in the name of God are the rest of this family hiding themselves? No one has missed the boy and his mother in four days. Tomorrow we'll have to put photos in the newspapers, that's all there is to it. We've been to all the children's health centres in the entire inner city. All that's left are a few sick or absent paediatric nurses that we'll have to visit at home. That sort of thing takes for ever.'

'We've knocked on virtually every door within three hundred yards of the discovery site. Same thing there: it's the ones who don't open the door or answer the phone who create a bottleneck in the investigation.'

'It's hard to believe you can be so anonymous in this city,' Petra sighed.

'It doesn't surprise me a bit. It's stranger that no one saw anything,' Sandén muttered.

'Not many people go past there at that time of night. At midnight in September it's pitch black and the park is poorly lit. Besides, the whole thing must have happened extremely fast. Think about it: he comes towards her, driving at high speed. It's dark; presumably he doesn't see the woman until it's too late. She flies headfirst right into the tree, the inset flies into the bushes, the pram in a different direction. He stops the car, rushes out to see what happened and finds her dead. Panics and decides to hide the body. Then he catches sight of that sand box and drags her over there; it's not far. Gets her down into the box, for some reason decides that he should empty her pockets – maybe to get her money, or make the police's work harder or something. Then he runs back to the car and drives off. All in less than two minutes, the re-enactment will show.'

'You're forgetting the boy,' Sandén pointed out.

'The driver didn't even see him. I think the insert ended up in the bushes from the collision and that the pram flew or rolled off somewhere. Then a passerby discovered the pram on the grass and pushed it up to the turning area.'

'Or else someone ran her over on purpose,' Sandén suggested. 'The father, for example. Maybe they were in a custody dispute and so he did away with her.'

'As she was pushing their son in a pram?' Petra sounded sceptical.

'Maybe the children have different fathers. Maybe he was only the father of the girl.'

'You don't believe that yourself.'

'You're right,' Sandén admitted. 'I'll do the rounds of the paediatric nurses who are off sick in the north and west suburbs during the afternoon; you take the rest.'

'Good,' said Petra. 'Tomorrow we'll release the pictures to the press and then I'll try to put together a reconstruction in Vitabergsparken at night. I'll talk to Conny and see whether he has any new angles.'

'He probably has his hands full too, I would think.'

'I haven't seen him since Sunday.'

'No, we keep missing each other. And then there's Einar, like the spider in the web,' said Sandén with a grin.

Petra let out a hollow laugh and pretended to shudder.

'He does what he's supposed to anyway,' said Sandén soothingly.

'But not a bit more.'

'It could be worse.'

'I know, but I hardly dare give him any work.'

'You'll have to learn to, if you're going to get anywhere.'

'How can a person be so surly and bitter?'

'What do we really know about what life's like for him, what reasons he might have for his behaviour?' Sandén philosophized. 'If we knew what he's experienced, maybe we'd love the guy for his positive attitude. Not everything is always as it seems, Petra, my dear.'

They gathered up the rubbish from the hamburgers on one tray, which Sandén set on top of the overflowing bin, and left the restaurant together. As they came out on

Götgatan, Petra's phone rang. She pulled it out of her pocket and glanced at the display: 'Blocked number.'

'Sjöberg,' she guessed. 'See you, Jens.'

Sandén left her with tired steps and a hand gesture that could possibly be construed as a wave.

'Hi, Conny, I was just about to call you.'

'I think it's best if you come in.'

'Right now?'

'No, but during the afternoon. We need to talk.'

Was that a sigh she heard? Sjöberg did not sound like himself. There was something . . . cordial missing from his tone.

'I'll be there as soon as I can,' said Petra. 'I –'

'Do that.'

Impersonal. Toneless.

'I need to talk to you too.'

'Hmm.'

Like Eeyore, thought Petra. He sounds like Eeyore.

'I'll see you later,' she said.

'See you,' said Sjöberg.

Her stomach knotted up as she ended the call.

* * *

'What did you really want?' Hamad asked.

He was sitting at his desk holding the phone between his chin and shoulder, trying to open a packet of sugar to add to his coffee.

'Huh?' Elise said blankly.

'When you were here earlier and talked to me. What was the real reason?'

He wanted to give her a chance to tell him what it was about. He felt sorry for the girl. She must think it was unpleasant to have to talk to the police and it made her nervous. Hamad had no intention of putting her off balance, but he wanted to hear her tell the truth.

'I wanted to know whether you knew who did it,' she answered lamely.

Hamad managed to tear off one corner of the sugar packet and emptied the contents into his coffee.

'But it wasn't just that, was it?'

Now he was giving her a hint that he knew. If she didn't take that bait she was an idiot. He stirred his coffee with a little plastic spoon. She did not answer.

'Elise, I'm a policeman. If I ask you a question, you have to answer.'

He regretted calling instead of going there. He would have liked to see her reaction now.

'I wanted to talk a bit to you or one of the others,' was all she said.

'And that was the only reason you came to the police station today?'

'Yes.'

'So when we'd had our little talk you went straight home?'

'Yes, I did.'

'Elise, I know that you went to the lost property department with a wallet. Why didn't you tell me about that?'

'Oh, yes, that. I didn't even think of it. That doesn't have anything to do with Jennifer,' Elise said, sounding indifferent.

'That's not for you to decide,' said Hamad sternly. 'Your sister was murdered and we're trying to solve the case. If you lie to me now or withhold something, how will I ever know if you're telling the truth?'

'I didn't mean to lie. I just didn't think of it.'

'You're still lying. You don't fool me. I gave you several opportunities to talk about what's really going on, but you didn't take them. Now tell me about the wallet.'

There was silence on the end of the phone. Hamad did not intend to let her off the hook. He took a gulp of coffee and waited.

'What do you mean, tell?' she said at last. 'I found it on the street and then I handed it in. Isn't that what you're supposed to do?'

'Where did you find it?'

'On the street, like I said. I don't know the name of the street.'

'When did you find it?'

'A few days ago. The day before yesterday, I think it was.'

'And you only turned it in today? Did you think about keeping the money?' Hamad asked, straight to the point.

A few seconds of silence, then she answered. 'Yeah, I guess I did. It was a lot of money –'

'Three thousand kronor. Yes, that's a lot of money. Keeping the wallet would have made you a thief, do you know that?'

'That's why I turned it in,' she defended herself.

'Who is Sören Andersson?' asked Hamad. 'Do you know him?'

She hesitated briefly before answering, 'Is it his wallet? No, I don't.'

'Why didn't you contact him yourself?'

'How would I know where he lives?'

'All that information is in the wallet. Address and phone number. And it was a lot of money. I'm sure you would have got a reward.'

'Maybe he's not a nice person. You have to be careful of strangers,' she said defiantly.

'Maybe you had a guilty conscience too, since you thought first about keeping the money.'

'Maybe so.'

Hamad had the feeling she was keeping something from him. Her story might very well add up, but why all the secrecy?

'Do you know what I think?' he asked.

Elise did not answer.

'I think you stole the wallet.'

Hamad waited for a reaction, but there was only silence. He continued.

'You took the wallet because you needed money. Then you changed your mind, so you came and handed it in to the police. Did the owner know it was you who took the wallet?'

'I found it, I said.'

'Why didn't you give the police your name? If you need money? Or you can't get a reward.'

'I don't want any reward. I didn't steal it; I found it on the street.'

'But now *I* know who found it anyway, so I can give your name to this Sören Andersson,' Hamad said provocatively. 'I mean, then you can get your reward –'

'You do that,' said Elise.

Hamad felt a sting of bad conscience about the girl, but even so he was satisfied at having taught her a lesson.

'You don't need to worry,' he said. 'I won't reveal who you are. But I would be grateful if you told the truth in the future.'

'Uh-huh,' she mumbled in response.

'Take care, Elise, and no more foolishness now.'

After the call he remained sitting there for a while, absent-mindedly fiddling with the wallet. The girl was lying, he was sure of it. In all probability she had stolen the wallet, but then she had thought better of it and that was good. Elise Johansson was simply yet another of these lost kids who thought it was easier to lie than to tell the truth. Who never hesitated to toss out a half-truth or a bald-faced lie, because it made things easier in the short run. She saw no reason to worry about repercussions or consequences; she lived for the moment with no respect for her surroundings, because she herself had never been shown any respect. Then he reminded himself that she had actually repented and turned in the money on her own initiative. Perhaps there was still hope for Elise.

Hamad glanced at the clock, sighed and got up from his chair. He decided to concentrate on the Jennifer Johansson case and leave her little sister to her fate for the moment. Then he took the wallet back down to the lost property department.

Tuesday Afternoon

As always, he told himself that nothing was decided, there were no definite plans. That was almost true: the thought of the solitary child had only occurred to him as he was reading *Aftonbladet* on Monday evening. But once he had talked to her he could not stay away. He would simply go there and check out the mood a little and see how the whole thing turned out. It would be just that. Of course, one thing usually led to another. Maybe she would be afraid, push him away. Then maybe he would coax her, make her realize that he only wished her well. He would put her in a good mood, spoil her a little so that she would see how nice he was.

First, of course, he would call and talk to her again. Make sure the circumstances hadn't changed. Then he would go up and ring the doorbell, hear the drumming of energetic little feet against the parquet floor as she ran up to the door to greet him. He imagined her bright little voice shrieking with delight when he arrived. Her new friend; they had a secret together. He reminded himself that before going there he would have to make sure it still was a secret, that no one else knew about her predicament and was on their way to help her.

If she was obstinate – if she changed her mind and no longer wanted him there – then maybe he would just leave. If it worked out like that naturally. He would not hit her; he would not hurt her. It just didn't feel right in this situation. No, he would restrain himself and give up. Or else he would whine a little, plead with her in a childish way, a way that children recognized. He might crouch down or get on his knees and put on his silkiest voice. 'Be nice, Hanna, let me stay. I'm so lonely.'

You could always try that. Appeal to a child's empathy. That was something they recognized, could identify with. She could be big and he would be little.

He would bring hamburgers from McDonald's; she couldn't resist that. He had heard how happy she sounded on the phone when he suggested that. Poor child, she obviously hadn't eaten properly for days. But she seemed to be managing fine; she was a child with a mind of her own. He would give her sweets too. Then they would take a bath. Wash her hair if she liked that; otherwise she could skip that, for the sake of domestic tranquillity. But he wanted her clean otherwise. Clean and smooth, with her skin softened after the warm bath, tender and smelling of soap.

He got up from the chair, crossing between the desks, and went over to the cloakroom where the toilet was. He closed the door behind him and locked it. Stood in front of the sink and looked at himself in the mirror. He was a nobody. He was an observer of the world around him, but he did not belong to it. As if to confirm this, he let his fingers run along the hollow in his neck between the collarbone, along the sternum and down to his navel, where for a moment, he let his index finger playfully twirl around, and then continue its journey downward.

He closed his eyes and found himself in the draught from

the rushing train. The endless train with all its carriages, with all its windows. He could barely fix his eyes on a single one of the people sitting inside before they were gone again. Gone and forgotten.

* * *

Barbro Dahlström, private detective, she thought as she tramped through the grass around the Barnängen allotments. From there she could see apartment buildings in several different directions. One direction however interested her more than the others. As she stood outside the fence by the row of plots at the far southern end of the park, she could see a white-plastered, 1920s-style, six-storey building. Across from it was a school building. It was the large yellow edifice of the Sofia School, which occupied an entire block in the angle between Skånegatan and Ploggatan.

She felt her heart skip a beat and hurried on to the little footpath that led over to Stora Mejtens Gränd. The closer she got to Ploggatan, the more she could see of the school's exterior facing the street. When she was finally standing outside the corner building, number 20, she could see the entire Sofia School rising up before her. It was a grand building, bright yellow and towering. The corner of the building, across from Ploggatan 20, was adorned with a number of vertical, dark-yellow ovals, which ended both above and below in a checked pattern of blue and red squares. Below these decorations the words 'PRIMARY SCHOOL' were written in big letters. And then, right at the top, a tower. A tower that might possibly house a beautiful princess.

Her excitement was tangible. She turned around purposefully and found herself staring through the window at yet another entrance hall. On the wall between the entrance and the grey internal doors hung a directory. Her eyes scanned eagerly through the dozen names on the list until they stopped at the one at the bottom. There was no doubt; she could see it clearly. Plain and simple: the small, white plastic letters formed the name Bergman.

Barbro had finally come to the right place.

Energized, she tugged at the door, but it was locked and would not open. The building didn't have an entryphone, but Barbro started to enter four-digit combinations on the code reader, hoping that someone would come through and open the door for her. At first she used only the most worn keys, but after a while she collected herself and started systematically to punch in combinations in numerical order. She realized that there were thousands of possible combinations, but she hoped in her eagerness that she would not have to try too many.

After 400 tries, with still no sign of a building resident or the postman, she was forced to give up. She wrote down all the names on the directory in the hall and started walking in the direction of the police station on Östgötagatan. With all due respect to the county detective unit, this had now become a matter for the Hammarby police.

Not until Barbro sat down did she let herself feel how her legs ached. She would not have lasted much longer, she realized that now. It had been foolish of her to go out on this desperate odyssey among the allotments, but now it was done. She had fulfilled the mission she had taken on, and she was proud of herself. Although she was a little angry too. Angry at the police, who had not done it themselves. She should be feeling like her work was done, but she wasn't at all. She had completed the most trying, arduous and time-consuming part, but the most important thing still remained. Now she had to get to the girl. By herself or with the help of the police.

She leaned back comfortably in one of the armchairs in the police-building lobby. She had been directed there by the pretty receptionist, as Deputy Police Commissioner Malmberg, she said, was in a meeting. Barbro had in most definite terms asked to speak with a police inspector, but the receptionist advised her not to wait for Inspector Sjöberg – who was the only chief inspector in the building at the present time – because there were already several other people in the lobby waiting to speak to him.

But Barbro insisted that come what may she wanted to speak to a person in authority, and to her surprise she was granted an audience with the deputy police commissioner himself. Perhaps this was too much, thought Barbro, but on the other hand he was a policeman too, presumably a capable one. She would not have to wait long, she was promised. The receptionist winked at her and said that she would give Barbro top priority.

'Mrs Dahlström, you can go up to the deputy police commissioner now!' the girl called from her place behind the counter.

Barbro nodded gratefully to her and took the lift up to the top floor, as she was told. Here there was another reception area, and the soon-to-be-retired lady in charge directed her to a nearby office. A sign said 'Gunnar Malmberg' outside the door, which was open. She stepped into the room and Malmberg, who appeared to be in his fifties, looked up at her with lively blue eyes from a tidy desk.

'Barbro Dahlström? Please sit down,' he said, showing her to one of the visitor's chairs.

He had a friendly, cultivated appearance; he was in shirt and tie, with his jacket hanging neatly on a hanger on the wall behind him. Barbro hoped that he would take her more seriously than his subordinate had when he had dismissed her on the phone.

'What can I help you with?'

Barbro felt she would have to make an effort to be firm with this policeman with his disarming smile.

'I called here on Sunday evening and spoke to one of your officers,' she said, getting straight to the point. 'I doubt that you heard about it, because I got the impression he didn't take my request very seriously. He referred me to the county detective unit, which proved to be a mistake, because the matter belongs here.'

The deputy police commissioner looked at her with an unchanged expression.

'This concerns a little girl I spoke to on the phone. She called me and asked for help.'

Malmberg leafed to a blank page on his notepad and wrote something down before he looked up at her again and said, 'Let's hear it. In what way did she need help?'

Barbro told about the call from Hanna while Malmberg took notes. Sometimes he smiled in recognition, and Barbro drew the conclusion that he had children himself.

When she told him about little Hanna's food preparation arrangements and how she had hurt herself, a wrinkle of concern appeared between his eyebrows. Barbro continued her story with the long walks among the allotments of Södermalm. Malmberg dropped the pen on the pad and put his hands behind his neck. With a smile that Barbro hoped was still friendly and not contemptuous, he listened further to what she had to say.

'I think I actually know where the girl lives,' Barbro paused for dramatic effect, and Malmberg looked at her with interest that she hoped was genuine. 'So now I think it's time for you to take over this investigation.'

The deputy police commissioner appeared to take the criticism with unruffled calm.

'Of course we will,' he answered. 'That was very responsible of you, Mrs Dahlström. Where do you think the girl lives?'

'At Ploggatan 20.'

Malmberg made a notation.

'You have to go there,' said Barbro. 'As soon as possible. I'm really worried about the girl.'

'I understand that, after all you've done to help her. We'll do what we can.'

Barbro got up from the chair and Malmberg followed her example, extending his hand.

'And do keep me informed,' she ordered with a smile, before leaving the office and closing the door behind her.

On her way to the lift she passed the receptionist and they exchanged friendly smiles. Just as Barbro was about to get into the lift she heard the intercom on the receptionist's desk beep, followed by a crackling order issued in the deputy police commissioner's voice.

'Inga, call up Holgersson. I have a job for him.'

* * *

Jamal Hamad had another gap between interviews with the solo male travellers. So far today he had done eight, and no one yet had behaved strangely or reacted unexpectedly to his now routine questions. All supplied credible accounts of their doings on the night of the murder; Sjöberg, for his part, had not stumbled across anything that aroused the slightest suspicion either.

Hamad stared blankly at the names before him. He did not know how many times he had let his eyes run over these endless lists, but he knew that somewhere here there was a significant name. He wished that one of the names would speak to him, would leap out, but the best he could do was to learn to recognize as many as possible. He hoped that sooner or later he would be rewarded for his diligence. That was how he worked: methodical, focused and persistent. Sjöberg, who lacked that sort of patience and seldom could stick to the same task for very long, relied on intuition and energy. Hamad relied on being systematic, on dogged zeal and stubborn perseverance. And as a result of these monotonous marathons, he had developed his already good memory. It was rare, but it happened and it would happen again. That creeping sensation would come over him: the seed of an idea, a sense that he ought to react. In the beginning he would not know to what he was reacting, but gradually it would come to him.

There was half an hour before he was due to question yet another of the passengers from the Finland ferry, and he decided to plough through another two pages of names before rewarding himself with a cup of coffee. There were two names left on the page when something clicked. This time it did not creep up on him; he saw it at once. His eyes wandered across the row, from the name and personal identification number to the telephone number and address. Every detail he had in front of him tallied with what he had seen a few hours earlier. The man whose wallet Elise had turned in, Sören Andersson, born in 1954 with an address on Katarina Bangata, had been one of the passengers on the Finland boat when Jennifer was murdered.

What should he do with this information? They now had a connection between Jennifer and a previously unknown fellow passenger. A lost wallet, Sören Andersson's wallet, handed in to the police by Jennifer Johansson's younger sister. How had Elise come across it? Naturally, she must have found it among Jennifer's possessions. The two sisters shared a room. Perhaps Jennifer stole it from Sören Andersson and Elise had found it and handed it in to the police.

But why in that case would Elise lie about that and pretend she found it on the street? Because she did not want to tarnish her sister's memory? No, that didn't add up. And it was in Elise's interest for her sister's murderer to be arrested. Does a man commit murder because his wallet was stolen? But maybe there had been something special in the wallet –

something that the man was determined to keep secret at any price. Maybe it was something that was no longer there, that wasn't there when Elise turned in the wallet. Thoughts were whirling around in Hamad's head.

Quickly he scanned the rest of the solo travellers and determined that Sören Andersson was one of the men scheduled to be questioned by Sjöberg, but who had not yet been contacted. He grabbed the telephone and called the lost property department.

'Sören Andersson, the one with the wallet that I spoke to you about – have you got hold of him yet?' he asked.

'Yes, we have. He's here now.'

'Keep him there for me. Detain him somehow, without making him suspicious. I'm coming down right away.'

He rushed down to the lost property department, but stopped in the corridor and took a few deep breaths, not wanting to be out of breath or seem excited. For a minute or two he stood like that before stepping into the office, hoping he seemed casual and relaxed. His eyes met the young policeman's, who signalled that this was the sought-after Sören Andersson he was talking to. Hamad went up to him and put a hand on his shoulder.

'Sören Andersson?' he asked calmly.

The man looked back at him with a blank expression. 'Yes?' he answered.

'I've been trying to get hold of you about a completely different matter,' Hamad said slyly. 'It's great that you happened to come in right now. Would you please come with me up to my office? It won't take long.'

'Sure,' answered Sören Andersson. 'Were we done with the formalities?' he asked the policeman at the counter.

The police officer smiled and nodded in reply, and Hamad gave him a grateful wink as he left with Sören Andersson.

He was tall and thin with sunken cheeks, and gave the impression of being relaxed. His hair was strawberry blond, thin and unruly, and seemed freshly washed.

'The reason I want to talk to you is that you were a passenger on the Finland cruise over the weekend where a young girl was found dead,' Hamad said when they had sat down on either side of his desk.

'I see,' the man answered with no noticeable reaction.

'I'm sure you were told by the Finnish police that you might be questioned again?'

'Yes, they mentioned that.'

'At the present time we are questioning all men who travelled alone across the Baltic, and from what I understand you travelled without a companion?'

'That's right.'

The man's expression did not show that he was uncomfortable in the situation or that he was worried about the questions he had to answer. Hamad thought that either Sören Andersson was a very good actor or he really had nothing to fear from the police.

'What was the purpose of your trip?' Hamad asked.

'Just a pleasure trip,' the man answered.

'So how did you spend your time? Did you meet anyone?' Hamad continued.

'No, I didn't meet anyone in particular. I danced a little. Ate and drank. Played the slots.'

'Did you win anything?'

'A few kronor.'

'Jennifer Johansson, which was the girl's name, was seen in the bar on board together with a man your age. Was that you?'

'No.'

'Are you quite sure of that?'

'Like I said, I didn't meet anyone. I didn't sit in the bar with anybody.'

'So our witnesses are not going to point you out?'

'How would that be possible?'

The man was cold as a piece of ice, showing no signs of uncertainty.

'You danced, you said?' Hamad continued.

'Yes, a little.'

'With anyone in particular?'

'With a few different women.'

'How many?'

'Five, maybe.'

'Anyone you talked to?'

'Not that much.'

'You didn't dance with Jennifer Johansson?'

'No.'

'You're sure of that?'

'Yes.'

Hamad asked him to recount in detail what he had done during the trip, and Sören Andersson described what he had been up to without leaving any obvious gaps in his story. He had slept alone in a two-bed cabin and gone to bed at one o'clock on the night of the murder. The man looked ordinary; there was nothing in his appearance or behaviour that might attract attention as far as Hamad could see. He showed him a photograph of

Jennifer Johansson and another depicting the clothes she had been wearing when she was murdered.

'Do you recognize her?' asked Hamad.

'No,' the man answered calmly. 'I've seen the pictures before, but I've never seen the girl.'

There was not much more Hamad could do, so he moved on to talk about Sören Andersson's current errand at the police station. As if in passing he tossed out his question, with a half-regretful, half-joking smile.

'And then you went and lost your wallet. Was it on the boat you lost it or – ?'

'No, it was before.'

'Was it stolen?'

'I don't think so. I must have left it somewhere or dropped it.'

He answered calmly and factually, without looking away, but Hamad's smile went unanswered. Sören Andersson showed no signs of anxiety.

'Where do you think it might have happened?'

'No idea. I didn't discover it until the next day.'

'Which was?'

'Last Saturday.'

'So you lost it on Friday?'

'Yes, I must have.'

'When do you think it happened?'

'In the afternoon or evening.'

'When did you last see the wallet, do you think?'

'When I was out shopping, about four.'

'Were you out in the evening?'

'I took a walk.'

'Alone?'

'Alone.'

'You have no family?'

'Sure. Wife and kids.'

'But they didn't want to go along on the Finland cruise?'

'They had other things to do.'

'Where did you get the money for the trip, since you'd lost the wallet?'

'My bank cards weren't in it.'

'Where do you usually keep them?'

'I leave them at home if I don't think I'm going to use them.'

'Why didn't you file a police report?'

'There was nothing of value in the wallet. A little money, but I didn't think I'd get it back.'

'And yet you did in the end anyway?'

'Apparently there are honest people.'

'Do you know who brought in the wallet?' asked Hamad.

'Evidently someone who wanted to remain anonymous.'

'Do you have any idea who that might be?'

'No.'

Brief, concise answers, no unnecessary digressions. Sören Andersson was a man of few words or a man who carefully avoided saying too much. Hamad decided it was time to end the interview.

* * *

If you take a walk at night with a pram in Vitabergsparken, you don't live far from there, Petra concluded. If you usually go to Blecktornsparken in the afternoons, that only strengthens that theory.

A number of tips had come in since the newspapers started reporting on the incident, but they were able to dismiss them all. Petra had visited all the paediatric health centres within a reasonable distance from Vita Bergen, even Liljeholmen, which was almost too far away. The private alternatives that existed in several places in the city had also been checked off the list. She had made home visits to a handful of paediatric nurses who had not been at work the last few days to ask whether they recognized the boy or his mother. Everywhere she had come up empty-handed.

They had no witnesses, no names. It was high time to submit the pictures to the media and ask the general public for help. Someone would find out that he had lost his wife by seeing the picture of a dead woman in the newspaper. Someone would turn on the TV and be met by their dead daughter's pale face. It was not how they usually worked. But they had to do something to move the investigation forward. Anything else was indefensible.

That was partly why Petra was now back at the station, even though there were still a few paediatric nurses left to check off. To discuss strategy with Sjöberg. To ask him for help with the reconstruction of the hit-and-run accident, if it had, in fact, been an accident. But there had also been something so ominous about his tone of voice on the phone that she was having a hard time concentrating on anything else. He had asked her to come in for a talk and she might as well bite the bullet.

She gave a slight shudder as she passed Sjöberg's door in the corridor. It was cracked open and she could hear him talking to someone in there. Calm and friendly. She went into her own office, hung her jacket on the hook behind the door and sat down at the desk to collect herself. Her mouth was dry; her heart was pounding loud beats in her ears. She could not remember being so nervous since her driving test. It was important to stay on Sjöberg's good side. It was hard not to be; he liked people, appreciated them for who they were, whatever they were like. But he was a person you did not want to let down; Petra had a strong feeling that somehow she had done that.

A light knock at the door made her jump in her chair.

'Nervous?' asked Gunnar Malmberg, deputy police commissioner, with a smile distinctly lacking in warmth.

Petra laughed and shook her head.

'No, I was just deep in thought.'

He stepped into the office and sat down in the visitor's chair across from her.

'A lot going on in your mind, I imagine?'

The smile was already completely gone.

'Yes, I'm working extremely intensively on a case –'

'I guess you have time for other things too?'

Petra did not understand, and squirmed a little in her chair, unable to think of anything to say.

'Outside of work.'

He was leaning far back in the chair with his legs apart and his hands clasped over his stomach. Handsome and smart in a well-ironed shirt, tie and jacket, he looked at her with an aura of self-assurance. Her brain worked feverishly trying to understand the reason for his visit.

'What were you doing last Friday, for example?'

'I was on a course all day, as you know,' answered Petra,

feeling surprise turning into irritation. 'Is this some kind of interrogation?'

Malmberg was the police commissioner's henchman. The police commissioner himself was an idiot, dense and ignorant, but with an ingratiating smile and the gift of the gab. It was Malmberg who did the work. Always one step behind the police commissioner, talented, shrewd and with a superficial charm that could impress anyone. Which he was not showing any sign of right now, as he studied her with a blank expression.

'Does that surprise you?'

'Yes, very much,' answered Petra, bolder now.

'What did you do after the course?'

'I went back to the police building and worked out in the gym. Then I had a beer with a colleague.'

'*One* beer?'

Inconceivable. What was he getting at?

'Do you suspect that I'm drinking too much; is that what this is about?'

'Just answer my questions, please. How many beers did you have?'

Petra rolled her eyes.

'Five, I think. So now you know.'

'Who were you out with and where were you?'

'When did you become an internal investigator?' countered Petra.

'I'm an internal investigator in this particular case, on orders from the police commissioner.'

Brandt, realized Petra. That lecher feels slighted and now he's trying to smear me.

'And I think you should be grateful for that,' Malmberg continued. 'That there aren't others involved, I mean.'

He added this last with a quickly passing smile that made her think of a father admonishing a child.

'So who were you out with and where were you?'

'I was at the Pelican with Jamal Hamad.'

'And when did you leave there?'

'At eleven-thirty, I think.'

'Together?'

After a moment's hesitation Petra answered, 'We left the bar together, yes.'

'And then?'

'What exactly are you looking for?'

'I am looking for exactly what you did then,' Malmberg answered.

'Ah, I understand,' said Petra with a contemptuous smile. 'I know that Brandt is interested in sex, but from that to mapping the sex lives of his staff . . . You can tell him that I did *not* hop into bed with Jamal and that I am *not* interested in hopping into bed with the police commissioner either.'

Malmberg's expression revealed nothing of what he was thinking. Factually and in an ice-cold voice he continued the questioning.

'But you stopped by the police station before you went home?'

'No, I did not.'

'The log from your pass card shows that you came in at 11.44 p.m. and left the building at 12.06 a.m.'

'But that's not right,' said Petra, feeling at a disadvantage in this mysterious interrogation.

She did not know what this was about, she did not know what they intended to punish her for, but it would amount to nothing. Then she suddenly remembered something.

'After the course Jamal and I went back to the station; I went up to the office and while I was getting my workout bag I put my pass card on the desk and left it there. We went down to the gym together, and he let me in. We left there together, took our bags to the office again and either I simply forgot to take the card from the desk or else it was no longer there.'

'In that case, why haven't you reported your lost pass card? You know that's what regulations prescribe.'

'Because it was here on the desk on Saturday when I dropped in. I hadn't even missed it. The main entry was open, I went straight up to the office and here it was.'

'So someone borrowed your pass card. Perhaps someone borrowed your computer too?'

'No,' said Petra. 'No one knows my password.'

'So what is it? "Westman" maybe?'

Petra tried a smile that was supposed to look superior.

'Nothing that easy.'

'Show me,' said Malmberg challengingly.

'My password? Never.'

'Your computer. Log in.'

While Petra logged into the computer he sat calmly, without trying to see what she typed.

'There,' said Petra. 'I'm in.'

'You maintain that your computer security is not compromised? That no one besides you could get into your computer?'

Petra nodded, but suddenly felt uncertain whether that was the right answer.

'Go into your e-mail,' Malmberg continued in a frosty voice.

Petra did as she was told without resisting. She had no obligation to accommodate him, but she wanted to get this whole thing over with.

'At 11.58 p.m. on Friday you sent a provocative e-mail to Roland Brandt,' said Malmberg, getting up from the chair and straightening his tie. 'He is deeply offended and is going to take action. The fact that you were drunk might possibly be considered an extenuating circumstance. Or aggravating. We'll get back to you when a decision has been made about whether drug treatment, suspension, transfer or termination will be necessary. Goodbye.'

The deputy police commissioner left the office with self-confident steps. Petra felt ready to cry, still not having a clue about what she was really being accused of. With a lump in her throat she double-clicked on the folder of sent mail.

* * *

The sun was going down and now there was probably only a short time to wait. Hanna had been longing all afternoon for evening to arrive because then, when it was dark outside, she would finally be rescued. By a nice man named Björn. He would bring food and sweets with him. Hanna could not wait any longer; she wanted it to be evening now.

In the morning, when there had been such a lengthy wait

ahead, she had felt very lonely. She lay on the floor in front of the TV, crying, for ages. She wanted Mummy so terribly that she could barely stand it. Her anger was gone now; she couldn't be angry at Mummy any more. She didn't think about Lukas at all. Only the loneliness was left. Loneliness that was so big her ears hurt. The silence in the apartment when the TV was turned off bounced back and forth in the rooms like a big thundering ball that would never stop. Right then she needed only Mummy, not even Daddy would do.

Hanna stopped crying when she ran out of energy, when her throat hurt so much that she was forced to stop. Then she lay in the same position for several hours just staring into space, her thoughts coming and going. She had not eaten a thing since morning; she did not have the energy to get up. Finally she fell asleep.

When she woke up a few hours later she felt better. She ate butter, straight from the packet, and uncooked cold potatoes from the refrigerator with the peel on. They weren't good, but it satisfied her a little and soon Björn would come with hamburgers.

She was sitting at the little table in her room, lining up her bookmarks in long rows when the phone rang. She ran out into the hall, climbed up on the chair and answered before it had rung more than four times.

'Hello?' she answered hopefully.

Perhaps it was Mummy finally calling!

'Is this Hanna?'

It was not Mummy's voice.

'Yes,' she answered, despite the disappointment. 'Who is this?'

'Sweetie, it's Barbro! How are you doing?'

'I think you're stupid,' said Hanna.

'I know you think this is taking a long time, but it was hard to find you, I must say.'

'You're lying.'

'Dear Hanna! If you only knew how hard I've been working to find you!'

'You're lying,' said Hanna again.

'May I speak to Mummy or Daddy?' Barbro tried.

'They aren't here. You know that.'

'Is there anyone there I can talk to?'

'No, I told you. You're stupid.'

'I've been looking all over for you, Hanna! Now I know where you live and I can call you too. Very soon a nice man will come and help you.'

'I know,' said Hanna.

'You knew that?' Barbro asked.

'Yes, because he called and said he would come.'

Then she remembered that she promised Björn that it was their secret, that she shouldn't tell that to anyone.

'My daddy is coming soon,' she said quickly.

'Do you mean that?' asked Barbro.

'Yes,' said Hanna. 'He's out buying hamburgers for us.'

'But . . . So you mean your daddy has come home again?'

'No, he's out buying hamburgers, I said that.'

'But that's just great, Hanna! So you won't be alone any longer?'

'Yes. Bye!' Hanna said brusquely and hung up.

Barbro had been able to get phone numbers for every household at Ploggatan 20 with the help of the Eniro website, except for one that had an unlisted number. She was prepared to make lots of calls that no one answered during the day, but to her great delight little Hanna answered at Barbro's third try.

After the girl so brusquely hung up on her, Barbro still felt uncertain. The conversation had taken a strange turn, which she could not really describe afterwards. What had been said really? Had Deputy Police Commissioner Malmberg been in touch with Hanna? Or that Holgersson? Was the father back, or had he simply never been away? She had tried to order her thoughts during the course of the call, but before she could do that it was over.

Barbro sat for a long time afterward, fingering the phone and considering whether to call again. Finally she got up with a sigh and went into the kitchen to put on water for tea.

* * *

Jennifer's personal possessions were kept in a shoebox. While she was alive it was absolutely forbidden for Elise to even touch the box, but now things were different. Jennifer was dead. Nothing could change that. She sat at their little table – you couldn't really call it a desk, but it served that purpose – and carefully raised the lid of the box. She felt a tug in her belly as she cracked open the entrance to her big sister's secret life.

Elise did not know what she had expected to find, but presumably something much more serious, much more forbidden than the jumble of meaningless trinkets she was looking at. A few bottles of perfume, costume jewellery that hadn't been Jennifer's style for years, a few letters from a girl in Skåne she remembered that Jennifer had been pen pals with years ago. There was also a bundle of school photos of Jennifer's friends from middle school, a pack of French cigarettes with no filters, a half-empty packet of birth control pills. And at the bottom: an address book.

Elise picked it up and leafed through it from the back. Only familiar names from Jennifer's circle of friends. Most were old friends, from primary school, but a few new names had been added more recently. Elise kept track of who Jennifer saw, even if she was seldom invited to join them. Then she found Joakim. 'Joakim Andersson,' it said; it was like Jennifer was savouring the name.

How many times had Elise done the same thing with friends when they looked through the school yearbook to rate good-looking guys? It was actually pretty silly, but there was a tingle in your stomach when you saw the address of a cute boy. She wondered whether guys did the same thing: drooled over the girls' meaningless street addresses. And now there it was again, that tingle in her stomach. Joakim was exciting, tall and grown-up – not like the spotty high-school boys she knew.

She closed the address book and picked up the bundle of school photos from the shoebox. She did not have to flick through many before she was looking into Joakim's grey-blue eyes. In the picture he did not have a beard, but she recognized him anyway. There was no mistaking those eyes. He looked a little dangerous too. Maybe it was the eyes that did it, those mournful eyes that seemed to be looking inwards instead of at her. And then there was the adultness and his way of holding Jennifer, as if he owned her.

And now he was available, it struck her. Now he wasn't Jennifer's boyfriend any more; now he was free to go out with whoever he wanted, do what he felt like.

Everyone said they were so alike, Jennifer and her. Elise didn't think so, but if that was how people saw them . . . Maybe he would too . . . ? She would give a lot to feel those arms around her. Joakim was probably really sad now. Besides, the police had their eye on him; he must be a suspect. But Elise could not imagine that – that Joakim could have murdered Jennifer, strangled her. No, not the way he held on to her that time she had seen them together. She imagined that he was depressed. He needed consolation, someone to talk to.

And who could be better in that situation than her? They were in the same boat, Joakim and Elise. Living in a vacuum from the loss of Jennifer. It might be worth a try. She looked up his address again and memorized it. He did not live far from her, only a few blocks away. She put Jennifer's things back in the shoebox, closed the lid and put it back in the cupboard. As if Jennifer could have discovered what she had done.

Elise caught up with a woman who had been out walking her dog and slipped into the building unnoticed. She stopped in front of the directory to see what floor Joakim lived on. There were two Anderssons in the building; she decided to go up the stairs to the second floor, where the first of them lived. She did not really know what she would say when she saw Joakim, but she was not exactly shy, so it would probably work out. She wondered whether Jennifer had ever been here. She had never said so, but why should she have? It struck her that maybe Joakim would not be home, but she felt sure that he was, given the circumstances.

Indeed, Joakim opened the door. He looked inquisitively at her without saying anything.

'Hi,' she said, smiling at him. 'Aren't you Joakim?'

'Yes,' he answered, smiling cautiously back.

He looked like he'd been in a fight, with a yellowish bruise around one eye.

'I'm Elise.'

Joakim looked at her in silence for a few moments, not revealing what he was thinking.

'You look alike,' he said.

'That's what they tell me.'

Neither of them seemed able to think of anything else to say.

'May I come in for a minute?' Elise asked at last.

'No, right now isn't a very good time,' Joakim replied, looking over his shoulder as if someone inside was not supposed to know she was there. 'Did you want anything in particular?'

'No. I just wanted to talk a little.'

'I'm sorry about your loss,' said Joakim, lowering his eyes.

Those words were so solemn somehow. It didn't sound natural when young people talked that way, but perhaps there was no other way to express it.

'I guess I should say the same thing,' said Elise.

'Yeah. What happened was terrible.'

'Are the police after you?' asked Elise, in an attempt to find some common ground.

'Yes, of course,' Joakim answered. 'Are they after you too?'

'They don't think I'm the one who did it, but they're always asking a lot of questions.'

'Tough,' Joakim nodded.

'Do they suspect you, or . . . ?' asked Elise.

'I suppose so. I guess they have to,' Joakim sighed.

'I don't think you did it anyway. You don't look like a murderer,' Elise said.

'Thanks,' said Joakim with a faint smile.

He felt above his eye with his middle finger, as if he wondered whether the bruise didn't tell a different story. There was an echo in the stairwell as the door shut down below.

'How does it feel?' asked Elise.

Joakim hesitated for a moment before he answered.

'Terrible, actually. It's as though life has . . . stopped. You don't know how you'll go on.'

'It's the same for me,' Elise hurried to say.

Actually she didn't know how she felt. She had not really had time to feel anything yet. It was hard to grasp that her sister had really been murdered. That Jennifer no longer existed. She had not really started to miss her yet. Joakim looked distressed, and she had a desire to hold him. Stroke his cheek, show him in some way that she cared. She heard someone approaching on the stairs from below and turned towards the sound. A man was on his way up the stairs, but she could not see his face because he kept his eyes looking downwards, towards his shoes.

She turned back to Joakim and was about to say something when she noticed how he froze. His eyes became blank somehow, as if he were no longer present. He was no longer looking at her but at the man who was approaching them. Elise immediately felt the tension in the air and lifted up her shoulders to defend herself against whatever was coming from behind. Both she and Joakim stood as if nailed to the floor. She did not dare turn around; she just stared at Joakim and tried to read in his expression how she should react.

'I see,' said a man's voice just behind her.

Joakim did not say anything. Elise did not move.

'What have we here?'

'Just a friend,' said Joakim.

* * *

That was the wrong answer; Joakim knew that. He could have said almost anything at all, but not that. He was expected not to have any friends. Especially not a girl. He could have said it was someone selling something or someone who had knocked at the wrong door. Anything at all, but not that. He had done it for Elise's sake, so she wouldn't wonder, for appearances' sake. But he should have known better.

'That's a pretty little friend you have,' said the man in a joyless tone, but the scorn in his voice did not escape Elise.

He was talking about her, perhaps to her, and she did what was natural, she turned towards the strange man with a forced smile, as if to say hello. But the smile disappeared and she could not get out a word. Joakim saw what was happening without understanding, so to rescue the situation he said quickly, in as neutral a voice as he could manage, 'She was just leaving, Dad.'

But the words disappeared into empty nothingness.

Elise, who could simply have raised her hand in farewell and left, stood as if frozen with her mouth open and could not tear her eyes from the man. Joakim's father, who was in mid-step to the doorway, had only to complete the motion and disappear into the darkness of the apartment. Instead he stopped and Joakim saw the contempt in his father's eyes as they devoured her from head to toe – one body part at a time – before he hissed, saliva foaming at his lips, 'Aren't you dead, you little whore?'

Only then was the spell broken and she ran for all she was worth down the stairs.

* * *

'Not a thing,' said Sjöberg. 'Nothing of interest has come out in any of the interviews.'

Hamad decided to suck on the sweet he had in his mouth and let the inspector complain for a while before he told of his own discovery.

'You look tired,' he said.

Sjöberg sighed. He thought briefly about Margit Olofsson's nightly disturbance of his sleep, the smell of her perfume that lingered in the air around him. He did not want to think about it, much less talk about it.

'Yes, there's probably more than one reason for that,' he said without going into detail. 'By the way, Nieminen called. Those Finnish consultants, Helenius and Grönroos, have never had any problems with the police. Or with the tax authorities. And they had completely legitimate reasons for their trip to Sweden, so they aren't dodgy – in that way at least. How have you been doing?'

'I've found a connection,' said Hamad. 'A connection between Jennifer Johansson and a previously unknown passenger on the Finland ferry.'

'What are you saying?' said Sjöberg, suddenly looking a little livelier. 'That's exactly what we need right now.'

'It's vague, but it's a connection. Unfortunately I'm not getting anywhere with it.'

'Let's hear it,' said Sjöberg.

Hamad described his meeting with Elise and Sjöberg listened with growing interest. The account continued with the discovery of Sören Andersson's name on the passenger list and his subsequent questioning of the man, without anything of interest arising.

'Well, I'm not happy with that,' Sjöberg maintained. 'Do his age and appearance match the description of the man in the bar?'

'Sure, it could have been him,' said Hamad.

'But that wallet . . . How did Elise get hold of it?' Sjöberg asked. 'Even if this is the connection we're looking for, how in the world do they hang together?'

'Jennifer can't have stolen the wallet on the boat, because Elise wouldn't have had it. Elise claims to have found it on Sunday; Andersson says he lost it on Friday.'

'Maybe he's lying,' Sjöberg suggested. 'Let's say that Jennifer stole it on the ferry and then hid it in the cabin or gave it to one of her friends. He killed her but didn't get his wallet back. One of the friends then gave the wallet to Elise, who handed it in.'

'But why should she lie about that?' Hamad asked.

'Besides, it's a bit of an overreaction to kill someone who stole your wallet. There must be more to it than that.'

'Drugs?' Sjöberg tried.

'Jennifer didn't do drugs.'

'We'll have to get Eriksson to research this Sören Andersson's past and see if we find anything there. It's going to be hard to pick holes in his story, especially if he made an effort to stay anonymous during the trip.'

'If he was the one sitting in the bar with Jennifer, then he failed at least once. He was seen.'

'There's only circumstantial evidence,' said Sjöberg. 'If we could connect him to the scene of the crime, we would have more to go on. We'll have to see what Lehto has to say about this character, but first we have to sound Elise out properly.'

A quiet knock on the open door caused them both to fall silent. Westman stood in the doorway, and Hamad thought she looked like a timid schoolgirl, like he had never seen her before.

'I'll pick you up in a while,' Sjöberg concluded the conversation in a voice that had suddenly taken on an authoritative tone. 'Close the door behind you.'

Hamad got up with a raised eyebrow, gave Petra a familiar pat on the back and left the office.

Petra sank down with a sigh on the visitor's chair where Hamad had just been sitting. She could feel the warmth left by his body as she met Sjöberg's eyes with a regretful expression.

'Okay now, Petra,' Sjöberg sighed in turn. 'I can see that you're uncomfortable.'

'I know what it is you want,' she answered. 'I just found out from Gunnar Malmberg. They're planning to fire me.'

Sjöberg shook his head and gave her a look that was unbearable.

He felt sorry for her. Not because she had been badly treated, but because she was . . . sick. Not to be trusted. A problem child. The black sheep of the force. Scandalous.

'Is that your biggest problem, do you think?' he asked, not concealing his disappointment. 'If I were in your shoes, I would pack up my things and leave this building. Do you understand how you've disgraced yourself? This is irreparable, Petra. You can't stay here.'

'It's bad, Conny, but nowhere near as bad as it appears.'

She saw that he was getting angry, but anything was better than disappointment.

'Petra, that's a pornographic picture.'

Sjöberg hissed out the words so they wouldn't be heard out in the corridor. Petra lowered her eyes.

'A picture depicting you in an unconventional intercourse position. In an e-mail that was evidently an invitation to the police commissioner! "Sexy, or what?" What the hell has got into you, Petra? Do you have a drinking problem or do you think you can screw your way to a higher salary?'

'You've seen the picture,' said Petra quietly.

'I've seen the picture because Brandt forced me to look at it. I looked for a second or two until I understood what the hell I was seeing, then I deleted it. Believe me, Petra, I am not the least bit interested in seeing you like that.'

Even when he was so upset, when he was telling her off, his eyes were friendly. Suddenly it occurred to Petra that he was not angry, he was sincerely sorry for her sake. She was close to tears now.

'Conny, I did not send that e-mail. I was not even here when it was sent,' she said as calmly as she could, feeling the lump in her throat growing.

'And that's not you in that damn picture either? Huh?'

'That is me in the picture, but I was unconscious when it was taken,' she forced out before the tears pricked her eyes. 'Besides, it's not a photograph, it's a frame from a film that was recorded when I was raped last autumn. And if you don't believe me, ask Rosén.'

Now she could no longer hold back her tears and in some way that was a release. She had not shed a single tear since the rape, but now it suddenly felt as if she had been waiting for this moment the whole time. Just to open up the floodgates and let her emotions out. And no more than that was needed to make calm the storm inside Sjöberg. Purely intuitively he let his loyalty, which for a few hours had been led astray, find its way home again. To Petra. To his Petra, whom he had never, ever doubted before. Instinctively he got up and went over to her. With both hands he turned her face up towards him, then took her hands and kindly pulled her up from her place on the chair. Then he took her in his arms with her head on his chest.

'Rosén?' asked Sjöberg gently.

He felt her nodding in his embrace, and they remained like that for a long time, while he stroked her hair and let her calm down.

The silence was only broken when Sjöberg pinched her softly on the neck and asked if she'd fallen asleep. Petra laughed and freed herself. She wiped her face with her sleeve and Sjöberg went back to his place behind the desk. Petra smiled a little self-consciously as she too sat down. She noticed that Sjöberg looked like he had had a weight lifted from his shoulders.

'Now let's take this from the beginning,' said Sjöberg, adopting his customary working frown.

For the first time in almost a year Petra described how she and Jamal had spent a November evening at Clarion's bar, how she started talking to Peder Fryhk with whom she later shared a taxi, about waking up in his house in Mälarhöjden, and about the hangover and the pain. It was liberating to be able to do it. It felt safe to have Sjöberg on her side, someone to talk to about what had happened, someone who understood what she was going through. She continued by telling him about her irregular investigation, how she succeeded in getting an acquaintance, forensic technician Håkan Carlberg, to help her with analysing samples. How the prosecutor had then put the anaesthetist and serial rapist Fryhk behind bars. Finally she told him about the Other Man, about the missing video recording, and about her worry that she might be revealed as the one who had convicted Fryhk.

Together they mapped out what had happened since last Friday: the course, the workout session, the visit to the bar with Hamad, and the exact times of entry, exit and the sending of the fateful e-mail.

'Someone had his eye on you last Friday, Petra. Someone knew exactly when he could execute this, and how.'

'And this someone has the film,' Petra added. 'There is

someone out there who raped me and who is sitting at home on the couch jacking off to this video.'

'In here,' said Sjöberg. 'There's someone *in here* who's doing that.'

Petra had not managed to think that far. There had been one catastrophe after another during the afternoon and she had not had time to stop and analyse. She had a vague idea that a skilled hacker could log into her computer from somewhere and send an e-mail that appeared to come from her. But of course Sjöberg was right. The Other Man was a policeman. A police officer who worked here in the building. And who had used her pass card and computer to direct suspicion at her.

'Who knows your password?' asked Sjöberg.

'No one. I told Gunnar Malmberg that too.'

'Do you have it written down anywhere?'

'No, only in my mobile phone and I always have it with me.'

'Have you changed passwords in the past year?'

Suddenly Petra realized where he was headed. The Other Man had been meticulous. He had even gone into her contacts list and snooped out her password as she was stretched out in Peder Fryhk's bed. It had been a naive hope that he would not know who she was. He had recognized her from the start. Petra shook her head with a look that showed she understood what Sjöberg meant.

'I assume you've tried to figure out who's been calling you at night?' Sjöberg continued.

'Prepaid cards,' Petra confirmed. 'A different number each time.'

Sjöberg nodded thoughtfully.

'But why is he doing this?' said Petra, throwing up her arms. 'He's so careful and so concerned about not being discovered. He doesn't appear on a single film frame, Fryhk is keeping his mouth shut, and according to Hadar he hasn't left a trace behind him.'

'Well, he has left *one* trace behind.'

'But we have nothing to compare it with.'

'Not yet. Do you know why men rape, Petra?'

'They say it's not so much about sex as about power.'

'Exactly. And he doesn't feel that he's finished with you. You put a spanner in the works for them and that can't be tolerated. He wants to pressure you properly. Get revenge. That's to our benefit.'

Our, thought Petra, feeling warmer inside. I'm not alone any more.

Sjöberg glanced at the clock.

'There was another thing too,' Petra said. 'Something unpleasant happened yesterday evening.'

Then she told him about the telephone call from Brandt and her meeting with him.

'So he probably wasn't really all that offended by that e-mail,' she noted in conclusion.

'What did you say he said after that business about Mathias Dahlgren?' Sjöberg asked.

'Something along the lines of "I thought we could continue a few flights up after we'd eaten".'

Sjöberg suddenly started laughing. Petra looked at him in surprise.

'You're not much of a slut, Petra! Don't you understand what he meant by that? Mathias Dahlgren's restaurant is on street level in the same building as the

Grand Hotel. That horny bastard probably reserved a room for the two of you there too!'

Still with an amused gleam in his eye, Sjöberg picked up the phone and dialled directory enquiries.

'Please give me the number for the Grand Hotel and then connect me with Mathias Dahlgren's restaurant. Thanks.'

Shortly thereafter someone picked up at the other end. Petra watched her superior wide-eyed without understanding at first what he had in mind.

'I would like to know if there was a reservation in the name of Brandt yesterday evening . . . No? . . . I see, eight o'clock . . . Around seven. Thanks very much.'

Without saying anything he winked at Petra and dialled another number.

'Roland Brandt here, Hammarby Police. I suddenly got a little worried that I forgot to cancel my room reservation yesterday . . . No, that's nice . . . A double room . . . Great, thanks.'

Sjöberg hung up and rubbed his hands together with a satisfied smile.

'Roland had a table reserved at Mathias Dahlgren for eight o'clock yesterday, which he cancelled at seven. Afterward he had envisioned a little tête-à-tête with you in one of the double rooms, but he had to cancel that too. He was clearly terribly offended.'

* * *

'What was that all about?' Hamad asked during the walk up to Ringen.

'What?' Sjöberg asked with feigned cluelessness.

'You and Petra behind closed doors. What kind of secrets do you have together?'

'Oh, I see, that. We were just talking about work.'

'Are things going that bad for her at work?' Hamad asked with a wry smile. 'She looked like she'd been crying her eyes out.'

'I didn't notice that,' Sjöberg answered curtly.

'Petra and I are good friends,' Hamad persisted. 'You can tell me –'

'I see, you are?' interrupted Sjöberg. 'Yes, I heard the two of you went out last Friday. Where were you?'

'At the Pelican having a beer.'

'For how long?'

Sjöberg quickened his pace a little, his eyes fixed on some indeterminate point up on the rise.

'I guess we left there around eleven-thirty. What about it?' Hamad sought eye contact without success.

'And where did you go after that?'

'Home. I went home. I had to get up early to –'

'And Petra?' Sjöberg continued.

'I guess she went home too! What is this? You don't think that Petra and I –'

'I don't think anything. Just pure curiosity.'

Hamad shook his head. Sjöberg walked on at a rapid pace without meeting his associate's eyes.

The party was already in full swing when they showed up at the Johansson family's apartment. It was depressing to see the company crowded around the kitchen table. Not so much for their own sake; the two policemen's thoughts centred mostly on Elise. Poor kid, thought Sjöberg. Apparently things had been like this her whole life. And now she did not even have a sister to share her fate with. They had agreed on a considerably harder approach to the girl this time, but their intentions slipped away when once again they saw at close range what life was like for her.

Elise was perched on the bunk with a pillow behind her back looking at a magazine when they stepped into the girls' room.

'Is it always like this?' asked Sjöberg, with a gesture towards the rest of the apartment.

Elise shrugged and tried to look indifferent.

'How are you doing?'

'Fine,' she answered without conviction.

Hamad took over and went straight to the point.

'I'm not satisfied with your answers to the questions I asked you on the phone,' he said in a somewhat harsher tone than really felt right.

Elise looked back at him with an unsympathetic expression.

'I think you have more to tell us about that wallet.'

'Well, I don't,' said Elise, turning her eyes away.

'When did you find it?' asked Sjöberg.

'I don't know. I think it was on Sunday.'

'Where did you find it?'

'On the street, I told you! I don't know the name of the street.'

A reaction anyway. It was clear that she did not want to talk about this and that energized Sjöberg.

'You're lying, Elise. And you know that we know you're

lying. Now you're going to tell us exactly where and when you found this wallet.'

Elise started browsing through her magazine. Sjöberg grabbed it with both hands and threw it on the floor. Elise winced. She had not expected that.

'We're trying to find the person who murdered your sister,' said Sjöberg with unruffled calm. 'All we're asking of you is that you answer a few questions. We want to know the truth. We need to know the truth in order to separate what's important and what's not. You're lying to us and that's not acceptable. You stole that wallet, didn't you?'

'No, I found it,' said Elise, but the self-assurance was no longer there.

'Then we'll see what Sören Andersson has to say about it. When we tell him that the girl who stole his wallet is fourteen, her name is Elise Johansson and she lives on Götgatan.'

'But that has nothing to do with it!' Elise cried out, clearly upset now.

'Doesn't have to do with what?'

'With Jennifer!'

'We'll decide that, not you,' said Sjöberg. 'When did you steal the wallet?'

'I didn't steal it! But it may have been on Friday that I found it,' she admitted.

'Why did you say Sunday if it was Friday?'

'I don't really remember, but it was probably last Friday.'

'Where did you find it?' Sjöberg went on.

'It was somewhere close to Vitabergsparken, but I don't know the name of the street. It's true!'

* * *

291

Elise watched with dismay as the two policemen exchanged glances, but she did not understand at all what those looks might mean. She felt only a growing sense of discomfort. She was prepared to do anything, almost anything at all, to get away from there, to escape those scrutinizing stares and questions about what she never wanted to think about again – something that had nothing at all to do with the murder of Jennifer. In her desperation she lashed out against the policemen, the way she might against her mother or her teachers.

'Why don't you do your job, you fucking pigs? Catch Jennifer's murderer and don't be after me all the time! I didn't murder Jennifer; I haven't done anything! And that disgusting dirty old man he has for a father, her damn boyfriend; he asked why I wasn't dead! Do you get how that feels, you fucking idiots! Do you get how it feels when people say you ought to be dead! I suppose you want me to die too? It would have been a lot better if *I'd* died instead, huh? Then everyone would have been happy. Damn, I wish I were dead, so I could escape you and all of your stupid questions and all this bullshit!'

* * *

Hamad and Sjöberg stood as if petrified, witnessing the fourteen-year-old Elise Johansson's adolescent outburst, but Sjöberg had to admit later that it was actually quite a relief. Elise had finally reacted like a normal teenager and that felt liberating in some way. It was a huge contrast to the fearful, cowering, self-denying behaviour that had marked her during their encounters so far.

'What was that you said?' asked Sjöberg, when the sound of her voice had ebbed away. 'Did Joakim's father ask you why you aren't dead?'

'Yes, he did,' answered Elise, still angry, but considerably more composed now.

She avoided his eyes and sat fingering both of her rings.

'You need to explain that.'

'"Aren't you dead, you little whore?" he said to me. Was that a nice thing to say?'

'In what context? When did you see him?'

'Before,' Elise said simply.

'This afternoon?'

'Yes.'

Thoughts were whirling in Sjöberg's head. He glanced at Hamad, but he looked equally perplexed. Neither of them could immediately verbalize just what was so strange, but it was clear to both of them that something was really wrong here.

'Where did this happen?'

'At Joakim's,' said Elise.

'I thought you didn't know each other,' Sjöberg pointed out.

'We don't, but I went there anyway. I just wanted to talk to him.'

'And then . . . ?'

'And then his dad came home from work or something. We were standing out in the stairwell. And then he caught sight of me and looked completely crazy. "Aren't you dead, you little whore?" Yes, that's what he said, "Aren't you dead, you little whore?"'

Sjöberg looked at Hamad, who was shaking his head in disbelief.

'That must have been unpleasant, Elise. What did you do then?'

'I just ran away from there. As fast as I could.'

'And Joakim?'

'Well, what could he do? He stayed there.'

'What in the world was that about?' asked Hamad when they had left Elise and were on their way back down to the police building.

'That was a strange story,' Sjöberg agreed.

'But is it true?'

'I actually think she was telling the truth this time. Her account was spontaneous, you might say,' said Sjöberg with a meaningful smile.

'Oh boy. Just wait till your kids reach that age.'

'God forbid.'

'But why did he say that? "Aren't you dead?" What does that mean?'

'It may mean that he recognizes Elise and thought she was the one who was dead. Then we have to ask ourselves: Why does he recognize Elise? It may mean he recognizes Jennifer, knows that she's dead, sees Elise, and thinks she's Jennifer. Where does he recognize Jennifer from? Do you think Joakim introduced them? Not very likely. However we look at this, we end up with two facts. One: He has seen one of the girls, or both of them, before.

Two: He thinks Jennifer and Elise look a lot alike. So alike that he can't really tell them apart.'

'That's a new idea,' said Hamad.

'He may have seen Joakim with Jennifer at some point. At a distance perhaps. And then he runs into Elise there in the stairwell. Elise reminds him of the only girl Joakim has ever gone out with – Jennifer – and so he spits that out. Contemptuously, because he didn't approve of their relationship. We know that, because that was why he assaulted Joakim that Friday evening.'

'Joakim's dad seems to be a truly unpleasant person,' Hamad observed.

Sjöberg could not help but agree and they walked side by side for a while lost in their own thoughts. When they reached the turning area outside the police building Hamad said, 'I have another idea.'

He stopped and Sjöberg did the same.

'What if Joakim's dad was also on the boat?'

'Wouldn't we have known that?' asked Sjöberg.

'How would we? We're staring our eyes blind at their names, whom they share a cabin with and so on, but I for one haven't investigated whether there was another passenger on board with the same address as Joakim.'

'Joakim would have said something.'

'Maybe he didn't know it himself.'

'They would have run into each other,' said Sjöberg. 'His reason for being on board must have been to take Joakim to task because he went even though he was forbidden to do so.'

'His reason may just as well have been to kill Jennifer.'

'In that case, why?'

'Because he's a sick bastard who doesn't tolerate being contradicted.'

'Well, he's no doubt sick,' Sjöberg observed. 'He abuses his twenty-four-year-old son, and holds him in a kind of prison as his extremely obese mother's caregiver. They also sleep together . . .'

'Who sleeps together?' Hamad wanted to know.

'Father and son.'

'Sleep together? In the same bed, or what?'

'In the same bed. A single bed besides.'

'You're joking. Why haven't you said anything about this?'

'I am now. We've had other, more important things to talk about, haven't we?'

'This is important! Suddenly Joakim's father is a person of interest in the investigation!'

'Jamal, I'm telling you this now because he's attracted our attention. There's no reason to start speculating about sensitive issues like incest on such flimsy grounds.'

'You're the one who said it, Conny. You said incest, so you were thinking incest.'

'The kid is twenty-four, Jamal. What can I do? Start an incest investigation on a twenty-four-year-old man? Joakim could report the matter himself if he wanted to. In theory he is perfectly capable of moving away from home and breaking contact with his family.'

'In theory, yes. But not in practice. He's chained to his sick mother.'

'And to his sick father,' Sjöberg agreed. 'Yes, I know. And we're stuck with our procedures. For that reason we'll let this rest for the time being. Until we need it.'

'You realize that Joakim may have been abused by his father the whole time he was growing up?'

'I realize that, yes,' Sjöberg sighed.

'In that case it would mean that the old bastard is not only incestuous but a paedophile,' Hamad pointed out.

'Now let's just take it easy. We can at least find out whether he was on board the boat before we start running away with this.'

'You've already completed the thought.'

'At the same time as you, I would think,' Conny Sjöberg concluded the discussion.

Their suspicions proved correct. Neither of them was surprised when a short time later in Sjöberg's office they determined that Göran Andersson, Joakim's father, had been among the passengers on board the Finland ferry that fateful night. Hamad filled a briefcase with papers and other things he thought he might need that evening. Neither of them could predict how the next few hours would turn out, so it was as well to be prepared. He felt they could do without running back and forth between the police building and the homes of those involved. Eriksson was briefed on the latest thinking and Lotten was ordered to cancel Sjöberg's and Hamad's remaining interviews for the day. They also asked her to send photographs of Göran Andersson and Sören Andersson to Nieminen. Then they took off for Joakim's apartment on Ölandsgatan.

No one opened the door, even though Hamad rang the doorbell several times. Not until Sjöberg called out to Joakim through the letter box were they let in. Joakim looked devastated, his eyes terrified.

'Why don't you open when the doorbell rings?' Sjöberg said harshly, clomping straight into the living room without taking off his shoes.

Hamad followed and Joakim slunk behind them like a shadow, without saying anything. A middle-aged man was sitting in an armchair with a cigarette in one hand and a rolled-up newspaper in the other. He looked at them with an indifferent air and struck the newspaper against his knees a few times before Sjöberg began to speak.

'Are you Göran Andersson, Joakim's father?'

'Yes. What's he done now?' he retorted, with an almost amused expression.

'Nothing, as far as we know. On the other hand we would like to have a few words with you.'

He took a few quick puffs on his cigarette before he answered, 'You don't say.'

Sjöberg turned on the record function on the MP3 player and set it on the coffee table without asking for permission. Göran Andersson followed his movements with his eyes, but said nothing.

'We have information that you were on board the boat where Jennifer Johansson, Joakim's girlfriend, was murdered. What do you have to say about that?'

Sjöberg made an effort to be strictly factual, without revealing what he was thinking.

'That might be true.'

'For what reason did you make that trip?'

'I guess a little getaway to Finland is never a bad thing.'

'You have a sick wife to take care of in there,' Sjöberg pointed out, gesturing towards the bedroom. 'It seems a bit irresponsible to leave her without supervision for more than twenty-four hours. What do you have to say about that?'

Göran Andersson's eyes flicked suspiciously from Sjöberg to his son.

'Has Joakim –' he said, before Sjöberg interrupted him.

'Joakim has nothing to do with it. I've been here myself and seen her. How can you take off on a Finland cruise with Joakim and leave a family member who is in need of constant care at home alone for such a long time?'

'We didn't travel together,' Joakim interjected.

'No one asked you to open your mouth!' his father shouted.

'I'm the one leading the conversation here,' said Sjöberg without raising his voice, giving the man in the armchair an ice-cold look. 'So you didn't travel together? Then I'm extremely curious about what business you had on that boat.'

'I wanted to check up on what Joakim was up to. He didn't have permission to go.'

'No permission?' Hamad interjected. 'As far as I know, you don't need your father's permission for anything when you're twenty-four years old.'

'As you've seen, his mother needs care.'

'And?' Sjöberg said with feigned surprise. 'Is that Joakim's job? Taking care of your wife?'

'Taking care of his mother is another way to look at it. Yes, that's the arrangement we have. The kid gets paid for it.'

'So, if Joakim happens to be away, you take the opportunity to go away at the same time? So that it's completely certain she gets no care? Mrs Andersson should have had professional help long ago. We're going to report this to social services.'

For the first time Göran Andersson looked bothered.

He did not answer, but instead took a deep drag on the cigarette before he put it out in the ashtray on the table.

'Were you aware that your father was on the boat?' Hamad asked Joakim.

'No,' Joakim answered quietly. 'Not until the morning. He showed up in the breakfast lounge.'

He did not dare look at his father when he answered. Nor could he stand to meet the eyes of the policemen. He stared down at the floor with his arms hanging at his sides.

'Why haven't you told us this before?' asked Sjöberg.

'Why should I have? No one asked. We didn't travel together.'

'But still,' Sjöberg attempted, 'you must have been very surprised when your father suddenly showed up out of nowhere.'

'Yes . . . I guess I was,' Joakim admitted.

'Afraid perhaps?'

Joakim did not answer.

'What did you talk about at breakfast?'

Sjöberg turned back to the father.

'The murder, of course,' the man answered. 'I guess that was all anyone was talking about that morning.'

'Did you know it was Joakim's girlfriend who'd been murdered?'

Göran Andersson was silent for a few seconds before he answered. 'I had my suspicions.'

'How's that? Had you met her?'

'No, I hadn't. But I knew her name.'

'Was it not the case,' Sjöberg suggested sharply, 'that you spent some time in the bar on Saturday evening together with Jennifer Johansson?'

For a fraction of a second Sjöberg thought he saw a shadow pass across Göran Andersson's face before he answered with a surprised laugh.

'Where in the name of God did you get that from? I've never seen her! Until they showed me a picture of her in the morning.'

'And if someone says they've seen you in the bar with her? What do you say to that?'

For the first time during the conversation Joakim looked over at his father. Sjöberg sensed both astonishment and fear in that look. A penny for your thoughts, Joakim, he thought before the father answered.

'That *someone* is not a credible witness.'

'I can tell you a thing or two about credibility,' Hamad said. 'A credible person does not assault his son. A credible person does not live his life in isolation with a seriously ill woman enclosed in a room without care. A credible person does not sleep in the same bed as his adult son.'

During the silence that followed his colleague's unexpected outburst, Sjöberg observed father and son and noted that Joakim was blushing and had turned his eyes down to the floor again, while his father's face was like stone. No one said anything for a long time.

'How do you know Elise Johansson?' Sjöberg broke the silence.

'Who the hell is that?'

'Elise is Jennifer's sister, and we know that you met her a few hours ago.'

'I don't know her.'

'Apparently you know her well enough to spit out a number of ugly things to her. "Aren't you dead, you little whore?" for example. Why did you say that to a fourteen-year-old who has just lost her sister?'

Göran Andersson recovered quickly and answered without any hesitation, 'She looked like that Jennifer. I thought it was her.'

'You can't very well have thought that, because you knew she was dead, didn't you?'

'All the more reason to be surprised,' Göran Andersson observed drily.

'So it was pure surprise that made you say that?'

'Yes, you might say that.'

'Who were you comparing her to?'

'What do you mean, compare?'

'Who were you comparing Elise to?'

'To Jennifer, of course. What kind of crazy questions are these?'

'But you'd never seen her, you say,' Sjöberg continued.

'I saw her on that picture they showed us, damn it.'

'Would that be enough for you to see a similarity between the sisters? A photograph?'

'Apparently,' Joakim's father answered coldly.

'I don't believe that,' Sjöberg continued tirelessly. 'You were with Jennifer in the bar, and that was the image you were comparing Elise with.'

'You can believe what you want.'

'But why did you call her a whore?' asked Hamad.

'I guess I thought she looked like one,' answered Göran Andersson with a crooked smile.

'Do you mean you would say the same sort of thing to anyone at all you think looks sluttish?'

'Anyone at all, I don't know exactly . . .'

Sjöberg did not intend to let him off that easily. He couldn't escape logic just by being shameless.

'You meet a girl in the stairwell outside. You maintain that you've never seen her before, and yet you say, "Aren't you dead, you little whore?" Now I want you to explain to me exactly what was going on in your mind when you said that. Otherwise we're taking you to the police station for interrogation.'

Göran Andersson let out a heavy sigh and finally answered reluctantly. 'There has been one girl in Joakim's life. One girl, and it was that Jennifer. I'd seen the picture of her the police showed. I didn't like it that Joakim was going out with her. She was a bad influence on him. He went to Finland with her, even though I'd told him not to. So when I'm coming up the stairs and I catch sight of Joakim with a girl who I think looks exactly like Jennifer in the picture, I guess something goes wrong in my brain somehow. I didn't really understand what I was seeing. I could only believe that it was her, but she was dead as far as I knew and it came out that way. Just like I said.'

Göran Andersson did not buckle under their pressure. Towards the end of this fruitless interview Hamad took a look around the apartment, and he too caught a glimpse of what Sjöberg had described to him: Joakim's grotesquely overweight mother and the bed he apparently shared with his father. There was nothing more the two policemen could accomplish at the Andersson family home right then. They were preparing to leave when Hamad once again felt forced to bring up what bothered him most.

'Why do two grown men share a bed? Can you explain that to me?'

He directed himself to the father, not to Joakim, but Göran Andersson simply dismissed him with a cold laugh.

'You've seen what's spread out in the double bed. Finally you get pushed off on to the floor, and then the only thing to do was move into the bed where there was still room.'

'But you could easily get another bed,' Hamad suggested sardonically.

'Do you think I'm made of money? The little bastard can move out if he thinks it's too cramped,' replied Göran Andersson, unrolling the newspaper he'd held rolled up in his hand during the entire interview.

Hamad tried to make eye contact with Joakim, but he was occupied by something stuck under his thumbnail. With faint hope that the father intended to devote himself to reading, the two policemen left the apartment.

'There's something about that insult that doesn't sit right,' said Sjöberg when they were down on the street.

'It doesn't mean much more than brat these days,' said Hamad.

'Yes, but for our generation. You don't blurt out such things just like that.'

'Maybe you don't, Conny, but the similarities between you and Göran Andersson are not exactly striking.'

'I don't know,' said Sjöberg doubtfully. 'Both of us are white-collar workers, roughly the same age . . .'

'With his vocabulary you'd think he cleans at the bank.'

'Stop right there. Maybe we shouldn't be so prejudiced.

With your appearance you'd think you clean at the police station.'

Hamad smiled fleetingly, but continued seriously. 'But you have to admit you seldom encounter someone like him when you go to the bank.'

'I'm sure he's not that way at work. It's just at home with the family that that side comes out. Dr Jekyll and Mr Hyde. He's not the only one who lets himself be provoked by the police.'

'He sounded like a longshoreman,' Hamad said.

'I don't think a longshoreman my age would call just anyone a whore.'

'You think maybe there's something more to it?'

'Who knows? I'm thinking about those two Finnish businessmen. Maybe they weren't the only ones Jennifer was misbehaving with on the boat.'

* * *

'Is your mum or dad there?'

Didn't the voice sound a little familiar?

'Who is this?' Hanna asked, curious.

There was silence on the line.

'Is it Björn?' asked Hanna. 'It sounds like Björn.'

'Yes, it's Björn. I thought I would just have a few words with your mum or dad, and make sure it's okay for me to come over and visit you this evening.'

'Mummy moved away, I told you. And Daddy is in Japan. You know that!'

'Sorry, I forgot. So do you still want me to come over?'

'Yes, you promised!' said Hanna. 'And you're going to bring sweets and hamburgers.'

'I'll do that. See you in a little while.'

'Bye!'

Excited and expectant, she put the receiver back in the cradle, but she had just climbed down from the chair when the phone rang again.

'Hi, this is Hanna. Is this Björn?'

'Holgersson, Hammarby Police.'

'You sound crabby.'

'Is your mother or father there?'

'They don't want to talk to you.'

'They can decide that for themselves. Would you please get one of them?'

'No, I won't.'

'Just do it now, please.'

'Why are you so angry?'

'Get them now, otherwise I'm coming to see you.'

That would not do, that crabby old man couldn't come here. Björn was coming and no angry policeman was going to spoil that.

'Daddy went to get hamburgers,' said Hanna, in a friendlier voice now. 'He'll be back soon. Wait a minute and you can talk to him when he gets here.'

'So you're not at home alone?'

Hanna hesitated only for a moment before she answered, 'No, Daddy's with me.'

'That's good to hear,' said the voice. 'Bye now.'

Hanna hung up, relieved at not having to talk to that nagging man any more. You could tell from his voice that he didn't like children. He had a voice like Aunt Hedda.

She had not even reached the floor when the phone rang a third time.

'Who is this now?' she answered, still irritated after the last call.

'Hi, this is Einar. I'm a policeman. I would like to speak to your mother or father.'

'Was it you who just called?' Hanna wanted to know.

'No, why do you think that?'

'Because he was a policeman too.'

'What are you saying? What was his name?'

'His name was Hammarby Police,' Hanna replied.

She heard him laughing at the other end. This policeman's voice sounded much nicer.

'So what did he want?' asked the policeman.

'He wanted to talk to Mummy or Daddy too,' Hanna answered truthfully.

'So did he?'

Hanna hesitated for a moment before she answered, 'Yes, he talked to Daddy.'

'I'd like to have a word with him as well.'

'That's not possible now, because he went to get hamburgers for us. But if you wait for a while, you can talk to him,' she added.

'Otherwise your mother will be just fine,' said the friendly policeman.

'But she's not home. Do you want to wait for Daddy?'

'I'll call again in a little while. Bye now, Hanna.'

When she was back in the living room in front of the TV the phone rang again. The phone is ringing off the hook, thought Hanna. Daddy always said that. But this time she did not even bother to answer.

Tuesday Evening

Hamad headed for the metro to Thorildsplan to confront the bartender Juha Lehto with the pictures of Sören Andersson and Joakim's father, Göran Andersson. It was Lehto's girlfriend who let him in. She was a short woman in her thirties with a cheerful, open appearance. For some reason it surprised Hamad that she spoke Swedish without a Finnish accent, but when he remembered that her name was Britt-Marie Lundholm it made sense.

'Juha is on the phone, but he's expecting you. Come in and have a cup of coffee. Do you drink coffee?'

Hamad suddenly noticed how hungry he was and in the hope of getting something edible to go with it he said yes. She showed him into the kitchen and he took one of the two chairs at the small kitchen table. He heard a male voice from inside the closed door to an adjacent room that he assumed was the bedroom.

'I have some rolls in the freezer I can heat up if you'd like.'

'That would be great,' said Hamad gratefully. 'Do you work at Viking Line too?' he asked, to avoid seeming to eavesdrop on the phone call going on in the background.

'No, I work at a shoe shop in the city,' she answered as she put the rolls on a plate and into the microwave.

They made small talk for a few minutes until the microwave beeped, just as the door to the bedroom opened.

Lehto greeted Hamad and sat down across from him. The girlfriend discreetly left the kitchen.

'Have you thought any more about what happened?' Hamad asked, taking a bite of one of the rolls.

It felt impolite to be eating in front of someone who wasn't, but he pushed the thought aside and tried to take small bites.

'Of course I have,' Lehto answered in his melodic dialect. 'It's pretty hard to think about anything else. But it feels like I've thought about it too much, if you know what I mean. It's like I don't know any more if I'm thinking about what happened or my memory of it.'

'I can understand that,' said Hamad. 'It's a common phenomenon in witness psychology. But you're aware of it anyway, and that's a good thing. So you have nothing to add to your previous testimony?'

'No, unfortunately not.'

From the briefcase Hamad dug out an envelope that he had prepared before leaving the police station, and from it he removed ten photographs depicting middle-aged men, only two of whom he knew.

'I'd like to know if you recognize any of these men,' he explained, placing the pictures in a row in front of Lehto.

Lehto sat quietly for a few minutes and Hamad studied his reaction with tense expectation. He could see the bartender's eyes running back and forth across the photographs. Finally Lehto revealed his thoughts.

'I recognized one of them immediately, but I wanted to be sure of myself and not say anything too soon. This is the man in the bar,' he said, pointing at one of the photographs. 'Small, mean eyes.'

Hamad picked the photograph up from the table and viewed it with satisfaction.

'You're sure of that?' he asked to be on the safe side.

'I'm completely sure of it,' Lehto confirmed.

* * *

Lisa's Café was open in the evening for once. Lisa was stocktaking and thought that this boring but necessary task would be more fun with customers around. Sjöberg was not much company, however, submerged in his own thoughts.

An extremely overweight woman, somewhat older than himself and possibly a little drunk, came into the café and sat down at the neighbouring table with her back to him. She was babbling ceaselessly about first one thing, then another with everyone in the place except Sjöberg, who had the good fortune to be at a kind of dead angle to her. He was not paying attention to what she was saying, but something about her reminded him of his night-time walk with Margit Olofsson. Perhaps it was the hennaed hair, perhaps something familiar in the voice, or perhaps simply her way of taking the whole world in her embrace. There was also the possibility, of course, that Sjöberg's musings had nothing to do with the talkative woman. Perhaps it was the short break in itself that allowed his thoughts to run away. Because whenever he was not occupied with something else she was always making an appearance. Margit. He barely knew her, and yet there was something about her that felt like home. There it was again, that word. Home.

In logical terms, Margit Olofsson was the opposite of home. Right now she was the greatest threat to everything the word 'home' stood for. She had rocked the foundations of his existence and there was nothing positive about that. Absolutely nothing. Yet here he was daydreaming back to that night. A walk, a kiss – that was all there was to it. But still, there was something else too. An aroma, warmth. Security? What kind of security is it that turns everything upside down? Push it away; shut it down.

In front of him was his second cup of coffee, a plate with an almost finished egg-and-anchovy sandwich and a tabloid that he was now leafing through again. Both his own case and Petra's got quite a bit of space today, and he noted that the paper's depiction of the police department's work was not particularly flattering. Even though they were working their butts off, they did not have anything concrete to report to the press. So the articles contained no new facts, only even sharper criticism of their work. But tomorrow they would get pictures of the dead mother and her boy – he and Petra had agreed on that – so then the reporters would have something to feed on. His musings were interrupted by a vibration in his pocket.

'Jamal here. We've identified the man in the bar.'

'No doubts?'

'Lehto was dead certain about it.'

'How many pictures did he have to choose from?'

'Ten.'

'That's good.'

'Where are you?'

'At Lisa's.'

'I'm on the metro between Thorildsplan and Fridhems-plan. There's a hold-up. Power cut. It might take a long time, they say. Have you finished eating?'

'More or less. Okay, out with it now, damn it.'

'I suggest you immediately make another visit to Ölandsgatan.'

'Of course.' Sjöberg ended the call, breaking into a big smile.

Fifteen minutes later he was sitting on the edge of the dark-green couch again, across from Göran Andersson. Joakim was not there this time; Sjöberg had asked him to go out for a while, so that he could speak to his father in private.

The father no longer looked so insolent; his gaze wandered and he avoided eye contact. It struck Sjöberg that perhaps Göran Andersson felt more secure when there were several people around than when he was subjected to a single individual's penetrating gaze. Possibly his son's presence may also have changed his attitude. For the worse, it seemed. The aggressiveness seemed to have run out of him completely now, and he seemed mainly uncertain rather than angry and condescending. Perhaps he felt the thumbscrews being tightened. Perhaps the police showing up twice in such a short interval had helped him to understand the seriousness of the situation.

'Okay, now. So, I'm back already,' Sjöberg began. 'It didn't take long for us to round up reliable witness information that unambiguously points you out as the person sitting in the bar with Jennifer Johansson a few hours before the murder.'

Göran Andersson fumbled with his cigarette pack and

finally managed to get one out, which he lit with a match. He glared at the MP3 player on the table and did not answer.

'You can continue to deny it, of course. That doesn't put you in a better light, as I'm sure you understand,' Sjöberg continued. 'Even if we still have no technical evidence that confirms this testimony, three independent witnesses, all of whom point you out, weigh very heavily in this context.'

Admittedly the two Finnish businessmen had not been confronted with the pictures yet, but Sjöberg saw no reason to reveal that fact right now. He studied how Joakim's father took a deep drag and coughed. He was off balance now; Sjöberg felt it instinctively. He blew out the smoke and followed it with his eyes for a while before he finally spoke.

'I sat with the girl briefly in the bar. But so what? I didn't kill her. I bought her a beer, nothing more.'

'According to our witnesses you were threatening her. What reason did you have for that?'

'Threatening?'

'They claim you were heavy-handed with her and said unpleasant things. Until someone came to her rescue. Did you know who she was?'

Göran Andersson let out a dejected sigh. 'Yes, I knew who she was.'

'How did you end up in the bar together? Did you follow her?'

'No, I didn't follow her. I was just sitting down in the bar when I caught sight of her. I knew immediately that it was her.'

'Joakim's girlfriend?'

'No, I didn't realize that until later. When the police

showed me the photograph and said her name. Jennifer – that's fairly uncommon.'

'What do you mean you knew who she was? Had you met her in some other connection?'

Göran Andersson took a few quick puffs on the cigarette and tapped off a pillar of ash against the edge of the now almost full ashtray on the table. The man must smoke like a chimney, Sjöberg thought. The contents of the ashtray had increased noticeably since he had last seen it just over an hour before.

'Yes, I had met her earlier,' Göran Andersson admitted. 'Or . . . I thought I had. Now I'm not so sure.'

'You're going to have to try to be a little clearer,' said Sjöberg authoritatively.

'A lookalike showed up. The sister, I mean. That Elise or whatever the hell her name is.'

'You can't tell them apart?' Sjöberg helped out.

'It doesn't seem like it.'

'So in the bar on the Finland ferry you didn't know that the girl you were talking with was Joakim's girlfriend, but you still recognized her from before?'

Andersson nodded.

'But today when Elise showed up, it occurred to you that maybe it was actually her that you'd met before,' Sjöberg summarized. 'Resulting in the attack in the stairwell.'

Andersson nodded again.

'Now we're getting somewhere. Why the aggressive treatment? Why did you call her a whore?'

Göran Andersson took a last puff on his cigarette and put it out. Sjöberg waited patiently until he had finished.

'Joakim was on his way out on Friday night. He was going

to meet Jennifer, he said. I couldn't allow him to do that, but then he got angry and said he was going on a Finland cruise with her the next day. It was completely out of the question for him to go along, so we had a little tussle about that.'

'A little tussle?' Sjöberg repeated. 'You beat him black and blue. That's called assault and it's a crime.'

Göran Andersson did not counter Sjöberg's accusations and did not look him in the eyes. Sjöberg saw how he was shrinking up into the little piece of shit that he was. The faulty structure was starting to shake on its foundations.

'I thought we'd agreed that he should stay home. Joakim fell asleep and I went to bed,' Andersson continued.

You beat him unconscious, you miserable creep, thought Sjöberg.

'When I got up a few hours later he was gone. He had gone out, even though he wasn't supposed to. I went out in my car to search for him. I drove around for a while, without success. On Skånegatan a girl suddenly came rushing towards me. She waved and waved and when I stopped she started banging on the door. She pulled open the door and got in on the passenger side and I asked what she wanted. She wanted a ride; she was in a hurry to get home, she said. I thought it seemed more like she was in a hurry to get away from there. She was drunk as hell too; she reeked of alcohol. "What will I get for it?" I asked. I wanted to mess with her a little; she did just get in the car without having the green light, so to speak. "I'll show you my pussy, you dirty old man, just drive!" she screamed.'

Göran Andersson fell silent and started fumbling for another cigarette in the pack.

'And you let her do that,' Sjöberg filled in.

'She just did it. As soon as I started driving she pulled up her knees and spread. She had on a very short skirt and no panties.'

'And so was this Jennifer Johansson or her sister, Elise?'

'I'm starting to think it was Elise, but I'm still not completely sure. The girl in the car and the one in the bar the next evening looked exactly alike to me and had similar clothes on.'

'Very short skirt?' asked Sjöberg.

'No, it was a leather jacket with pockets and buttons and shit on it. And they had the same slutty look.'

'What did you and Jennifer talk about in the bar?'

'I asked her if she was drunk again. She looked puzzled and didn't seem to recognize me. I told her she should knock it off with the whorishness, but she was completely blank. That's what makes me think now that she wasn't the one in the car; it was the other one instead. Because *she* on the other hand looked completely terrified when she caught sight of me.'

'And then what happened? In the bar, I mean.'

'Some guy she knew came and she went off with him.'

'And you?'

'I left the place.'

'Did you see her again during the trip?' asked Sjöberg.

'No, I didn't see her again. And I didn't kill her,' Göran Andersson added. 'Why the hell would I have done that?'

'You've been lying pretty freely up till now,' Sjöberg pointed out sharply.

'But, what the hell! When I realized who'd been murdered and that someone might have seen us together . . . I didn't want to admit that.'

'Innocent people tell the police the truth as a rule,' said Sjöberg, glancing at his watch. 'I have to ask you to come to the station tomorrow. We'll need your fingerprints and samples for DNA analysis.'

'I've got a job to take care of –'

'So do I,' Sjöberg ended the conversation.

* * *

A few yards from them, but so far away she was in another world, her own world, Kerstin was trying to hear what they were talking about. She had turned off the wall-mounted TV for once; she had recognized the voice. It was the policeman's voice, the one with the friendly eyes who had talked to her as if she were a thinking person, as if she understood. He had been upset, raised his voice, but he had talked *to* her, not *about* her. He was going to contact social services, he said, take her away from here. Was that what they were talking about out there? She was ready for it now, felt that life perhaps still had something to offer. She had rid herself of Göran; it had taken time, but now he no longer existed for her. She no longer existed for him. During the past few years she had seen him only a few times.

Kerstin had once been beautiful. Interested in fashion and careful about her appearance. She worked in one of the concession shops in NK's men's department. Göran could not tolerate that she spent her days there, surrounded by men. Because of that, she had never gone back to work after her maternity leave. He had loved owning her, showing her off. But when someone looked too long he hit her. Not right then, but afterwards, when no one was watching. It was an impossible equation to solve, and she was weak, could not put up any resistance. She did not dare leave him, did not know any other way to live.

But she found a way. When Joakim was born she had a hard time getting rid of all the pounds she put on during pregnancy. Göran criticized her, wanted her to be beautiful, perfect. He didn't stop hitting her, but it happened less often. Other men stopped eating her with their eyes and Göran lost interest in her as a woman. It was a more comfortable way to live. When he was gone she sat at home and did nothing. Watched TV and ate. She and Joakim took care of each other. As she grew, Göran shrank, as a person and as a man. He became ashamed of her, forbade her to show herself. Finally she disgusted him; he did not want to see her at all, did not want to hold her. Did not even want to hit her.

But she had Joakim. Kerstin's world consisted of Joakim and herself. To Joakim she was someone. He took good care of her, made sure she was clean and had enough to eat, and kept her company. They talked to each other. If it hadn't been for her, he would have left home long ago. She did not want to begrudge him that. Since the policeman with the friendly eyes had been there that morning, they had talked about the future, she and Joakim. He had money now; he had worked hard and saved. When they took her away he would go with her. He would get a

318

life of his own, but he would continue to be part of hers. He assured her that she would get healthy, and she wanted to believe him, she felt ready to try.

The door closed; it was not quite time yet.

* * *

Finally, finally, finally the doorbell rang! It must be Björn arriving, because now it really was evening. It was completely dark outside and the children's programmes she had been watching had finished a long time ago. Hanna rushed out into the hall and called loudly so it could be heard outside.

'Hello! Is that Björn?'

'Ssh, take it easy,' a voice hissed through the letter box. 'Is that you, Hanna?'

'Yes, it's me,' Hanna whispered back.

'Is anyone else at home?'

'No, just me.'

She was so excited she could not stand still. She clapped her hands together in front of her chest and her feet tramped eagerly on the spot. Her secret friend had finally come!

'Do you think your keys work?' she asked anxiously, but she got no answer, because the letter box closed with a bang.

She stood attentively, looking at the closed door and listening for sounds from outside. Suddenly there was a rattle in the lock and she could see the knob on the inside moving a little. Hanna made small, expectant hops, then she ran up to the door and pulled on the handle, but nothing happened. She backed up a few steps and heard another key being put in the upper lock now and twisted around. The handle was pulled carefully down and now the door was really opening! In the doorway a man appeared; he had a finger to his lips as a signal to remain silent. Hanna did not say anything, but her whole face was one big smile. The man slipped quickly into the hall and quietly closed the door behind him. Only then did he answer her smile and get down on his knees on the rug. The tension was released and Hanna threw herself into his arms. Björn – the only one who had listened to her. It was almost as if Daddy had come home.

She could not see his face now when they were hugging, but she felt his big, warm hands as he caressed her hair and back, and it felt so nice to have someone with her again. She wanted to fall asleep like that, right there in Björn's soft embrace, but then her eyes fell on the familiar paper bag he had set down on the floor when she came running towards him, and hunger got the upper hand.

'McDonald's!' she cried.

He set her down on the floor and stood up.

'Of course!' he said with a smile. 'A promise is a promise.'

He looked at her as she stood there beaming at him.

'You're a pretty little person,' he said. 'How old are you, Hanna?'

'I'm this many,' answered Hanna, waggling the three fingers that she held up in the air before him. 'But soon I'll be this many,' she continued, raising another finger.

'How clever you are to manage all by yourself here at home,' he praised her. 'But it smells a little bad in here. I think we'll have to take a bath once we've eaten.'

'Yes!' said Hanna. 'Are you going to take a bath too? Are you dirty?'

'I'm probably a little dirty. If you want, we can take a bath together.'

Hanna was not used to this. Her parents never bathed with her. They always said the bathtub was too small, that it was cramped to sit in if you were a grown-up. But Björn – he didn't care about that; she had made a really good secret friend.

'Of course,' said Hanna. 'But first I want to eat hamburgers.'

She took him by the hand and led him into the kitchen. Half-empty and empty packets lay in a mess of melted ice and food scraps. The kitchen didn't smell that good either, but he didn't scold her like Mummy would have.

'Is there another table we can sit at?' he asked. 'Then we won't have to clean in here,' he added with a wink.

That's a good idea, thought Hanna. 'We can sit in my room, because you can't eat in the living room. Everything's so nice and expensive there.'

She went ahead of him into the children's room and sat down on one of the little chairs by the little table. She swept the bookmarks and toys on to the floor with her arm and looked up at her secret friend with a happy smile.

'Now we can eat!' she said, pulling him down on to the chair beside hers.

Just as they were about to begin the phone rang. Hanna got up and started running towards the hall.

'Don't answer, Hanna,' said Björn. 'Don't worry if it rings. I'm here now.'

Hanna stopped in the doorway.

'But what if it's Mummy!'

'It's not. Sit down.'

Another ring.

'But what if it's the police!'

'The police?' said Björn, looking concerned.

'There was an angry policeman who called and said that he would come if he didn't get to talk to Daddy,' Hanna explained.

A third ring sounded in the apartment.

'Where's the phone?' asked Björn, suddenly getting up and rushing out of the room.

'In the hall!' Hanna called after him.

Just after the fourth ring, Hanna heard Björn's calm voice from out in the hallway.

'Hedberg residence . . . Of course . . . I understand . . . No problem . . . Bye.'

* * *

Einar Eriksson had called that number many times without getting any answer. When someone finally picked up it was a little girl, who said that her father was only out for a little while. That proved to be correct. Eriksson removed the Hedberg family at Ploggatan 20 from his list.

* * *

Hoping that the train would soon start moving, Hamad decided to stay seated. The alternative was to go by foot to Fridhemsplan and then look for a bus that might take him in the direction of Skanstull. While he waited he took the opportunity to call Westman, whom he had not had a glimpse of in several days. Except when she – as he interpreted it – left Sjöberg's office in tears a few hours earlier.

'It's Jamal. How are you doing?' he asked gently.

'Fine,' Westman answered curtly. 'How are things going for you?'

'Moving along. Was something wrong before?'

'No, why do you think that?'

'Petra, I *saw* it. Tell me what's happening.'

'Nothing is happening.'

'Don't try. I could see on your face when you went into Sjöberg's office that you were prepared for the worst. I heard in his voice that he wasn't very happy either. Did he reprimand you?'

'On the contrary,' Westman answered cryptically.

'Later he basically interrogated me about what we were doing last Friday evening,' Hamad continued stubbornly. 'Did something happen after we went our separate ways?'

'Nada. Nothing.'

'Okay, then I guess there's nothing –'

'Okay.'

Hamad sighed audibly and gave up.

'You know you can come to me, Petra. *If* there is something. See you.'

'All right. Thanks for calling anyway.'

'You're welcome,' he muttered to himself as he stuffed the phone into his pocket and went back to staring alternately out of the window and at his watch.

*

The train was stuck between stations for forty-five minutes. The satisfaction of getting Joakim's father identified as the man seen in the bar with Jennifer gradually diminished as time passed. It was sheer luck. If Elise had not gone to see Joakim and run into his father, perhaps they never would have discovered it.

Andersson. That was not a name that leaped out at you when you were staring intently at long lists. And another Andersson had also shown up as a person of interest in the investigation: Sören Andersson. It struck Hamad how their interest in him had suddenly diminished. How had that happened? Hamad tried to replay the conversation with Elise Johansson. They had pressured her concerning Sören Andersson and his wallet. After a lot of evasion she finally admitted that she had acquired it on Friday and not on Sunday as she had said earlier. But she still refused to admit that she had stolen it.

Then she blurted out that bit about Joakim's father, which they had quickly followed up. All suspicion was now focused on him. Correctly perhaps, but where did *Sören* Andersson go? Could it be pure coincidence that Elise shows up at the police station with a wallet that belongs to a passenger on the ferry where her sister was murdered? The thought was gnawing at him during the whole journey back to Södermalm. He tried several times to call Sjöberg, but he seemed to have his phone turned off. Not until Slussen did he get a response. They agreed to meet outside the barriers at the metro entrance at Skanstull.

* * *

Sjöberg took his jacket from the hook, pulled it on and stuffed the MP3 player in his pocket. He went out to the corridor and was walking in the direction of the stairs when it struck him that perhaps he ought to check in with Petra before he took off. He turned and went over to her office a little further down the corridor. The door was open and she was sitting at the desk, looking as if she was working. He knocked softly on the doorpost and stepped in. She looked up at him with a tired smile.

'Have you heard anything?' he asked, sitting down on the visitor's chair with his hands pushed down in his jacket pockets.

'No, I'm still here,' Petra answered a little wearily. 'Have you heard anything?'

Sjöberg shook his head.

'No news is good news,' he answered, without for a moment believing that. 'But we're going to get through this, don't worry.'

Petra sighed and set her elbows on the desk, letting her chin rest on her thumbs.

'Thanks for your support, Conny. I appreciate it.'

'The centre of gravity, Petra. Make sure you have your centre of gravity in the right place when they come after you.'

Petra straightened up and leaned back in the chair with a laugh. She laced her fingers behind her neck and suddenly looked completely relaxed, almost at peace, Sjöberg noted. Maybe that thing about centre of gravity wasn't so silly after all.

Yet another knock at the door and the deputy police commissioner stepped into the room with a serious expression. Sjöberg gave him a tired glance and then looked at his watch.

'Gunnar,' he said guardedly. 'Are you here this late?'

'Good that you're here, Sjöberg. I need to talk to both of you. We've looked at your case now, Westman, and have decided that we should go easy on you. At the police commissioner's recommendation we're choosing to avoid court. On condition that you resign. That way this will stay between us, and you'll be spared the embarrassment of being fired . . . and the gossip among your colleagues that would follow.'

Factually and without a trace of Schadenfreude. He was simply doing his job. Petra sat as if petrified as the information sank in.

She did not know how to react. Was this positive – losing your job but escaping jibes in the corridor?

'Court?' said Sjöberg. 'What would the classification of the crime be in that case?'

'Sexual harassment, of course,' answered Malmberg, standing with his legs apart and his hands in his trouser pockets.

He looked like a well-ironed cowboy. On most men this would have appeared pathetic, but for him it seemed quite natural. A ten-pointer, thought Petra. A winner on all levels. Sjöberg was thinking nothing of the kind as he sat, still with his hands in his jacket pockets, lightly tapping his fingers on the MP3 player.

'And how would you define sexual harassment?' he asked, with stoic calm.

'Well, in this case it's rather simple,' said Malmberg with a joyless smile that revealed a perfect row of teeth. 'Do I need to describe the content of that e-mail to the police commissioner?'

'Not at all,' Sjöberg replied. 'I'm thinking like this: Let's say that a high-level superior calls a female employee – who is in a subordinate position – into his office, and entices her with a reservation, already made, to one of Stockholm's best restaurants and a room at the city's finest hotel. When she says no, he tries to pull her on to his lap and caresses her behind. Would you characterize that as sexual harassment?'

'Of course, Sjöberg,' laughed Malmberg, 'but that never happened.'

'And if I can prove it?' Sjöberg continued, and Petra could almost see sparks flying from him now. 'You can tell the police commissioner from me that I have confirmation from Mathias Dahlgren that there was a table reserved by Brandt for eight o'clock yesterday evening. And I have confirmation from Grand Hotel that Brandt reserved a double room there yesterday, and that it was cancelled at the same time as the restaurant reservation.'

A raised eyebrow was all that revealed that Malmberg had not been prepared for this. Petra held her breath as she followed the exchange.

'And I should thank you for this, Petra,' said Sjöberg, now suddenly waving the MP3 player. 'It was prudent of you to have it turned on. It will come in handy at the hearings.'

Suddenly she realized what he was up to and a broad smile spread across her face, still leaning back in the chair with her hands behind her neck. The only thing to do was play along.

'No problem, Conny. You can take care of it for now.'

'What do you mean, hearings?' asked Malmberg.

His neutral facial expression had suddenly shifted to something more human.

'What Westman and I were just discussing,' Sjöberg answered calmly. 'We intend to file a report against the police commissioner for sexual harassment. There are also clear elements of abuse of authority as well, which we think we may pursue further.'

Petra listened attentively, completely taken by surprise by Sjöberg's initiative.

'I knew nothing about this,' said Malmberg, starting towards the door. 'I'll have to talk to the police commissioner and hear what he says.'

'Tell Roland I'm sorry if I offended him,' said Petra, strengthened by Sjöberg's priceless improvisation.

Malmberg suddenly stopped and turned towards them with a decisive look.

'I suggest we agree that this conversation never took place,' he said. 'I feel sure that the police commissioner will share my understanding.'

'I haven't heard a thing,' said Sjöberg with a wink in Petra's direction. 'And I haven't seen any provocative e-mail either,' he added to be on the safe side.

'Deal,' muttered Malmberg.

'By the way, Gunnar,' Sjöberg added. 'Brandt promised to give Sandén's daughter a trial as an assistant in reception. Please see to it that that's done.'

'Sure,' answered the deputy police commissioner resignedly and he left the office.

* * *

'Before you tell me how it went with Göran Andersson, I just want to say one thing,' Hamad began when he met Sjöberg at Skanstull. 'So that it doesn't drown in other interesting facts like last time.'

Sjöberg nodded attentively.

'I think we dismissed the suspicions against Sören Andersson far too casually. When Joakim's father showed up in the investigation, we focused all our attention on him. There's nothing strange about that, but I just want to point out that we're not through with Sören Andersson. That's all I wanted to say.'

'You're very right, Jamal. Elise was up to no good last Friday and now we're going to talk to her about that. This time we won't give up until she tells us the whole truth.'

Once again they made their way to the Johansson family apartment at Ringen, while Sjöberg briefly recounted how the conversation with Göran Andersson had developed.

Elise was in bed, fully clothed under the covers, listening to music on her iPod. She had earphones on and did not hear when they knocked, so they stepped into the room unannounced. Hamad closed the door behind them to dampen the commotion from the kitchen and living room where life went on as usual. Elise sat up with a start, giving them a somewhat harried look. Sjöberg thought her eyes looked red and wondered whether reality had finally caught up with her.

'Hi, Elise. Here we are again,' said Sjöberg apologetically, throwing out his arms.

Elise pulled the earphones out and started tapping on her iPod. She did not answer, but reached for her cigarettes while she got out of bed. Then she sank down on the floor with her back against one of the cupboards. Hamad did the same, but Sjöberg considered himself too old for such things and sat down on the only chair in the room.

'Now we want to hear what really happened last Friday night,' said Sjöberg. 'We know more or less what you were doing, but we'd like to hear it in your own words.'

'Has he – ?' Elise began, but stopped herself.

'Has who?' Sjöberg echoed encouragingly.

'Has anyone said anything?'

'Someone has said something, yes. But now I want to hear you say it.'

'Say what?'

'What you were doing last Friday. We know you're not doing too well right now, Elise, but you have to talk. It's important. We think you can help us find the person who murdered Jennifer.'

She tapped a cigarette out of the pack and put it in her mouth. Sjöberg tossed her a box of matches from the desk, and no one said anything until she had lit her cigarette.

'I'm just so scared,' she said with a sigh, and for the first time she looked Sjöberg in the eyes without immediately turning away.

There was silence for a few seconds before she continued.

'I know you're going to think I'm a slut, but I was drunk and stupid and . . . Well, I guess it's genetic,' she said, nodding towards the door. 'But I am never, ever going to do it again. I've learned that at least.'

*

Then Elise finally told them. It felt liberating. She was ashamed of her story, but it was still good to get it out. As if some of the shame released its hold on her. She told them how she and Jennifer had been sitting there on the kitchen floor, with their mother and her friends carrying on in the background, smoking and drinking. How they had chatted about this and that, nothing important, just keeping each other company.

As she painted the picture of how she and her big sister had spent their last moments together, it suddenly became so clear to her. The loss of someone to share this fate, her childhood with, hit her like a kick in the gut. She felt the tears welling up in her eyes and the words sticking in her throat, but she didn't care. It was so nice just to share her thoughts with someone. So she talked, while the tears streamed down her cheeks. She told them how the intoxication had put her in a good mood, made her strong and brave. How on that final evening she had unexpectedly got to borrow her sister's new leather jacket, how she had met Nina down on the street, Nina who had money and who whispered and pointed out the 'paedophile' to her, the disgusting old man who groped little girls. She told them how she had gone up to him and made her idiotic offer. Which she would regret for the rest of her life.

She walked three steps behind him all the way to the car park at Bjurholmsplan, where he had left his car, a dirty white Opel. He unlocked the door on his side and got into the driver's seat, then leaned over to the passenger door and opened it for her. She looked around before she got into the car, as if to make sure that no one noticed them and understood what they were going to do.

Elise felt exhilarated and wild. It was one of those divinely inspired intoxications where all the barriers come down and the rules loosen up and become meaningless. She imagined that this was how it felt to do drugs; it was like you put yourself outside your real self, become immortal and just live life here and now. She was bubbling inside. He drove silent and resolute through lively blocks, single-mindedly headed towards more deserted areas. She tried to talk to him, but he was taciturn and uninterested. Asked what he was going to do over the weekend; she was going to Åbo on Viking Line, she lied to make herself interesting, but he wasn't going to do anything, didn't want to talk about anything. She studied him covertly as he drove with his eyes rigidly fixed on the street ahead of them. How old could he be? Fifty maybe, or seventy? Hard to say: he was an old man anyway. Not clean. Greasy hair hung down over his ears and he had an unfashionable old man's jacket on. His hands on top of the steering wheel were skinny and hairy. His profile was okay, but the skin on his face had large pores, and it was greasy too.

He turned on to a side street. On one side were several slumbering houses with the lights turned off, and on the other a number of sweet little allotment cabins. It was calm and deserted; there was no one out and about at this time of day. In the turning area where Vitabergsparken started he stopped and turned off the engine. When the car lights were turned off it became almost completely dark around them. Elise did not know what to do. The situation was completely new to her, but she did not want to appear inexperienced. He turned slowly towards her and looked at her with empty eyes. Not at her face; his gaze swept across her body.

'The money first,' she managed to say.

Her heart was pounding in her chest, but for some reason she did not feel the least bit afraid. He did as she said and pulled the wallet out of the inside pocket of his jacket, took two hundred-kronor bills out and put them in her outstretched hand. She quickly put them in her jacket pocket while he set the wallet down by the gearstick, between them. She followed his hand with her eyes and it came towards her and settled on her bare thigh. He moved it a few times up and down along her leg and she heard him begin to breathe more intensely.

'How old are you?' he asked.

'Sixteen,' Elise lied, not really knowing why.

'What's your name?'

'Jennifer,' she answered, as if to further confirm her age.

'Pull up your sweater,' he ordered her, and she did as she was told.

'Turn this way,' he said, and she turned towards him.

It felt stupid to just sit there, with her sweater up to her neck, and watch as the strange man started touching himself outside his trousers to the sound of heavy breathing. She remained sitting like that for several minutes and she did not move an inch during that time. Then he unbuttoned his trousers and pulled down his zip, then raised himself up a little on the seat and with some effort pulled his trousers and pants down to his knees. This was a strange sight: a man exposing himself in a dark car and she herself beside him with bare breasts.

'Take off your knickers and sit so I can see you,' he ordered her.

Elise wriggled the knickers off under her skirt and put them in her pocket. She crawled up with both feet on the seat and legs tight together, but his hand was there at once prying her knees apart. She stayed seated that way, with her back resting uncomfortably against the door and her legs parted, while he started stroking himself back and forth and moaning as if he were in pain. He wanted to touch her and again and again his free hand groped between her legs. But Elise stuck to her guns and pushed his hand away each time.

'Not that,' she said firmly.

'What the hell?' he complained, while his hand worked faster and faster and the expressionless, introverted gaze fixed on her crotch.

Elise thought he was repulsive with his nasty moaning and she tried to think about something other than the image of herself together with that creep. Her eyes moved from his hard dick and the hairy hand's rhythmic movements to the wallet lying there at her feet. It would be so easy, she thought, just to take it and run away. With her head start she would be gone by the time he got his trousers on and ran after her or got the car started.

Now his moans were louder and more drawn out. She realized that it was almost over and just as it started squirting, her hand was there grabbing the wallet. Before he could react she had the door open and was on her way out of the car. She did not bother to slam the car door behind her, just took to her heels and ran, ran for all she was worth.

'You little whore!' she heard from inside the car behind her. 'What the hell are you doing? I'm going to . . .'

That was the last thing she heard him say. She ran and ran and not until she was a fair distance away did she hear a car engine gunning. The tyres squealed and the car thudded; maybe he drove into a lamp post or something. Then it was quiet. Before she disappeared around the street corner she turned around and looked back at him one last time. Now he was out of the car and looked as if he intended to chase after her on foot. But she was faster. After a span of time that felt like an eternity, a car, a green Toyota, came slowly from a cross street, and she rushed out in front of it and waved her arms at the astonished driver who stopped the car. She banged hard on the window on the passenger side and pulled open the door.

'You have to give me a ride; I'm in a hurry to get home!' she commanded breathlessly, throwing herself on to the seat and pulling the door shut.

The driver eyed her curiously without making any move to do as he was told.

'Just drive, damn it!' she screamed, surprised at her own assertiveness.

'Well, well,' the man sighed, letting the car start to roll. 'So what do I get for it?'

'I'll show you my pussy, you dirty old man!' Elise screamed, *creeping up in the seat in the way she had just done, with legs parted and with no knickers on under her skirt.*

It did not feel nearly as dramatic this time; now it was more like a punishment, a punishment for all the sick bastards out there in the world who didn't care how she was doing. She remained sitting like that for a long time and the man studied her now and then while he drove, but he drove away from Vitabergsparken, away from the white Opel and that was all she cared about. When her pulse started to normalize and the adrenaline subsided, she put her feet on the floor, cleared her throat and said in as normal a voice as she could manage, 'You can let me off at Ringen, please.'

He did not answer, but drove her where she wanted without further comment.

'I don't know what got into me,' Elise ended her story, drying her cheeks with the back of her hand.

'You were drunk,' Sjöberg observed calmly. 'You're fourteen years old and fourteen-year-olds should not drink alcohol.'

'What will you do with me now?'

'Nothing,' Sjöberg replied. 'Your future is in your own hands. But if you need someone to talk to, I can help you with that.'

* * *

Barbro intended to stop early and rest after her adventurous few days, but thoughts of the little girl would not leave her alone. She wandered back and forth in her apartment, stopping now and then by the living-room window and looking down at the street outside. Beyond the parked cars along the pavement, the barberry hedge that surrounded the building opposite and its neglected lawn glistened in the glow of the streetlights. A quiet rain was falling over the city and she was grateful that it had held off until now. Someone had optimistically set out several paper bags full of newspapers for recycling outside the entrance, but it seemed probable they would collapse before morning.

She wanted to call that Holgersson, but she expected he had gone home for the day and it was highly unlikely that they would give out his mobile or home number. You had to assume that the police were doing their job, she thought with a sigh. At Hanna's no one answered. Barbro had done what she could, and it appeared that the girl was now in good hands. Whether it was the father who was with her or the police who were on their way, it was all the same; Hanna was taken care of, and that was the main thing. Barbro could let the whole thing go.

But something wouldn't let her. Thoughts were grinding through her head, and she could not get the last conversation straight.

'Well, you've gone to all this trouble,' she thought out loud. 'You'll just have to finish what you've started . . .'

With sudden determination she went out into the hall and pulled on her rubber boots. She took the raincoat down from the hanger and before she had put it on she was in the stairwell locking up.

After a fifteen-minute wait outside the building on Plog-gatan she was let in by a middle-aged woman with a stressed appearance. The woman held the door open for her and, to Barbro's great relief, did not bother to ask why she wanted to get into the building without an entry code. Instead she rushed up the stairs, leaving Barbro by herself.

Barbro took the lift up to the fourth floor, where her eyes immediately fell on the Hedberg family's name plate. She remained standing outside the door for several minutes and listened attentively for sounds from inside the apartment. There was definitely someone inside; that was unmistakable. She could make out one child's voice at least, and a male voice besides. True, things were quiet, as far as she could judge, but at least two people were without a doubt awake in there. Barbro rang the doorbell numerous times, but no one opened up for her. She leaned down and called into the letter box, 'Hanna! Are you there? It's Barbro! Open for me, Hanna dear?'

She rang again, for longer this time. No reaction. And after her attempts to make contact with the people in the apartment, she could no longer make out any sounds from inside. She took off her raincoat and folded it into a thick bundle that she set on the cold step right outside the door. There she sat down to wait, for what she did not know. But this time she did not intend to give up right away.

* * *

A fine, gentle summer rain was falling, even though it would soon be October. Sjöberg and Hamad were walking hurriedly in the direction of Sören Andersson's address on Katarina Bangata.

'Are you thinking what I'm thinking?' asked Hamad, as he wiped away a raindrop that was hanging on the tip of his nose with the back of his hand.

'Do you mean Vitabergsparken?'

'Yes,' Hamad confirmed.

'Same place, approximately the same time . . . Two dead people. This sounds like almost divine intervention.'

'Do you believe in such things?'

'Hardly,' Sjöberg said.

'What do you think happened?' asked Hamad.

'I think poor Jennifer Johansson was murdered because she let her sister borrow her jacket,' said Sjöberg quietly.

'Because someone believed that Elise was a witness to something she never saw,' Hamad continued.

'Witness to something she still has no idea happened,' Sjöberg filled in. 'That Sören Andersson ran over a woman in Vitabergsparken.'

'We have to call Petra.'

'They're still working on identifying the victim. We'll take Sören Andersson first. Maybe he can enlighten us on that point.'

'He hides the body and empties her pockets. And then he murders his only witness in cold blood.'

'Wrong person besides,' Sjöberg observed.

'From no criminal record to double murderer in one day. That's one cold-blooded bastard!' Hamad exclaimed.

Sjöberg phoned Einar Eriksson and asked for the entry code to Sören Andersson's building. It took him forty-five seconds to supply it, and then they went in. A grey-haired woman who looked considerably older than her fifty-three-year-old husband opened up for them. Sjöberg, who knew that she was roughly his own age, assumed there were good reasons for her premature ageing.

'Sören's not home,' she said timidly after they introduced themselves.

'What time do you expect him back?' Sjöberg asked politely.

'Not later than midnight, I would think. He has to work tomorrow.'

She blinked nervously up at the considerably taller chief inspector.

'Do you know his whereabouts?' asked Sjöberg.

'He was going to visit a friend, but he didn't say who.'

'We just want to ask a few routine questions,' Sjöberg lied, 'but it can wait until tomorrow. Do you happen to know whether he took the car?'

The woman turned around and glanced towards a stripped bureau by the wall with a mirror above it. On the bureau was a little ceramic bowl, and Sjöberg noted the car keys in it.

'I don't think so,' Mrs Andersson answered with some hesitation.

'Where is the car parked?'

She looked at him perplexed, but answered without objections.

'He usually leaves it by Bjurholmsplan.'

'What kind is it?' asked Sjöberg with an easy smile.

'It's an Opel,' she replied. 'An old white Kadett. Would you like to take down the registration number too?'

They did.

*

'We'll put the apartment under surveillance,' said Sjöberg when they were down on the street again. 'Then we'll rest a little until they arrest him. I think we both need a little sleep. But let's just take a look at Bjurholmsplan first. See if the car is there.'

'What do we do if it is?'

'Call in the technicians.'

And sure enough there it was. It was both rusty and unwashed. On one front door they immediately caught sight of a dent, but it seemed to originate from a carelessly opened car door in a car park. They walked around the car from either direction and by the right front bumper they stopped and looked at each other. It was seriously dented and Sjöberg crouched down to illuminate the damaged metal with the little flashlight he had on his key ring.

'What do you say?' he said, turning his face up towards his associate.

'I say it looks like a car that ran into a pram – and the owner of a pram,' Hamad observed. 'Are there fragments of blue paint?'

'Looks like it,' said Sjöberg. 'Call Hansson.'

The technicians were soon on the scene and Sjöberg explained the situation to Gabriella Hansson.

'So you have a perpetrator, a weapon and a victim,' she said, giving Sjöberg a meaningful smile. 'In other words, only one slight detail remains . . .'

Sjöberg made an irritated grimace, took the mobile phone from his pocket and entered Petra Westman's number.

'How's it going with the identification?' he asked.

'Not good,' sighed Westman. 'We still have no name for

the victim. But we're quite certain it's a Swedish woman who lives in the vicinity. With the pictures in the paper tomorrow it should be resolved.'

'I think we have the perpetrator,' said Sjöberg. 'And the car.'

'What are you saying?' said Westman astonished. 'How did you – ?'

'Our paths cross, Petra. I think we're working on the same case.'

'What the . . . Have you arrested anyone?'

'Not yet. He's not at home. We have surveillance on the building, so we'll arrest him when he shows up and question him immediately.'

'Now you have to explain . . .'

Sjöberg briefly recounted what he and Hamad had concluded, and when he was finished Westman sighed deeply and repeated what Hansson had just said.

'Only one slight detail remains . . .'

'To be sure,' Sjöberg agreed, 'but perhaps the perpetrator himself can help us with that information. Go home and go to bed, Petra.'

Sjöberg ended the call and threw some words of encouragement to the forensics team before he left with Hamad.

* * *

Jens Sandén was finally on his way home to the house in Bromma after yet another fruitless day of searching for someone who recognized the unfortunate woman or her son. There still remained to visit only one person on the list, a nurse on sick leave who worked at a private paediatric clinic on Östermalm. He had left her until last, because she lived not far from him in Stora Mossen.

All the spaces in the car park outside the small apartment building area were occupied, so he parked his car carelessly halfway on to the grass. He made his way into the building with the help of the code Eriksson had supplied him with and saw on the directory that she lived on the third floor. He went up the stairs and was about to ring the doorbell when his mobile phone rang. He considered not answering but changed his mind when he saw on the display that it was Jessica. Jenny, after many ifs, ands and buts, had let herself be talked into having Jessica stay with her overnight.

'Daddy, I have to tell you something,' she began in a tone of voice that worried Sandén.

'Are you at Jenny's?' he asked anxiously.

'Yes . . . or no, I went outside to phone. I didn't want to call you while she was listening.'

'Okay, get to the point.'

'Jenny was extremely definite that I couldn't get here until quarter past eight,' said Jessica, 'so I promised not to. Punctuality is important to her, you know. But I was already here by five to eight, so I decided to wait outside the front door until quarter past so she wouldn't be upset.'

'And?' said Sandén, who feared the worst but could not imagine what that might be.

'I was playing with my mobile phone and it was truly not my intention to spy or anything, but I happened to notice that at eight o'clock sharp a man came out of Jenny's apartment.'

'But I'll be damned . . . Was is that Pontus?'

'No, it wasn't.'

'Then it must have been that damn Yugoslavian. The one we talked about this morning . . .'

Sandén sighed and was about to continue when he was interrupted by his daughter.

'Yugoslavian?' she said hesitantly. 'What do you mean?'

The lights in the stairwell went out and he was surrounded by darkness.

'I thought Mum told you. There was some guy named Dejan there –'

'She told me,' Jessica interrupted again. 'But this was a little old Swedish man, retirement age. His name was Kjell-Erik.'

'Well then, that's nice to hear,' Sandén laughed in relief.

'No, Daddy, I don't think you would say that.'

He felt his stomach knotting up without really understanding why.

'When I came up at quarter past eight she had just showered,' Jessica continued. 'I asked her about the man I'd seen.'

Everything was swimming before him and he felt like he had to sit down. He fumbled for the handrail in the darkness and managed to sit down on the steps without hurting himself.

'She only knew his first name. But he was yet another "friend of Pontus". It turns out that there are quite a few so-called friends who show up there. Some, but only a few, give her a little money. A tip, I guess.'

Sandén did not know what to say, sitting there in the dark on the cold stone floor in a strange stairwell, but his heart was pounding so that it boomed in his ears.

'Daddy, I'm sorry to have to say this, but I think Jenny is a prostitute. I think that idiot Pontus is keeping her as a whore in her own home and that he keeps the money for himself.'

'I'm going to kill that –'

'No, Daddy,' said Jessica in such a calm, determined voice that he lost his train of thought. 'You're not going to ruin your life and ours for a little piece of shit like that. If you do that, I'll never forgive you. You're not going to do anything. We'll talk about this later tonight. I'm taking Jenny home to Mum now.'

'Thanks . . .' was the only thing he could say before the call was over.

* * *

It was the best thing she'd eaten in her whole life. Never before had a hamburger tasted so good. Hanna talked without interruption as they ate. The words welled out in floods between bites. Her secret friend – Björn – did not say much, but that didn't matter. He listened to her and smiled in a friendly way, and didn't get mad when she spilled something.

'Are you a man or a boy?' Hanna wanted to know.

'What do you think?' he asked back.

'An old boy,' Hanna giggled, and then Björn giggled too.

They understood one another. When Hanna happened to get a little ketchup on her nose, Björn put ketchup on his finger and smeared it on his own nose. Hanna laughed at him and he looked happy. Mummy would not have liked that. But that didn't matter any more.

Björn wanted them to take a bath as soon as they'd finished their food, but Hanna wanted sweets first.

'You brought sweets, didn't you, Björn? You said you would,' said Hanna.

'I have sweets with me. But can't we take a bath first, and save the sweets for later?'

'But I want sweets now,' said Hanna.

'Then we'll have a few sweets now, but save most of them until after the bath,' Björn decided.

Hanna agreed to that. Björn went out in the hall and took a big packet of sweets from his jacket pocket. Hanna waited for him at the table in the children's room. Then the doorbell rang. Hanna leaped up from the chair and rushed out into the hall.

'Someone's coming!' she called, but Björn silenced her with a finger over his lips.

'We're secret friends,' he whispered. 'No one else can be with us.'

'But if it's Daddy . . .' said Hanna, but he put his hand over her mouth.

'You don't want to share the sweets with other people,' he coaxed. 'And Daddy has his own key; he wouldn't ring the doorbell.'

Hanna complied and they slipped quietly back into the children's room and Björn closed the door behind them. They sat there quietly for a while and listened to the doorbell ringing again and again.

'Hanna! Are you there? It's Barbro! Open up, Hanna dear!' was heard from outside the front door.

Then Hanna smiled and whispered to Björn, 'It's just that silly Barbro. She lies like a rug.' Daddy always said that. It sounded funny, thought Hanna.

She poured sweets on to the table and divided them carefully into two roughly equal piles.

'You only get three sweets before the bath,' Björn suggested.

Hanna nodded in agreement and took a fistful of sweets and popped them into her mouth. Björn looked at her as if he meant to say something, but he only shrugged. He studied her blankly while she chewed.

'Now let's take a bath,' he said.

* * *

After sitting for a while on the cold stairs recovering, Sandén stood up with a groan. He suddenly felt very old, and very unhappy. He wanted to go home, immediately, but decided to make a final effort before giving up for the day. He was standing outside the paediatric nurse's door anyway.

The woman who opened it did not look as sick as he felt; she was dressed and her hair was done.

'Jens Sandén, Hammarby Police,' he said, holding up his police ID with a slightly trembling hand.

'Come in,' said the woman, who appeared to be in her forties. 'I was expecting one of you to stop by.'

Sandén stepped into the hall and took the envelope of photographs out of his inside pocket – he had lost track of how many times he had done that. He was out of breath, but hoped that it was not noticeable as he tried to act normally.

'Excuse me for bothering you, but this won't take long,' he apologized. 'I've been running around tormenting paediatric nurses all day.'

'That's no problem. It's just a cold and I feel much better. I'll be back at work tomorrow. Won't you come in?' she asked politely.

'No, thanks. I'm on my way home. I just need to show you a few photographs. They're not very cheerful, these pictures. I want to warn you in advance. You see, a dead woman was found in Vitabergsparken. Perhaps you read about it in the papers?'

She nodded.

'We also found a little boy in a pram insert in the bushes,' Sandén continued. 'He's in no danger; he's being treated at a hospital and is almost recovered. But it's been more than sixty hours since we made the discovery, and no one has contacted us yet about these missing persons. We haven't been able to identify either of them, so that's why I'm running around talking to nurses. This is what the boy looks like,' said Sandén, holding up one of the pictures in front of her.

She studied the photograph for a while in silence, but then shook her head.

'It's hard when they're that little,' she said. 'They change so quickly at that age. How old is he?'

'We think he's about five months old.'

'No,' she said. 'That doesn't ring any bells. Do you have a picture of the mother too?'

'Yes, I do. She was dead when she was photographed

and it's not that pretty to look at. You'd better brace yourself.'

She crossed her arms and nodded. He pulled out one of the photographs and showed it to her. She answered almost immediately.

'The boy's name is Lukas,' she said, swallowing. 'Lukas Hedberg. He was born sometime in the middle of May. Pretty big for his age. I don't remember the mother's name. She's very nice. Was very nice,' she corrected herself. 'There's a girl too, Hanna – she must be three or so. Let's see . . . March, I think. Born in March 2004. What happened?'

'We don't know for sure,' Sandén replied, 'but it looks like she was run over by a car when she was out pushing the pram. A hit-and-run accident.'

'Good Lord,' the paediatric nurse said indignantly. 'And little Hanna –'

'We have to find out where they live,' Sandén interrupted. 'The relatives must be informed as soon as possible. You don't happen to know the address, do you? Or the parents' first names so I can call information?'

She thought quietly for a few moments, then said, 'Home visit. We make a home visit to our children when they're newborns. I'm sure I have the address in my diary.'

Her handbag was hanging on a hook in the hall and she took it down and pulled out the diary. Sandén was sweating profusely and felt like he needed to sit down again, but he could not very well sit down on the floor in the hall.

'Let's see here. May, I said . . .'

She quickly leafed back through the diary until she came to the end of May, then took more time over each page, examining her notes. Sandén was standing close by, following her finger as it ran over the pages.

'Here it is,' she said at last, turning her face up towards him.

'Home vis. Lukas Hedberg, Ploggatan 20,' Sandén read. 'You've been an invaluable help. I have to call the station.'

He took the phone from his pocket but could not focus his eyes on the keypad. His thumb moved over the numbers, but he could not tell if he was hitting the right ones. He managed to press four times. Then he collapsed on the hallway floor.

* * *

Hanna showed her guest the way to the bathroom. The bathtub had not been drained since she had last used it. Björn pulled the plug and let the cold, murky water run out of the tub before he rinsed down the sides with the shower head. Then he filled it again with clean, hot water.

'Should we put bath beads in the water?' Hanna suggested. 'Then it smells nice.'

'Sure,' said Björn. 'If you think so.'

Hanna gathered up some of the variously coloured bath beads from a drawer and scattered them in the water.

'Are you going to take off your clothes?' asked Björn.

'You too?' asked Hanna.

Björn nodded and started unbuttoning his shirt. Hanna tore off all her clothes before Björn had even finished with his buttons. She bounded up to the bathtub, climbed over the edge and sat down.

'Daddy has one of those too, although it's a lot littler,' Hanna observed, as Björn raised one leg over the edge of the tub.

He gave her a warm smile in response and lowered himself across from her with a sigh of pleasure.

* * *

Barbro could not relax. The situation was absurd. Either everything was fine in the apartment and she should just forget all this and go home to bed. Or else something was wrong, really wrong. And what good did it do to sit here in the stairwell staring out into the darkness? She had done a lot of things right the past few days, but this – it just felt cowardly. She might as well end with guns blazing – wasn't that the most important thing? What other people thought should make no difference. Even if she were a hysterical female disgracing herself. She had to follow her own conscience and do what felt right to her.

There was a three-year-old in there who had told her that she was home all alone, that she had to find food for herself and had hurt herself. Now suddenly there was a grown man with her, but what kind of strange character was it who didn't open the door when the bell rang? Who didn't even yell at her to go away when she shouted through the letter box. Instead he had kept quiet and hidden somewhere in the apartment. That was not normal, it just wasn't. If Hanna's father believed that Barbro was a lunatic who was trying to disturb them, he would have called the police. Which would have made her happy. But he hadn't done that – he refused to communicate with her, and he withdrew into the apartment with the little girl.

What if something horrible was going on in there? What that might be Barbro could not imagine, but the more she thought about it, the more obvious it seemed to her that something was not right. And what was she doing, really? She ought to be slapped. Get up now, Barbro, and take hold of the situation. Don't be one of those people who only stand and stare.

* * *

A fragment of a thought fluttered past as she passed Hamad's darkened office on her way to the coffee machine. She put a teabag in the brownish cup and noted that she ought to clean it with salt to get rid of all the old stains that weren't removed in the dishwasher. She put it in the machine and pushed the button for hot water. Squeezed out the teabag with a spoon and tossed it in the wastebasket, added milk from the refrigerator. And there it was – that unpleasant feeling that you get when you know you haven't followed a thought to its conclusion. Because you were interrupted, because you couldn't, or because you didn't want to, didn't dare. Petra tried to shake off the feeling, and took a biscuit from the cupboard although she didn't really want one.

She took the teacup and started walking back to her office. Stopped outside Hamad's door, which was open, inviting an unannounced visit. But he was not there. Sjöberg and Hamad were up at Bjurholmsplan; she and Eriksson were the only ones in the offices on this corridor.

Eriksson almost always worked with his door closed, unwilling to subject himself to the friction of encounters with other people. Petra remained standing outside Hamad's room, staring into the darkness. Come back, thought. What were you trying to tell me? It was close now; it was there knocking again, but would she let it in?

She saw herself sitting in Clarion's bar one fateful November night; saw herself exchange a fleeting smile with a charming anaesthetist over Jamal's head. Who made an early exit, leaving her in the clutches of a serial rapist who drugged her and dragged her home with him. To then film and rape her together with . . . someone. The Other Man. What bad luck, Jamal, that you didn't stay longer, then we could have left together.

She saw herself sitting with Jamal in the commotion at Pelican. Noisy, cosy, warm and convivial. As it always was with Jamal. They could have left together then too, but he had other plans. He wasn't taking the metro; he was going to walk home. Home?

They had worked out together after the course, but had they done that? Sometimes; sometimes not. There were periods when she didn't see him as she struggled with her machines and weights. When she was boxing with the sandbag in the adjacent room, he was still at the machines. Or was he? When she showered, he showered too; but how long did that take? Thirty minutes, like her, with shoulder-length hair that had to be washed and blow-dried? Or ten minutes, like most guys?

And his warmth, his eyes, his way of embracing her? What did that mean? His way of being close to her and yet inaccessible? Near and far. He had just separated from his wife, but she didn't really know why. How well did she really know him? Very well, and not at all.

Petra glanced back along the corridor and slipped into Jamal's office, closing the door behind her. In the darkness she groped her way up to the desk and sat down at the computer. Dragged the mouse back and forth a few times, until the screen lit up and the computer asked for a password. Jamal never changed passwords; he always used the same one: Maryam, his mother's name. Petra quickly went through his e-mail, but to her relief found nothing of interest. Then she clicked on 'My Pictures' but there was only one folder: 'Sample pictures', a default folder with images of mountains, sunsets, flowers and winter scenes. She was just about to log out when something made her open the folder of sample pictures anyway. And there it was at the very bottom, the picture of her in Peder Fryhk's bed; the picture that had been sent to the police commissioner.

Petra took a deep breath, not knowing what to do. After a moment's deliberation she deleted the picture, emptied the virtual wastebasket and logged out. Without any idea whatsoever of how she should deal with this.

She got up and was just about to leave the room when her mobile phone rang. It lit up the office for her and she quickly made her way to the door, opened it as quietly as she could and went out into the corridor before she answered.

'Jens?' she said, but there was no one there.

All she could hear was a woman's voice in the background. She drew the conclusion that Sandén had called her accidentally and was about to hang up, when something the woman was saying made her change her mind.

'Stora Mossen,' she could make out. 'Third floor. I need

an ambulance immediately. I'm a nurse myself and I think in the worst case it may be a stroke.'

'Jens!' shouted Petra. 'What's going on?'

Rumbling in the receiver, racket and noise.

'Hello!' she cried, even louder now. 'Is anyone there?'

The door to Einar Eriksson's office opened and he came out and looked at her questioningly.

'I think something has happened to Jens,' Petra explained. 'I'm trying to make contact, but –'

'Hello,' she suddenly heard the woman's voice in her ear. 'I have a policeman here whose name is Jens Sandén. He collapsed and I've called an ambulance. Are you a police officer?'

'Yes,' said Petra. 'What happened?'

'I can't explain it, but I know he's very concerned that you should know that the address is Ploggatan 20. Do you understand?'

'Ploggatan 20,' Petra replied, with her heart in her throat. 'I understand.'

'The boy's name is Lukas Hedberg. He has a three-year-old sister whose name is Hanna Hedberg. I have to go now.'

'Hedberg,' mumbled Petra, but the woman had already hung up.

Eriksson and Petra stood staring at each other for a few moments before the information sank in.

'But I talked with the girl this afternoon and with her father just now,' said Eriksson with a puzzled expression.

'And they weren't missing any family members?'

Eriksson shook his head with a frown.

'Then it wasn't her dad,' Petra said. 'We have to go there. Do you know where it is, Einar?'

'By Vitabergsparken. Ploggatan is an extension of Stora Mejtens Gränd. Or the other way around. But Sjöberg and Hamad are in the vicinity. We'll send them there if it's urgent.'

'It is,' said Petra, speed-dialling Sjöberg.

* * *

There was a terrible racket in the stairwell, someone hollering and screaming and hammering with something that sounded like metal. Sjöberg and Hamad quickly ran up the stairs to the fourth floor. A dozen people were assembled there watching with amusement an elderly woman who was crouching down, banging the cover of the Hedberg family's letter box. When Sjöberg caught sight of Barbro, he could not conceal the start of a smile.

'You can go home now,' he said to the curious observers, holding up his police ID so that they could all see it. 'We'll take over here.'

Hamad herded them away and made sure they scattered. Sjöberg extended his hand to Barbro and helped her up.

Barbro greeted them quickly, without taking the time to smile back at the policemen.

'I've been ringing, but no one opens. But I know someone's in there.'

'Really?' said Sjöberg, putting his ear to the door.

He kept it there for a minute or so before he gave up.

'There's not a sound coming from inside,' he said. 'Are you sure someone's there?'

'Yes, I am,' Barbro replied. 'Before I rang I listened for sounds from inside the apartment, just like you. I heard both a child's and a man's voice. I called to Hanna through the letter box, but then it went completely quiet. I think it's very strange that no one opens the door when you ring –'

'Yes, you might think that,' said Sjöberg. 'They may be busy with something . . . May I ask, what's your business here exactly?' Barbro briefly told him how she had been phoned by little Hanna on Sunday evening, and how after several days of toil she had managed to find the address. She also let it be known that she suspected that the police had not been very quick in their handling of the matter. Sjöberg could hardly believe his ears, but realized that this woman clearly had a mind of her own and was worth taking seriously.

'You haven't spoken with Hanna again, after that first conversation?' he asked.

'Yes, I have,' Barbro admitted. 'But Hanna was mad at me and did not want to talk.'

'Mad at you?'

'She thought I'd betrayed her. I did promise that I would rescue her. But she said she wasn't alone any more – or actually that someone was on their way here. At first I thought it must be the police, but then she said it was her daddy . . .'

'But you didn't really believe that?'

'Yes, I guess this sounds strange, but . . . no. She said it in a way that sounded as if she changed her mind while she was talking. I can't really put it into words; I don't remember exactly what she said. First I got the impression that the police were on their way here, then suddenly Daddy was home and going to get hamburgers for her.'

Sjöberg pushed the doorbell a few times and the angry

bell signal was heard clearly and audibly out in the stair-well, but no other sounds.

'Call Westman and ask if we should go in,' Hamad suggested.

'I'll go down to the street,' said Sjöberg. 'It's not neces-sary for the whole building to hear what we're talking about.'

'I'll stay here,' said Barbro, as she rang the doorbell. 'In case something happens.'

'I'll stay here with Barbro,' said Hamad, 'and continue to make a disturbance. Go down and call now, Conny.'

Sjöberg went down to the street and wandered towards Vitabergsparken while he called. He filled Westman in, and she promised to call back as soon as she had spoken to the prosecutor about a search warrant. She kept the bad news about what had happened to Sandén to herself for the time being.

While he waited Sjöberg sat down on a bench in the park and looked out over the crime scene in the autumn dark-ness. Could it be the case, he thought, that a little girl had spent four whole days alone, locked in an apartment while her mother was in the morgue? The thought was dizzying. And where had the father been all this time? It was almost inconceivable that the mother would have left her three-year-old alone at home. Unless she was desperate for some reason. What was she doing out in the middle of the night?

He looked over the lawns around him. His eyes fell on the bushes where the boy was found. He imagined the child lying there in the pram insert. Inconsolable to start with, but then sleeping, perhaps unconscious. He shook off the unpleasant thoughts and thought instead about his own family. His own children who were down with chickenpox at their grandparents. Imagined Åsa chasing back and forth between healthy and sick children who demanded attention – each in their own way. She had help from her parents anyway, he consoled himself.

His gaze wandered back to the bushes, and it suddenly struck him that the little boy had tonsillitis. He was reminded of when Maja, his own five-year-old, had tonsillitis as a baby. How she screamed without stopping during a flight to Greece. Disturbed everyone on the plane. Åsa and he took turns carrying her around, but nothing helped. She could not sleep, would not take her dummy; Calpol had not helped.

Suddenly it was clear to him what had happened. A single mother with a sleeping three-year-old and a baby with tonsillitis. She was desperate. At last, exhausted, she left the big sister sleeping alone at home and went out for a walk. Only a short walk in the immediate vicinity so the child would have a chance to fall asleep. Fall asleep, and fall silent. That's what had happened. One time. A single time, in desperation she left her three-year-old home alone, and it had ended badly. Very badly.

The phone rang.

'I can't get hold of Rosén,' said Westman, stressed. 'But Einar has found out that the father's name is Carl Hedberg and the mother is Cecilia Hedberg; both are registered at that address.'

'In any case no one's opening the door for us,' said Sjöberg. 'But reportedly the three-year-old is in there with a man.'

'Then that must be the father.'

'Of course it might be the father, but why doesn't he answer the door? Why hasn't he reported his wife's disappearance? I think it's someone else.'

'The keys,' said Westman suddenly.

'What keys? What do you mean?'

'She didn't have any keys with her. The victim had no keys on her when we found her.'

'We have to go in,' said Sjöberg.

'I'll keep hunting for Hadar, so at least we have a search warrant.'

'Make it quick. I'm going to catch hell for this, but we're going in now. Send a couple of cars and an ambulance.'

Sjöberg was already running towards the apartment building at Ploggatan 20 before he ended the call. He entered the code and was halfway up to the second floor when the door closed behind him. He took two steps at a time and when he appeared Hamad and Barbro Dahlström looked worriedly at him.

'We're going in now,' said Sjöberg breathlessly, and without waiting for an answer he tugged on the door handle with all the strength he could muster. The door offered no resistance, but instead flew open and hit him on the chin and chest, but he barely noticed it. Hamad slipped into the lighted apartment; Sjöberg gestured to Barbro to stay where she was and then followed Hamad. From the hall they went into a living room, where they stopped and listened for sounds. Through one of the doorways in the living room they caught a glimpse of a bedroom, and from there the sound of splashing was heard. Hamad went into the bedroom quietly with Sjöberg right behind him. Through a half-open door they could see a tiled floor, and they slipped carefully over to the doorway. Jamal watched Sjöberg soundlessly form his mouth into one, two, three, and then Hamad rushed into the bathroom with Sjöberg at his heels.

* * *

In the bathtub a fully grown man was sitting. Naked, with his hand over the mouth of little Hanna, who was sitting on his lap looking wide-eyed at the policemen rushing in. Hamad stopped for a moment and stared at the hollow-eyed fifty-three-year-old and his catch. A terrified three-year-old girl whose mother he had killed. Hamad had barely understood what he was seeing before he was at the edge of the bathtub tearing Hanna out of the man's arms.

'It's Sören Andersson,' he said to Sjöberg, who mutely let his eyes wander between the little girl in his colleague's arms and the disrobed man in the tub.

Then Hanna started to scream. Not a scream full of despair and sorrow, but a three-year-old's furious, defiant howling.

'It just rang and rang! We were taking a bath!' she screamed.

Again and again the same thing: that they didn't have time for the bath because the doorbell was ringing the whole time. Sjöberg grabbed a bath towel from a hook on the wall and placed it over her where she was hanging in Hamad's arms. Hamad pulled her towards him, but she was stiff with rage and flailed her arms around. Barbro had defied the instructions she'd been given and slipped up to the doorway. With her hand to her mouth she became a witness to the incomprehensible scene playing out in the bathroom. Hamad forced his way out to the bedroom with the hysterical child and sat down on the edge of the bed with her, trying to calm her with gentle words and caresses.

Barbro looked from Hanna in the arms of Hamad to Sjöberg who calmly stepped up to the bathtub, took Sören Andersson by the neck and pushed his head down under the water. It felt like an eternity before she could get herself to react and she saw the pale, hairy arms flapping around the naked body in the water. Then her legs came to life and she went up to Sjöberg resolutely and placed her hand on his arm.

'That's enough now, inspector,' she said calmly. 'I didn't see that. Get him out of the tub now.'

Then she gave him a friendly pat on the arm and Sjöberg released his hold on Sören Andersson, whose head came up out of the water panting and snorting. Sjöberg threw him a towel and ordered him to get out of the bathtub. Barbro left the bathroom and sat next to Hamad on the bed and with his help lifted the girl over on to her lap and repeated in a calm, firm voice the same words, over and over.

'Little Hanna, Barbro's here now and everything's going to be all right . . .'

Patiently she repeated the chant until the girl calmed down and finally, exhausted, fell asleep with her head against her shoulder.

From out on the street sirens were heard.

* * *

It was almost two a.m. when Sjöberg rang her doorbell. She smiled at him when she opened the door, but he did not smile back. He looked at her with eyes red from crying without saying anything. He was completely exhausted and tears were running down his cheeks. He embraced her without a word and burrowed his head down into her soft, reddish-brown hair. They remained standing like that for a long time before in a whisper she suggested that they should sit down. He sank down on the floor with his back leaning against the wall and she sat down beside him and took his hand and placed it in her lap.

'You can tell me now if you want,' she whispered.

And he told her. The words flew out of him like sparks from a bonfire; they were blinding but brief, burned out, extinguished and replaced by new words. She let him talk without interruption, without curious questions that interfered. She listened to stories about people in prison; a woman in a coffin and a girl in a public toilet; grown men in invisible chains and a child in a bathtub; a woman imprisoned in her own body and the invisible bonds between daughters and mothers, sons and fathers. He told her about a woman in a window and a man that fell. About how sometimes you didn't know what you were seeking, but you still had to keep searching anyway; how sometimes you found something you didn't know you were looking for.

Several hours later, as he lay beside her on the rug, emptied of words and thoughts and tears, and their hands were woven together and he felt her gentle breath against his cheek – nothing warned him, no barriers went up, no inner voice told him that what happened shouldn't happen.